A SENSE OF WONDER

A SENSE OF WONDER

Samuel R. Delany,

Race, Identity,

and Difference

JEFFREY ALLEN TUCKER

Wesleyan University Press

Middletown, Connecticut

Published by Wesleyan University Press,
Middletown, CT 06459
© 2004 by Jeffrey Allen Tucker
All rights reserved
Printed in the United States of America
5 4 3 2 1

LIBRARY OF CONGRESS CATALOGING-IN-PUBLICATION DATA
Tucker, Jeffrey Allen, 1966–
A sense of wonder : Samuel R. Delany, race, identity, and difference / Jeffrey Allen Tucker.
    p. cm.
Based on author's Ph. D. thesis, Princeton University, 1997.
Includes bibliographical references and index.
ISBN 0–8195–6688–8 (alk. paper)— ISBN 0–8195–6689–6 (pbk. : alk. paper)
1. Delany, Samuel R.—Criticism and interpretation.   2. Homosexuality and literature—
United States—History—20th century 3. Science fiction, American—History and
Criticism.   4. Difference (Psychology) in literature.   5. Identity (Psychology) in
literature.   6. Race in literature.   7. Gays in literature.   I. Title.
PS3554.E437Z93 2004
813'.54—dc22   2004000521

For my mother
and in memory
of my father

And it can be said in particular of

Wonder that it is useful in making us

learn and retain in our memory things

we have previously been ignorant of.

For we wonder only at what appears rare

and extraordinary to us. And nothing can

appear so to us except through our hav-

ing been ignorant of it or through its

being different from things we have

known, for it is in virtue of this difference

that it is called extraordinary.

> —René Descartes,
>
> *The Passions of the Soul*

CONTENTS

ILLUSTRATIONS

ACKNOWLEDGMENTS

This book began as a doctoral dissertation at Princeton University. My heartfelt thanks go to Arnold Rampersad and to Wahneema Lubiano, both of whom encouraged the project from early musings to completion and represent a level of intellectual achievement to which I continue to aspire. Thomas Keenan, Wendy Chun, Mike Lee Davis, and Gavin Jones read drafts of the dissertation and offered valuable suggestions. Andrew Ross, Jeffrey Sammons, and Brad Verter provided vital textual and information resources. And Gayle Wald and Cornel West provided inspiration and encouragement, perhaps unknowingly, when needed.

My thanks also go to Samuel R. Delany, a writer whose works have offered the greatest pleasures and challenges imaginable, and who has walked the fine line between being this book's topic and its author's advisor with an admirable combination of grace, sincerity, and respect. I am grateful for the letters, books, articles, and e-mail messages he has sent me and for the attention, critiques, and support he has lent to this project, which is all the better for them.

I am indebted to colleagues who have read drafts of the manuscript and passed on useful comments and suggestions. My sincerest thanks in this regard go to Douglas Crimp, John Ernest, Grant Farred, Hal Gladfelder, Nesha Haniff, John Michael, Marlon Ross, Craig Sellers, Heather White, Sharon Willis, and most especially to Bruce Simon. Revision of the dissertation began in earnest with the composition of Chapter 5, which grew out of conversations with and suggestions made by Joseph McLaughlin, Dean McWilliams, and Robert Miklitsch. However, I should note that—to borrow one of Delany's own formulations—the book's errors and eccentricities are my own.

This book was completed with the assistance of a National Endowment for the Humanities Summer Stipend and the University of Michigan Center for African and Afro-American Studies' DuBois-Mandela-Rodney Postdoctoral Fellowship. I also thank the University of Rochester College of Arts and Sciences and the Department of English for supporting my candidacy for these awards.

The Special Collections Department at Boston University's Mugar Memorial Library was hospitable and helpful during two summer trips to view the Delany Collection; I wish to thank the entire staff and, in particular, director Howard Gotlieb, Sean D. Noël, and J. C. Johnson.

Judith Jackson Fossett's friendship and advice have been indispensable, especially in this project's final stages. My thanks also go to Edward K. Chan, Michael DePorte, Thomas Di Piero, Lester Fisher, Kevin Gaines, Thomas Hahn, Randall Halle, David Halperin, Darrick Hamilton, Sarah Higley, Nalo Hopkinson, Bette London, James Longenbach, Eric Rabkin, Kane Race, Brad Verter, and Penny Von Eschen. Betsy Huang and Vasudha Kurapati provided intelligent and enthusiastic bibliographic and editing assistance, for which I am grateful.

For all that she has given me—including her strength, support, and patience—I most especially thank Belinda Redden.

INTRODUCTION

If Samuel R. Delany did not exist, we would have to invent him. That is to say, he represents, to my mind, the ideal postmodern intellectual. His work regularly achieves that to which many contemporary intellectuals aspire: a readership across various lines of academic discipline, among "highbrow" intellectuals and a more general, "popular," readership. The first African American science fiction (SF) writer to win multiple Hugo and Nebula awards, the genre's highest honors, Delany, a 2002 inductee into the Science Fiction Hall of Fame, has been a trailblazer for black SF writers who have followed such as Octavia E. Butler, Steven Barnes, Nalo Hopkinson and others.[1] In 1969, SF writer and editor Algis Budrys called him "the best SF writer in the world."[2] Black Canadian fantasy author Charles Saunders sees him as "a giant in the genre [whose] name is mentioned in the same breath as those of Asimov, Bradbury, and Clarke."[3] Author Ursula K. LeGuin identifies him as SF's "finest in-house critic"[4] in recognition of, among other work, *The American Shore* (1978), *The Jewel-Hinged Jaw* (1977), and *Starboard Wine* (1984), his volumes dedicated to SF criticism. Delany has also been identified as a representative of the New Wave of SF that emerged in the late 1960s, an association that Delany denies since he was not really part of that group of writers associated with the British periodical *New Worlds*.[5] His writing demonstrates a mastery of SF, literary and intellectual history, and literary criticism, and engages with the most vital social and political issues of his times: race and racism in America, gay liberation, feminism, the AIDS crisis, and more. Bruce Sterling identifies him as one of the major influences on cyberpunk SF, another designation the author contests in deference to other SF writers, especially women writers, of his generation.[6] The quality of Delany's prose has prompted author and critic Charles Johnson to praise his "attention to music and the mutability of language."[7] Moreover, Delany's creative representations of the pleasures and breadth of human sexuality have contributed to his winning of the Bill Whitehead Award for Lifetime Achievement in Lesbian and Gay Writing. His writing participates, often simultaneously, in multiple academic discourses, such as science fiction, African American studies, gay and lesbian studies, and critical theory.

Delany is a writer not unlike some of the inventions of his own imagination or the subjects on which he has trained his formidable intellect. In characters such as Lobey from *The Einstein Intersection* (1967), Mouse from *Nova* (1968), and the Kid from *Dhalgren* (1975)—well-traveled adventurers who are as skilled in battle as they are in creative artistry— a reader may see versions of Delany's own multifarious career, which has included stints as musician, editor, comic-book writer, critic, and professor as well as award-winning author. Reed Woodhouse has commented that Timothy Hasler—the gay science fiction–writing philosopher, whose murder is investigated by a graduate student in *The Mad Man* (1995)—bears some resemblance to the novel's author.[8] Delany's writing is "cruel" in the same sense that Antonin Artaud's theatre is, as Delany himself puts it, "not because of its violence or its pain but because of its rigor, its demand for committed audience attention, for complete artistic dedication."[9] He is a skilled writer and a remarkably successful autodidact with a keen mind and wide range of interests; his description, therefore, of poet Hart Crane— most definitely not "a common-sensical, super-average man"[10]—fits Delany pretty well. An appreciation, therefore, of the multiplicity of the author's identities, activities, and audiences is crucial to this book's assertion that he is an intellectual who has made important contributions to discussions about race and identity, and to the diverse field of African American studies.

A Sense of Wonder begins by situating itself as a participant in recent debates about the status of the categories "race" and "identity" among left-liberal intellectuals. Chapter 1, "Dangerous and Important Differences," acknowledges that there is support to be found among Delany's fiction and criticism for the characterization of the author as a skeptic of identity politics; however, in the interest of asserting that such categories still have their uses, this chapter also reads Delany with attention to the significance of racial, cultural, and generic specificity in his works. Moreover, it seeks to refute the evaluations of some critics who have found Delany's writing insufficiently racial in content.

This study continues with an analysis of *Dhalgren* (1975). Its setting, the city of Bellona, draws all kinds of people to it, prompting Robert Elliot Fox to compare it to 1960s San Francisco, "the countercultural Mecca." Fox describes the novel as "a labyrinth with many dead ends,"[11] but a degree of race consciousness may assist the reader in finding his or her way. The use of repetition as a thematic and structural principle links *Dhalgren* to black cultural traditions, and the novel is invested in exploding a variety of sexual myths, particularly those about black men. *Dhalgren* is also very much a novel of its time, a significant distortion of its present, in that it not only represents various countercultural movements of the late 1960s and early 1970s, but also speaks of and to that era of urban uprisings in America.

Delany tries his hand at SF's paraliterary cousin, known as "fantasy" or "sword-and-sorcery," in his four-volume *Return to Nevèrÿon* series, which chronicles the life of Gorgik, from youth, to slave, to Liberator. Concomitant with Gorgik's quest to free all slaves in the empire of Nevèrÿon is a quest to satisfy his sexual desires, which are attached to the collars that slaves wear. But the series is not only an implementation of what Fox identifies as Delany's "semi/er/otic strategy;"[12] it is also a meditation on the institution of slavery, and an investigation of the ways in which sexual and social freedoms link to and inform one another.

The simultaneity of a *distinction* between and the *imbrication* of contexts is repeated with considerable force in Delany's Hugo Award–winning memoir *The Motion of Light in Water* (1988), one of the most important texts in the tradition of African American autobiography to appear in the last two decades. *Motion* demonstrates not only the constructedness of identity but also what Robert Reid-Pharr calls "the essentially permeable and thus impure nature of all American identities."[13] *Motion* can be read as a textbook on the poststructuralist conception of identity as "plural and 'intersectional' . . . relational and differential."[14] Split subjectivity is figured in *Motion*'s conceptual double columns; therefore it can be seen as revising or reapplying the theory of DuBoisian double consciousness, which Delany suggests may "apply even more to gay culture than to black—or rather, by the focus on black *gay* life, the split is chiseled deeper."[15] Delany may appear to be immersed in a Rinehartian "vast seething, hot world of fluidity"[16] in *Motion*, but I prefer to see his identity as at once multiple *and* locatable. The text's title image recalls Delany's refractive master trope, and is not a figure for suspension above identities, but rather an emblem of the multifaceted jewel of identity and the permeability of boundaries. *Motion* does more than recite the "race, class, gender, sexuality" mantra; it explores, to quote Kobena Mercer, "the complexity of what actually happens *in-between* the contingent spaces where each variable intersects with the others."[17]

My reading of *Atlantis: Model 1924* (1995) similarly seeks to locate the text in the tradition of African American literature through an appreciation of its representation of the unlimited semiosis of memory and its inventive variation on the African American migration narrative. *Atlantis* offers an opportunity to consider the pros and cons of a certain kind of identity-critique and of a consciousness of the very real social and political experiences of constructed identities.

The Mad Man (1995) represents how, in recent years, Delany's paraliterary focus has shifted from SF to what his alter-ego, K. Leslie Steiner, has called "antipornography"[18] and what he himself has called "transgressive fiction," which the author describes as "that fiction that has something in it to offend *every*body."[19] I will refer to this genre, perhaps simplistically, as pornography. *The Mad Man* is not Delany's first published work of this type; it was preceded by *Equinox* (1994), previously titled

The Tides of Lust (1973), and *Hogg* (1995), his pre-Stonewall novels, the latter of which gave expression to the author's hostility toward a hetero-sexist society, an anger that had no socially constructive outlet prior to the modern Gay Rights movement. They can be best described by borrowing Andre Gide's evaluation of Antonin Artaud's 1947 improvisational lecture, cited in Delany's essay "Wagner/Artaud." That is to say, they are "atrocious, painful, almost sublime at moments, revolting also, and quasi-intolerable."[20] For analyses of *Equinox* and *Hogg*, I am afraid that one must turn to more intrepid critics than myself.[21] So what makes *The Mad Man*, a novel featuring meticulous descriptions of sexual acts involving excrement, any different? In addition to the fact that practically all of the sexual situations in *The Mad Man* assume or require informed consent, the novel is representative of Delany's insightful, provocative, and sizable constellation of writings on the HIV/AIDS crisis, which continues to demand our attention and action and has had a disproportionate impact on the African American community. *The Mad Man* is a synthesis of fictional styles—pornography, detective fiction, satire of academia—but it is also AIDS activism at its best due to its paraliterary status, its representation of sex as a life-affirming act, its direct confrontation with the difficult and discomforting issues of disease and death, and its method of speaking back to, and thinking critically about, medical discourse on HIV transmission.

The chapters that follow are not limited to intellectual pronouncements about cultural politics but are meant to convey my enthusiasm and appreciation for the works of one of our most gifted writers and the sense of wonder they evoke.

1

DANGEROUS AND IMPORTANT DIFFERENCES

SAMUEL R. DELANY AND THE POLITICS OF IDENTITY

> For my part, I confess that the only "universal" commodity that I feel at all certain
> about is the hydrogen atom.
> —Stephen Henderson, Introduction to *Understanding the New Black Poetry*[1]

> "You are different." That is what La Dire said. "You have seen it is dangerous to
> be so. It is also very important."
> —Samuel R. Delany, *The Einstein Intersection*[2]

Samuel R. Delany is an exemplary writer whose finely crafted writing covers vast stretches and diverse types of fertile intellectual ground. Yet that very multiplicity suggests that different readers who come to his writing seeking different things, "invent" different Delanys, conceptions of the author that conform to their own desires, agendas, and politics. The author and his writing, therefore, constitute a contested terrain onto which this book enters to challenge the invention of him as a skeptic of the politics of "identity," perhaps even challenging such inventions that are shaped by Delany himself.

The Return of the Universal

These are hard times for "identity." David Palumbo-Liu notes that "when the word is mentioned these days, it tends not to meet with a straightening of the back and a defiant stare, nor even a wince and a evasive move, but rather a resigned sigh—'Oh, *that* again?'"[3] Just over a decade ago, however, Kobena Mercer wrote that "just now everyone wants to talk about identity."[4] This situation was because the status of "identity" was changing from something evident and stable to something problematized and disrupted. In 1989, Stuart Hall recognized that "the question of identity" was returning "with a particular kind of force" due to the crisis that Mercer identified; Hall named the "four great decenterings in intellectual life and in Western thought that have helped to destabilize the question of identity": (1) the Marxist argument that "there are always *conditions* to identity which the subject cannot construct. *Men and women make history but not under conditions of their own making*"; (2) the Freudian theory of the unconscious which suggests that the self is "grounded on the huge unknowns of our psychic lives"; (3) the influence of Saussurian linguistics on the realization that the self's utterances play off of pre-existing language systems for their meaning: "In order to speak, in order to say anything new, we must first place ourselves within the existing relations of language"; and (4) the destabilization that occurs when "Western discourses of rationality" are revealed to be what Michel Foucault called "just another regime of truth."[5] The end of the 1980s also appears to be a significant turning point for the status of "identity" according to the editors of a recent issue of *New Literary History* entitled "The End of Identity Politics?" They point out that it was at this moment, "after a decade of groundbreaking work on race, class, and gender, [that] a number of influential critics turned a skeptical eye toward identity."[6] These critiques have targeted, in particular, essentialism, what Diana Fuss describes as "a belief in the real, true essence of things, the invariable and fixed properties which define the 'whatness' of a given entity," a belief that tends to naturalize human behaviors, thus minimizing the possibility for structural change.[7] One of the most famous critiques of identity has been Judith Butler's *Gender Trouble* (1990), which advanced a theory of performativity, that gender is not an identity that exists as much as it is an act that is performed: "there need not be a 'doer behind the deed,' [rather] the doer is variably constituted in and through the deed." Butler's work interrogated the privileging of gendered identity in feminist politics and argued that through performativity, "the postulation of a true gender identity would be revealed as a regulatory fiction."[8]

The ramifications of such critiques of identity for the ongoing black liberation struggle have been immense, requiring a reconsideration of what is meant by formulations such as "black identity" or "the black community." Hall's "New Ethnicities" (1989) speaks of and within a specifically British context, but it is nonetheless relevant to debates about "identity" for people of African descent in the United States. The essay identifies the results of an encounter between black cultural politics organized around a unifying and apparently stable category, such as "The Black Experience" and "a Eurocetric, largely white, critical cultural theory which in recent years, has focused so much analysis of the politics of representation," in particular, "the discourses of post-structuralism, postmodernism, psychoanalysis and feminism."[9] What happens when these worlds collide is "the end of the innocent notion of the essential black subject," a recognition that "'black' is essentially a politically and culturally *constructed* category." This encounter, therefore, is "dangerous and difficult" because "it may seem to threaten the collapse of an entire political world," one that was based on simplistically pitting "the bad old essential white subject" against "the new essentially good black subject."[10] Of her gender-critique, Butler claims that the "troubling" of identity "need not carry such a negative valence,"[11] the truth value of which is demonstrated in the very welcome results of critiques of "black identity": an acknowledgment of the diversity within black communities and individuals along lines of class, gender, and sexuality (for starters), necessitating "forms of solidarity and identification which make common struggle and resistance possible but without suppressing the real heterogeneity of interests and identities." Indeed, Hall notes that this encounter produces "relief" at "the passing away of what at one time seemed to be a necessary fiction. Namely, either that all black people are good or indeed that all black people are *the same.*"[12]

More recently a number of cultural, social, and political theorists have argued for a conceptual move beyond the particularities of racial, gender, and sexual identities. Palumbo-Liu summarizes such arguments by saying, "These critics argue that, whatever salutary value feminist, queer, or critical race and ethnic studies have had, they have caused the left to veer off-track and into the minutiae of finer and finer distinctions of special interest groups, each claiming priority over the others."[13] We should subordinate identity-based interests, these arguments claim, to a program that will yield more universally transformative results. With "identity" laboring under the weight of so much scrutiny, one is reminded of the rhetorical question that Young Emerson puts to Ralph Ellison's perplexed narrator in *Invisible Man:* "Identity! My God! Who has identity any more anyway?"[14]

As hard as times are for "identity," they may be even worse for "race," a category notoriously deployed as part of the oppression, exploitation, and extermination of entire communities of people. But "race" is also a category around which those same communities have organized collective responses to the forces that threaten them. Any biological scientist or anthropologist can tell you that, quite evidently, we are one, human, race, and the groupings that we call "races" are the most constructed of categories. Philosopher Lucius Outlaw cites, for example, an essay by anthropologist Frank B. Livingstone, titled "On the Non-existence of Races," that declares, "there are no races, there are only clines," physiological differences that, genetically speaking, are only incrementally detectable.[15] In recent years, however, this simple and rather obvious fact has been asserted with considerable zeal by intellectuals in America. Walter Benn Michaels, for example, has consistently argued that race is an error of logic and that any deployment of the category is necessarily essentialist and, therefore, logically and ethically bankrupt.[16] Philosopher Kwamé Anthony Appiah's 1986 essay on W. E. B. DuBois asserts that "race is relatively unimportant in explaining biological differences between people," and molecular biology bears out his assertions: "for two people who are both Caucasoid, the chances of difference in genetic constitution at one site on a given chromosome are currently estimated at about 14.3 percent, while for any two people taken at random from the human population, they are estimated at about 14.8 percent." As for DuBois, although he "thought longer, more engagedly, and more publicly about race than any other social theorist" of the twentieth century, Appiah argues that he never really theorized "race" in a way that divorced itself completely from the biological. By the end of the essay, Appiah appears to doubt if such a conception of "race" is even possible:

> The truth is that there are no races: there is nothing in the world that can do all we ask "race" to do for us. The evil that is done is done by the concept and by easy—yet impossible—assumptions as to its application. What we miss through our obsession with the structure of relations of concepts is, simply, reality.[17]

Appiah develops similar ideas in *Color Conscious* (1996), in which he argues "against races" and "for racial identities." He again states that race has no biological meaning, but also claims that race has only a tenuous grasp of the cultural meanings often ascribed to it. Appiah criticizes the notion that cultural forms such as jazz or hip-hop, coded as "black," necessarily and exclusively "belong" to and are shared by African Americans via some form of "cultural geneticism." He recognizes that people still think in important racial terms, which is why the language of race remains significant, but demotes race consciousness to the realm of superstition when he compares it to witchcraft: "We may need to understand talk of 'witchcraft' to understand how people respond cognitively and how they act in a culture that believes in witches, whether or not we think there are, in fact, any witches." The current language that we use to talk about race is merely "the residue, the detritus," and "the pale reflection of a more full-blooded race discourse that flourished in the last century." Moreover, a healthy respect for the diversity of the African diaspora and an urge to get past the truly pernicious language of racial authenticity, which he calls "scripts," prompts Appiah to suggest "a more recreational conception of racial identity," one that "would make African-American identity more like Irish-American identity . . . for most of those who care to keep the label" and to prevent racial identity from "becoming the obsessive focus, the be-all and end-all, of the lives of those who identify with them."[18]

As diverse as skepticisms of race and identity are, they perhaps indicate a change in opinion toward the ideal of universalism. The universal was once, very recently, scrutinized and critiqued as a discourse of exclusion and totalization; Enlightenment aspirations to address, as Dick Hebdige outlines, "a transcendental subject, to define an essential human nature, to prescribe collective human goals," were implicated in histories of European colonization and male domination.[19] The universal appears to be making a comeback, however, with a vengeance and from a different political position. Left-liberal critics who are frustrated with the particularisms of identity politics, "have begun to reconsider the universal as a productive theoretical category," to see the universal in a dialectical relationship with the particular. "The functional independence of a specific identity group," for example, "is often predicated upon the universalist claim that all such groups should have the right to self-determination."[20]

One of the more compelling variations of this new universalism, and the most relevant to this study of an African American writer most famous for his works of science fiction, is expressed in Paul Gilroy's recent book, *Against Race*. In its concluding chapter, "'Third Stone from the Sun': Planetary Humanism and Strategic Universalism," Gilroy considers "the racial politics of temporality," criticizing the millenialisms of race-based nationalisms—whether Ku Klux Klan or Nation of Islam—as "fascist" and argues against Afrocentrism's "intense desire to recover the lost glories of an African past." Like Appiah, Gilroy finds certain types of "race-speak" to be outdated:

> Changes in communication and infomatics mean that the past's claims are qualitatively different now. For good or ill, they are weaker than they were, and the ebbing away of the brutal colonial relations that gave such a distinctive meaning to "race" is draining them further. This historic transformation is another aspect of the contemporary crisis of raciology that was sketched at the start of this essay. It is one more compelling sign that "race" is not what it was.[21]

Instead, he advocates a future-oriented humanism rooted in black cultural traditions:

> I suggest that, in moving into a new stage of reflection and aspiration that tallies with our novel circumstances as we leave the century of the color line behind, we need self-consciously to become more future-oriented. We need to look toward the future and to find political languages in which it can be discussed.[22]

Gilroy's futurism is an antiracist project that cuts its ties with racial thinking "in the interest of a heterocultural, postanthropological, and cosmopolitan yet-to-come."[23] It is distinguished by its fearless reliance on past and present imaginings of human contact with extraterrestrial beings. His chapter's Kantian epigraph suggests that the commonality of the "human race" is asserted "when one thinks of it as a species of rational beings on earth, compared to those rational beings on other planets, sprung as a multitude of creatures from one demiurge."[24] Gilroy cites Frantz Fanon's declaration of independence from an identity rooted in the history of colonialism—that he is "not a prisoner of history"[25]—as well as Richard Wright's claim that his own antiracism positioned him "ahead" of the West.[26] The multiracial humanism of the most popular SF television program in history, *Star Trek,* is singled out for staging the first televised interracial kiss and for counting the Rev. Martin Luther King Jr. among its most notable and visionary of devotees. Gilroy even considers films such as *Independence Day* and *Men in Black,* which he seems to recognize as rather facile, watered-down cinematic SF fare, as significant in their illustrations of the Kantian image of a humanity united across racial and ethnic differences against common extraterrestrial enemies. Gilroy finds models for a black-based humanistic futurism in the R & B and funk music produced in the 1970s and 1980s by artists such as Earth, Wind, and Fire, whose lyrics can be interpreted as addressing both race-specific and universal issues and themes, and whose visual styles mixed African and science fiction imagery. "Our challenge," Gilroy concludes, "should now be to bring even more powerful visions of planetary humanity from the future into the present and to reconnect them with democratic and cosmopolitan traditions that have been all but expunged from today's black political imaginary."[27] Gilroy's project calls for, and performs, the visionary "work of the imagination" that Appiah says "we need to begin," which requires "recogniz[ing] *both* the centrality of difference within human identity *and* the fundamental moral unity of humanity."[28]

The cultural logic of Gilroy's vision has been given more recent musical expression in the contemporary British electronic music of artists such as Nitin Sawhney, who announces his intention to transcend the cultural boundaries imposed with a racial identity in the title of his album *Beyond Skin,* and 4Hero, whose *Creating Patterns* features a track entitled "The Day of the Greys," perhaps heralding the arrival of a new race, either extraterrestrial or multiracial (or both). These musicians employ a cut-and-mix style, derived from hip-hop's techniques of digital sampling bits of recorded sound, to create both syntheses and collages of various musical styles and traditions including hip-hop, R & B, jazz, dub, electronica, and central and southern Asian.[29]

"Collage" is also the emblem for the "cosmopolitan" ideal advanced by Ross Posnock in *Color and Culture* (1998), which makes the following bold and immensely valuable argument: African Americans were the first modern American intellectuals. It was W. E. B. DuBois, Posnock contends, who followed the Dreyfus Affair, observed how the Dreyfusards were "scorned as *déracinés* and branded with the imprecation of *Les Intellectuels*," and ultimately "imported the tradition of modern intellectuals into the United States."[30] Now is the time to make such an argument, Posnock claims, for two reasons: First, the return of the public intellectual to at least some prominence in the United States during the 1990s—most notably in the person of figures such as Cornel West, bell hooks, Henry Louis Gates Jr. among others—which can only be seen as "a continuing black achievement" (1). Second, postmodernism and "its tribal conception of politics founded on a romance of identity" is, according to Posnock, dead. He advances "a left-liberal skepticism" of cultural pluralism, better known as identity politics" (3). A major, and laudable, aspect of this work is its interrogation of the notion of authenticity, which Posnock locates at the center of racial identity movements: "identity politics (practiced by whites and blacks alike) has long dominated, fixated on racial difference and the question of what and who is authentically black" (3). The rage for authenticity has, for example, stigmatized black male intellectuals as effeminate, an association that Posnock traces back to Booker T. Washington's dismissal of liberal education and his "[opposition of] the black intellectual to what is natural, manly, and virtuous" (26).[31] He cites Appiah's desire to escape authenticating "scripts" as representative of "the desire of black creative intellectuals for options other than race responsibility" (25). This valorization of African Americans as the first and most representative of modern American intellectuals challenges the received notions that "the post-war Manhattan literati centered in and around *Partisan Review* and Columbia University" known as the New York Intellectuals "defined the public intellectual," whereas black intellectuals have been regarded as "particularists, bent on creating a nationalist, vernacular folk culture of uplift" (7). Posnock contends that black intellectuals have instead pursued the ideals ascribed to the New York intellectuals, chief among them "cosmopolitanism." Theorizing cosmopolitanism as a black declaration of the right to access culture on the other side of the color line, "a democratic challenge to the obdurate belief that high culture is a private citadel of white privilege" (3), Posnock endorses this ideal over claims of cultural possession, of which he, like Appiah, is highly skeptical. This cosmopolitanism informs his book's slogan: "color has no culture," a phrase attributed to Alain Locke who, like DuBois, serves as an example of Posnock's prototypical "antirace race man" (10). Posnock acknowledges that the claim that culture has no color may sound strange to "postmodern ears," which may detect in it "the rhetoric of a liberal humanism by now synonymous with a (pseudo) universalism that was actually the property of white men" (12). And he acknowledges that "color-blind ideals are appropriated routinely for conservative political use" (12); however, he maintains that black intellectuals have consistently deployed "universalism" against white supremacy. Like Gilroy, Posnock cites Dr. King as an example. Noting that this "cosmopolitan universalism" has been "held under suspicion during the reign of postmodernism" (21), Posnock announces, in a chapter titled "After Identity Politics," that the new universalism is more self-conscious and self-critiquing than the previous. "Universalism returns," he states, "not in nostalgic defiance but chastened, neither positing a 'view from nowhere' nor seeking to bleach out ethnicity and erect a 'color-blind' ideal. Rather, it stands in reciprocal relation to the particular" (21). That "postmodernism is waning" is heralded not only by the return of the universal, but also by what Posnock sees as "a growing chorus of thinkers busy writing postmodernism's obituary" (3). In the academy, "identity politics is at last losing prestige" and "the glamorous provincialisms that congregate under the names multiculturalism and Cultural Studies are revising their tendency to absolutize ethnicity and race" (25). The "postmodern fascination with hybrids, cyborgs, mestiza consciousness, creolization and the transnational" is dismissed, using Walter Benn Michaels's formulation, as "just another turn of the essentialist screw" (25). So as "the epoch of postmodern tribalism wanes," Posnock explains, a "democratic cosmopolitanism awaits a hearing it has never really been granted" (294).

What makes Posnock's work particularly relevant to my project is his characterization of Samuel R. Delany as a descendant of ostensibly "cosmopolitan" black intellectuals. Although we arrive at widely differing readings, the goal of Posnock's work is similar to my own: to locate Delany within traditions of African American thought and culture. But Posnock does so by emphasizing Delany's inheritance of the "antirace race man" mantle. Delany differs from some of his intellectual ancestors who experienced the "black (/) intellectual" formulation as an internal conflict, whereas he embraces this split as an aesthetic model. The double columns Delany asks the reader of his autobiography, *The Motion of Light in Water* (1988), to imagine constitute one example. Born into a middle-class family, Delany never had to struggle to gain access to the realm of white culture, unlike figures who preceded him like James Baldwin, who ultimately succeeded at attaining access to, and comfort with owning, Western cultural traditions. Indeed, Posnock sees Baldwin as opening doors for subsequent generations of black intellectuals like Delany. Moreover, Posnock suggests a congruity between multiple splittings of the self, a refusal of race as a locus for identity, and a collage aesthetic present in both Delany and playwright Adrienne Kennedy's writing:

> Kennedy and Delany remake the antirace race lineage by abolishing the obligation to represent the race. Disrupting conventional coherence, they favor the paratactic disorientations of collage as a thematic and structural principle. Their collages frustrate the demand of identity and anticipate (and in one instance resist) the current decline of identity politics. (9–10)

Posnock cites a number of Delany's own statements that demonstrate the SF author's reluctance to serve as representative for the race or any other group identity. Consider Delany's recognition of how issues related to his race, gender, sexuality, and profession inevitably shape his writing without defining it:

> The constant and insistent experience I have as a black man, as a gay man, as a science fiction writer in racist, sexist, homophobic, America, with its carefully maintained tradition of high art and low, colors and contours every sentence I write. But it does not delimit and demarcate those sentences, either in their compass, meaning or style. It does not reduce them in any way.[32]

In his refusal to represent the race, Delany, according to Posnock, is similar to Charles Johnson, whose *Being and Race* (1988) celebrates Delany as "a model of genuine excellence for future black fiction" and criticizes cultural nationalist movements like Négritude and the Black Arts Movement as deeply problematic attempts at "image control," successful only as "a retreat from ambiguity, the complexity of Being."[33] Posnock also sees Delany as an antirace race man who effectively refutes interrogations of his racial authenticity—"why," Delany says, "as a black writer, my work wasn't, in effect, blacker"—from white critics:

> Look, I *am* black. Therefore what I do is part of the definition, the reality, the evidence of blackness. It's *your* job to interpret it. I mean, if you're interested in the behavior of redheads, and you look at three and think you see one pattern, then you look at a fourth and see something that, for some reason, strikes you as different, you don't then decide that this person, despite the color of his hair, isn't really red-haired—not if you and yours have laid down for a hundred years the legal, social, and practical codes by which you decide what hair is red and what hair isn't, and have inflicted untold deprivations, genocide, and humiliations on those who've been so labeled by that code.[34]

Even here, however, we can see a degree of race consciousness, an awareness of the history and politics attached to race in America, on Delany's part, even though his referral to "codes" suggests the history and historicity, the artifice and arbitrariness, of race and racial attribution. But the main meaning that Posnock takes from this statement, though by no means an improper or unimportant one, is a resistance to imposed racial scripts: "do not let the category (the 'pattern') become proscriptive" (260). Delany's aesthetic is therefore characterized as one of iconoclasm, devoted to subverting preconceptions and "perched upon that refusal to be caught in the net of predictable expectations attached to racial and gender markers" (45). It is figured by what Posnock understands to be Delany's master trope, in which the author's willful transgression of markers that delimit culture, a "fascination with blurred boundaries," becomes "a structural and thematic motif of simultaneity that he names 'suspension,'" particularly in works such as *Motion* and *Atlantis: Model 1924* (46). For Posnock, Delany's writings represent one of several "significant efforts to escape the reductionism of the ideology of 'authenticity,' which fixates upon particularity or difference" (21).

Delany's writings do provide a reader with the materials necessary to invent an author who conforms to the contours of the new universalism, who brings intense intellectual pressure to bear on "identity" and identity politics, who emphasizes the illusory aspect of race, invests in humanistic visions of the future, and offers models of "cosmopolitan" identity in both fictional characters and in collage aesthetics. Posnock calls Delany "a skeptic of identity politics" (266); if this is so, perhaps it is because Delany is a skeptic of efforts to specify an agenda for any identity, whether it be a politics of the self or the features of a cultural genre. For example, in the second chapter of his *Metamorphoses of Science Fiction: On the Poetics and History of a Literary Genre* (1979), renowned critic Darko Suvin lays out the assumptions on which his analyses are based, including "(1) that no field of studies and rational inquiry can be investigated unless and until it is at least roughly delimited; [and] (2) that there exist literary genres, as socioaesthetic and not metaphysical entities."[35] In addition to this rationale for the definition of SF, Suvin provides one of his own: "a literary genre whose necessary and sufficient conditions are the presence and interaction of estrangement and cognition, and whose main formal device is an imaginative framework alternative to the author's empirical environment."[36] Although Delany believes that SF can be "described," he produces a sharp and sure critique of the felt need for definitions and "the dream of scientificity" informing it:

> But this notion that SF *is* somehow definable is an idea that haunts the academic discussion of SF as much as it haunts the informal discussion that

has filled the fanzines since '39. If SF were definable, then it would be the only genre that was! No one has found the necessary and sufficient conditions for poetry. No one has found the necessary and sufficient conditions for tragedy, for the novel, for fiction. If SF is, as Suvin calls it, "a full fledged literary genre," why should it be the single one to *have* necessary and sufficient conditions?[37]

Delany's approach to SF is more along the lines of a New Genre theorist. "*All* genres resist definition," he claims prior to invoking Jacques Derrida's "*La loi de genre*" and its suggestion of the impurity of genres.[38] Genres, like genders, can be bent; that is their purpose, as well as Delany's own, according to the author.[39] Delany has also frequently asserted that SF is not simply a kind of writing, but also a way of reading. The example he uses to demonstrate this point is in the very different meanings that the same sentence—that is, "Her world exploded."—has in a work of SF and in a work of "mundane" fiction. The SF reader learns to read such sentences in a different way from readers who are unfamiliar with SF, with a heightened sensitivity for the possibilities of literal meaning.[40] Delany's analysis of SF shifts emphasis away from what the genre *is* to how it is read, in a fashion similar to the way Butler's critique of identity shifts the focus from ontology to performativity.

This refusal to define SF carries over to Delany's reluctance to accept "definitions" of identity, particularly gay identity. In a recent interview, he characterizes the critique of identity as a productive development: "Identity politics is sustaining a necessary and clarifying attack/analysis, one that will doubtless leave it forever changed into something more flexible and useful, more provisional and provisioned."[41] The case can be made, however, that Delany himself participates in this "attack/analysis." His essay "Coming/Out" interrogates the notion that a single event—that is, coming out—can define a person's life, even if it can "change" it. Heterosexuals, as Delany points out, never commemorate the moment they discovered they were straight because that would suggest it would be possible to be otherwise: "The rhetoric of singular discovery, of revelation, of definition is one of the conceptual tools by which dominant discourses repeatedly suggest that there is no broad and ranging field of events informing the marginal." This fact, he contends, applies to class, race, and (para)literary genre as well as sexuality.[42] Delany demonstrates the mutability and contextuality of "coming out" itself by describing the difference between the pre- and post-Stonewall meanings of the phrase, between, respectively, a sexual act and declaring one's sexuality in public. Moreover, he uses his essay as an occasion to map out the "philosophical paradox" presented by "identity" and "difference," terms that one might expect to inform each other, but, according to Delany, instead move in opposite directions:

Differences are what create individuals. Identities are what create groups and categories. Identities are thus conditions of comparative simplicity that complex individuals might move toward, but (fortunately) never achieve—until society, tired of the complexity of so much individual difference, finally, one way or the other, imposes an identity on us.

Identities are thus, by their nature, reductive. (You do not need an identity to become yourself; you need an identity to become *like* someone else.) Without identities, yes, language would be impossible (because categories would not be possible, and language requires categories). Still, in terms of subjects, identity remains a highly problematic sort of reduction and cultural imposition.[43]

Elsewhere, Delany states that "gay identity" can be deployed all too easily "in terms of heterosexist oppression of gays" as "a strategy for tarring a whole lot of very different people with the same brush," even as it can be used "in terms of gay rights" as a "strategy" for purposes of organizing for justice and equality. "Gay identity," therefore, "requires analysis, understanding, interrogation, even sympathy, but never an easy and uncritical acceptance."[44] This logic, and the sense that identity can be both reductive and an imposition, informs the interrogation of the possibility of defining either gay identity or SF.

Indeed, Delany applies his genre theories and his resistance to reductionisms to the contexts of race as well as sexual identity, contending that "worrying about the purity of the genres on any level is more futile than worrying about the purity of the races."[45] Delany's "Wagner/Artaud," a long essay on the exemplars of modern and postmodern aesthetics, respectively, identifies a "conceptual screen" shaped by ideals of aesthetic unity against which intellectuals like Hegel and Nietzsche worked, a screen congruent with ideals of aesthetic unity "put forth by Aristotle and Poe" and linked to race and the most noxious uses to which that concept has been put:

> This nineteenth-century reductionism, this plea for a unity in which all that is anomalous can be ignored, this appeal to rationalism over empiricism, is behind the whole deadly concept of race; by the end of the century we will see its fallout in the virulent anti-Semitism of the Dreyfus Affair, in what we now speak of as British imperialism, and in Rhodesian and South African racism. Such reductionism when essentialized becomes the philosophical underpinning of this century's totalitarianisms, whether Hitler's or Stalin's . . .[46]

Delany's denunciation of not simply racism, but race in its entirety as "deadly" and his reference to the anti-Semitism against which the Dreyfusards fought, which gave DuBois what Posnock claims was his model of modern intellectualism, provide further material for inventing Delany as an antirace race man. His skepticism toward identity is matched by his challenging of race as a meaningful concept. For Delany, the category signifies "a system of political oppression grounded [à la Appiah] on a biological fantasy."[47] But this "crime" that has been committed against people of African descent in America "is not a matter of a 'great race' treated as an 'inferior race'"; rather, it is in "a complex of lies, contradictions, and obfuscations [that is] fundamental to the very notion of race."[48] Is the meaning of race, however, limited to "oppression"? According to Delany, "anything 'positive' in the system associated with 'race' can be translated into terms of class—as class conflicts alone can explain the obfuscation, lies, and unspeakable cruelties that are the oppressive system itself."[49] Moreover, Delany finds it difficult to extract "race" and "racism" from each other given these concepts' intricately related careers, from Gobineau to David Duke: "In a society such as ours," he says, "the discourse of race is so involved and embraided with the discourse of racism that I would defy anyone ultimately and authoritatively to distinguish them in any absolute manner once and for all."[50] It is for this reason that Delany sees the lower case "b" in, for example, "black studies" as "a *very* significant letter, an attempt to ironize and de-transcendentalize the whole concept of race, to render it provisional and contingent, a significance that many young people today, white and black, who lackadaisically capitalize it, have lost track of."[51] Like Appiah, who attributes a "thought experiment" about racial identification to a conversation with Delany,[52] the SF author finds the language of race to be outdated, and matches the philosopher's "witchcraft" example with his own comparison of the "attempt to transcendentalize the notion of race itself" to the persistence of pre-Copernican astronomical discourse: "People still use geocentric rhetoric such as 'sunrise' and 'sunset' who are quite aware of—and wholly in concurrence with—the heliocentric vision of the solar system," he explains. "But the abuses of essentialism are much closer to us than the abuses of the Inquisition. . . ."[53] So Delany may be correct in saying that he is "at a rather problematic position" when confronted with "the current debates" about the meaning of race, "in which melanists contest with culturalists, who contest with Afro-centrists,"[54] particularly given the way that he, as Posnock states, "displaces" race with sexuality.[55] "I am a gay man," Delany states; "which is to seize only another marginal and problematic index in the discussion around so sexually and heredetarily laden a notion as race."[56] In his own way, therefore, Delany has cogently mapped out the limits of the categories of identity and race.

The visions of future worlds in certain of Delany's works of SF can similarly be seen as attenuating the significance of race. Humans of various racial heritages and configurations abound in the futuristic worlds of Delany's SF, but rarely, if ever, do characters make race the center around which their identities are constructed; more rare are examples of characters oppressed, harassed, or disenfranchised solely or primarily due to their racial makeup. Delany tells his bibliographers that at least some of his SF purposefully envisions a world without the racial conflicts ours has known, a world "where things have changed":

> In most of my futures, the racial situation has changed, and changed for the better. As a young writer I thought it was very important to keep an image of such possibility before people. . . . I don't ever remember subscribing to the idea that "being black doesn't matter." I wanted to write about worlds where being black mattered in different ways from the ways it matters now.[57]

Such a world may be one in which Appiah's vision of recreationally deployed racial identities is realized. The same could be said to be congruent with Gilroy's visions of "planetary humanism" and a description of Delany doing what he describes elsewhere as "the SF visionaries' job," which is "to provide mental practice in dealing with a whole *range* of different situations . . . different from what we have now *and* different from one another."[58] Delany describes this enterprise in "The Necessity of Tomorrows," a 1978 address at the Studio Museum in Harlem, blocks away from the building where both his childhood home and his father's funeral home business were located. "Necessity" opens with a description of his father's enterprise as well as "Mr. Lockley's Hardware and Houseware Store," which featured a metal gate with "many vertical black shafts, hinged to the numerous diagonals with rollers at their ends, between,"[59] compelling the nine-year-old Delany to touch and then rattle it before his father arrived to give a stern admonishment. Delany was fascinated with how the gate "rippled, like a curtain" (25), suggesting a web or a net and a metaphor for "society itself": "Each person represented a juncture. The connections between them were not iron struts, but relations of money, goods, economics in general, information, emotions" (26). The young Delany applied this insight to his own experience, which was "not a typical Harlem childhood" (26) in that his family was comfortably middle-class. "We lived in a private house . . . and had a maid" (26). He attended the Dalton School, "a private school at Eighty-ninth Street just off Park Avenue" with very different demographics than his Harlem neighborhood; Dalton was "overwhelmingly white, largely Jewish," many student children of "millionaires, literary lights, government officials, and theatrical personages" (26). His "twice daily" travels between Harlem and Park Avenue constituted "a journey of near ballistic violence through an absolute social barrier" (26). In language that echoes W. E. B. DuBois's figures of "double-consciousness" and "the veil," he describes his childhood musings over the relation between "these two gates, two webs, two nets": "In gross terms, the white one seemed to surround the black, holding the black one to its place and keeping it rather more crushed together in less space" (27). The primary connections between these webs were economic: "white landlords and absentee store owners" exported money out of Harlem, whereas black workers employed by whites brought it in (27). Connections between these webs were nonexistent: "Their absence was the barrier I crossed every time I left for and returned from my school," Delany says; "Their absence *was* the violence" (27). This is "the racial situation" that could be improved upon in the pages of a SF text. For Delany, the 1950s were a decade of immense technological and social change, symbolized by his memory of hearing both "Sputnik and Little Rock reported on the same September afternoon radio newscast" (27).[60] It was then that Delany became an avid reader and found African American literature, namely the works of James Baldwin, Chester Himes, and Richard Wright, to be "as wonderful as science fiction"; though these texts were backwards looking, rooted in the past, like "history" (28). There was no denying the accuracy of their representations of "the racial situation": "They certainly said that the condition of the black man in America was awful" (28). But, Wright and Himes in particular "seemed to say as well that, in any realistic terms, precisely what made it so awful also made it unchangeable." This was fairly incongruent with Delany's understanding of his world, which "was clearly exploding with racial change from headline to headline" (28). SF, with its typical—but by no means "necessary" or "sufficient"— orientation toward the future provided an alternative, but through a most unusual source. Robert A. Heinlein's Hugo Award-winning *Starship Troopers* (1959), a classic SF novel set in the future about humanity at war against a hostile alien race, provided Delany with "a galaxy of marvels" (30). It also featured some of the most militaristic content in the genre's history, brazenly lampooned by Paul Verhoeven's 1997 film of the same title.[61] But what is significant about the novel, for Delany's purposes in "Necessity," is that well into it, the narrator-protagonist, as he happens to look in a mirror, comments on the dark color of his skin. This casually mentioned detail—"He was not caucasian at all—indeed, and it gets dropped in the next sentence, his ancestors were Filipino!" (30)—signified that in the world of *Starship Troopers* race certainly had very different meanings than it did in middle-twentieth-century America:

> [A] among the many changes that had taken place in this future world that I had been dazzled by and delighted with, the greatest was that the racial situation, along with all the technological changes, had resolved itself to the point where a young soldier might tell you of his adventures for 200 pages out of a 300-page novel and not even *have* to mention his ethnic background—because it had, in his world, become that insignificant! (30)

"Necessity" contends that visions of "a racially improved world" (31) such as the one in *Starship Troopers* are vital toward creating racial justice in the here and now, even if Heinlein's novel provided "only an image—not at all an explanation of how to accomplish it," and an image Delany has repeatedly felt compelled to revise (31). He explains, however, that "one cannot *revise* an image until one *has* an image to revise" (31). The vision of a society in which race means differently—where it is not used to segregate, to alienate, to disenfranchise, to harass, or to oppress— provides a goal, a horizon, to work toward: "If science fiction has any use at all," Delany states, "it is that among all its various and variegated future landscapes it gives us images *for* our futures" (31). Concluding his address to what the reader assumes is a predominantly black audience by saying, "We need images of tomorrow; and our people need them more than most," Delany appears to pursue, like Gilroy, the liberation of people of African descent from "blind history, economics, and politics beyond our control" and the cultivation of "clear and vital images of the *many* alternatives, good and bad, of where one *can* go" (35).

If "Necessity" provides Delany's analog to Gilroy's visionary humanism, the collage aesthetic championed by Posnock and employed in the cut-and-mix stylings of contemporary electronic musics is represented by the Mouse in Delany's *Nova*. Mouse is an orphaned gypsy youth, and a master of an instrument known as the sensory-syrynx. In the thirty-second-century galactic society in which the novel is set, there is a concern about "cultural solidity"[62]—that is, the authenticity, integrity, and purity of cultural traditions—that usually manifests itself in the form of academic lectures and/or cocktail party conversation. By the end of the novel, Mouse's starship-mate Katin Crawford, a Harvard alum from Luna at work on an outdated art form known as the novel, is sharply critical of such arguments. "They're all just looking for our social traditions in the wrong place," Katin contends; "There *are* cultural traditions that have matured over the centuries, yet culminate now in something vital and solely of today" (220). Moreover, he identifies Mouse as not only the heretofore elusive topic of his novel, but also as the best embodiment of the culmination and development of the galaxy's culture. The sensory-syrynx allows Mouse to integrate various sensations and artistic genres from across a range of cultural traditions, as an admirer's request suggests: "Come on, kid! Give us the mosaics on the San Sophia ceiling again before you do the Parthenon frieze—and make 'em swing!" (14). Mouse's mastery of the syrynx prompts Katin to celebrate him as a collagist par excellence, who gives expression to the cultural logic that followed in the wake of the psycho-economic innovations, plugs and sockets that put workers into intimate contact with the tools and products of their labor, of twenty-third-century philosopher-psychologist Ashton Clark:

"You've collected the ornamentations a dozen societies have left us over the ages and made them inchoately yours. You're the product of those tensions that clashed in the time of Clark and you resolve them on your syrynx with patterns eminently of the present—" (220)

Mouse appears to exemplify Posnock's "cosmopolitan collage," which, with Katin's critique of "cultural solidity," lends further support to the case for Delany as a skeptic of identity politics, antirace race man, and visionary.

A Fabulous, Formless Blackness

Here I must say that I do not completely agree with the critiques of race and identity just described and apparently endorsed and performed by Delany—or more accurately, their deployment as critiques of social movements called "identity politics." As valuable as such critiques can be as strategies against racisms that reduce the diversity of African American communities to a single type, or against languages of authenticity that employ a similar logic, it is my belief that "identity" and "race" still have their uses, particularly for African Americans. In other words, I am not prepared to throw the baby of identity out with the bathwater of authenticity and chauvinism, no matter how grimy that bathwater may be. To borrow Diana Fuss's formulation regarding essentialism, a practice that she astutely argues is not as important to critique or endorse as much as the politics and/or aesthetics behind it, "identity" and "race" are categories that I would like "to preserve," that is, both "to embalm" and "to maintain."[63]

Stuart Hall's "Ethnicity: Identity and Difference" speaks specifically about "ethnic" groups in England whose marginality has been reinforced by their linkage to an "ethnicity," a term that he seeks to rearticulate and redeploy. His insights apply to a variety of groups, however, particularly those who have organized around various politics as racial, gender, or sexual constituencies. The essay's summation of the decenterings of identity, including "the great stable collectivities of class, race, gender and nation" (12), as well as those categories' encroachment "from above" in the form of universalizing forces of global capital and "the interdependency of our ecological life"—or the HIV/AIDS crisis—as well as "from below" in the form of even more particular identities (13), leads to the conclusion that identity is something that is constructed. As he says of his son's claims to a Jamaican identity, "he can't just take it out of a suitcase and plop it on the table and say 'That's mine'" (19). Hall also addresses identity as a process and its location within the split between Self and Other.

He even acknowledges that "there is some language for the notion of doing without identity altogether," language that characterizes the Self as "a kind of *perpetual signifier* ever wandering the earth in search of a *transcendental signified* that it can never find" (15). Ultimately, however, Hall is justifiably reluctant to give up on identity: "While there are certain conceptual and theoretical ways in which you can try to do without identity, I'm not yet convinced that you can" (15). This is because marginalized groups simply cannot contest the unjust aspects of their marginality without it:

> There is no way, it seems to me, in which people of the world can act, can speak, can create, can come in from the margins and talk, can begin to reflect on their own experience unless they come from some *place,* they come from some *history,* they inherit certain cultural traditions. (18)

Hall explains that in order to speak, one must have a place from which to speak. You and your addressee have to know, as the colloquialism goes, where you are coming from:

> What we've learned about the theory of enunciation is that there's no enunciation without positionality. You have to position yourself *somewhere* in order to say anything at all. (18)

From this perspective, history is not a retrograde realm in which the self is mired, but a source for the materials with which the work of constructing identities can be performed by marginalized constituencies:

> They need to honor the hidden histories from which they come. They need to understand the languages which they've been not taught to speak. They need to understand and revalue the traditions and inheritances of cultural expression and creativity. And in that sense, the past is not only a position from which to speak, but it is also an absolutely necessary resource in what one has to say. (18–19)

The raced subject may no longer be "innocent" of the class, gender, and sexual differences (among others) that split it; however, that loss of innocence has not occasioned the loss of racial/ethnic identity's efficacy or usefulness as a platform for speaking—one of many, upon which others can be erected and others extracted.

The absence of any biological meaning of race and the common humanity of us all deserve frequent and repeated declaration and celebration, particularly as a response to persistent racisms at both personal and institutional levels. But I am not the first to point out that despite being scientifically bankrupt, race continues to have immense powers to shape our world. As Appiah's counterpart on the topics of philosophy and race, Lucius Outlaw, puts it, "That 'race' is without a scientific basis in biological terms does *not* mean, thereby, that it is without any social value, racism notwithstanding."[64] Given the history of its deployment by racist regimes, denunciations of race as "evil" and "deadly" in and of itself are understandable, and to be supported when deployed strategically against specific racisms. But there *is* a distinction between "race" and "racism," despite their intertwined careers, which such arguments sometimes obscure. I find Michael Omi and Howard Winant's concept of "racial formation" a much more practical, appropriate, and sophisticated approach because it acknowledges that racial meanings are multiple, that they contest with one another, that the meaning of race is contextualized.[65] For example, "race" is a concept central to the Ku Klux Klan, as it is to the NAACP; only a fool, however, would draw a moral or political equivalence between these groups. Each formation indicates a different racial meaning. Outlaw most appropriately draws attention to the meaning of race for "the lived experiences of those within racial groups," to an "[appreciation of] the integrity of those who see themselves through the prism of 'race.'" I will hazard the following generalization: African Americans know that there is no such thing as race. This does not stop African Americans from passing on narratives of our history, creating and listening to black music, cooking certain recipes, reading African American literature, speaking "black English," and organizing politically and in other ways with the specific purpose of combating racism. "We must not err yet again," Outlaw states, "in thinking that 'race thinking' must be completely eliminated on the way to emancipated society."[66] Whatever it may be in the future, at present, for many African Americans, race is a constitutive, though not necessarily dominant or privileged, element of many black identities.

I am not prepared to limit "identity," specifically racial identity, solely to the realm of the provisional and the political. This is because for at least some African Americans, a degree of racial pride is a necessary part of day-to-day survival in a racist society. Appiah acknowledges that racial identity may be "historically, strategically necessary" for this reason, but he wants to ask further "whether the identities constructed in this way are ones we can all be happy with in the longer run."[67] Perhaps, perhaps not; but the subsequent question is what it will take to make the practice of provisional racial identities a practical reality. Any answer that does not take into account persistent derogations of blackness, as well as what George Lipsitz calls "the possessive investment in whiteness," is incomplete.[68] Given the persistence of anti-black attitudes and practices, both in the academy (white students harassing students of color for simply being present on campus, white fratboys masquerading in blackface makeup, students writing racist graffitti aimed at instructors and courses on classroom blackboards) and in "the real world" (racial profiling, black overrepresentation among incarcerated Americans, white firefighters' refusal of a symbolically multiracial memorial statue), it appears that the greatest stake in racial categories can be located in efforts to maintain and advance white privilege. To tell African Americans on the receiving ends of such antagonisms that race does not exist strikes me as both a feeble and patronizing response. But it seems as if Appiah's visions lay the responsibility for transforming black identities and the social and political conditions that give them shape primarily on the shoulders of black people.

We must remember that "identities are often not embraced voluntarily but rather forced upon individuals and communities by homophobic, sexist, and racist power structures."[69] Attacks on identity politics, therefore, are attacks on the conceptual tools that raced groups, women, and sexual minorities have used to recognize and organize themselves in order to critique, to speak back to a centered subjectivity that does not need an "identity politics" because they have not had an identity imposed upon them. "Identity politics is a rejection of interpellation and an insistence upon public re-identification," according to Grant Farred; "it represents the political effort to increase minority agency, to challenge and reconfigure the ways in which the dominant group positions and 'sees' (publicly understands) its marginal constituents." Perhaps the most obvious example of this is the radical—though hardly unproblematic—rearticulation and redeployment of the term "nigger" in contemporary hip-hop culture. Farred sees this phenomenon as evidence that those who have been interpellated as a demonized identity have "wrested the authority for themselves," and "they now police the use of the historically pejorative, determining who can use it, where it can be applied, and, most importantly, who is prevented from invoking it."[70] "Queer" has a similar recent history as an epithet, appropriated by those it interpellated, and redeployed as a locus of identity, community, and resistance against anti-gay bigotry. If we understand "the struggle for identity" as enabling and enabled by, as Farred puts it, "the capacity of marginalized groups to . . . simultaneously acknowledge, reject, and reinscribe the disjuncture between 'identities imposed' and those desired," perhaps the "recreational, provisional" blackness that Appiah champions can be seen as a long-range goal toward which identity politics works.

I, for one, am extremely sympathetic to, and thankful for, critiques of racial authenticity such as Appiah's debunking of racial "scripts." As an African American who was teased throughout childhood and high school for "talking proper," as a student of literature in English who has longed to study the British Romantics with the same frequency as African American literature, as a music lover who is as much a fan of U2, Nirvana, and Radiohead as Charles Mingus, Bob Marley, and The Roots, I am most appreciative of Appiah's—and, for that matter, Delany's—declarations of an autonomous identity that is not confined by narrow racial expectations, from other African Americans as well as from whites. Too often, one's race threatens to eclipse all the other things that one is. As Appiah quite appropriately notes, in addition to our racial, sexual, and religious subject positions, "we are also brothers and sisters; parents and children; liberals, conservatives, and leftists; teachers and lawyers and auto-makers and gardeners; fans of the Padres and the Bruins; amateurs of grunge rock and lovers of Wagner; movie buffs; MTV-holics, mystery-readers; surfers and singers; poets and pet-lovers; students and teachers; friends and lovers."[71] Such a realization does not mean, however, that my "blackness" is not a valued part of my own "multifarious" identity. It is indeed the place from which I do a large part—though not the entirety—of my speaking, personally, professionally, socially. Does choosing to speak as a "black writer" necessarily preclude that writer's engagement of, activation of, other aspects of the self? Has identifying as a black writer kept bell hooks from her work as a feminist or Toni Morrison from writing on Woolf and Faulkner? Although individual identity and group identity politics come into conflict, as in DuBois's "unreconciled strivings" and "warring ideals," they also combine, connect, and coexist.

The current critique of identity politics coming from certain left-liberal intellectuals appears to be nostalgic for an earlier era for Left politics. Farred identifies the arguments in Todd Gitlin's "Organizing Across Boundaries" as endorsing a "universalist" politics that hearkens back to "the 1960s when the Left was a more coherent, structured organization." According to Farred, intellectuals such as Gitlin and Wendy Brown lament the "splintering" of the Left into various identity movements. Whereas some would like to turn back the clock, Farred's sketch of the history of identity politics, however, locates its "roots" within the New Left. Paralleling the development of Cultural Studies in the academy, identity politics, Farred contends, "gave cultural articulation to the achievements of the Civil Rights, Black Power, Stonewall, students', and women's movements of the 1960s and 1970s" and served as "the 1980s corollary of the 1960s' 'cultural revolution.'"[72] He explains that identity movements were generated by groups "who had constituted [the Left] but were never recognized as central to its functioning," groups that became conceivable as a result of the interrogation of the privileging "class" received as a category of analysis and organization, especially after working-class constituencies were hijacked by the Reagan-Thatcher Right:

Out of the history, disjunctures, and the ideological contestations within the New Left emerged not only profound black, female, and gay wariness of class as an organizational instrument, but the fracturing of that political category into distinct constituencies; these disjunctures enabled a series of new resistance strategies. . . . Groups once presumed to be only problematically part of the working class now took up positions at a distance from it. Blacks, gays, women, and greens insisted upon their difference from not only the hegemonic class of the New Left leadership, but also from the unfissured working class.[73]

Farred contends, however, that these new movements cannot be seen as being in opposition to the New Left. "The 'struggle' was never abandoned; it was simply refashioned by the 'new social movements'"; the New Left was "superceded by a younger, more fluid, and mobile manifestation of itself."[74] Farred's sketch suggests the problems with translating, as Delany puts it, the positive meanings of race into terms of class. Class no longer sustains a privileged or central position relative to race. Indeed class and race are categories and identities that intersect and make a difference to each other; there are a range of black experiences and white experiences across class difference. Similarly, it is to be expected that blacks and whites who occupy the same economic class—lower, working, middle, or upper—have different experiences. To say that one is translatable into the other seems factually wrong and, frankly, smacks of the orthodox quasi-Marxism espoused by the Brotherhood—"Why do you fellows always talk in terms of race!"[75]—and criticized in *Invisible Man* by Ralph Ellison, who can hardly be called an essentialist given his familiarity with, and assertions of, the hybridity and multiplicity of American and African American identities. "Everybody intuitively knows that everyday life is so complex that no singular belief system or Big Story can hope to explain it all," Kobena Mercer says; "we don't need another hero."[76] Neither race nor class, nor any other category on its own, will suffice.

Palumbo-Liu identifies a more disturbing aspect of the new critiques of identity politics, of "postethnic thinking," in the tendency to "overplay the economic" and "downplay" the continuation of "prejudice against those who are particularly *identified.*"[77] Anti-identity politics rhetoric is also too easily co-opted by what Farred identifies as the anti-P.C. backlash. "There is no censure for being against 'political correctness,'" Farred observes, and "there are few easier ways to score political points than to disavow or bash 'P.C.-ness.'"[78] "You're just being P.C." is merely code for the speaker's desire to maintain a certain privilege and to resist antiracist, antisexist, or anti-homophobic language.

Gilroy's humanistic futurism also raises concerns about how it could be rearticulated in direct opposition to its ideals. Criticisms of race consciousness on the basis of the claims that it makes about the past neglect of what Farred calls "a struggle for and about a history—a past and a present that has been misrepresented, silenced, muted, mutilated, or even obliterated, a past that has to be reclaimed and reconstituted in the present."[79] For example, arguments that race is not what it once was provide ample ammunition for the conservative critics of Affirmative Action and jeopardize the possibility of discussing, let alone advocating for, reparations for slavery. The world certainly has needed and continues to need its visionaries, but the visions they generate must be cognizant of, and germane to, the lived experiences of raced groups. "The idea that we are all somehow mixed is a notion with which any group of reasonably intelligent undergraduates will agree," states Robert Reid-Pharr; "The problem stems from the fact that this agreement does little to change the actual conditions of living Americans."[80] Cultivating images of future racial harmony is fine, but that project must be tempered by a vigilance against what Terry Eagleton identifies as a "bad utopianism," which "grabs instantly for a future, projecting itself by an act of will or imagination beyond the compromised political structures of the present."[81]

A number of critics have argued convincingly that what really matters in the debate over identity politics is not "identity" as much as the politics.[82] Judith Butler's *Gender Trouble* actually concludes on this note: "The deconstruction of identity is not the deconstruction of politics; rather, it establishes as political the very terms through which identity is articulated."[83] This is a position I agree with in general, but given the value of race pride as sustenance and a shield against continuing attacks on black humanity, I do not see African Americans opting out of identity because of its constructed or phantasmagorical nature any time real soon. And if we do face "the end of identity politics," I must concur with Robert Reid-Pharr that before dancing on the corpse's ashes "we must at the very least offer an alternative that speaks to the realities of people's lives."[84]

Given my position on the status of "race" and "identity," I have an investment in "inventing" a Delany that is different from Posnock's anti-race race man, from a humanistic futurist, and from a skeptic of "identity politics." I choose to recognize his own characterization of how he speaks very much from a specific position, one shaped not by race alone, but also by his sexuality and the genre with which he is most associated:

Well, I see myself as writing from a particular position. That position is black; it's gay; it's male; and it's far more contoured by the marginal workings of science fiction than what I take to be the central concerns of literature, that is, those concerns organized around "the priority of the subject."[85]

Delany's conversation with Anthony Davis and Henry Louis Gates Jr. transcribed in *Silent Interviews,* about opera, Malcolm X, and race, is an example of Delany speaking very much as a black man to other black men, specifically about the black incursion into what had been previously understood, particularly by white opera critics, as predominantly white cultural space that Davis's opera *X* and its audience represented.

SF may indeed provide images of the future where "the racial situation" is much improved, but to assert that the genre necessarily features a futuristic orientation would be incorrect. Delany is known for asserting that, contrary to Gilroy's characterization of the genre, "science fiction is not 'about the future'"; rather, it is "a significant distortion of the present that sets up a rich and complex dialogue with the reader's here and now."[86] As with all texts, works of SF are documents of the historical moment in which they are produced. "The 'future,'" Delany explains, "is the most common writerly convention science fiction uses to accomplish this [distortion], but it is not the only one." He identifies the parallel universe as another convention; cyberspace/virtual reality in cyberpunk SF is a more recent device. All of these conventions provide the SF author with the space to create a world similar to and significantly different from the one he or she shares with the reader. Indeed the difference between the world in a work of SF and "the real world" are of great importance to Delany. "Necessity" not only expresses the impact of *Starship Troopers'* vision of a future world where race mattered differently, but also demonstrates the significance of the difference between fictional and factual worlds. Isaac Asimov's robot stories are cited as 1950s SF that "veered close" to addressing America's changing racial landscape. The famous "Three Laws of Robotics"—1) A robot may not injure a human being, or, through inaction, allow a human being to come to harm. 2) A robot must obey the orders given to it by human beings except where such orders would conflict with the First Law. 3) A robot must protect its own existence as long as such protection does not conflict with the First or Second Law[87]—provide an analogue for "a white ideal of what the 'good Negro' ought to be."[88] But if the primary utility of SF is its images of the future, "its secondary use," Delany says, "is to provide a tool for questioning those images, exploring their distinctions, their articulations, their play of differences" (31). Reading Asimov also prompted the young Delany to ask questions about the incongruities between robots and African Americans: "Just exactly how does the situation of the robots in these stories *differ* from the reality of the racial situation of my world?" (29), a questioning that he claims led him to be "a far more astute observer of our own racial situation than I might otherwise have been" (29). The similarities and differences between the world of a SF text and that of the reader are characteristic of "the marginal workings of SF" and central to what makes SF in general, and Delany's work in the genre specifically, so fascinating and so significant for African American Studies.

As his conversation with Davis and Gates and his discussions of Heinlein and Asimov demonstrate, Delany's belief that race does not exist does not keep him from addressing race and racial issues. For example, speaking "as a black reader," he has taken William Gibson to task for the Rastafarians in *Neuromancer* (1984), whom Delany describes as "a powerless and wholly nonoppositional set of black dropouts."[89] His more extensive response to Helen Vendler's reading of Rita Dove's poetry serves as something of a template for this book's response to readings of Delany by critics like Posnock. For a 1999 issue of an *American Literary History* symposium on "The Situation of American Writing," Delany and twenty-five other writers responded to short set of questions, beginning with:

> No matter how strict your sense of career as an individual endeavor, do you also find that your writing reveals a connection to any group—political, religious, cultural, national, international, racial, class, gender, sexual, or other? Do you see your development as a writer as contiguous with the interests of any such larger group? Do you see this development as linked in any way to the socioeconomic circumstances of your upbringing?[90]

In his overview of these questions, Delany, following the examples of Roland Barthes and Michel Foucault, critiques the "positivity" that enables the construction of an author as "authoritative, intentions wholly present to himself, centered in the current of some mainstream society" (331–32). He is also quite candid about his belief that "all art is political" because everything is and because art is an expression of the very political practice of asking questions about the world (333), as well as his "farther to the left than not" position on issues such as "African American rights, women's rights, gay rights" (334). However, Delany sees "writing as a practice" as "not in any *necessary* way allied to any of these categories" (333). His response to the final question about "scholarly assessments of contemporary writing" (220), contends that Vendler's reading of Dove "staggers into the same slough of political positivity in which [the] opening questions were mired" (344). Vendler states that "the primary given for the black poet Rita Dove has to be—as for other black writers in America—the fact of her blackness," which Delany finds ludicrous. It is not that he believes Dove's racial subject position is not an important lens through which to read her poetry, but that it, or any other aspect of her identity, could be privileged and prioritized as a "primary given," which is a concept that Delany states "needs to be jettisoned if the criticism is to reach any level of sophistication" (344). Vendler follows with the claim that "no black has blackness as sole identity"; as true as this statement is, it is merely an attempt, Delany contends, at "defusing her opening totalization," and proves to be "entirely absorbed by what Derrida analyzed as the logic of the supplement" (345). Vendler later judges "the best poem" in Dove's first volume, "a poem of perfect wonder," to be "Geometry," in which Dove "has not a word to say about the fraught subject of blackness" (346). Delany's response to this reading is insightful, to the point, and a bit charged:

> One would have to be culturally deaf not to hear, beneath Vendler's explicit argument, that, somehow, in this poem, as it is placed not in Dove's book, but in Vendler's exegesis, after the "stagy" and "unsuccessful" historical poems about blackness that don't quite work, an implied contention that somehow, by writing a poem that "has not a word to say about the fraught subject," Dove has herself, like her house, expanded, expanded *beyond* blackness into the realm of pure poetry by writing a poem that is, rather than about blackness, "about what Geometry and poetic form have to say about one another." And, to put it gently, I just don't think this is the case. I don't think this is how blackness figures either in the lives of black men and women, nor in the art of most black writers, nor in *this* poem: a primary given that, somehow, the writer must expand beyond (impossible, however, because it *is* a primary given) to achieve a poetry of pure wonder. (347)

Delany points out that the praise Vendler gives Dove's "Parsley" is because the poem displays sympathy for both a white dictator and his black victims and that she contends that in *Thomas and Beulah* "The things that make Thomas unhappy are not his blackness and his oppression by whites—not at all" (347). "Who in the *world*," Delany asks "is Vendler talking down to like that?" (347). For him Vendler's claim that "for the most part the handsome poems Dove has written . . . do not take blackness as one of their themes" is an attempt "to teach [Dove] why the 'poetry of wonder' is attainable once she or he has expanded beyond blackness" (348).

In a more direct response to the question of whether his writing demonstrates his identification with any particular group, Delany acknowledges that his writing probably betrays an interest in, for example, African Americans, homosexuals, and men because of his own subject position(s). But he contends that the "primary givens of his life" are not "primary givens of his writing," and are instead "at best provisional material *for* writing" (350). The presence of the features that mark his writing as "African American" or "gay" are not the products of some involuntary "cultural geneticism"; rather, Delany purposefully chooses to address issues of race and sexuality. Vendler's mistakes, I would contend, are the mistakes that scholars like Posnock make with regard to Delany, portraying him as black writer whose evasions of the parochialisms associated with racial identity have enabled him to produce sophisticated art. To echo Delany, I do not think that this is how race operates in his writing, which to be appreciated requires attentive reading along with awareness of the author's commitment to difference and to SF.

Worlds of Wonder

> [D]espite its superficial resemblance to realistic or naturalistic twentieth-century
> fiction [science fiction] is fundamentally a drastically different form of literary art.
> —Joanna Russ "Toward an Aesthetic of Science Fiction"[91]

According to John Clute and Peter Nicholls' *Encyclopedia of Science Fiction* (1993), "sense of wonder" is "a term used to describe the sensation which, according the cliché of fan criticism that goes back at least to the 1940s, good SF should inspire in the reader." Rather than a quality within the work of SF itself, it is a response by the reader to the work. Attempts have been made to specify this sense further by linking it to "transcendence" or "the sublime."[92] Delany attributes the phrase to SF author, editor, and critic Damon Knight, who "lifted" it from W. H. Auden's "In Memory of Sigmund Freud"[93]:

> but he would have us remember most of all
> to be enthusiastic over the night,
>   not only for the sense of wonder
> it alone has to offer, but also
>
> because it needs our love. . . .[94]

Knight's volume of SF criticism, *In Search of Wonder* (1956) attributes the phrase to SF historian Sam Moskowitz and asserts that "science fiction exists to provide . . . the sense of wonder," which he describes as

> some widening of the mind's horizons, no matter in what direction—the
> landscape of another planet, or a corpuscle's-eye view of an artery, or what
> it feels like to be in rapport with a cat . . . any new sensory experience, im-
> possible to the reader in his own person, is grist for the mill, and what the
> activity of science fiction writing is all about.[95]

Gary K. Wolfe's *Critical Terms for Science Fiction and Fantasy* notes that the "sense of wonder" may precede Auden's poem, as "wonder" was prominent in titles of pulp magazines that emerged in America during the late 1920s and were popular in subsequent decades, for example, "*Worlds of Wonder.*"[96] Despite its possible links to these roots of the genre and its intersection with high-modernist literature, however, the term has not been in good standing in SF for a long time. Darko Suvin, in *Metamorphoses*, says that the sense of wonder is "another superannuated slogan of much SF criticism due for a deserved retirement into the same limbo as extrapolation."[97] According to Clute and Nicholls' *Encyclopedia*, the response can be produced by even the most "badly written" examples of SF, particularly those that have not evolved from the genre's primordial origins in pulp magazines. The term has therefore been associated with adolescent first encounters with SF's "lowest form, pulp prose"; the sense of wonder is also understood to be easily "counterfeited" in SF through the inclusion of "something a) alien, and b) very, very big." For these reasons, the term has been derided among some SF readers, those who are "likely to use it ironically, spelling and pronouncing it 'sensa-wunna.'" It would appear that times are as hard for the "sense of wonder" as they are for "identity" and "race." Nevertheless the term "may be necessary if we are to understand the essence of SF that distinguishes it from other forms of fiction" and identifies "feelings that seem too honest and strong to be dismissed as youthful illusion."[98]

Delany's own illustration of the sense of wonder does indeed identify what makes SF special, that is, both enjoyable and distinct from other genres, particularly "literature." The introduction to *Empire* (1978), a collaboration with artist Howard V. Chaykin, which Delany has since humbly called a "glorified comic-book,"[99] suggests that hierarchical thinking is at least partly a result of our experience with the force of gravity: "Almost everything is measured on this same, imaginary scale that runs from *down* to *up*, from *lower* to *higher.*"[100] Delany asserts that the image most associated with SF, a rocket ship, is a useful antidote for verticality:

> Consider: a rocketship takes off. It goes up, *higher* and *higher;* and still *higher.* At a certain point, after escape velocity is passed, it decreases acceleration and, inside, suddenly "up" and "down" cease to exist . . . Everything is in free-fall.[101]

This ship's encounters with other star systems and planets generate a series of decenterings. The Earth, the ground on which vertical measurement systems are based, ceases to be the center of the universe, and is now seen to be revolving around a sun. Interstellar travel then reveals that that sun, the center of a solar system, is part of galaxy of stars. And that galaxy is one of countless others. According to Delany, SF's decentering process is what makes it appealing:

This experience of constant de-centered de-centeredness, each decentering on a vaster and vaster scale, has a venerable name among people who talk about science fiction: "the sense of wonder."[102]

SF's almost routine tendency to present alternatives—in this case, an alternative perspective, an alternative point of view—is what distinguishes it from the literary. SF is a type of "paraliterature," which Suvin describes as "the popular, 'low,' or plebeian literary production of various times, particularly since the Industrial Revolution,"[103] a field which also includes, according to Delany, "comic books, pornography, film and television scripts, advertising copy, instructions on the back of the box, street signs, popular song lyrics, business letters, journalism—in short, the graphic flood from which most of the texts each of us encounters over any day come."[104] Paraliterature is the generic Other against which literature defines itself. "Just as (discursively) homosexuality exists largely to delimit heterosexuality and to lend it a false sense of definition," Delany explains, "paraliterature exists to delimit literature and provide it with an equally false sense of itself."[105] Hence the dismissive attitude toward SF one may encounter at, for example, a meeting of the Modern Language Association. The difference between SF and literature is also mapped out in Delany's "*Dichtung und* Science Fiction," which notes that since "about the last quarter of the nineteenth century," literature has been characterized by its prioritization of the subject, "of the self, of human consciousness," whereas SF is characterized by its prioritization of the object, "i.e., the world, or the institutions through which we perceive it," not to the exclusion of the subject, but with a emphasis on how the subject is "excited, impinged on, contoured and constituted by the object."[106] If we return to Delany's example of sentences that not only mean differently but also must be read differently depending on whether they are found in a literary fiction or paraliterary SF (e.g., "Her world exploded.") it is evident that in a work of SF such a sentence prompts its reader to ask, the following questions: "What in the portrayed *world* of the story, by statement or implication, must be *different from ours* in order for this sentence to be normally uttered? (That is, how does the condition of possibility in the world of the story differ from ours?)"[107] In other words, in the fictional world in which the event that "Her world exploded" signifies is set, it is possible for a woman to own or govern a planet (assuming that the belonging implied by the pronoun "her" does not indicate place of origin). In the reader's reality, the technological, social, economic, and political systems that make the sentence's literal meaning meaningful are, obviously, absent. An individual female, is not able to own or govern an entire planet. Delany provides another example in "*Dichtung*":

But even the most passing mention by a SF writer of, say, "the monopole magnet mining operations in the outer asteroid belt of Delta Cygni," begins as a simple way of saying that, while the concept of mines may persist, their object, their organization, their technology, their locations, and their very form can change—and it says it directly and clearly and well before it offers any metaphor for any psychic mystery or psychological state. Not to understand this object-critique, on whatever intuitive level, is to misread the phrase as science fiction.[108]

Kenneth James's introduction to Delany's *Longer Views* cites the preceding passage and Barthes's observation in *Mythologies* that "things lose the memory that they once were made"[109] in order to illustrate how critical theory, SF in general, and Delany's writing in particular, offer "ways of scrutinizing things which may seem eternal, totalized, and systemic, and questioning their totality, interrogating their systematicity."[110] Such scrutiny is fundamental to the writing of SF. In response to the question, "Where do sf writers get their crazy ideas?" Delany answers, "From watching all there is *very* carefully."[111] James states that Delany's example demonstrates SF's tendency to reveal conventional ways of structuring reality as exactly that, matters of convention as opposed to nature: "even the most conservatively inclined science fiction," James says, "if it is in any way sophisticated *as* science fiction, must keep a certain margin of imaginative space open for the apprehension of the historicity of objects, landscapes, and social institutions."[112]

SF, therefore, focuses on, to borrow from Delany's *The Mad Man*, "the systems of the world," the structures that both shape and are inhabited by subjectivities. The language of SF prompts the reader to conceptually build upon, around, and in place of the structures known to him or her, altering them in order to conceive the science-fictional world. This possibility of alternatives informs Delany's emphasis on the importance of "the difference between the science-fictional world and the real world" in "Necessity"; it adds a layer of meaning to his assertion that SF is "a significant distortion" of present reality. SF regularly offers its readers alternative systems of the world, whether social, political, ideological, cultural, economic, sexual, all of these, or other. "The SF writer's overarching theme," Delany says, "is likely to be the discovery that the world itself is negotiable."[113] Earl Jackson Jr.'s characterization of Delany's SF as "imagining it otherwise,"[114] therefore, is quite appropriate. According to James, the political ramifications of this practice, of which Delany is cognizant and takes full advantage, are considerable, particularly in the context of his racial and sexual subject positions:

> For a gay black man such as Delany—or for anyone of whatever social position committed to a critique of or intervention in a status quo which

seems to derive much of its strength from a whole series of discursive and coercive exclusions and oppressions—the recognition of the relativization of discourse to rhetoric is a tremendously empowering political truth.[115]

The sense of wonder, therefore, identifies the effect of SF's challenges upon the reader and speaks to the genre's palpably radical potential.

Worlds of Difference

In its engagements with and affinities for critical theory, as well as its analyses of structures discursively inscribed as "natural," Delany's writing strikes this reader as quintessentially postmodern, a term that may be considered by some to be either outmoded ("That's *so* 80s!") or "waning." I want to suggest "postmodernism" is still relevant, however, especially when considering Delany's career and his writing, which aspires to the multiple.

"Postmodernism" has been employed in a variety of academic disciplines including literature, politics, sociology, architecture, visual arts, music, and the like. It has been associated with decentered subjects and Derridean deconstruction, characterized by Fredric Jameson as "the cultural logic of late capitalism" and an awareness of modernism's "dominant, but dead" status, described by Jean-Francois Lyotard as "incredulity toward metanarratives," and identified by Dick Hebdige as the negation of totality, teleology, and utopia. Ihab Hassan's "catena" or "paratactic list" of postmodernisms includes "indeterminacy, fragmentation, decanonization, self-less-ness, depth-less-ness, the unpresentable, unrepresentable, irony, hybridization, carnivalization, performance, participation, constructionism, and immanence."[116] Both celebrated and derided, encouraged and cautioned against (sometimes simultaneously) throughout its career, postmodernism is like the transuranic element Illyrion in Delany's rollicking early SF novel, *Nova;* both are "psychomorphic and heterotropic" (31), that is, "many things to many people."[117] As Steven Seidman puts it, postmodernism is "a rhetorical figure whose meaning is linked to the use to which it is put in a particular social context."[118]

Whatever locales of meaning "postmodernism" has visited, SF has probably already been there. Delany's 1990 Afterword to his novel *Stars in My Pocket Like Grains of Sand* (1984) cites Kim Stanley Robinson's response to Fredric Jameson's 1984 essay, "Postmodernism, or the Cultural Logic of Late Capitalism," a response that sees the embodiment of Jameson's descriptions of postmodernism in Delany and Robinson's genre of choice. The split between modern and postmodern culture parallels the emergence of the "New Wave" of SF emerging in the mid- to late 1960s.

"Post–New Wave SF" is noted for bringing an "added esthetic richness" to the lowly paraliterary genre, thus blurring the boundaries between "high" and "low" or "popular" art in a typically postmodern way. Robinson and Delany see a postmodern pastiche of other fictional forms, "detective fiction . . . earlier modes of SF," in the SF of writers such as Roger Zelazny, John Varley, and William Gibson, whose works resist readings that search for modernist depth. Robinson's point, according to Delany, is that "if you're looking for the new, postmodernist art, clearly it's already emerged,"[119] and its name is science fiction.

It is SF's postmodern ability to decenter, which produces the sense of wonder, that is most significant, particularly with regard to race. Robert Young interprets postmodernism as the decentering of white, Euroupean-derived culture, because it is accompanied by "a deconstruction of . . . the concept, the authority, and assumed primacy of, the category of 'the West.'"[120] Young claims that postmodernism can best be understood as European history and culture no longer having the status of "History and Culture," no longer occupying "their unquestioned place at the centre of the world."[121] Delany's Afterword makes a similar argument, specifying further the subjectivity his work has an interest in decentering. Jameson "inclines" away from "a radical poststructuralist position" that contends that a central subjectivity has always been an "ideological mirage" and toward an "historicist position" that sees the "once-existing central subject" as having "dissolved . . . in the world of organizational bureaucracy."[122] Delany "incline[s] the *other* way":

> I think that any time when there was such a notion of a centered subject, especially when related to the white, western, patriarchal nuclear family, not only was it an ideological mirage, it was a mirage that necessarily grew up to mask the psychological, economic, and material oppression of an 'other' . . .[123]

The scrutiny that SF and critical theory apply to the systems of the world is similar to that which Delany seeks to bring to bear on the construction of a centered—white, male, heteronormative—subject, often at the core of a putative universal humanism. Hence postmodernism's association with a politics of difference, "wherein many of the voices of color, gender, and sexual orientation, newly liberated from the margins, have found representation," culturally and politically.[124] The postmodern goal is not to divide and separate people into polarized identities, but instead to recognize the constitutive characteristics within—and between—groups, which is an essential step toward redressing unjust differences in terms of political power, social status, and cultural recognition. As such, Wahneema Lubiano interprets the significance of postmodernism to African Americans in particular as "a 'name' that allows certain of us African Americans to organize our response to modernism's blind spot in regard to people of color" and as "a general epistemological standpoint for engaging/foregrounding what has been left out of larger discourses, a consideration of certain kinds of difference and the reasons for their historical absences."[125]

Lubiano goes an important step further by training this postmodern sensitivity to difference upon black identity. "It is necessary to be able to see when color hangs us all," she says, "as well as when gender or sexuality adds weight to the tree limb."[126] The black postmodernism that Lubiano theorizes involves a recognition of the end of the innocent black subject heralded by Hall. That "end" does not require an abandonment of black identity; but rather, a critical self-reflexivity that acknowledges that certain constructions of "blackness" have marginalized black women and black gays and that both black identity and black liberatory politics have "frequently been stabilized around particular conceptions of black masculinity."[127] Phillip Bryan Harper's *Are We Not Men?* (1996) reveals, for example, that "debates over and claims to 'authentic' African American identity are largely animated by a profound anxiety about the status specifically of African American *masculinity*."[128] White supremacy collapses people of African descent into a single type, a danger black nationalisms have flirted with out of a blindness to the multiplicity of black identity. In hindsight, it appears as if diverse black identities have been produced—or more accurately, brought to collective attention—through a manner comparable to nuclear fission, as if the denigrated blackness imposed by white supremacy and the exalted blackness of black nationalism collided like atomic particles, producing other particles of identity, as well as some light and a lot of heat. But the diversity of people of African descent is not a new phenomenon; differences of gender, class, sexuality, geography, generation, education, and the like, instead of dividing the black community, have constituted it. A black politics of difference, therefore, must engage in the business of "build[ing] those forms of solidarity and identification which make common struggle and resistance possible but without suppressing the real heterogeneity of interests and identities."[129] As Harper states, "African American social difference must be acknowledged, attended to, engaged, and interrogated, rather than denied or deemed inadmissible, and this belief constitutes both a theory of cultural-critical practice and a political position."[130] African American postmodern culture thus represents the variety of "the black experience," the diversity of "the black community," and the multiplicity of "black identity." There is a fundamental contradiction, therefore, in Posnock's argument. The same postmodern investment in difference, which he dismisses with the racialized language of "fetishization" and "tribalism," actually asserts the vast diversity of black identities and issues available for black intellectuals to explore.

Delany's career has been a series of cultural expressions of a politics of difference. With Lubiano's formulation in mind, his entry as a writer into the previously all-white field of SF can be seen as a postmodern intervention. He claims that he never intended his participation in the genre as an act of transgression. However, given the harangue from an éminence grise prior to Delany's reception of the Nebula Award at the 1968 banquet, which dismissed SF like Delany's as "pretentious literary nonsense," the author notes that "transgression inheres, however unarticulated, in every aspect of the black writer's career in America."[131] The marginality of Delany's chosen genre parallels that of his racial and sexual subject positions, all of which provide him a vantage point from which his SF can observe and analyze the center:

> For a number of reasons, from my racial makeup to my sexuality to my chosen field of writing, SF—or even because, in this society, I've chosen to write at all—my life has always tended to have a large element of marginality to it, at least if you accept a certain range of experience that overlaps those of an ideal, white, middle-class, heterosexual male as the definition of centrality.[132]

As this statement suggests, the marginality of Delany's life is paralleled by the marginalization of SF as a genre, of which he takes full advantage. For Grant Farred, identity politics represent marginalized groups challenging hegemonically imposed identities by inhabiting those identities, being "'ontologically' aware of (or 'invested in') their public subjectivities in order to respond to them."[133] The wound can only be healed by the sword that caused it. Something similar happens with SF, which contributes to a kind of "genre consciousness" in Delany. There is a strong similarity between hip-hop's rearticulation of "nigger," gays' and lesbians' rearticulation of "queer," and Delany's embrace and deployment of "paraliterature." This is not to equate SF with new social movements or to suggest a *necessary* affinity between SF and such movements. The point is rather that, according to Delany, the genre's marginality is "one of the most forceful and distinguishing aspects of science fiction"; it enables SF's critique of the object. From this marginal position, it is "at its most honest and most effective."[134] Delany may contend that SF or any genre is impure and undefinable and has said that he has "never *proclaimed* [his] work SF, proudly *or* humbly."[135] But he frequently celebrates SF's distinction from the literary in terms of its language, scope, and object-critique:

I feel the science-fictional enterprise is richer than the enterprise of mundane fiction. It is richer through its extended repertoire of sentences, its consequent greater range of possible incident, and through its more varied field of rhetorical and syntagmatic organization. I feel it is richer in much the same way atonal music is richer than tonal, or abstract painting is richer than realistic.[136]

There is a kind of "genre pride" to Delany's response to the worn-out "literature is good; science fiction is bad" cliché; instead of suggesting that SF is like literature, he purposefully identifies its difference from the literary. He also criticizes uninformed attempts to legitimize SF by conflating it with its privileged opposite, as in the application of the term "speculative fiction," which has a specific history of usage, but more often than not means little more than "high-class SF" or "SF I approve of and wish to see legitimated."[137] Attempts to make this paraliterary genre seem more literary, that is, more respectable, by claiming that its roots can be found in the writing of figures like Edgar Allan Poe, Mary Shelley, or even Plato, are well-intentioned and can even lead to fascinating interpretative possibilities, but these attempts often fail to recognize the pulp magazines dating back to the late 1920s as the real precursor to what we call SF. "There's no reason to run SF too much back before 1926," Delany contends, "when Hugo Gernsback coined the ugly and ponderous term 'scientifiction.'" The pulp magazines that Gernsback pioneered were dismissed as frivolous, anti-intellectual "trash" because they were inexpensive, and therefore regularly purchased by the young and the poor. This particular "high culture/low culture" split, therefore, has been at least partly a matter of economic class. SF has inherited the stigma imposed upon these magazines, as well as "a new way of reading, a new way of making texts make sense."[138] The academy's attempts to absorb SF without a respect for the genre's history demonstrates the blindness described in the first [and last] tale in Delany's *Return to Nevèrÿon* series, "The Tale of Gorgik": "It is precisely at the center that one loses the clear vision of what surrounds, what controls and contours every utterance, decides and develops every action."[139] The perspective offered by the margin may have something to do with why so many of Delany's characters are either artists, criminals, or both. *Dhalgren*'s Kid is a poet/vagabond; *Nova*'s Mouse is a musician/thief whose sensory-syrynx, like Lobey's sword/flute in *The Einstein Intersection,* can kill as well as create. In *Empire Star* (1966) the Lump tells Comet Jo that "the only important elements in any society are the artistic and the criminal, because they alone, by questioning the society's values, can force it to change."[140] The politics of difference, therefore, also apply to the cultural politics between the literary and the paraliterary.

A closer look at Delany's fiction reveals an investment in the politics of difference, demonstrated in representations ranging from the dangers produced out of a fear of difference to characters embracing difference as an important social and cultural value. Much of the author's earliest published writing, which he claims "yearned to be at—was suffused with the yearning for—the center of the most traditional SF enterprise,"[141] figuratively and/or explicitly highlights such attitudes toward cultural and/or racial difference. For example, in *The Ballad of Beta-2* (1965), a student of galactic anthropology interprets a ballad of the Star Folk, humans who left Earth in starships to travel through the galaxy centuries ago, and learns that those who deviated from the statistical norm were ostracized, labeled as "One-Eyes," tried in court, and even executed as part of fascistic obedience to and enforcement of a narrow definition of "humanity." Because the One-Eyes were among the most competent of these travelers, their persecution jeopardized the Star Folk's very mission. A similar social opposition between "Norms" and individuals actually referred to as "different," is seen in *The Einstein Intersection*, set on a future Earth that humanity has abandoned and is now inhabited by beings who have imperfectly interpreted human legend and myth and made it their own. The novel pits a dark-skinned Theseus/Orpheus figure named Lo Lobey against a white-skinned Billy the Kid–type psychopath with tremendous mental powers known as Kid Death, whom Emerson Littlefield describes as "inhumanly white," and "a caricature of the classic Aryan type, with his blazing red hair, green eyes, and skin 'as pale as Whitey dying.'"[142] Kid Death kills Lobey's lovers, Friza and Dorik, because they were "different," even though he himself is "different," that is, possessing remarkable abilities.

Nova prominently features Lorq Von Ray, a mulatto starship captain. The crew of his ship, the *Roc,* is ethnically and racially diverse, including a gypsy, an Asian woman, and two crewmen of African descent, as well as white characters. Each pair of crew members hails from a different sector of the galaxy identified in part by economic class. Mouse and Katin are from Draco, the home of Red-shift Ltd., a company that has a monopoly on spaceship manufacturing due partly to the high price of Illyrion. Draco includes Earth and the solar system it inhabits, and its galactic reach "extended by the vastly monied classes of Earth" (93), whereas the Pleiades Federation, the home of Tyÿ and Sebastian as well as Lorq, is home to predominately middle-class settlements. Idas and Lynceos are twins who used to mine Illyrion on Tubman B-12 in the Outer Colonies, whose population "comes from the lowest economic strata of the galaxy" (80). The sectors' class identities generate their own cultural logics. Inhabitants of the Pleiades Federation speak in syntax-refracting dialect. Moreover, Lorq's quest to snatch seven tons of Illyrion from a collapsing and exploding star is his response to his father's prediction that the Outer Colonies will lower the element's price and continue to develop distinct cultural traditions, both of which will trigger an independence movement and prompt Red-shift to strike out at both the Colonies and the Pleiades. Difference is also an issue with the novel's fictional author, Katin, who enters the storyline with a fondness for the "beauty" of moons, which "is in variations of sameness" (26). By the end of the novel, however, he has cultivated an appreciation for the cut-and-mix pastiche of different cultures and traditions in Mouse's sensory-syrynx compositions.

A similar pattern is performed by Customs Officer Daniel Appleby in the Nebula Award–winning *Babel-17* (1966). The novel's protagonist is a female Asian poet named Rydra Wong. Captain Wong needs Appleby's assistance in assembling a crew for her starship, the *Rimbaud,* and has him accompany her to Transport town, one of a sequence of similar locales in Delany's fiction, including *Dhalgren*'s Bellona, *Trouble on Triton*'s UL Sector, and *Nova*'s City of Dreadful Night, that are precursors to cyberpunk's interzones. Robert Elliot Fox identifies such settings as "fictive analogues to the Dionysian impulses of the 1960s and of the perennial underside of labyrinthian urban complexes like New York."[143] Transport personnel proudly display their "cosmetisurgery," a body modification technique that surgically fits ornaments such as jewels, lights, or implanted fangs, onto the body. "They're all so weird" Appleby decides, "That's why decent people won't have anything to do with them."[144] He even goes so far as to call them "perverts" (43). Near the end of the novel, however, the reader finds Appleby making a stop at "Plastiplasm Plus (Addendums, Superscripts, and Footnotes to the Beautiful Body)" (191), where Rydra's psychiatrist, Markus T'mwarba, observes as the nerves in the Customs Officer's shoulder are attached to a cage that releases a miniature spark-spitting dragon. Appleby's decision to get his own cosmetisurgery is a result of the example of Rydra Wong, whose comfort level with Transport personnel and ability to use language to "cut through worlds" (204) had a delayed effect on the Customs Officer: "She managed to say so much to me in that one evening, so very simply. . . . And half the time she wasn't even looking in my direction when she said it" (195). By foregrounding Asian and black characters and dramatizing a "centered" subject's revision, his deconstruction, of the opposition between Custom and Transport identities, *Babel-17* does the *important* work of introducing multiracial characters to SF while critiquing the *dangerous* impulse to naturalize difference.

Similar examples abound in what could be called "The Later Delany." Both Earl Jackson Jr. and Carl Freedman note the subversion of the reader's expectations, a maneuver that is characteristic of Delany, with the dragon hunts in *Stars in My Pocket Like Grains of Sand.* On Marq Dyeth's homeworld, hunters target dragons with radar-bows that do not injure the prey but instead transmit its consciousness to the hunter, who is rewarded by temporarily seeing the world from the dragon's point of view. The hunter, therefore experiences "a sense of wonder" not unlike Knight's cat-rapport. Freedman identifies the hunts as an example of Theodor Adorno's concept of formal freedom: "difference . . . not simply tolerated . . . but actively *desired,* sought, and embraced."[145] The disavowal of difference is punished in the creation myth told by Raven, a masked warrior-woman from the Western Crevasse in "The Tale of Potters and Dragons," from *Tales of Nevèrÿon.* According to Raven's story, women are "daughters of Jevim," the first woman, whereas men are descended from another woman, Eif'h, created to be Jevim's companion. Eif'h pursues "the pure and unpolluted essence of the act" of god's creation, "which is, of course, not the way to praise the act at all—for the act is always manifest in difference, diversity, and distinction"; as punishment, therefore, god beats Eif'h on her loins, breasts, and face, transforming her into a "'man, which means broken woman."[146]

Critics have commented on the politics of difference informing Delany's *Trouble on Triton* (1976), subtitled "An Ambiguous Heterotopia." The novel's Appendix B cites as an epigraph Michel Foucault's *The Order of Things* (1966), which distinguishes "heterotopia" from utopia:

> *Utopias* afford consolation: although they have no real locality there is nevertheless a fantastic, untroubled region in which they are able to unfold; they open up cities with vast avenues, superbly planted gardens, countries where life is easy, even though the road to them is chimerical. *Heterotopias* are disturbing, probably because they make it impossible to name this *and* that, because they shatter or tangle common names, because they destroy "syntax" in advance, and not only the syntax with which we construct sentences but also that less apparent syntax which causes words and things (next to and also opposite one another) to "hold together." This is why utopias permit fables and discourse: they run with the very grain of language and are a part of the fundamental *fabula;* heterotopias . . . dessicate speech, stop words in their tracks, contest the very possibility of grammar at its source; they dissolve our myths and sterilize the lyricism of our sentences.[147]

In *Demand the Impossible* (1986) Tom Moylan reads Delany's invocation of Foucault as an announcement that *Triton* will not "afford consolation" or offer its reader a utopian "fantastic, untroubled region." Instead, the novel's heterotopia "contests the very possibility" of utopia. *Triton* is not a utopian "blueprint or a party line," Moylan explains, but rather an exercise in "the practice of imagining a radical other to what is," what Delany would call a significant distortion of present reality.[148] Moylan states that "heterotopia is to post-capitalist, post-modern, post-Enlightenment, post-industrial society as utopia was to capitalist, bourgeois society."[149] The novel depicts an ideal society, but not one characterized by unity, totality, or singularity, but by the enormous multiplicity of subject positions available to be occupied. On the Neptunian moon, there are "forty or fifty sexes, and twice as many religions" in addition to a multitude of political parties and communes.[150] It is this kind of multitudinous blossoming of identities to which Judith Butler's critique aspires, "a radical proliferation of gender" that will "*displace* . . . gender norms."[151] Moylan's analysis of *Triton* also illustrates the convergence of the science-fictional mode of reading and the genre's prioritization of the object. In the "alternative landscape" of the novel, the Solar System's Inner Planets are at war with the Outer Satellites, emblematizing the conflict between protagonist Bron Hellstrom and his love/sex interest, The Spike. Therefore, the statement that "they were worlds apart," according to Moylan, "no longer has a merely metaphorical meaning."[152] Earl Jackson Jr.'s *Strategies of Deviance* sees the margin's critical response to the center figured in the conflict between the "Inner Planets" and the "Outer Satellites" in the novel. Indeed, as Jackson points out, what qualifies as the marginal in *Triton*—namely Bron's archaic presumption of the centrality of his straight, white, male subjectivity—is hegemonic in the reader's world.[153] As Moylan notes, Bron's "sentences trail off into uncomprehending confusion;" it is his "speech" that is "desiccated," his "words" that are "stopped in their tracks."[154] An anti-essentialist approach to identity that emphasizes its constructedness is similarly demonstrated, according to Jackson, by Luna, which "naturally" would be classified a satellite, but politically is counted as a member of the "Inner Worlds."[155] Similarly, there may be some gender trouble on Triton, in that Butler's theory of parodic repetitions of gender appears to be on display. On Triton, gender—as well as race and sexuality—can be changed as routinely and with as little fuss as we might change a hairstyle. Bron's friend Sam is a black man who used to be a white woman; though, interestingly, the object of hir desire, white women attracted to black men, remained the same, suggesting that only an exterior, sociopolitical identity has changed. As Edward K. Chan has observed, the characters in the novel are all in some form of "drag" or "costume." Chan acknowledges that the novel can be read as asserting the performativity of identities: "Relegated to the background, racial and gender differences are really optional, cosmetic issues; they are flattened." But this does not empty social identities of meaning as much as they reframe them as categories embraced through affiliation as opposed to those hegemonically imposed. "We are meant to understand the social fabric of *Triton,*" Chan states, "as a field of unlimited subject positions and infinite choice." Whereas utopia is associated with "the erasure of social difference," Chan associates heterotopia with "the maintenance of social difference, a 'resignation' to its inevitability," which is not "a negative proposition" if received with "the gift [of] the loosening of reified epistemologies," that is, the destruction of the syntax that structures the discourses that naturalize, essentialize, and hierarchize identity.[156]

Robert Elliot Fox finds enough evidence among Delany's writings to assert that the author "has been devoted throughout his career to a vision of multiplexity, of pluralities of being."[157] "Multiplexity" comes from Delany's *Empire Star,* which opens with a Proustian epigraph—"Truth is a point of view about things"—that asserts the importance of multiple perspectives. *Empire Star* is the circular tale of Comet Jo, one of a colony of humans processing plyasil on the moon Rhys. Jo plays the ocarina and wields "brass claws on his left hand" (3), and is one of the earliest in a line of Delany's characters skilled at both art and weaponry. The story is told by Jewel, the survivor of an organiform ship that crashes on Rhys and whose dying companion entrusts Jo with the mission of taking a message to Empire Star at the center of the galaxy. Jewel, who crystallizes after the crash, is "multicolored, multifaceted, and multiplexed" (6), which makes him a perfect choice to narrate the story "from the point of view called, in literary circles," he tells the reader, "of the omniscient observer" (4). Jo, on the other hand, is rather simplex and confused about exactly what message he is to take to Empire Star and why. An elderly female mentor named Charona explains by having Jo walk underneath what's called "the Brooklyn Bridge," an allusion to the bridge across which Delany and Hacker walk while discussing SF in Delany's autobiography, in order to observe the light passing through its holes. The simplex view is merely of random dots of light. As Jo walks, he gains a complex view, observing that the lights appear to blink on and off. But as he runs under the bridge, "the rate of flickering increased, and suddenly he realized that the holes were in a pattern, six-pointed stars crossed by diagonals of seven holes each. It was only with the flickering coming so fast that the entire pattern emerged" (16). The Brooklyn Bridge, therefore, is less an image of suspension than of multiplexity, the awareness that different truths are to be gained from different perspectives. Jo eventually joins the crew of a transport ship, whose Capt. Elmer and first mate Ron are based on the men with whom Delany worked on shrimp boats in the Gulf of Mexico. Jo's job is to play therapeutic music for the ship's cargo, a race of slaves known as the Lll, who (re)built much of the Empire. A woman named San Severina, the owner of seven Lll, takes a liking to Jo and explains that the Lll are "the shame and tragedy of the multiplex universe.

No man can be free until they are free" (30). San Severina recognizes Jewel as a crystallized Tritovian, a member of the race that is spearheading the movement to liberate the Lll, which, she suggests, has something to do with Jo's message. San Severina has Jo meet the Lump, "a linguistic ubiquitous multiplex" (40), that is, a kind of computerized being, on Luna. The Lump, initially masquerading as Oscar Wilde, is based on Delany himself: he is partly mechanical but has the mind of an Lll; similarly, Delany is descended from black slaves. Commenting on the current "suffering" of the Lll, the Lump says that "even the Lll can't agree on what's so awful about their situation" (71), a statement that speaks to the different social, political, and cultural strategies—from assimilation, to pro-integration advocacy, to black nationalism—from which African Americans chose during the mid-to-late 1960s. Like the light-complexioned Delany, the Lump could pass (for a computer, that is), but he refuses to do so on principle. His response to being revealed as a Lll is to point out, "some people can tell right off. That's better than the ones who sit around and talk to you for an hour before they get around to asking" (56–57), expressing the frustration Delany may have felt toward whites unsure about his racial identity. The name of the Lll on whose consciousness the Lump's is based is "Muels Aranlyde," an anagram of the author's name; and the Lump's favorite writer is also one of Delany's, SF author Theodore Sturgeon.

The Lump instructs Jo further in the ways of multiplexity. "Sometimes one must see through someone else's eyes," he says (68), so he has Jo put Jewel in his eye. The experience is initially painful and disorienting for Jo, who suddenly sees many things, from many perspectives, simultaneously. Lump warns Jo away from "spiral staircases" (69) an allusion to Marcel Duchamp's *Nude Descending a Staircase* and the painter's multiplexed technique, that is, representing an image from multiple points of view, "all at the same time" (68). Jewel's multiplexity allows for some rather clever narrative maneuvers. When told that the most multiplex thing to do when unsure is to "ask questions" (66), Jo, who is trying to "order perceptions multiplexually" but states that he is still "not used to it" (66, 67), asks why he must join Prince Nactor's army. Jewel says that "*the army is going* [Jo's] *way*" (67), but the reader may momentarily wonder who Prince Nactor is and where Jo got the notion that he had to join the Prince's army in the first place. In the next paragraph, Jewel explains:

> Incidentally, between the time that Jo said, "I'm not used to it," and the time he asked his question, the radio had come blaring on, and Prince Nactor's voice had announced that all humans in the area were up for immediate conscription, to which Lump had said, "I guess that takes care of your problem." So there's nothing mysterious about Jo's question at all. I want to stress, for those who have followed the argument to this point, that multi-

plexity is perfectly within the laws of logic. I left the incident out because I thought it was distracting and assumed it was perfectly deducible from Jo's question what had happened, sure that the multiplex reader would supply it for himself. I have done this several times throughout the story. (67)

Empire Star, therefore, not only asserts the fact of differences in points of view, but also cultivates the reader's own multiplexity, his or her ability to order their perceptions and those of others in a meaningful pattern, which is not a bad definition of reading, period. As Jo increasingly feels as if all that he is experiencing has happened before and that everyone knows what is going to happen except him, Jewel reveals the content of his message: "*Someone has come to free the Lll*" (67). The novel concludes when Jo and a younger version of San Severina arrive at Empire Star, also called Aurigae, "the largest star in the galaxy . . . an eclipsing binary star" rotating around a single point in space (83). The immense gravitational forces there create a hole in time and space. "The temporal present joins the spatial past there with the possible future, and they get totally mixed up," Lump explains to Jo; "Only the most multiplex of minds can go there and find their way out again the same way they went in" (83–84), which is exactly what they do. "The multiplex reader," Jewel states, "has by now discovered that the story is much longer than she thinks, cyclic and self-illuminating" (89). Numerous characters are revealed to be past or future versions of other characters, for example, Lump and Muels Aranlyde, Charona and San Severina, Jo and Norn, who crashed on Rhys with Jewel and told Jo to take a message to Empire Star.

Jewel is emblematic of *Empire Star*'s oft-stated motto: "The truth is always multiplex"(35); and in his crystallized form, the Tritovian represents the best candidate for Delany's master trope. A perusal of Delany's titles reveals the prominence of jewel imagery and of light's refraction: for example, *The Jewels of Aptor, The Jewel-Hinged Jaw,* "Time Considered as a Helix of Semi-Precious Stones," *Driftglass/Starshards, The Motion of Light in Water,* "Prismatica," and so on. Delany attributes "his obsessive use of the image of the jewel" to the influence of a 1950s television show, *Tom Corbett: Space Cadet:* "Tom and his cronies encountered some mystical jewels; and watching them on television, I thought the glittering objects the program used to represent them were the most beautiful things I'd ever seen."[158] But he also reads the figure of the jewel as representing the values that inform a politics of difference:

> They reflect and refract the light that passes through them. In so doing, they shatter unitary images. Look through them and things become at once fragmented and multiple. The refractive quality of cut gems is a metaphor for analysis, brilliance, and pluralism.[159]

As white light passing through a prism is refracted into a multitude of colors, a spectrum—an image employed by both the gay rights movement and the Rev. Jesse Jackson's "Rainbow Coalition"—so have *grand narratives,* totality, and utopia been problematized by a spectrum of previously marginalized voices. The refraction of light performed by jewels are symbols of this postmodern investment in multiplicity.

Appropriately, such imagery is prominently featured in another of Delany's circular texts, *Dhalgren* (1975), set in the burned-out American city of Bellona. The only inhabitants left are scavengers and those drawn to the city seeking freedom from mainstream society. Traditional laws and political and social structures are in abeyance, replaced by a kind of orderly anarchy. Before entering Bellona, the novel's protagonist, known to himself and others only as "Kid," meets an Asian woman who leads him to a cave where he finds a bladed hand-weapon called an orchid, and a chain of prisms, mirrors, and lenses looped together. He takes it and later discovers that some of Bellona's remaining population wear similar "optic chains." "Prism, Mirror, Lens" is the working title of a multi-tracked musical composition recorded by one of Kid's love interests. It is also the title of a Marilyn Hacker poem and that of *Dhalgren*'s first chapter. More significantly, Delany uses the image to figure the historicizing, decentering effect and ability of SF:

> By much the same process that poetry expanded beyond its beginnings in ritualistic chant and incantation to become a way to paint all that is human and etch much that is divine, so s-f became able to *reflect, focus, and diffract* the relations between man and his universe, as it included other men, as it included all that man could create, all he could conceive [emphasis added].[160]

The optic chain figures Delany's critique of totalizing discourses: "I don't have *a* personal vision. I have any number, many of them quite contradictory. I distrust people with only one—especially if it's too complete, and they want to thrust everyone into it."[161] Again, if we recognize light as a figure of the Enlightenment, the reflection, diffraction, and distortion of light by Delany's optics can be seen as a postmodern response to Enlightenment humanism. The optic chain represents multiplexity, an awareness of a range of different subject positions and points of view. In this manner, Delany's works meet what Andrew Ross identifies as SF's need to approach "the task of living differently and living with difference" and constitute one of "the diverse challenges, on the part of women, sexual minorities, and people of color, to a universalist interpretation of history" that is "exercised in the name of universality."[162] If Delany has a master trope, this is it.

But the "chain" is just as significant as the "optics" in this image because it serves as a figure for articulation, in the sense of what Stuart Hall calls "the form of connection that *can* make a unity of two different elements, under certain conditions . . . a linkage which is not necessary, determined, absolute and essential for all time."[163] Religion, to use Hall's example, "has no necessary political connotation"; its associations with politics radical and conservative, liberating and oppressive, are constructed, not natural. This semiotics of the political suggests that political meanings can be detached and reattached in new formations like so many little plastic bricks. And there is no reason to assume that different liberation movements always have each other's best interests at heart. Kobena Mercer cites the example of black activists on the issue of education in late–1980s England "participat[ing] alongside the New Patriotic Movement" in anti-gay demonstrations; "homophobia became hegemonic over racism" and "an 'unthinkable' alliance between black people and the National Front" was created.[164] Given the persistence of what Kendall Thomas has identified as African Americans' "jargon of authenticity" and that jargon's persistent reliance on homophobic language,[165] any liberatory black cultural politics worthy of the name must be continuously, vigilantly, disarticulated from anti-gay bigotry and articulated to movements for recognition of, and equality and safety for, gays and lesbians. Therefore, the links in the optic chain can symbolize the articulation of black liberation politics with gay liberation politics, which is given cultural expression in Delany's writings, and, ideally, in this straight black reader's analysis of those writings. Delany proves the merit of Mercer's claim that "black gay and lesbian artists are producing important work on the question of identity . . . because they have made strategic cultural and political choices out of their experience with marginality which situate them at the interface between different traditions,"[166] but to identify those choices and strategies necessitates the lending of a certain amount of credence to categories of "identity," "tradition," and "race."

To Make a Science Fiction Writer Black

In short, the aim of this book is to read—or invent—Delany as an African American writer, though not to make blackness his "primary given," or to marginalize his many other identities. Delany's race is a field that overlaps, intersects, and is contiguous with his other identities. But given that, as Ross Posnock notes, with Delany's inclusion in the *Norton Anthology of African American Literature* (1997), he is now "officially regarded as canonical,"[167] one may reasonably ask, "What is at stake, in making an argument that appears to be so very obvious?"

Although Delany's African American literary canonicity is to be celebrated, it prompts questions as to the extent to which his work has been part of recent scholarship and teaching in the field. In his reading of *Stars in My Pocket Like Grains of Sand,* Carl Freedman cites and praises Robert Elliot Fox's *Conscientious Sorcerers* (1987), a volume that analyzes and compares "The Black Postmodernist Fiction of LeRoi Jones/ Amiri Baraka, Ishmael Reed, and Samuel R. Delany." Delany, Freedman says, is "the most original and accomplished male novelist to have emerged in the African American tradition since the era of Baldwin and Ellison," an assertion with which I concur. But Freedman acknowledges there is little support for such claims coming from scholars of African American Studies: "look for any reflection of [Delany's] achievement in the mainstream forums of Black Studies, and you will, with few exceptions, look in vain."[168] How then do we account for this African American silence on SF in general and Delany in particular? Freedman laments what he sees as an effect of the general marginalization—among writers, in the publishing industry, and in the academy— familiar to SF for decades. As with white supremacy's denigrations and demonizations of blackness, the construction of SF as an "Other" is organized around the kind of misconceptions and myths about the genre that James Morrow catalogues during Delany's interview of him:

> I keep running into people who, when I identify myself as an SF author, assume I must be into weird stuff: UFOs, ESP, harmonic convergences, holistic healing, and so on—constructs that ironically, I might use to explain what science is *not,* or to upbraid pseudo-science. And who can blame them? For the average consumer, of the *X-Files* and the George Lucas product, this kind of irrationalism is what "SF" now *means.*[169]

I hate to generalize or to presume to know other people's thoughts, but the narrow conceptualization of SF described by Morrow is what academics, regardless of their field, have in mind when they say "I don't like science fiction." Such statements come from people who, clearly, have not read much SF. (Can you imagine someone walking up to you at a meeting of the MLA and saying "I don't like sonnets"—without having read any?) Delany caricatures such attitudes through the persona of S. L. Kermit, a fictional archaeologist whose letters reveal his half-serious concerns about the ribbing he will receive from his well-heeled colleagues for being associated with the genre after receiving copies of Delany's Nevèrÿon fictions from the author's alter ego, K. Leslie Steiner:

> It sounds like she's gotten me involved, somehow, in this 'SF,' as she used to call it. (She actually would try to get me to *read* the stuff!) If that's what she *has* gotten me involved with, I shall never be able to set boot in the mahogany-panelled halls of the Spade and Brush Club again. (Professor

Loaffer will guffaw and bang me on the shoulder, and invite me for a pint, and ask rude questions about flying saucers until I have to say something rude in retort. Professor Cordovan, on the other hand, will not say anything at *all!*)[170]

Kermit's attitudes are based on very real situations Delany has experienced. *The Motion of Light in Water* includes a section on Sue, a graduate student who begs off from reading any of Delany's writing out of a felt obligation to read only from "an ideal list of Great Literary Works . . . the works you were supposed to read," and a concomitant fear that "she might actually find one of these non-canonical works as entertaining, if not as intelligent, as she clearly found in her confrontations with classical writers," which "would itself threaten all the unexpressed and unanalyzed notions that made the idea of a canon valid."[171] He also has a more direct response to the knee-jerk dismissal of SF, saying "It's highly moral, hugely indignant, rigidly class bound, and drenched in social exclusions."[172]

To the extent that scholars of African American literature have adopted this snobbery—and, to be fair, scholarly interest in SF writers like Delany, Octavia Butler, and Nalo Hopkinson within Black/African American Studies appears to be on the rise—it is especially unfortunate, not to mention counterintuitive. Walter Mosley, best known as the author of the Easy Rawlins detective stories, has recently embraced SF as a genre perfect for African American exploration, noting, like Kenneth James, that it "allows history to be rewritten or ignored" and is "made to rail against the status quo."[173] Mark Dery has noted the use of SF imagery and themes in the music of Jimi Hendrix, Parliament/Funkadelic, and Sun Ra.[174] John Akomfrah's 1996 documentary film *The Last Angel of History* traces further connections between the SF of Delany and Butler and the sonic innovations of dub master Lee "Scratch" Perry as well as the electronic musics currently being produced by black artists in America and England. Moreover, one might reasonably expect more of an affinity between cultural fields that share histories of being ignored and denigrated in the academy. "It is particularly ironic and depressing," Freedman says, "to find such marginalization practiced by those whose own field has suffered from a closely similar denigration and malign neglect by hegemonic literary canons."[175] Perhaps this is yet another example of Hall's theory of articulation, a linkage one might expect is not necessarily in effect and requires effort, energy, and attention to create.

One fact that may impede such an articulation is that, quite simply, the genre has, for most of its history, been dominated by white (and male) readers, writers, editors, and characters, almost totally excluding black representation. Black Canadian fantasy author Charles Saunders, writing in "Why Blacks Don't Read Science Fiction" (1980), explains that "a black man or woman in a space-suit was an image beyond the limits of early science fiction writers' imaginations." According to Saunders, for much of its history in North America SF has been "akin to the proverbial driven snow [or] as white as a Ku Klux Klan rally."[176] The lack of black characters is in part an effect of easy utopianism in SF of the 1940s and '50s; the universalist vision of a future in which humanity is united across racial lines in opposition or comparison to extraterrestrials, is, as with postmodernism, someplace SF has already been. In worlds where race does not matter, representation of raced groups does not matter; hence the paucity of black characters. And when black characters did appear in the "colorblind" SF of this era that, as Robert Crossley says, "imagin[ed] a future in which race no longer was a factor," they "often embodied the white liberal fantasy of a single black character functioning amiably in a predominantly white society."[177] There was also an actively policed "veil" in SF, a line that blackness could not cross. Consider, for example, legendary SF writer and editor John W. Campbell's rejection of what would later become Delany's novel *Nova* for serialized publication in *Analog* magazine. Campbell told Delany's agent, "For Heaven's sakes, he's got a Negro for a protagonist! It's a good book, but our readers aren't going to be able to identify with that."[178] Such conditions were not conducive to cultivating a black SF authorship or readership. Without black readers, SF will continue to have few black writers. But Delany says that the readership is here now:

> Why is SF still so overwhelmingly white? I wish I knew. There're lots of African-American SF readers—many more today than there were when I entered the field in '62, by hundreds of percent. I meet them at conventions. I meet them at academic conferences. I meet them at bookstore signings. Why haven't the writers followed?[179]

If Delany is correct about black SF readers, the writers may be on their way, and there may be some validity to Walter Mosley's recent prediction that "there will be an explosion of science fiction from the black community."[180] Perhaps that explosion is already happening; a number of black SF writers are publishing and achieving prominence including Delany, Butler, Hopkinson, Mosley, Steven Barnes, and writers in related genres such as Saunders, Tannarive Due, and more. The dawn of the new millennium saw the work of these writers and others collected in a volume entitled *Dark Matter*, edited by Sheree Thomas, which should go down in history as a landmark in African American literature.

Perhaps the principle obstacle facing African American SF writing, however, is the discourse of black authenticity. I will never forget the conversation I had with a cousin who inquired about the topic of my doctoral dissertation:

"I'm writing about Samuel R. Delany," I said.

"I've never heard of him before. Who's he?"

"Well, he's probably best known for being the first award-winning African American science fiction writer," I offered.

"Oh, no," my cousin replied with deadly earnest, "We don't do that. We leave that kind of stuff for white folks."

The discourse that fixes SF and African American culture as mutually exclusive categories is spoken by—or speaks through—whites as well as African Americans, which have led to some staggeringly inaccurate assessments of Delany's work in particular. A review essay in a 1993 issue of *The Nation* includes "Sam Delany" in a list of cyberpunk SF authors, including Bruce Sterling, John Shirley, Rudy Rucker and others, and describes the group as "so white and middle-class that maybe hacking is a form of suburban flight."[181] Although "middle-class" may accurately describe a position Delany has occupied for much, though not all, of his life, he is a black man who was born and raised in Harlem and whose adult life has been spent predominantly in New York City. In response to a critic who asked about the ostensibly low degree of blackness in his work, as if blackness is something you could measure, Delany's reply asserts his investment in combating white supremacy and declares his independence from narrow preconceptions of what "black writing" can or should be:

"If *you* [the critic] wrote, 'Behind a deceptively cool, even disinterested, narrative exterior you can hear the resonances of the virulent anti-white critique that informs all aware black writing in America today,' I would think you were a downright perceptive reader" (italics, incidentally added) [Delany's note]—all of which he chose to quote in the final version of his article. I suppose this was my way of saying: "Hey, my experience as a black American runs all through my work. But why do you assume its traces will be such stereotypes?"[182]

Delany follows with the claim that, with regard to his writing, the policing of black identity is a job that white critics have taken up more readily than African American critics:

But somehow black critics—and three or four, if not five or six, have written the odd article on me—just don't seem to be all that interested in how black a black writer's work is; or, when they are, they express that interest in—how shall I say?—a different tone of voice. The white, worried about some black's "blackness," always seem to be expressing the troubling anxiety that, indeed, you may not really *be* black, and that, therefore, somehow they've been fooled, taken in, or duped, either by your manipulative intentions or by some social accident—whereas the black critic is perfectly aware that you *are* black; I mean if you're born black in this country, you're going to know what it means to *be* black in this country; they're just kind of curious, therefore, to know what's going on with you.[183]

Without completely denying the truth value of that statement, however, it is important to note that the discourse of authenticity is as much, if not more, an intra-racial phenomenon as an inter-racial one. Moreover, some black critics have been very interested in "how black" Delany's work is. In an article entitled "The Future May Be Bleak, But It's not Black," Thulani Davis acknowledges that Delany's worlds have a "multiethnic, multisexual-preference" character similar to works by Ursula K. LeGuin and Marge Piercy, but concludes that "Delaney's [sic] people are black in fact, if not so much culturally."[184] Greg Tate has been similarly concerned about what he senses as the failure of the race of Delany's black characters to signify in a conspicuous fashion:

> I've always found Delany's racially defused futures problematic because they seem to deny the possibility that the affirmative aspects of black American culture and experience could survive assimilation. By which I mean not just obvious things like the genius present in black music, speech, and style but the humanity and range of personas born of black people's sense of communion.[185]

As Davis does, Tate notes that Delany's works may feature African Americans and other of people of color, but claims that "the race of these characters is not at the core of their cultural identity."[186] Delany responds to Tate's criticism by acknowledging the conventionalisms of his early work, his writing up through *Nova*, published during that multiple-eventful year of 1968, after which he "sat back and decided to figure out what I was really doing here"; he now doubts that Tate has been similarly perturbed by his work since *Dhalgren*.[187]

A Sense of Wonder, therefore, is an attempt to counter the invention of Delany as divested from "race" and to respond to readings of his works that fail to appreciate their meaningful engagements with race and other issues within the wide scope of African American Studies. It is an analysis of selected Delany texts since, and including, *Dhalgren*, with a sensitivity for what I see are the qualities that mark its participation in African American cultural traditions. In a way, I am simply asking of Delany's writing what Toni Morrison asks of her own in "Unspeakable Things Unspoken": "Other than my own ethnicity—what is going on in my work that makes me believe it is demonstrably inseparable from a cultural specificity that is Afro-American?"[188] Moreover, it is an earnest taking up of the challenge that Delany lays down before critics who question whether his writing is sufficiently black, a challenge that deserves restating: "Look, I *am* black. Therefore what I do is part of the definition, the reality, the evidence of blackness. It's *your* job to interpret it." "If you're a critic," he says, "tell me an *interesting* story."[189] Here, Delany reminds me, as he does Kenneth James, of Laurie Anderson, a multi-genre artist not too far away perhaps from *Nova*'s Mouse, who instructs her audience, "Hey, Sport. *You* connect the dots. *You* connect the pieces."[190] This is, as James's introduction to *Longer Views* notes, the task that Delany sees as facing "the radical reader," that is, to "respond to" the author's "suggestions," their "raw material."[191] In these instructions to the reader I hear the echo of the following statement by Roland Barthes, "an *obiter dictum,*" Delany says, "I've been impressed with enough to repeat, I'm sure (a hundred, two hundred times?), far more, I'd guess, than Barthes ever did," that is, "Those who fail to reread are obliged to read the same story everywhere."[192] By reading and rereading through the prisms and lenses and against the mirrors of African American literature and history—and by building on existing scholarship on Delany by scholars of African American literature such as Mary Kay Bray, Robert Elliot Fox, Sandra Y. Govan, and Jane Branham Weedman[193]—perhaps this reader can generate a new story that will serve not as the last word on Delany, but as a point from which further conversations can grow, as a reading that subsequent views of this treasured writer can confirm or contest.

I choose to view Delany's racial identity as Robert Elliot Fox does, "not [as] a limiting factor . . . but rather an opening of the aperture of our heretofore narrowly focused cultural vision, enabling 'discoveries' of what was always present but studiedly masked or unacknowledged."[194] The time for African American racial pride is far from over, but it must be synthesized with an acknowledgment of the multiple ways in which we identify, and it must not inhibit engagement with groups organized around other identities. Poet and activist Audre Lorde said that "too often, we pour the energy needed for recognizing and exploring difference into pretending those differences are insurmountable barriers, or that they do not exist at all."[195] Ultimately, *A Sense of Wonder* seeks to navigate a path through Delany's writing between the Scylla of universalisms and disavowals of "race" and "identity" made without regard for their progressive and constitutive uses, and the Charybdis of a discourse of race nationalism and racial authenticity that allows the immensity of race in America to blind us to the multiplicity of being.

2

CONTENDING FORCES

RACIAL AND SEXUAL NARRATIVES IN *DHALGREN*

> Fire.
>> That is their way of lighting candles in the
>> darkness.
>> A White Philosopher said
>> 'It is better to light one candle than to curse the
>> darkness.'
>>> These candles curse—
>> inverting the deeps of darkness
> —Gwendolyn Brooks, "The Third Sermon on the Warpland"[1]

> No lights in any near buildings; but down those waterfront streets, beyond
> the veils of smoke—was that fire? Already used to the smell, he had to breathe
> deeply to notice it. The sky was all haze. Buildings jabbed up into it and disap-
> peared.
> —Samuel R. Delany, *Dhalgren*[2]

Dhalgren (1975) is one of SF's most important novels. Delany's circular
metafiction of eight hundred-odd pages about the experiences and writings of a man known only as (the) Kid, who wanders into, among, and
out of the post-apocalyptic "warpland" of an American city named Bellona, has generated the strongest of responses from readers, such as that
of black Canadian science fiction author Nalo Hopkinson:

> *Dhalgren* blew my brain apart and reconfigured the bits. Talk about getting
> hacked. It was years before I'd begin to find words to express what I found
> so revolutionary about it, and when I discovered that Delany is black I wept.[3]

Hopkinson's response emphasizes the significance of Delany's racial subject position as a context for reading *Dhalgren*. Yet it suggests that she
learned of the author's race only *after* reading the novel, that the novel

itself did not indicate that it was part of the cultural traditions of people of African descent in North America. But *Dhalgren*'s most significant features have to do with how it operates as a text that exhibits formal characteristics associated with black culture, addresses American racial history, and investigates the construction and meanings of racial difference.

The narrative that Delany himself tells about *Dhalgren* is of the novel's role as the marker of a major shift in his works' cultural politics. Although his work up to 1968's *Nova* had been fascinating in its own right, Delany has said that his early works presented few challenges to traditional "space opera" narratives, plot-driven melodramatic space adventures with roots in early pulp fiction that have inspired science fiction action epics such as George Lucas's *Star Wars* films. "Some of that earlier work of mine," Delany states, "yearned to be at—was suffused with yearning for—the center of the most traditional SF enterprise."[4] Delany states that it was in 1968, before he started writing *Dhalgren*, that he "sat back and decided to figure out what [he] was really doing . . ."[5] After the breakup of Heavenly Breakfast, the commune/rock band of which Delany was a member,[6] the author dedicated himself for almost five years to the creation of "a major science fiction project . . . what was to become *Dhalgren*."[7] The "initial idea," Delany explains, "was to write a series of political novels—five, in fact—in which factors of modern life I'd seen burgeoning throughout the previous decade—in the counter-culture of the sixties—eventually worked to bring down five very different kinds of governments: one, an even more extreme form of North American–style consumer-industrial capitalism than we actually have; another, a highly repressive collectivism; one was a classical parliamentary monarchy; another was a regular fascist dictatorship; still another was a corrupt bureaucracy that ran on bribes and payoffs. . . ."[8] Revising his drafts in San Francisco in early 1969, Delany decided to write a single volume set in the present as opposed to the far-off future settings of many of his previous fictions. Although those earlier books were being republished, the loyal fan base that Delany had built up, as well as fellow SF writers and critics, would wait eagerly for new Delany material for six years.[9] SF author Frederick Pohl, then an editor at Bantam Books, got his company to buy and publish the new novel, which appeared in bookstores, with "A Frederick Pohl Selection" stamped on the cover as a mark of SF authenticity and quality, in 1975.

The range and intensity of the novel's initial reception is notable. *New York Times Book Review* critic Gerald Jonas found its circularity "daring and defensible,"[10] and author Theodore Sturgeon all but praised it to the high heavens. Labeling the novel "the very best to come out of the science fiction field," Sturgeon compared "Delaney" [sic] to "Homer . . . Shakespeare . . . [and] Nabkov" [sic], exclaiming that "the usefulness of *Dahl-*

gren [sic] to you and me is beyond question. Having experienced it, you will stand taller, understand more, and press your horizons back a little further away than you ever knew they could go."[11] Perhaps nothing surpassed the extremity of Sturgeon's praise, except that of Harlan Ellison's criticisms. Ellison, editor of the SF compilation *Dangerous Visions* (1967) in which Delany's short story "Aye, and Gomorrah . . ." first appeared, made his disappointment with Delany's latest effort as clear as can be, calling it "a tragic failure" and "an unrelenting bore of a literary exercise afflicted with elephantitis, anemia of ideas and malnutrition of plot and character development." Ellison claimed that he could not even get halfway through the novel,[12] which may raise questions about the validity of his critique. However, he was not alone; another critic claimed that only one out of thirty informally polled readers had actually finished the book.[13] Some expressed doubt as to whether *Dhalgren* could be classified as SF, or even as a novel. In the November issue of *Fantasy and Science Fiction* Algis Budrys stated that it was "not science fiction, or science fantasy, but allegorical quasi-fantasy."[14] Perhaps SF author Lester Del Rey's evaluation in *Analog*—"For the number of pages per dollar, it's a bargain. And that's the only good thing I can find to say about it"[15]—was the harshest that *Dhalgren* received.

    Dhalgren was nominated for, but did not win, the Science Fiction and Fantasy Writers of America's Nebula Award; it did not receive a nomination for the World Science Fiction Society's Hugo Award. Seth McEvoy has written that "of the nearly 100 reviews [of *Dhalgren*] . . . at the time, mostly appearing in science fiction fanzines [amateur magazines privately circulated among active SF readers], most of them were hostile and negative."[16] There were likely fewer fanzines and reviews at the time, with a larger ratio of positive reviews among them. Regardless, *Dhalgren* has to be considered a commercial success despite, or perhaps because of, its negative critical reception. Delany himself has suggested that given the number of copies sold, whatever amount of controversy that existed around the novel itself actually constituted its acceptance within the SF community.[17] *Dhalgren* sold over half a million copies in its first two years of publication, making it one of the best-selling science fiction novels of all time.[18] Since its publication, the novel has sold over a million copies worldwide, its appeal reaching beyond the usual SF readership.[19] In 1984 McEvoy estimated that over 90 percent of *Dhalgren*'s buyers had been readers who did not usually read SF.[20]

    In his introduction to the 1975 Gregg Press edition of *Dhalgren*, Jean Mark Gawron looks at this possible difference in reception between SF readers and non–SF readers and hypothesizes that the reason for any degree of antipathy toward the novel from the former group "may simply be a question of certain fixed expectations not being met."[21] *Dhalgren* may not have been the book that SF readers were expecting, but that is because the novel purposefully subverts a SF reader's expectations. What causes the buildings in Bellona to burn continuously? How is it possible that two moons appear in the night sky? Why does the sun appear to swell to a monstrous size? These questions are never answered definitively; and when the expectation of an explanation is raised through the introduction of a character like Captain Kamp, an astronaut who has seen the Earth from space, it is not fulfilled: "Frankly, I can't tell what's wrong," Kamp tells Kid, "I still haven't been able to figure out what's happened here" (459). "To enter *Dhalgren* is to be progressively stripped of various certainties, many of these having to do with unspoken, often unrecognized, aspects of the reader's cultural contract with the author," states SF author William Gibson in his foreword to the 1996 edition of the novel; "There is a transgressive element at work here, a deliberate refusal to deliver certain 'rewards' the reader may consider to be a reader's right."[22] For example, each member of the scorpions, a predominantly black gang that Kid eventually joins and later leads, wears an "optic chain" whose links are loops of prisms, mirrors, and lenses, and a "light-shield," a device that projects a hologram of an insect, animal, or fantastic beast—"SPIDER DRAGON LIZARD FROG BIRD OF PARADISE SCORPION MANTICHORE GRIFFIN" (554)—around the wearer. The reader may reasonably wonder what kind of animal Kid will turn into once he receives his own projector and batteries; perhaps the holographic creature will figuratively reveal something about Kid's character in particular or the novel in general. Bunny, the go-go dancer at Teddy's, a gay bar that is Bellona's social center, gives voice to such ruminations in conversation with Kid: "How exciting, to anticipate your glowing aspect, to puzzle over what you'll turn out to be" (360). However, once Kid finally activates his light-shield, he realizes that its projection is invisible to the wearer. Because Kid's consciousness guides the narrative, in several rhetorical forms, his holographic image is invisible to the reader as well: "(I don't know what I am.) He looked down at the cracked pavement. (But whatever it is, it's blue.) The halo moved with him across the concrete" (598). The narrative teases the reader further by suggesting that Kid will eventually discover what he transforms into: "He wondered how long before he would finally get someone aside and ask" (598). But Kid never does ask; in fact, he simply turns his light-shield off.

Douglas Barbour identifies a conversation between Kid and Tak Loufer—a gay industrial engineer, who, like Kid, wields a bladed, brass hand-weapon called an "orchid"—as *Dhalgren*'s most specifically targeted response to the genre's conventions. As they try to determine the nature of the disastrous event to which Bellona was subjected, Tak, an avid

SF reader, hypothesizes that "the whole thing is science fiction" (372). He explains to Kid "the Three Conventions of science fiction" and how Bellona appears to follow each of them:

> First: A single man can change the course of a whole world: Look at Calkins, look at George, look at you! Second: The only measure of intelligence or genius is its linear and practical application: In a landscape like this, what other kind do we even allow to visit? Three: The Universe is an essentially hospitable place, full of earth-type planets where you can crashland your spaceship and survive long enough to have an adventure . . . in Bellona you can have anything you want, as long as you can carry it by yourself, or get your friends to. (372)

Tak's explanation is, clearly, ironic. Barbour convincingly asserts that Tak's characterization of the city is not so much false as it is incomplete: Bellona *Times* publisher Roger Calkins, George Harrison—a god-like cultural icon—and Kid are certainly important figures in Bellona, but their "powers" are more cultural and social than physical and material. Although Calkins represents what authority figures the city has left, his direct effect on other characters' lives is hard to gauge. And although Kid's poetry may serve as an example of applied genius, his possible madness and unstable memory, which inform the novel's fragmented representation of events, suggest an unusual type of mind.[23]

As a further example of the novel's manipulation of SF expectations, consider that the reader may reasonably wonder how these holographic projectors, optic chains, and orchids have been made available to the inhabitants of Bellona in the first place. The reader may just as reasonably expect that eventually, perhaps toward the novel's end, Kid will discover an explanation that will answer all of these questions. Likewise, some explanation other than the one Kid fears—his own crumbling sanity—about why he frequently sees red eyeballs when he looks into people's faces would seem to be in order. When Tak leads Kid to the warehouse of Maitland Systems Engineering, the reader teeters on the brink of an epiphany. The warehouse indeed contains crates full of orchids, optic chains, projectors, and "RED EYE-CAPS" (555). At least some of these items appear to have been imported from other countries, though no further explanation for their existence is given. Gawron notes that although the warehouse episode appears exactly at the place in the novel where the reader expects his or her questions to be answered, it is not the "source" of meaning in the novel, "merely one of numerous crossover points in the matrix," meticulously crafted to suggest a significance where only the arbitrary resides.[24]

The title of the novel is similarly arbitrary, designed to further create and confound expectations. The reader may expect the name "Dhalgren" to refer to an important character, place, activity, or concept. It appears as the surname of "William Dhalgren," an item in the list of names Kid finds in his notebook. At the party Calkins organizes in his honor, Kid meets "Bill," a reporter for the Bellona *Times* and Calkins's assistant. Kid later reads a letter from Calkins that features "RC; wd" (659) at the bottom of the page. At the Dionysian dance of scorpions and commune-ists in the city's park, Kid spots "Bill," concludes that he is William Dhalgren, and shouts "I know who you are! . . . I *know* . . . !" (783). But as Gawron explains, there is no definitive evidence offered to the reader, or to Kid for that matter, that Bill is in fact William Dhalgren.[25] Traditional SF hopes are also frustrated by the fact that Kid does not engage in the obligatory climactic battle with an antagonist. The novel's final chapter, "The Anathēmata: A Plague Journal," a transcript of Kid's journal with editor's notes, missing pages, and marginalia, features an entry describing a meeting with the mysterious Roger Calkins. But it is no showdown between a swash-buckling adventurer and an evil genius; instead, it is a conversation at a monastery about poetry, politics, and good and evil. A few pages later, in one masterfully self-referential stroke, the journal not only describes Kid's experience of reading his journal, but also anticipates the reader's response to the novel:

> My life here more and more resembles a book whose opening chapters, whose title even, suggests mysteries to be resolved only at closing. But as one reads along, one becomes more and more suspicious that the author has lost the thread of his argument, that the questions will never be resolved, or more upsetting, that the positions of the characters will have so changed by the book's end that the answers to the initial questions will have become trivial. (755–56)

The novel's thwarting of expectations, what Gawron identifies as "the manner in which it creates a growing sense of pattern, which ultimately is never realized,"[26] is one of its most significant features. In "Of Sex, Objects, Signs, Systems, Sales, SF, and Other Things," an essay written in response to a request for Delany's own thoughts on *Dhalgren*, the author suggests that these subversions of expectation may help combat the market-driven conventions that stifle creativity within the genre:

> In a field like SF, with not quite 325 original SF novels produced this year [1975] from substantially less than that number of writers—and most of these novels in a commercially fixed form the writers themselves would be the first to admit was dead from the outset—it is not so preposterous for a writer

to hope that a single work, fermenting in the acknowledged live area of the field, might loosen and recontour the web of possibilities, charging that web at each repositioned intersection of possible word and possible word.[27]

One may choose to read the novel's subversion of expectations as consistent with Ross Posnock's universalist interpretation of Delany's works and his contention that they evade racial specificity. According to Posnock's argument, as Delany's autobiography *The Motion of Light in Water* (1988) and novella *Atlantis: Model 1924* (1995) subvert the expectations that the reader brings to African American literature, so does *Dhalgren* subvert the reader's expectations of SF. Such a reading might seek to understand the novel's setting and protagonist as suggesting Delany's disinterest in identity politics, especially considering that Gawron describes Bellona as a place of "inconstant boundaries" and Kid as "a man of many backgrounds . . . equally unfixable . . . half-Indian, half-white, half-mad, half-named, bisexual, one-shoed, ambidextrous, willful, labile, poet, and hero."[28] Gawron even uses "suspension," which Posnock claims is Delany's "master trope," to characterize Bellona's fictive distance from the "real world."[29]

On the subject of universalism, however, consider the significance of *Dhalgren*'s optic chains composed of prisms, mirrors, and lenses. References to distortion, reflection, refraction, and illusion abound in the novel, particularly in Kid's first-person soliloquies that adorn the third-person narrative of the first six chapters like carefully accessorized jewels. In Chapter VII, "The Anathēmata," Kid's journal contains a reference to the brain's ability to "refract the jewelry of words into image, idea, or information" (762). Barbour suggests that the optic chain, with its loops and diffractions, is a proper figure for the global shape of the novel.[30] This suggestion is congruent with Jane Weedman's claim that the novel dramatizes Kid's efforts to construct his own multiplex consciousness[31]— Delany's revision of W. E. B. DuBois's concept of African American double-consciousness presented first in *Empire Star* (1966)—which represents the novel's events from multiple perspectives, as opposed to a single, "universal," one. Accompanying the scorpion called Pepper, for example, Kid thinks, "You meet a new person, you go with him, and suddenly you get a whole new city" (318). This idea echoes throughout Delany's works including *Flight from Nevèrÿon*'s "The Mummer's Tale" and *Return to Nevèrÿon*'s "The Tale of Rumor and Desire." *Dhalgren* demonstrates its investment in the multiplicity represented by the optic chains when Madame Brown, a black lesbian psychiatrist, tells Kid, "I *trust* people who have them just a little more than those who don't" (116). Barbour also describes Bellona as a radically multicultural city, "a construct in which no social group is central."[32]

Instead of pursuing universalism and diminishing the significance of race in Delany's works, the reader would have a better chance at making sense of this challenging novel by reading it, as a number of literary critics have, with a sensitivity to its resonances with black cultural forms and as a text that addresses the meanings of racial difference.[33] *Dhalgren*'s creation and subsequent subversion of formal expectations, for example, can also be recognized as a specifically African American characteristic. In "Repetition as a Figure of Black Culture," James Snead discusses how black music tends to create a beat that serves as "the listener's horizon of expectation." A musical form such as jazz, for example, "sets up expectations and disturbs them at regular intervals . . . that it will do this, however," Snead explains, "is itself an expectation." In black music, the disturbance of expectation is accomplished through the addition of another or other beats or rhythms or through repetition by a method known as the "cut," a seemingly unmotivated abrupt return to or rearticulation of the beginning.[34] Snead's theory seems particularly applicable to the apparently circular global shape of *Dhalgren*, suggested by the syntactic fit between the novel's opening—"to wound the autumnal city" (1)—and the closing words of the novel and of Kid's journal: "I have come to" (801). Chapter 1 shows Kid entering Bellona after the city has suffered some catastrophic event, while the final chapter of the novel shows him and others fleeing the city during another or perhaps the same catastrophe. Exiting Bellona, Kid meets a woman on her way into the city, to whom he gives his orchid; this woman is reminiscent of one of the women who give Kid an orchid when he enters Bellona in Chapter I; both appear to be (Eur)Asian sculptors. When musician, teacher, and love interest Lanya Colson offers Kid a notebook with a charred cover that already bears his own writing, he does not recall or recognize it, although he eventually (re)uses it as his journal. When he "first" picks up the notebook at this moment, it contains entries about a riot, lightning, fires, and trapped children, all of which Kid experiences by the end of Chapter VI and/or are described in entries in Chapter VII's transcript of his journal, partially burned in a fire at the gender-specific dwelling in which Lanya and other women live and work. Snead states that "In black culture, the thing (the ritual, the dance, the beat) is 'there for you to pick it up when you come back to get it.' If there is a goal in such a culture it is always deferred."[35] This statement accurately describes an event and an aesthetic that are rare at work in *Dhalgren*: Kid's journal is there for him to pick up when he comes (back) to Bellona to get it. The narrative goals the reader usually expects in SF—the explanations and confrontations that, as recently discussed, the novel does not provide—are playfully deferred. As the passage from Delany's journal that serves as an epigraph to the penultimate chapter of *The Einstein Intersection* states, "endings to be useful must be inconclusive."[36]

Improvisation is another end to which this aesthetic is put. Snead explains further that "without the organizational principle of repetition, true improvisation would be impossible, since an improviser depends upon the ongoing recurrence of the beat."[37] More than one reader of *Dhalgren* has commented on Kid's "charm;"[38] no doubt part of this charm is the way he improvises his way through experiences in Bellona. "[Kid] observes," Barbour writes, "but he does not try to explain."[39] It may be more accurate to say that Kid observes, and sometimes participates, in a way that is simultaneously critical and nonjudgmental. Like that of David Jones, the author of the long poem that gives *Dhalgren*'s final chapter its name, Kid's aesthetic appears to be one with Pablo Picasso's: "I do not seek, I find."[40] Kid goes with the flow: When the sun swells to monstrous proportions in the sky, for example, Kid alone does not succumb to fear, but instead is inspired to begin an improvised destructive scorpion-like run of his own.[41] Improvisation and the subversion of generic expectations are thus linked structurally and thematically by way of the figure of repetition in *Dhalgren*.

This understanding of *Dhalgren*'s participation in an African American tradition of repetition and improvisation is based on an understanding that the shape of the sequence of the novel's events is a loop instead of a line. Like *Empire Star*, *Dhalgren*'s plot appears to run along a circular temporal path. However, Barbour, Gawron, and Mary Kay Bray have all noted that the novel's global shape may be more accurately described as a mobius strip,[42] a three-dimensional circle with a twist in it that causes the outside part of the loop to become the inside and vice versa (figure 1). In an "Author's Note" that accompanied an earlier unpublished draft of the novel, Delany compared *Dhalgren* to one of M. C. Escher's illustrations of a mobius strip, suggesting that the novel should be read and reread so that the relationship between its parts could be appreciated:

> Such a strip, needless to say, is only fully enjoyed the second time over: One passes the same space, but on another surface. By extension, if you read Part One, then Part Two, then read Part One *again*, Part One, I suspect, will seem rather different, in light of what come after—or does it come before?[43]

A twist in *Dhalgren*'s loop occurs almost exactly in the middle of the novel. After watching Ernest Newboy leave Bellona at the end of Chapter IV, Kid turns back toward the city at the beginning of Chapter V, ruminating over the psychic dislocations produced by his amnesia and ambidexterity and worrying about what the disturbing visions of red eyeballs say about his mental health. He then meets Denny, a teenaged scorpion and Escher fan who matter-of-factly offers to fellate Kid and later forms a three-way sexual-emotional relationship with him and Lanya. But as they enter Denny's nest, Kid has an intense, mobius-shaped experience:

The whole tape of reality which he had been following had somehow over-turned. It still continued; he still followed. But during some moment when he had blinked, days had elapsed and everything right had shifted left: Everything left was now right. (388)

As a figure of repetition with a difference, the mobius strip is also a figure for the practices of looping and sampling in contemporary hip-hop culture. The rearticulation of a beat, lyric, or passage from another musical text in a different context, or the repetition, or "looping" of such a fragment inverts or otherwise changes that fragment's meaning.[44] As Snead explains, repetition implies transformation: "Whenever we encounter repetition in cultural forms, we are indeed not viewing 'the same thing' but its transformation."[45] *Dhalgren* represents repetitions and transformations that occur in language.

Douglas Barbour points out that *Dhalgren* maps the repetition of language as Kid transforms experience into writing.[46] Part 2 of Chapter I begins with a first-person soliloquy in which Kid reflects on a mysterious scratch he sees on someone's leg, most likely that of Milly, a member of the commune in the park and a friend of Lanya. The soliloquy features its own moments of repetition and difference:

It is not that I have no past. Rather, it continually fragments on the terrible and vivid ephemera of now. In the long country, cut with rain, somehow there is nowhere to begin. Loping and limping in the ruts, it would be easier not to think about what she did (was done to her, done to her, done), trying instead to reconstruct what it is at a distance. Oh, but it would not be so terrible had one calf not borne (if I'd looked close, it would have been a chain of tiny wounds with moments of flesh between; I've done that myself with a swipe in a garden past a rose) that scratch. (10)

Part 3 of Chapter II features Kid reading the following passage from his notebook:

It is not that I have no future. Rather it continually fragments on the insubstantial and indistinct ephemera of now. In the summer country, stitched with lightning, somehow, there is no way to conclude . . . (76)

In Chapter VII, the transcript of Kid's journal, a similar passage appears as a record of a thought Kid has during a conversation with the scorpion known as D-t:

While we talked I recall thinking: It is not that I have no future. Rather it continually fragments on the insubstantial and indistinct ephemera of then.

In the summer country, stitched with lightning, somehow, there is no way to conclude; but here, conclusion itself is superfluous. (699–700)

These passages render an experience, the reading of the record of that experience in the journal, and the journal's record of a memory of the experience. The statement does not merely repeat itself throughout the novel, but significantly changes its content and meaning depending on its temporal context and form. Barbour calls the novel a "phenomenological map of Kid's physical, mental and emotional response to the whole surround which is Bellona as he experiences it."[47] The novel transforms its language so as to "mirror" Kid's experiences in and of different rhetorical forms. In "Of Sex, Objects, Signs, Systems, Sales, SF, and Other Things," Delany describes the text he wanted *Dhalgren* to be as one that features "richly detailed slabs of experience itself . . . done with a rich web of language."[48] Moreover, the transformations hint at the myriad possible connections between the novel proper and Kid's journal, which are represented by another model for *Dhalgren*'s global shape, a Klein bottle (figure 2), which is suggested in an unpublished author's note:

> To the reader who wishes to take the trip *three* times or more (the invitation is, naturally, open), and who begins to note, once familiarity with the material has allowed movement in more spurious directions than dead on, that the "outer" novel and the "inner" notebook are connected in more complicated ways than the "outer" and "inner" surfaces of a twisted paper band— indeed, more like the "external" and "internal" lugs of a Klein bottle—I can only suggest that this is just partially accident.[49]

Dhalgren is the fictional equivalent of a Rubik's Cube. The reader can read and reread the novel in order to tease out the connections between novel and notebook—perhaps through those first-person passages that pop up in the first six chapters—which means that, contrary to its detractors' claims, *Dhalgren,* as McEvoy argues, participates in the tradition of classic, Campbellian, problem-solving SF even as it deviates from that tradition.[50]

As its transformational process indicates, *Dhalgren*'s fascination with language extends to an exploration of rhetorical types. As with other epic novels before it such as Herman Melville's *Moby-Dick* and Ralph Ellison's *Invisible Man, Dhalgren* is a rhetorical tour de force. The novel contains third-person narrative interspersed with first-person soliloquies, with a journal appended. It also features newspaper stories from Calkins's Bellona *Times,* sermons from the Reverend Amy Tayler, small talk at the party at Calkins's estate, a psychiatric session between Kid and Madame Brown, a letter from Calkins to Kid, bar chat at "Teddy's," a conversation between Kid and Calkins at the monastery that looks a lot like a confessional, and plenty of pillow talk (even when there are no pillows). "About Five Thousand Seven Hundred and Fifty Words," Delany's presentation as part of a 1968 Modern Language Association convention panel, reveals the author's interest in the different values placed on different types of discourse. According to Delany's scholarly alter ego, K. Leslie Steiner, *Dhalgren* is "lush with [the] juxtapositions, embeddings, and transformations" of different types of discourse in an effort to experiment with the social "weight" attached to them.[51]

To illustrate how *Dhalgren* pits discourse and rhetoric, differing explanatory narratives, against each other, Steiner offers yet another model for the novel's global structure, the Necker cube (figure 3). This familiar optical illusion allows the viewer to see the cube in two ways, so that the cube's interior and exterior switch places. Although *Dhalgren* has often been criticized as a novel in which nothing is resolved, Steiner argues that for any one of its mysterious events the novel offers at least two methods of resolution, often presented in or represented by different and contesting rhetorical forms; the reader of *Dhalgren,* like the viewer of the Necker cube, can therefore alternate between the explanatory narratives.[52] Snead's discussion of black music provides a similar example: "There are at least two, and usually more, rhythms going alongside the listener's own beat."[53] Therefore, the reader of *Dhalgren* "listens" alternately to rhythms generated by each explanatory narrative as well as by his or her own reading. Steiner argues that the point is not to choose one narrative over the other, but to observe the tension between them, the way in which the narratives are constantly contested.[54]

An example of contending alternative narratives is provided by "Bellona's oldest paperboy," Joaquim Faust, who explains that "nobody has the story really straight" on what started a riot in Jackson, the part of town where most of the city's African American population resides: "Some people say a house collapsed. Some others say a plane crashed right there in the middle of Jackson. Somebody else was talking about some kid who got on the roof of the Second City Bank building and gunned somebody down" (73, 72). And the fragmented journal entries that constitute Chapter VII can be reconstructed in several different chronological orders. The reader can alternate between these explanations and orders as one alternates between the two simultaneous images of the Necker cube. Steiner suggests that these contested narratives are presented in, or represented by, different rhetorical forms, as with the journal transcript of Chapter VII and the preceding six chapters of the novel proper. Considering that the narrative shifts from third to first person in Chapters I–VI, and that the first-person consciousness of the journal in Chapter VII could only be Kid's, Steiner notes that it is possible that Kid's consciousness is behind

Fig. 1 M. C. Escher's "Mobius Strip II" © 2003 Cordon Art B.V.—Baarn—Holland.

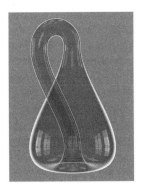

Fig. 2 Klein Bottle © John M. Sullivan.

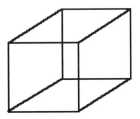

Fig. 3 Necker Cube

both the novel proper and the journal.[55] The journal's description of Kid's exit from Bellona mirrors—in the sense that it both resembles and reverses—the structure of Chapter I's dramatization of Kid's entrance into Bellona. Again, in the journal Kid gives the bladed, brass hand-weapon called an orchid to an "Oriental" (798) woman who is entering the city as he is leaving it, whereas in Chapter I he receives the orchid from a similar woman, one of a group, who is exiting the city as he is entering it. (Both women resemble another who has sex with Kid, and then promptly turns into a tree, at the novel's outset.) Because it is unlikely that both of these separate but so similar events "really" occur, Steiner suggests that either the journal sequence is "real" and the beginning of the novel is Kid's hallucination, or the novel is "real" and the journal contains a fiction Kid imagined or hallucinated and wrote down: "If Kid really left the city, he never truly entered it," Steiner states; "If Kid really entered the city, he never truly left it." Again, the point is not to choose one narrative over the other, but to observe how the narratives—rendered in different rhetorical forms (novel, journal)—interrogate each other, how they exist in contention with each other.[56]

Steiner's Necker cube hypothesis is crucial to understanding *Dhalgren* as a novel that not only illustrates but also performs the ways in which different narratives about reality vie with one another for social, political, and ideological privilege. Mary Kay Bray identifies the similarity between the novel's enigmatic epigraph, "You have confused the true and the real," and the African American experience of double-consciousness, identified by W. E. B. DuBois in *The Souls of Black Folk* (1903). For Bray, *Dhalgren* activates its own double-consciousness by initiating and ironically dismantling dominant literary narratives that have been fundamental in shaping an American cultural identity: quest and initiation, innocence and experience, romantic individualism, and so on. In so doing, the novel demonstrates that the country's "reality" is one in which many groups, particularly African Americans, have been excluded from the archetypal myths held as American "truths." This analysis is sound and highly instructive, but Bray concludes her analysis by assigning a "nonjudgmental" quality to *Dhalgren* because of the novel's formal innovations and the clash of narratives it offers. "The fact is," she claims, "this is a structure which does not point outward to any external message but continually returns its focus on itself"; and Bray surprisingly leaves the significance of *Dhalgren,* and of literature in general, up for grabs: "The country cannot be taught by *Dhalgren* or any other book, and it cannot be learned by readers of books. The experience of America is one of the experiences of *Dhalgren.* What the reader does with that experience is up to him or her."[57] But Bray's confidence in *Dhalgren*'s neutrality ignores the challenge that the novel's counternarratives make to socially privileged narratives of "certain knowledge," narratives which present themselves as "common sense" or "truth." It is a technique Delany cultivates in *Dhalgren* and later deploys to remarkable effect in his writings on the HIV/AIDS crisis. Steiner argues that the reception of any knowledge, no matter how factual, is a process of belief, which involves a modicum, if not a leap, of faith, and is therefore ultimately "a mystical occurrence."[58] This critique of commonly held "truth," of dominant ideologies, is most cogently performed by one of *Dhalgren*'s principal statements on race, in which "the true and the real" converge and challenge each other: its refutation of the myth of the black rapist.

Delany describes myths as "the stories a society can bear to tell about itself."[59] "Of Sex, Objects, Signs, Systems, Sales, SF, and Other Things" makes it clear that because of his own subject position(s), Delany is invested in the interrogation of myths about marginalized groups of people, "blacks, women, the mentally ill," and those marginalized on the basis of their sexuality; the author insists that his interest in myths about the marginal stems from a desire to "set matters straight," which is achieved in part by *Dhalgren*'s radical valorization of supposedly "abnormal" sexual acts.[60] In "Sex, Objects" Delany suggests that, in addition to being vexed by *Dhalgren*'s subversion of expectations, the novel's harshest critics are troubled by the sex in it. It is not that they feel there is too much. (For the record, according to one estimate, 36 of the 879 pages in the novel's first edition feature explicit descriptions of sexual acts.)[61] Nor is it a matter of these critics bearing antipathy toward representations of homosexuality and bisexuality. "These readers," Delany states, "are perfectly willing to respond to a 'sympathetic portrayal of the social problems of those who deviate sexually from the statistical norm.'" What is most distressing to *Dhalgren*'s critics, the author claims, is the novel's decentering of a sexual norm and its interrogation of the notion that sex necessarily dictates the form of social structures: "They are at first confused by and angered with a presentation that completely subverts the entire subtext that informs a discourse of 'social problems/sympathetic/sexual deviate/normal' in the first place."[62] It is here that Delany first explicitly articulates the counter-theory that informs *Dhalgren* and many of his later works:

> There's a prevalent theory that society, in some mysterious way, is and will always be a mirror of some mysteriously eternal sex act, i.e., standard missionary position. This theory, of course, is nonsense. Every sex act, from the most "normal" to the most "perverse," is an internalization of one or another set of social parameters. Once internalized, however, they are sexual and no longer social—save in their social *effect* as sexual behavior.[63]

Delany identifies two sources of "the sexual/social myth that the good society takes its form from the most socially condoned sexual act"; one is a nineteenth-century ideological formation reinforced by and articulated through fiction, whereas the other is a modern confusion about psychoanalytic theories about sexual repression:

> First, there is a mental template that was worked into the very form of fiction (among social entities) by the same industrial forces that contoured so much of the rest of the rhetoric of the nineteenth-century novel—forces that compelled people, to the extent of their identification with, or even their contiguity to, the white male, middle-class nodes of power, to see the working class in general, racial and religious strangers in particular (as they represented, in large amounts, possible additions to the labor market), and the unstable (do they work or don't they? Are they property or aren't they?) status of women in a radically revalued patriarchal society, as perennial threats to the order of things. The second factor—the twentieth century's addition—was to lay over this basic template a muzzy misreading of Freud, that saw ". . . sex as the source of all things."[64]

To combat this "sexual/social myth," which he calls "pure literary excrescence,"[65] Delany has adopted as his "rubric" Michel Foucault's suggestion to "get rid of the Freudian schema . . . the schema of the interiorization of the Law through the medium of sex."[66]

It is in challenging this schema that *Dhalgren* most rigorously investigates meanings of racial difference. In his "Meditations" on the novel, Robert Elliot Fox argues that "race and racism" are central to it, most evidently so "when they overlap with the psychosexual, with patterns of desire."[67] The locus of these issues is George Harrison, a black man whose notoriety in Bellona has much to do with what is perceived to have been his rape of a white teenager, June Richards, during the riot in the city's black community. There is no unmediated representation of this incident in *Dhalgren;* the only information the reader receives about it comes from stories and descriptions told by other characters. The discursive authority about the rape is the Bellona *Times.* The reader, along with Kid, first receives a description of the newspaper story from Joaquim Faust:

> "There's supposed to be one set of pictures; of this *big* buck, getting after this little white girl . . . a whole *lot* of stink about them pictures. 'Rape' is the nasty word they didn't use in the paper but rape is what it was." (71)

Faust goes on to tell Kid that Calkins's publication of the photos of George and June was only the beginning of a scandalous portrayal of George as a sexual menace:

"People was saying Calkins shouldn't've printed them. But you know what he did? . . . He went down and hunted up the nigger in the pictures and had somebody interview him; and he printed *every* thing. Now if you ask me, what he shouldn't have printed was that interview." (71)

Fox suggests that Faust's use of the racist epithet "nigger" indicates that he may have retrograde racial attitudes of his own,[68] but the "paperboy" articulates at least some awareness that Calkins's portrayal of George—as if he were Bellona's own Willie Horton—impedes the efforts of Bellona's black community toward social and political empowerment:

"I mean, Calkins is all interested in civil rights and things. He really is. The colored people in this town had it bad I guess, and he was concerned with that. Really concerned. But that nigger had the dirtiest mouth, and didn't use it to talk nothing but dirt. I don't think he even knew what a newspaper interview was. I mean, I know the colored people got it rough. But if you want to help, you don't print a picture of the biggest, blackest buck in the world messin' up some blond-headed seventeen-year-old girl, and then runnin' two pages of him saying how good it was, with every other word 'shit' and 'fuck,' and 'Wooo-eeeee,' how he's going to get him some more soon as he can, and how easy it's gonna be with no pigs around! I mean not if you want to help—do you?" (71)

The newspaper's representation of George is exactly what Delany parodies "so we will always recognize it" in "Sex, Objects," a model of blackness that sustains and is generated by the sexual/social myth: "All peoples who are not by heredity and/or active bonds of control fixed to the centers of bourgeois power are seething masses of dull, inarticulate sexuality."[69] And judging from the comments of other characters, Calkins is less interested in "civil rights" than in sexual stereotypes. Ernest Newboy tells Kid that he tried to convince Calkins to refrain from publishing Kid's poems, not because the poems were bad, but "Because Roger is not in the business of publishing poetry. Often unintentionally, he ends up in the business of sensationalism. Sensationalism and poetry have nothing to do with one another" (291). Tak declines Kid's invitation to join him and his nest of scorpions at the party at Calkins's estate celebrating the publication and success of *Brass Orchids,* Kid's book of poetry. When Kid asks, "Don't you want to see what happens when all us freaks get turned loose in there?" Tak cryptically replies, "Not terribly. But I suspect Calkins does" (552). Bunny, the go-go dancer, refuses the invitation with words that make Tak's meaning clearer: "As far as Calkins is concerned, or any of them up there," Bunny tells Kid, "you, me, or anybody you know just going up to make an appearance, is putting on a performance" (579).

Kid's predominantly black band of "freaks" has been invited primarily to provide a "*frisson*" of exoticism and danger for Calkins's mostly white, bourgeois guests.[70] According to Bunny, Calkins's willingness to open the party to the scorpions has a lot to do with his ownership of Teddy's: "Negroes and homosexuals, dear! Negroes and homosexuals! Having been lumped together in so many clichés for so long, we are *beginning* to learn" (579). Bunny refuses to perpetuate stereotypes about the "deviant" and/or "hyper-" sexuality of these groups in order to feed Calkins's and others' voyeuristic appetites.

According to Steiner, *Dhalgren* frequently undercuts the *Times*'s authority because the novel's events occur differently from how the newspaper reports them. Sporting arbitrary dates and absurdist headlines such as "ONLY ONE HUNDRED YEARS TILL THE DEATH OF HARLOW!" (45), the *Times* claims that after the water main break and subsequent power outage, the entirety of the city's African American population left the Lower Cumberland Park area of Jackson; but that is precisely where George, Dragon Lady, and other members of the black community reside.[71] Calkins's paper also advertises a new collection of Kid's poetry without his assent and before the volume is complete.[72] On the way to the party, the scorpions have fun with a *Times* article about them that overestimates their number by an order of magnitude and portrays them as a "rowdy band of black and white youths . . . terrorizing residents [and] committing acts of vandalism" (592). Kid's journal, however, reveals that the scorpions spend most of their time sleeping or staying in their "nest." At the party, Kid and the scorpions are introduced to Bill, Calkins's secretary and right-hand man, and most likely the "someone" who interviewed George and shaped the public image of him in the *Times*. Bill admits that he has never met Nightmare or Dragon Lady, although he has written about them. He tells Nightmare, "I was under the impression that the various gangs—nests—kept at each others throats," to which the scorpion simply responds, "Naw, it ain't like that . . ." (601). Bill's lack of familiarity with scorpion terminology and his distortions of the scorpions' activities make the *Times*'s representations of George's rape of June even more suspicious, and lend weight to what Eddy Richards, also known as the scorpion called Tarzan, tells his sister June: "The newspaper says a lot of things that aren't true, you know?" (568). The newspaper's discursive authority, therefore, is repeatedly challenged. That Kid wipes himself with a page from the *Times* just about says it all.

Calkins's newspaper provides a narrative of the sex act in which George and June engage that one must read critically. Given *Dhalgren*'s figurative and structural investment in multiple consciousness, it is important to look at the rape from other points of view. June Richards's behavior provides another context for interpreting her relations with George. She wanders around Bellona looking for George, biting her knuckle, and inquiring after him at his headquarters and at Teddy's, where Kid offers to obtain for her a poster of George from the Rev. Amy Tayler's church. When Kid asks why she is "so hung up on him [George]" June replies, "I don't . . . know. You wouldn't understand—if I told you"; and when Kid asks June what happened between her and George, she tells him, "Go read about it in the *Times!*" (195). Her next response expresses both confusion and exasperation with having to explain her behavior, prompting her to again accede to the dominant explanatory narrative:

> "The night the . . . black people had the riot? I was out, just walking around. There was lightning. And that immense thundering. I didn't know what had happened. And then it . . . I didn't even see the man with the camera until— It's just like it showed in the paper!" (195)

June's evident fixation on George raises questions about her brother Bobby's fall down the Labrys Apartments' elevator shaft; she may have feared that Bobby was going to tell their parents about the poster of George that Kid brought to June. Bobby's death provides another Necker cube moment in the novel in which two explanations are offered for a single event: Although June claims that while moving the Richards's rug she accidentally backed Bobby into the wrong elevator door, Kid, and the reader, cannot help but wonder if she pushed Bobby down the shaft to protect the secret of her obsession with George from her parents. Mary Kay Bray suggests that *Dhalgren* reverses "character stereotypes in . . . the black man–white woman rape plot, in which George is the knowledgeable, sensitive individual and June is driven by her lusts, perhaps even to murdering her brother."[73] June's explanation, however, is actually the more terrifying one. When Kid considers the possibility that Bobby's death truly was an accident, he concludes, "that means it's the city. That means it's the landscape: the bricks, and the girders, and the faulty wiring and the shot elevator machinery, all conspiring to *make* these myths true" (249). What Kid means, according to Jean Mark Gawron, is that there exists "the grim possibility that in Bellona it really does bring down death and destruction for a black man to have sex with a white woman. In Bellona it really *is* wrong."[74]

Besides the rape itself, the reader must also consider the images of George as a hypersexed black male from other perspectives, particularly that of the city's black community. Fox points out that Bellona's George Harrison is more *Soul on Ice* than the Beatles, and that the posters of him in various nude poses that appear in the city are "a visual equivalent of the sexual braggadocio (phal*logo*centrism) found in a good deal of contemporary rap music." Therefore, it is entirely possible that the popularity of the George posters depends on a repetition, recontextualization, and rearticulation of myths about black sexuality. What "would have gotten [George] lynched under different circumstances," Fox explains, is what makes him an "idol," especially among other black men.[75] There is always another way to look at things in *Dhalgren*, however. When Kid goes to the Reverend Amy Tayler to obtain a poster for June, he is first shown a series of head shots of George, as well as a new nude poster, before he identifies the other nude shot that he was looking for. Although she calls her church "interfaith [and] interracial" (73), the Rev. Tayler focuses her ministry toward the black community. When Kid asks "why do you have stuff like this [the posters] here?" she explains, "The poor people in this city—and in Bellona that pretty well means the black people—have *never* had much. Now they have even less. . . . We have to give them . . . something" (191). But some of the posters are more popular than others: "We've given out quite lots of the first one you saw," she tells Kid; "'That one,' she pointed to the one he held, 'isn't in quite as much demand'" (191). It could be that Bellona's black community demonstrates its own critical awareness of myths of black sexuality by preferring the head shots of George to the crotch shots, pictures that represent his identity and subjectivity instead of his mere sexuality.

Bellona's gay counterculture provides another context for the meaning of George's posters, one of which Kid encounters as part of a multiracial homoerotic triptych in Tak's abode. Tak later replaces two of this set of three posters with more of George. At Teddy's, George has, as Kid puts it, "a pretty heavy fan club" (323). And George is perfectly comfortable with being desired by the crowd at Teddy's; somewhat paradoxically he tells Lanya "I ain't got nothing against faggots" (213) and explains to Kid, "they [Bellona's gay male community (are)] good guys" (362). In this context, Fox's assertion that the posters represent "a different kind of 'wanted' poster than one marking him the target of slavecatchers, vigilantes, or bounty hunters"[76] suggests that the gay consumption of these posters rescues the meaning of black male sexuality from the realm of demonized social threat and releases it into the domain of desired sexual object, thus extracting sex from society further. A similar logic operates in several of Delany's works, with varying levels of success. But the fetishization of black male sexuality on the part of white gays is by no means unproblematic. Tak's description of his idol to Kid demonstrates that sexual fetishization and social oppression can easily go hand in hand:

> "Yeah, that's George—George Harrison. . . . Some of the boys at Teddy's got him to pose for that. He's a real ham. That ape likes to get his picture taken more than just about anything, you know? Long as he doesn't get too drunk, he's a great guy. Ain't he beautiful? Strong as a couple of horses, too." (100)

Admiration of George's physical "strength," desire triggered by his "beauty," and a racist reference to him as an "ape" go hand-in-hand here. With his ineffectually removed swastika tattoo and explicit—though perhaps ironically so—support of "white supremacy" (295), Tak represents what Kobena Mercer has identified as gay styles with "racist and fascist connotations . . . connotations of masculine power" that are "traditionally associated with *white* masculinity."[77] In contrast to Mercer and his own characterization of Tak, however, Delany has argued that Nazi emblems and clothing are sexualized simply because "what is forbidden is eroticized,"[78] which perhaps demonstrates how difficult separating sex and society really can be.

In the introduction to *Brother to Brother* (1991), Essex Hemphill writes that "the post-Stonewall white gay community of the 1980s was not seriously concerned with the existence of black gay men except as sexual objects. In media and art the black male was given little representation except as a big, black dick." Hemphill identifies one of the best known and most controversial of such representations in photographer Robert Mapplethorpe's *Black Book* (1986), specifically its "Man in Polyester Suit," which bears some resemblance to the nude George posters: a close-up of the flaccid penis of a black man, as the title suggests, in a polyester suit. "What is insulting and endangering to black men is Mapplethorpe's *conscious* determination that the faces, the heads, and by extension, the minds and experiences of some of his black subjects are not as important as close-up shots of their cocks," Hemphill states; "It is virtually impossible while viewing Mapplethorpe's photos of black males to avoid confronting issues of objectification."[79] Delany has also commented on Mapplethorpe's photography. His long essay "Shadow and Ash" includes the suggestion that critiques of "Man in Polyester Suit," such as those of Hemphill and Mercer, fail to appreciate the picture's "generic ambiguity," its confusion of the boundaries between artistic and advertising photography, wherein its most significant transgression lies.[80] Delany states that the answer to Hemphill and Mercer's question, "What do Mapplethorpe's images say to our wants and desires as black, gay men?" is "not necessarily conditioned one way or the other by being black alone."[81] The photo is also "funny," according to Delany, in that it is the visualization of an old joke told at the expense of white men. Such comments could conceivably be seen as supporting Posnock's evaluation of Delany as a black intellectual who deprivileges race, as a context for meaning. Hemphill and Mercer's critiques suggest, however, that one of the things black gays "desire"—in the nonsexual sense of the word—is respect. Moreover, the racial mode of meaning—initiated by Mapplethorpe, not the black viewer—*is* very much an issue, and the real joke that the photo invokes may be the racist one about how white supremacy views a black man regardless of economic security, political power, or academic achievement—all three of which are signifieds of the titular suit—as nothing but a "Nigger." Delany, however, does include a brief but sharp critique of "Man in Polyester Suit" in "The Rhetoric of Sex/The Discourse of Desire" as part of a response to a cultural discourse with no respect for difference: "Gay black male, look at Mapplethorpe's Man in Polyester Suit. There's something there (haven't we all been told?), universal, transcendent, aesthetic—good for you. Just swallow; and always insist to yourself that what must be swallowed is something other than the self-respect that is not, of course, his."[82] Delany's assertion that race is not the sole determinant of a black gay man's response to Mapplethorpe can be more productively characterized as his attempt to posit multiple, or multiplex, responses to the racial fetishism in which gay whites engage. Delany, therefore, parallels Mercer, who has written a two-part chapter that inveighs against Mapplethorpe's racial fetishism and revises that critique so as to distinguish it from the claims of homophobic and/or anti–NEA (National Endowment for the Arts) interests. Both writers speak as gay black men, and, therefore, multiply split subjects.[83] It is perhaps fitting, then, that *Dhalgren* allows for multiple perspectives on the reframing of George's sexuality by Bellona's white gays, alternating in Necker cube–fashion between celebration and criticism.

The account of what happened between George and June that most convincingly works as a counternarrative against the *Bellona Times* account is provided by George himself in a conversation he has with Lanya, who confronts him about June in order to find out what really happened out of concern for her friend Milly, a rape survivor. George explains that the type of sex he enjoys involves the woman "fighting and beating and scratching and crying . . . and moaning No, no, don't do it, but crawling back for more between trying to get away and a few yesses slipping out every once in a while" (208). Although his encounter with June during the riots may have appeared to be violent, according to George, it was a consensual sexual act: "[F]rom the way she was looking at me, I knew! I knew what she wanted and I knew how she wanted it. And I knew I wanted it too" (209). When Lanya thinks that she is simply hearing excuses, George makes a point of telling her that he thinks rape is "very, very sad" (210). He is also aware that the kind of "thing" he is into transgresses racial taboo, that "it's the one they all afraid of . . . between little-bitty white girls and big, black niggers" (210). When Lanya asks George what he thinks will happen when June finally finds him for another sex act, he simultaneously boasts of the magnitude of their performance and mocks the sexual/social myth by predicting that it will bring another apocalypse to Bellona:

"Well, she gonna get closer, and closer, just circling—and circling, and closer and closer, till—Blam! And the sky gonna go dark and the lightning gonna go roll over the night, wide as a river and slow as the sea, and buildings gonna come toppling and fire and water both gonna shoot in the air, and people gonna be running and screaming in the streets!" George winked, nodded. "Gonna be just like last time." (212)

For George, Bellona's apocalypse is a figure for the anxiety the *Times* and the rest of society suffers over him and June: "When we get together again," he explains, "*we* just gonna be doing our thing. *You* all is the ones who gonna be so frightened the city gonna start to fall down around your head" (212). After this explanation, it is hard not to agree with the reasoning that motivates Lanya to confront George, which she articulates by asking Milly, "Don't you find reality *more* fascinating than a flicker of half-truths and anxiety-distorted perceptions?" (202).[84]

What makes stereotypes of black males with insatiable sexual appetites especially vicious is that they reinforce stereotypes of black women as "chronically promiscuous"; Angela Davis identifies the myth of the black whore as an ideological formation that has historically blinded white America to black women's cries of rape.[85] *Dhalgren* may initially seem to reinforce this stereotype in a passage in Chapter 7, "The Anathēmata," where the scorpion known as Risa has sex in quick succession with a number of male scorpions, including Kid. Risa is described in Kid's journal as a black woman: "Her hair was stiff and long, like a spray of dark water that had shot from her head and frozen" (674). It is perhaps this passage that prompted the *Review of Contemporary Fiction* to describe *Dhalgren* as "sexy and sexist."[86] Watching a scorpion named Glass take his turn with Risa, the racially mixed Copperhead exclaims, "That nigger can fuck!" (676). Upon reflection, Kid writes in the journal's margin, next to his earlier entry, about this statement: "Re-reading this, it occurs to me that the written words don't let you know whether Copperhead meant Risa or Glass"; in keeping with *Dhalgren*'s attention to spoken language Kid notes, "His tone of voice did, though" (675). Without access to Copperhead's tone of voice, the reader of *Dhalgren* cannot tell to whom he was referring—another Necker cube moment, perhaps. But even though the scorpion called California claims that Copperhead and Glass "are having themselves a fuckin' contest" (671)—a Necker cube–like statement he must repeat, emphasizing the word "fuckin'" so as to clarify his meaning—Kid's observation raises the possibility that it is Risa who is exercising agency, that it is she who is doing the "fucking." Karen J. Bartlett has argued that Risa's assertion of "the desiring orifice" is a subversive sexual act "performed and controlled by a woman for her own satisfaction."[87]

She prevents men from defining the terms of her sex act when she tells Kid, "That was all mine. You just can't have any part of it" (684).[88] The gender ratio is reversed but the gender location of agency is the same at the women-only dwelling called the House, where Lanya and thirteen other women "ball" two male scorpions, Copperhead and Revelation. Risa is therefore neither rape victim nor indiscriminate libertine but, rather, like Lanya and, more significantly, like June, a woman who is actively engaged in the purposeful satisfaction of her own sexual desires.

Those desires would be deemed "abnormal," because they deviate from the received notions of "normal" sexuality (i.e., one woman and one man of the same race in missionary position) as well as of established gender roles (i.e., active male, passive female) that inform the "sexual/social myth." "People are scared of women doing anything to get what they want," Lanya tells George, "sex or anything else" (211). In the margins of his journal, Kid contemplates, for the sake of argument, the possibility that those desires are truly pathological—"Could it be that all those perfectly straight, content-with-their-sexual-orientation-in-the-world, exclusive-heterosexuals really *are* (in some ill-defined, psychological way that will ultimately garner a better world) more healthy than (gulp . . . !) us?"—before concluding "No *way!*" (720). Those desires are congruent with the forms—but, significantly, not the content—of sociopathic behaviors. As Bartlett suggests, *Dhalgren* is set in a space where certain sexual signifiers are decoupled from their negative, antisocial connotations or signifieds, disrupting the sexual/social myth. Bellona, named after a Roman war goddess, is a site where racial and sexual meanings clash.[89] Steiner observes, "Inside the city all myths/fictions/signs—literary and social—are shattered, revalued, and recombined."[90] Calkins's perpetuation of the myth of the black rapist through the representation of George in the *Times* is an attempt to fix the meaning of George's blackness. But the characters who inhabit Bellona seek to define their identities and sexual behaviors in their own new ways. Bunny has created a gender-refracting identity for him/herself, for example, which manifests itself partly in how [s]he is referred to. As Pepper explains to Kid, "Bunny is a guy, you know? But she likes to be called 'she'" (318).

The urge to define one's identity in one's own terms is at work within Bellona's black community as well. The names on the street signs in Jackson constantly change, at least sometimes due to the efforts of the city's black citizens. The scorpions' practice of (re)naming themselves, described in Kid's journal as "onomal maliability" (695), is one of the novel's most distinguishing characteristics. The importance of defining and redefining the terms of one's sexual, social, cultural, and political behavior is a highly significant theme in *Dhalgren*. It is a theme echoed in the words of Black Power leader, and Delany's former high school classmate, Stokely

Carmichael[91] in 1967, in referring to a text whose title features its own light-manipulating trope, Lewis Carroll's *Alice through the Looking Glass:*

"When I use a word," Humpty Dumpty said in a rather scornful tone, "I mean just what I choose it to mean, neither more nor less." "The question is," said Alice, "whether you can make words mean so many different things." "The question is," said Humpty Dumpty, "who is to be master." That is all. That is all. Understand that . . . the first need of a free people is to define their own terms.[92]

This contiguity between *Dhalgren*'s themes and the struggle for black liberation suggests that the novel should be read not only in a black cultural context, but also in a black historical context. Although science fiction often takes its readers into the far-flung future, each text is a product of its own historical moment. "Science fiction does not try to predict the future," Delany has stated; "rather it offers us a significant distortion of the present."[93] *Dhalgren,* written over a span of almost five years (1968–1973), is a significant distortion of the late 1960s and early 1970s. Americans' fears of nuclear warfare, spawned from an increasingly frosty Cold War with the Soviet Union, inform the "absolute panic of the Bomb" (419) that Kid felt as an undergraduate at Columbia University. Opposition to the American war in Vietnam, particularly that articulated by the nation's youth, is represented by Jack, a deserter from the U.S. Army. The first page of the novel features a cryptic first-person reference to student riots that evoke student protests at Columbia as well as the 1970 shooting of students by National Guardsmen at Kent State. Kid tries to show Lanya those same words in the notebook, which inexplicably appear as "student happenings" (33). The counterculture of the era, in which Delany participated as a member of Heavenly Breakfast, is represented by the commune in the park to which hippies John and Milly belong. The scorpions bear some resemblance to the tough, Hell's Angels biker–type squatters encountered in *Heavenly Breakfast.* And there is a nod toward the Stonewall uprisings, generally considered to be the point of origin of the gay and lesbian liberation movement and a signpost in Delany's life as well, in the placement of gay culture in the novel's background. As Bellona's refraction of the myth of black male sexuality transforms George from social threat to sexual idol, Teddy's, a gay bar not unlike the Greenwich Village establishment raided by the NYPD in 1969, becomes its city's social center. But *Dhalgren* most evidently conjures images of the era's uprisings in urban, predominantly black, neighborhoods and provides a reading of their relevant social, political, and economic factors. Weedman and Bray's identifications of the congruence of *Dhal-*

gren's "true v. real" epigraph and Du Boisian double-consciousness makes it possible to read the novel as a window onto what Robert Gooding-Williams calls "the perpetuation of a contradiction between the practice and the promise of American democracy."[94]

Most of the action in *Dhalgren* is set outside of Bellona's Jackson–Cumberland Park area, but one character asserts that, more than anything George has done, the poverty and desolation there are central to what has been happening to the city. Paul Fenster, a visiting black leader from the South, explains to Kid, before refuting Tak's attempts to identify as black on the basis of his gayness, that he does not necessarily believe that George is innocent of wrongdoing: "I don't approve or disapprove [of George]," he explains to Kid and Tak, "Sadism simply isn't my bag. And I don't hold with anybody committing rape on anybody" (284). Moreover, Fenster is concerned that the "to-do" over George is "the worst sort of red-herring" (284) in that it shifts attention away from more immediate concerns, such as the living conditions of Bellona's black population, most of whom are unable to leave the city. For them, the city is truly "a map of violences anticipated" (702). As bad as conditions are in general, they are significantly worse in Bellona's black neighborhoods. When Kid asks about George, Fenster calls the incident with June "past noise" and claims that "there're real problems that have to be dealt with now," pointedly asking Kid, "Have you ever *walked* up Jackson Avenue?" (283). When Kid answers that he has only crossed the Avenue instead of taking it into Bellona's black neighborhood, Fenster says, "Well, take a good look around it, talk to the people who live there before you go on to me about any of that George Harrison horseshit" (284). When the water main breaks in Jackson's Lower Cumberland section, the situation just gets worse, as Nightmare explains to Kid: "You got to watch out, down there . . . I mean it's getting pretty hungry, down there. Since the water main broke, it's just been sort of terrible. Two guys I know already got killed, down there. Yesterday. And somebody else two days before that" (542). The visiting poet Newboy provides an accurate representation of Bellona as a site of urban devastation that is all too real:

"There are times, as I wander in this abysmal mist, when these streets seem to underpin all the capitals of the world. At others, I confess, the whole place seems a pointless and ugly mistake, with no relation to what I know as civilization, better obliterated than abandoned." (354)

Kid fears that Bellona's "landscape" may be conspiring to make the myth of the black rapist come true and summon the destruction of the city, but Delany also uses this term at the beginning of the "random galaxy of notes" that closes "Sex, Objects."[95] "Landscape" applies to SF's attention to structures—what Delany calls elsewhere "the priority of the object"—that house and provide context for a character's subjectivity. The margins of Kid's journal contains a torrent of seemingly unrelated ideas, including a reflection on "not thinking but the way thinking feels. Not knowledge but knowledge's form" (732). The term also speaks to the ways in which human actions affect the material world—as with, to use Delany's examples, the greenhouse effect or the planting of trees—which in turn affect human psychology. An environment becomes the medium for the inscription of human actions upon it, constituting a sign system, a language, or "landscape": "a dense, interlocked web of the detritus of haphazard human action and/or intentional human undertaking which affects our psychology." As with any language, Delany explains, syntax affects meaning: "A new building encountered in a section of the city where all the buildings around it are new has one meaning; a new building encountered in a section of the city where all the buildings around it are decrepit slums has another." Each language unit—or "seme"—changes the meaning of its syntactic neighbor and of the neighborhood in general: "soot in the air (one seme) defaces a new building (another seme) creating a new seme—a grimy building—with a new meaning for the city itself. An unused sewer main beneath the street (one seme) collapses and causes a tenement (another seme) to drop a wall and collapse at one corner." After a chain of signs gets going, Delany states, it may be hard to identify the human author, or "intention on the part of the initial human actors," that started it all. But when human beings are brought back into the picture, the landscape alters both its own meaning and the human lives it encounters and incorporates, often with dire results: "The abandoned, half-ruined building where people have been injured and have fled from it is a different seme (with a different meaning) from either an overcrowded tenement or an abandoned sewer main." Delany eventually finds himself repeating Sartre quoting Marx: "The means of production affect the political, spiritual, and economic life of the people."[96] When Kid asks Lanya "Do you think a city can control the way the people live inside it? I mean, just the geography, the way the streets are laid out, the way the buildings are placed?" (249–50) and writes in his journal, "(Does the City's topology control us completely?)" (697), the novel is advancing Delany's concept of "landscape" further.

Consider, then, the effect that the conditions in Jackson have on the black lives there. It is not beyond the realm of possibility that due to such conditions, the riot described to Kid by Joaquim Faust—occurring before, during, or after Bellona's apocalypse, depending on how the reader sequences the novel's events, or most likely constituting it—ensues:

"The niggers. The first night, I guess it was. When all that lightning was going on. They went wild. Swarmed all over. Broke up a whole lot of stuff around here. . . . See if you can get hold of the paper for that day. People say you never seen pictures like that before. They was burning. And they had ladders up, and breaking in the windows. This guy told me there was a picture of them climbing up on the church. And breaking off the clock hands. Tearing each other up, too." (70–71)

Bellona represents very real, "autumnal"—"decaying and declining"—urban American terrain.[97] Steiner states that "the deliquescent and quintessentially American cityscape of Bellona" is "duplicated in how many photos of burned-out central Harlem, depopulated Buffalo, dying Detroit and half a dozen other towns."[98] Such comments suggest correspondences between the conditions in Bellona and those that contributed to the most striking of the urban uprisings of the 1960s. Like those uprisings, *Dhalgren* demands that attention be paid to a part of America previously ignored. In his introduction to the novel, William Gibson notes that during "the singularity that overtook America in the nineteen-sixties . . . a city came to be"; however, "the city was largely invisible to America."[99] After Kid receives his orchid and enters Bellona, the narrative describes the city's invisibility:

> This parched evening seasons the night with remembrances of rain. Very few suspect the existence of this city. It is as if not only the media but the laws of perspective themselves have redesigned knowledge and perception to pass it by. Rumor says there is practically no power here. Neither television cameras nor on-the-spot broadcasts function: that such a catastrophe as this should be opaque, and therefore dull, to the electric nation! It is a city of inner discordances and retinal distortions. (14)

Robert Elliot Fox points out that before the uprisings of the 1960s, America's ghettoes were invisible to the nation's collective consciousness "because the country had bought the illusion that the cities were steel-and-glass monuments to success and was unwilling to explore what lay in the long, deep shadows."[100] Reporting on the aftermath of the 1965 Watts, California, uprising, civil rights pioneer Bayard Rustin writes of "an unemployed black youth" who tells Rustin that "We won," on account of the fact that despite the 34 deaths, 1,000 injuries, 4,000 arrests, and $200 million in property damage, "we made the whole world pay attention to us. The police chief never came here before; the mayor always stayed uptown. We made them come."[101] Within a week of the Watts uprising, a record amount of guns were sold to whites, whose "desire for vengeance"[102] is paralleled in *Dhalgren* by the armed whites, including Jack and someone named "Reb", that Kid and the scorpion called Glass find stalking George's headquarters and joking about shooting him in retaliation for the scorpions' "run" on the white-owned Emboriky's department store.

The 1967 uprising in Newark, New Jersey, resulted in twenty-five deaths (all but two black), ten million dollars in property damage and twelve hundred arrests.[103] The following year, the National Advisory Commission on Civil Disorders reported, among other things, that "for the past twenty years the White [*sic*] middle class had been deserting the city for the suburbs"; for example, "Between 1960 and 1967 . . . the city switched from 65 percent white to 52 percent Negro and 10 percent Puerto Rican and Cuban."[104] The city's police force and political leadership, however, remained almost exclusively white. According to Fenster, before the catastrophe that visited it, Bellona was 30 percent black. "Now, even though you've lost so many people," he tells Tak, "bet it's closer to sixty" (282). As Fox states, "the 'fright flight' that so drastically reduced the population of the city was also a 'white flight'" comparable to what happened in Newark and continues to happen in American cities to this day.[105] The riots in Detroit that same year involved a confrontation of "the true and the real" when the *Detroit News* reported the presence of black snipers, "turn[ing] a 169-square block area north of West Grand Blvd. into a bloody battleground," when, in fact, no such snipers existed.[106] Godfrey Hodgson cites John Hersey's *The Algiers Motel Incident* (1968), an account of white law enforcement killing three black men who were socializing with two white women during the unrest.[107] Detroit produced its own "bloody arithmetic" that year: approximately 40 deaths, 2,250 injuries, 4,000 arrests, and $250 million in property loss.[108] The images of Newark and Detroit televised across the nation—"billowing smoke, gutted stores, looters and burning dwellings"—match descriptions of the city of Bellona.[109]

Although Gibson stops short of suggesting that *Dhalgren* is a "map" of that "city that came to be," he commends Delany for expressing "the unmediated experience of the singularity" of the 1960s, "free of all corrosion of nostalgia."[110] But Delany's commentary on cyberpunk author Gibson suggests that *Dhalgren* is also relevant to more recent events. Although *Nova* can be seen as an influence on cyberpunk—the SF sub-genre characterized by computer console "cowboys" who "jack" into computer systems in urban near-future settings—because of its representation of humans interfacing with machinery via "plugs and sockets," *Dhalgren* has its own thematic relationship to the style that Gibson, among others, made famous. Gibson's 1982 short story "Burning Chrome" begins with its protagonist reflecting on his (ab)use of a memory-stimulating drug: "Clinically they use the stuff to counter senile amnesia, but *the street finds its own uses for things."*[111] The rearticulation, recycling, and purposeful misuse of technology in the urban site that this statement represents made it a cyberpunk slogan in the 1980s. Delany claims that the slogan lost touch with "the anger, the rage, the coruscating fury from the streets toward the traditional use" of technology. Such a disconnection, Delany argues, was "no longer possible after the uprising that followed the acquittal of Rodney King's police thugs [in 1992]. To stand in the midst of the millions of dollars of devastation in Los Angeles and say, with an ironic smile, 'The street finds its own uses for things' is beyond irony and into the lunatic."[112] The 1992 L.A. uprising was the worst of its kind: 52 deaths, 2,383 injured, 4,000 businesses destroyed, approximately 500 fires, and property damage and loss approaching $1 billion.[113] Among other things, the uprising was a response to the "not guilty" verdict rendered by the Simi Valley jury that saw a videotape of King's beating; it was the result of raced subjects having their own expectations of justice subverted, further illustrating the gap between American ideals and the lived experiences of African Americans that Weedman and Bray identify as being at the core of *Dhalgren.* "Many of the very black Americans who had been victimized by the LA police believed that the videotape of the beating would once and for all educate white America about a form of racist repression that black Americans endure in everyday life," writes Jerry Watts; "Generally speaking, blacks expected whites to be appalled by the divergence between professed American democratic values and the black urban reality."[114] Instead, the police officers were acquitted, not despite the videotaped evidence, but with its assistance. The defense, according to Judith Butler, succeeded in convincing the jury to read the tape "as evidence that the body being beaten was *itself* the source of danger, the threat of violence, and, further, that the beaten body of Rodney King bore an intention to injure, and to injure precisely those police who either wielded the baton against him or stood encircling him."[115] The verdict, therefore, demonstrates how the black body, viewed through the distorting lens of white supremacy, is "always already" seen as a threat, as George is seen in the pages of the Bellona *Times.* The similarity between the defense's argument and George's representation in the newspaper is more apparent when considering LAPD Sgt. Stacey Koon's claim that King "shook it [i.e. his posterior] at" white patrol officer Melanie Singer,[116] a representation of black masculinity congruent with the stereotype that Delany's "Sex, Objects" parodies: "In him sex and aggression are one. . . . should he ever fail to repress, and that sexuality/anger should break free, he will destroy himself and all he has achieved in a single sweep, probably taking the odd bourgeois-born woman with him."[117] Moreover, to the degree that the site chosen for the trial's relocation, the bourgeois enclave of Simi Valley, was seen as "the normalized community: white, suburban, middle-class, male, straight, and law-abiding,"[118] it represents exactly the type of putatively centered subjectivity that *Dhalgren* in particular and Delany's work in general have an investment in decentering.

The poverty and desolation in Jackson are not necessarily the sole cause of Bellona's own urban uprising. Upon Kid's entry—or return—to the city at the beginning of the novel, Joaquim Faust tells him that one explanation for the riot is that a white sniper shot and killed a black victim. Although Kid detects what may be a plot to assassinate George in Chapter V, according to his journal it is Paul Fenster who is shot. Kid has fearful premonitions of the violence that will ensue following the killing: "(. . . There's going to be a riot! With Fenster shot, the blacks are going to be out all over Jackson and there's going to be a debacle from Cumberland Park too . . .)" (760). Fenster bears some similarity to the Rev. Martin Luther King Jr. who was assassinated months before Delany began work on the novel. Before he leaves Bellona, Newboy thanks Fenster: "I've really enjoyed the talks we've had. They've opened up a great deal to me. You've told me a great deal, shown me a great deal, about this city, about this country" (293). It is Fenster who initiates a day school for Bellona's children that Lanya manages. Joaquim Faust describes Fenster to Kid as a "colored man up from the South, some civil rights, militant person" (71). More telling, however, is Tak's flippant description of Fenster as "my favorite rebel-who-has-managed-to-misplace-his-cause" (282). Tak corrects himself by adding that Fenster's cause actually "went somewhere else when he wasn't looking" (282). There is a sense that most of the people in Bellona who would be interested in fighting for social justice have left the city. The scorpion called Nightmare informs Kid that "all the brainy niggers in Bellona had sense enough to get out" (498). At Calkins's party, Fenster bemoans the ironic "Tarzan and the Apes" routine put on by a few of the scorpions and longs for an earnestly progressive racial spirit to manifest itself: "You know, guys who come to parties like this in berets and talk about liberating the furniture: Now I'm pretty into that. But I guess that type all had sense enough to get out of Bellona while there was some getting" (612).

Though not a perfect analogue, the frustration Fenster feels working in Bellona parallels Dr. King's frustrated attempts at the end of his career. The application of nonviolent tactics that had succeeded in Birmingham failed in March of 1968. In Memphis, Dr. King led a demonstration that became a melee with police shooting at demonstrators and black youths fighting back. This incident marked a point in the shift of consciousness for some African Americans away from Dr. King's tactics of non-violent intervention and toward the militant slogans of Black Power politics. Four days later, King was assassinated. The initial reaction of most of black America was an overwhelming sense of loss and sorrow; however, this was quickly followed by unrest in over one hundred U.S. cities, involving looting and arson in urban areas and resulting in thirty-seven deaths, twelve in the nation's capital. Godfrey Hodgson quotes one black Washingtonian as saying "This is it, baby. The shit is going to hit the fan. We ought to burn this place right down."[119] Hodgson's description of the aftermath in Washington is strikingly similar to that of Bellona, *Dhalgren*'s "burning city" (11): "By dawn on April 6, a pall of black smoke from those fires hung over the national monuments."[120] At the end of Chapter VI, Kid and George walk into Jackson, which has erupted into flames: "Niggers done set the whole of Jackson to burning, don't it look like?" George asks (648). He recognizes that the water main break has aggravated the situation and fears that "everybody going to starve" (648). The neighborhood-wide conflagration also forces George and Kid to enter an inferno to rescue, according to Kid's journal, five children. But George is able to find something energizing and wondrous about the blaze: "Look at that burn up like a motherfucker;" he tells Kid, "It's beautiful, huh? Like walking on the sun" (648). George's tone echoes that of the speaker in Gwendolyn Brooks's "The Third Sermon on the Warpland" (1969), who views the flames of urban unrest as both motivational "candles" and as a "curse" cast upon the "darkness" of racial injustice in America.

There are important differences between the unrest of the 1960s and the 1992 L.A. uprising. Not simply a black versus white phenomenon, the 1992 "postmodern bread riot" included black, white, and Latino participants and highlighted conflicts within and between different racial and ethnic communities, black antagonism toward Korean-owned and operated businesses in particular.[121] But there are similarities as well, to which Delany's novel speaks. "If [*Dhalgren*] makes any social statement," Delany states, "it's that when society pulls the traditional supports out from under us, we all effectively become, not the proletariat, but the *lumpen* proletariat."[122] The L.A. uprising was a response to the deterioration of South Central L.A. as a result of the removal of exactly those supports, including reduced federal support for community-based organizations and social programs as well as economic divestment from the area.[123] In comparing the 1992 uprising to Watts, Gerald Horne suggests that "even if the LAPD had been transformed profoundly in the aftermath of the 1965 revolt, the 1992 civil unrest still might have happened because of the deteriorating economic environment facing so many in the city."[124] Of course, it is the antagonistic behavior of police toward African Americans that links these uprisings. The LAPD's treatment of black motorists played a role in both Watts in 1965 and Los Angeles in 1992. Newark was ignited by a white police officer abusing a black cab driver, and Detroit by a police raid on a "blind pig"—an illegal, after-hours drinking establishment—whose black patrons were often excluded from other, predominantly white, bars.

The response of conservative American politicians to the 1960s uprisings was to begin a right-wing movement to roll back the social and political advances of African Americans, in part through what Michael Omi and Howard Winant identify as the "rearticulation" of those gains. The 1968 presidential campaign saw "die-hard segregationist" George Wallace running as the "law and order" candidate, using "law and order" as what Omi and Winant identify as "code words": "phrases and symbols which refer indirectly to racial themes, but do not directly challenge popular democratic or egalitarian ideals (e.g., justice, equal opportunity)."[125] "Law and order" indirectly evoked distorted images of the recent riots, of chaotic blacks as a threat to whites and their security. Hodgson notes that most whites believed that "what happened in Watts was that the blacks rose, and rioted, and sniped, and killed white people," even though almost all of the victims of death and destruction in Watts and Detroit were black.[126] Wallace's "law and order" strategy yielded surprising election gains in Northern metropolises such as Philadelphia, Milwaukee, and Detroit, and the use of "coded anti-black campaign rhetoric" was suggested to the Nixon campaign that year, helping to put Nixon in the White House.[127] Criminologists John Galliher and James McCartney explain that during the Nixon administration "the United States appeared to become increasingly orderly after the tumult of the 1960s, which included urban ghetto riots and campus antiwar demonstrations"; however, they also argue that this apparent state of order "was not a result of the rule of law, for the evidence presented at the Watergate investigation shows that the Nixon administration was systematically and routinely violating criminal laws."[128] Although the sinister articulation of "law and order" succeeded in gaining Nixon the presidency, Watergate showed that the bond between "law" and "order" that many Americans have understood as innate was largely arbitrary.[129]

Dhalgren presents a similar challenge to received notions of "law and order" as part of its subversion of expectation. Gawron states that "the mechanics of expectation" exist in order to make "specific correspondences in the world for imposing order." Bellona itself is a space where law and order become decoupled from one another and lose their ideological privilege. As the periodic violent and vandalizing "runs" performed by the scorpions show, Bellona can indeed be chaotic. Also, as Kid's attempt to mug a passerby and Lanya's experiment with prostitution show, it is in some ways a city without traditional laws or law enforcement, though it would be a mistake to categorically label Bellona "lawless" or disorderly. Gawron states that in *Dhalgren* "the emblems of disorder are made instruments of order."[130] The scorpions are portrayed as a wild, destructive gang in the *Times*, for example, and the visiting astronaut known as Captain Kamp mistakes them for racketeers. But Bunny is able to understand the scorpions as "the only effective law enforcement organization in the city" (322) and interprets them as such to Kid and Pepper: "You scorpions do more to keep law and order in the city than anyone else. . . . I rather like the way it works here, because, since you *are* the law, the law is far more violent, makes much more noise, and isn't everywhere at once: so it's easier for us good people to avoid" (322). The scorpions are unlike Calkins, a shadowy figure whose panoptic authority seems to be all-pervasive, and they do enforce what rules there are in Bellona, as Kid learns when they beat him up after he trespasses on Calkins's property. Back at "Teddy's," Lanya asks Kid why he was attacked, to which he replies "I don't know. Shit. They just wanted to beat up on somebody, I guess," but Tak promptly corrects him: "No. That doesn't sound right. Not scorpions. Everybody's too busy trying to survive around here just to go beating up on people for fun" (87). As Tak explains to Jack, Bellona is "a strange place, maybe stranger than any you've ever been. But it still has rules. You just have to find them out" (87). The ability to learn Bellona's system of rules and operate in accordance with them is a key to survival in the city. Those who are unable or unwilling to understand end up isolated like Mrs. Richards in her self-imposed exile in the Labrys Apartments, alienated and antagonistic like Fenster's most likely assassin Jack, or at the very least, perplexed like Captain Kamp, who, observing the unconventional attire, or lack thereof, of the scorpions, admits, "I guess . . . I'm just not used to it" (608).

If Bellona's rules seem somewhat arbitrary, it is because *Dhalgren* demonstrates that laws in general are made, and are not "natural." Similarly, the power of law is assigned as arbitrarily as the date is in Bellona, determined by whatever date Calkins prints on the front page of the *Times*. Gawron explains that the novel illustrates how "power is something that accrues to social entities merely because of their position in the network."[131] As with its sexual signifiers, Bellona's refractory terrain is a space in which social signifiers, such as "law and order," can be decoupled from their received signifieds, such as traditional police and government, and affixed to new signifieds, creating new social meanings and social structures. Martin Duberman writes that the urban uprisings, the student antiwar protests, the feminist movement, and the Stonewall uprising of the late 1960s were manifestations of a zeitgeist of interrogating "arbitrary authority": "Over and over, the question was being raised: 'Who makes the rules—and by what right?'"[132] It is in its radical dismantling of law and order that *Dhalgren* is most evidently a sign of those times, as opposed to an open-ended testament to a neutral relativism.

The effect of entering Bellona for the reader who opens Delany's novel is the same as the Reverend Amy Tayler's sermon's description of the experience of having crossed the city's limits:

> "Don't you know that once you have transgressed that boundary, every atom, the interior of every point of reality, has shifted its relation to every other you've left behind, shaken and jangled within the field of time, so that if you cross back, you return to a very different space than the one you left? You have crossed the river to come to this city? Do you really think you can cross back to a world where a blue sky goes violet in the evening, buttered over with the light of a single, silver moon?" (480–81)

Dhalgren, therefore, encourages its readers to look at American society from radically new perspectives, to re-evaluate racial, class, gender, and sexual hierarchies that are too often taken to be "natural." Like the archetypal monster Grendel, an approximation of whose name Kid mistakes for "Dhalgren," the novel roams the boundaries of "inside" and "outside," and, like the Necker cube, troubles those distinctions.[133] In short, it leaves the reader with a dazzling, decentering, sense of wonder.

3

THE EMPIRE OF SIGNS

SLAVERY, SEMIOTICS, AND SEXUALITY
IN THE *RETURN TO NEVÈRŸON* SERIES

Clearly, no authentic human relationship was possible where violence was the
ultimate sanction. There could have been no trust, no genuine sympathy; and
while a kind of love may sometimes have triumphed over this most perverse
form of interaction, intimacy was usually calculating and sadomasochistic.
—Orlando Patterson, *Slavery and Social Death*[1]

'We are lovers,' said Gorgik, 'and for one of us the symbolic distinction
between slave and master is necessary to desire's consummation.'
'We are avengers who fight the institution of slavery wherever we find it,'
said Small Sarg, 'in whatever way we can, and for both of us it is symbolic of
our time in servitude and our bond to all men and women still so bound.'
—Samuel R. Delany, *Tales of Nevèrÿon*[2]

Fredric Jameson has described Samuel R. Delany's *Return to Nevèrÿon*
series as "a major and unclassifiable achievement in contemporary American literature." The tetralogy—which includes five stories in *Tales of Nevèrÿon* (nominated for the American Book Award in 1979), the novel
Neveryóna, three stories in *Flight from Nevèrÿon*, and three in *Return to
Nevèrÿon*[3]—certainly has a way of defying certain generic binaries. Is it
fiction or criticism, pop culture or high art? The series has been read as
all of these, but rarely with an acknowledgment of its correspondences to
the histories of people of African descent in America. The *Return to Nevèrÿon* series participates simultaneously in the discourses of African American Studies and semiotics, the intersections of which are located at the site
of a critique of oppressive social relations and a vindication of the right
to sexual freedom.

The series represents Delany's most significant foray into the paraliterary genre known as "fantasy," or "sword-and-sorcery," a sub-genre that often shares publishers, writers, and readers with SF. Sword-and-sorcery fictions are often set in some prehistoric civilization—what Delany calls "an aspecific, idealized past"[4]—and generally feature scantily clad sword-wielding heroes and/or heroines (with the physiques of bodybuilders or swimsuit models), magicians who wield sorcery for the causes of good or evil, and fantastic creatures such as dragons or demons. Quests, intrigue, and quasi-mythical deities are often sprinkled into the mix as well. Delany has described the language of sword-and-sorcery as "written with a sort of verbal palette knife—an adjective-heavy, exclamatory diction that mingles myriad archaisms with other syntactical distortions meant to signal the antique: the essence of the pulps,"[5] referring to the pulp fiction magazines emerging in the late 1920s and early 1930s that were the original paraliterary outlets. Robert E. Howard (1906–1936), an American writer whose works were among the many Delany read as a youth, produced numerous fictions still popular and influential today; the most famous include such characters as King Kull, Red Sonja, and Conan the Barbarian. Howard's fictions, the novels of J. R. R. Tolkein, Fritz Leiber's Lankhmar stories featuring Fafhrd and the Grey Mouser,[6] and Michael Moorcock's Elric of Melniboné books among others have inspired a host of subsequent sword-and-sorcery heroes and series. "Dungeons and Dragons," the internet-based "EverQuest,"and similar role-playing games are pop-culture descendants of such works that continue to share with sword-and-sorcery fiction a popularity beyond its stereotyped audience of white suburban male adolescents.

For some readers the sword-and-sorcery genre has something of a paraliterary second-class status, but it would be a mistake to assume that these books are a mere sidetrack in the career of a Nebula Award–winning author of relatively "respectable" SF. Delany's first SF novel, *The Jewels of Aptor* (1962), has recognizable elements of sword-and-sorcery, and the author wrote an introduction to *Alyx* (1975), Joanna Russ's sword-and-sorcery fiction named after its female protagonist. According to Delany, the *Return to Nevèrÿon* series is among the "more important" of his works. "They've occupied me, almost obsessively, for more than ten years," the author said in a 1986 interview, "Hour for hour, more work has gone into the Nevèrÿon texts than anything else I've ever written."[7] But when Delany claims that one of the aims of this series is "to articulate for adults the hidden and subterranean [erotic] currents that are forever at play in the largely infantile genre of sword-and-sorcery," he demonstrates an awareness of the general disfavor with which some have looked upon the genre: "There are many SF and fantasy writers," Delany states, "who honestly feel that my work for the last fifteen or more years [i.e., the *Return to Nevèrÿon* series] has been wholly misguided, if not deranged . . . since the genre *is* infantile, why not simply leave it behind and go do something else?"[8]

But when *Tales of Nevèrÿon* was first published in 1979, *New York Times Book Review* critic Gerald Jonas labeled it "superb SF."[9] In 1988, Jonas described *Return to Nevèrÿon* as the work of "one of SF's finest writers at the top of his form."[10] The language of these stories is dense, complex, and noticeably *un*like "the essence of the pulps." The series' thrills, however, are decidedly more intellectual than its periodical ancestors' were; Kathleen Spencer observes that in the series' opening story, "The Tale of Gorgik," which is repeated at the end of the series, there are "no villains to murder, no ladies to rescue, no dramatic slave rebellions, not even a daring escape."[11] Even Delany himself—in the guise of K. Leslie Steiner—half-jokingly writes that "Proust's opening twenty-thousand-word analysis of the bedtime preparations of a chronic invalid is hard-boiled action-adventure compared to any of [*Tales*'] soporific, if not somnolent, narratives."[12] Like *Dhalgren,* the series must be read and re-read to be fully appreciated, or to some extent even comprehended. The reader attends to the series in much the same way as Gorgik listens to the conversations of the royalty upon his arrival at the High Court of Eagles, "with the relaxed attention of an aesthete hearing for the first time a difficult poem, which he already knows from the artist's previous works will require many exposures before its meanings [*sic*] clear" (*Tales* 50). What is immediately apparent about these books, however, is that they feature an innovative mixture of fantastic fiction, metafiction, and critical theory, which has dazzled many enthusiastic readers. It is Delany's postmodern attempt to execute a highly artistic literary project within a tradition with its roots in popular pulp fiction that characterizes his work in general and the *Return to Nevèrÿon* series in particular.

Similarly, it is the series' "play" between "literature" and "theory" that informs Jameson's reading of the series as "unclassifiable." Constance Penley notes that the series positions itself "on a borderline between literary practice and critical theory." Steiner announces its central themes as "power, sex, and narration itself."[13] Chapters begin with epigraphs from some of the most important scholars of literary and critical theory: Edward Said, Gayatri Spivak, Michel Foucault, Julia Kristeva, and others. In a manner similar to *Dhalgren,* these theoretical insights and allusions cause the texts to subvert the reader's expectations has of a "sword-and-sorcery" book.[14] Delany himself has described the series as an exercise in "the genre equivalent of gender bending,"[15] no doubt with an awareness that "gender" and "genre" stem from the same etymological root.[16] Acknowledging the series' gen[d]re-bending qualities, Wesleyan University

Press has cross-listed the series under "Literature," "Fantasy," and "Gay Studies." The books are *not* listed under "African American Studies," however, which is quite surprising, especially given the significance of Delany's racial heritage, the racial makeup of the characters, and the centrality of the topic of slavery to the series' overall narrative.

File under "African American Studies"

The reader of the *Return to Nevèrÿon* series does not have to look far for evidence of its relevance to the interdisciplinary field of African American Studies. Although the setting of these stories is temporally and geographically unspecified, there are plenty of examples to suggest that the books are about people of color. The preface to *Tales* is attributed to Delany's alter-ego, K. Leslie Steiner, who is self-described as"your average black American female academic, working in the largely white preserves of a sprawling midwestern university, unable as a seventies graduate student, to make up her mind between mathematics and German literature" at the time she wrote the 1974 translation of a 900-word pseudo-artifact from 4500–5000 B.C. called "the Culhar' Text."[17] Also known as "the Missolonghi Codex," the Culhar' is the ostensible basis for the *Return to Nevèrÿon* series. Steiner hypothesizes that the setting for these stories is Mesopotamian or Mediterranean, and claims that "arguments can be made for placing it in either Asia or Africa" before noting that "its weather and immediate geography (sun, fog, rain, but no snow, in a city on the sea surrounded by mountains) make it sound like nothing so much as prehistoric Piraeus—or San Francisco." In the appendix to *Tales*, Steiner's friend and colleague, archaeologist S. L. Kermit, offers more inconclusive clues to the setting in his comments on the Culhar', once thought to be "humanity's first writing,"[18] which was found and purchased in Greece in the nineteenth century and is currently stored in Turkey.[19] Although the series is not very specific about its supposed historical and geographical location, it makes a point about announcing its difference from the majority of other sword-and-sorcery fictions, where the "aspecific, idealized past" in which they are set is usually an approximation of medieval Western Europe.

As ambiguous as the texts are about their location in time and space, they are very precise in their rendering of the racial diversity of Nevèrÿon's inhabitants. Nevèrÿon is a land in which dark-skinned people tend to rule and white people tend to be ruled. The empire's people can be divided into two general racial groups: multi-classed people of color described as either "brown" or "black," and "barbarians," whose blond, blue-eyed, and pale-skinned appearance marks them as Caucasian. Such a classification is congruent with the understanding of the series' chief protagonist, Gorgik, who as a child observes the prostitutes on the Bridge of Lost Desire in the capital city of Kolhari:

> . . . most of them [were] brown by birth and darkened more by summer, like the fine, respectable folk of the city (indeed, like himself), though here were a few with yellow hair, pale skin, grey eyes, and their own lisping language . . . bespeaking barbaric origins (*Tales* 30).[20]

The physical descriptions of the members of Nevèrÿon's aristocracy frequently include racial markers. Vizirine Myrgot, "a bottomless well of cunning and vice" (*Tales* 38, *Return* 228) who takes the scarred Gorgik from the obsidian mines at the base of the Faltha Mountains to serve as her sexual plaything at the Court of High Eagles, is introduced as having "tan skin and tawny eyes" (*Tales* 37, *Return* 228). When Gorgik first stumbles upon the Child Empress Ynelgo at a party in the Court to which he was not invited, he focuses on "her large eyes, close to the surface of her dark brown face" (*Tales* 57, *Return* 247). As an older woman, Ynelgo wears "her dark hair cornrowed severely over her head."[21] Madame Keyne, a wealthy Kolhari merchant, is described as having a dark face and "dark fingers."[22] And Lord Anuron, like other men in Nevèrÿon, has "nappy black hair" (*Return* 41). The series' most important characters, though not aristocrats, are clearly people of color as well. Delany has described Gorgik the Liberator as "a green-eyed black man."[23] In *Flight*'s *The Tale of Plagues and Carnivals*, the author makes a trip to a Third Avenue movie house in search of "one of the Saturday afternoon regulars" there, whom, his lover Ted claims, is "the *exact* image" of Gorgik (*Flight* 351). Delany is quite surprised, however, to see that Ted's "Gorgik" is "blond (!?), most likely Polish"; therefore, the author explains, "it would never have occurred to me to think he resembled my character." "Well," Delany concludes, "to each his own Liberator" (*Flight* 351).

Another of the series' most prominent characters, Pryn, the protagonist of *Neveryóna*, is also black. Pryn is the daughter of a soldier in the imperial army whose death was reported by another soldier whom her mother described to the child as "as black as your father" (*Neveryóna* 31). During her journeys throughout Nevèrÿon, Pryn befriends a dancer named Vatry, whose complexion suggests even further diversity of color among Nevèrÿon's populace:

> Instead of the rich nut brown Pryn assumed the normal complexion of all around her not specifically foreign, Vatry's face and shoulders had a yellowish cast, and she was spotted, hairline to hands and feet, with coppery freckles (*Neveryóna* 195).

Moreover, Pryn, herself "a loud brown fifteen-year-old with bushy hair" and a "heavy, short girl" (*Neveryóna* 15), is "not," as Madame Keyne describes her, "traditionally beautiful" (Delany, *Neveryóna* 97), and certainly not the typical Barbie-doll heroine or obligatory love/sex–interest appearing on the covers of most sword-and-sorcery paperbacks and comic books.

Because of differences in skin color and language, Nevèrÿon's barbarians, who come from the wooded southern regions of the country, are easily distinguished from the rest of the populace and suffer at least some disenfranchisement as the label "barbarian" might suggest. Such social and political marginalizations inform the familiar syntax of the bigotry of Clodon the bandit: "Lazy, dirty sorts, barbarians. I'm glad we don't have any around here—though I knew some when I lived in Kolhari. Oh, a few of them could be just as nice as you or me" (*Return* 135). Old Zwon, the potter, expresses a similar attitude about the women in barbarian families that have recently moved into Kolhari: "No grace about them at all. Uncivilized and nasty-tongued to boot—those you can understand for the accent" (*Tales* 209). In Nevèrÿon, slavery is not based on race as it was in the antebellum United States. Both Sarg, a pale barbarian, and Gorgik, the dark-skinned son of the employee of a city merchant, become enslaved; however, many of Nevèrÿon's slaves are barbarians, especially in the Empire's southern reaches. The racial ideology that enables distinctions between "yellow-haired barbarians" and "brown respectable folks" (*Flight* 194) informs and is informed by cultural difference. Male barbarian names tend to end in "-yuk," for example, and the barbarian language, as Zwon notes, has its own distinct sound, which Pryn chauvinistically imitates as "ba-ba-ba-ba-ba" (*Neveryóna* 300). But such differences do not prohibit what one might call an "interracial" relationships between Gorgik and Small Sarg as well as between Nari and Zadyuk, the friends of Pheron, a Kolhari weaver who succumbs to the titular sickness in *Plagues and Carnivals*. The correspondence between the social relations of Nevèrÿon's barbarians and its dark-skinned population and the social relations between black and white Americans is most strongly suggested by an incident a smuggler observes on the Bridge of Lost Desire in *Flight's* "The Tale of Fog and Granite." Emerging from the downstairs urinal-trough, he hears a barbarian youth pestering a robed citizen:

'Where you think you going, fine Kolhari man? Come on, tell me. Tell me, now! Afraid I'll rob you? Afraid I'll beat you? You don't have to be afraid of me, city man!' (*Flight* 34).

The robed figure, bearing signs of a higher socioeconomic class, ignores the barbarian as best as he can, but the youth persists until an older barbarian interrupts—"Hey, barbarian . . . why do you talk like such a fool?" (*Flight* 35)—and drags the younger barbarian off. The template for this episode is revealed in *Plagues and Carnivals* (alternately titled "Some Informal Remarks Towards the Modular Calculus, Part Five"), in which the plague that annihilated Norema's people on the Ulvayn Islands appears in Kolhari, afflicting the homosexual male prostitutes and patrons of the Bridge of Lost Desire in particular. The fictional plague is modeled on the emergence of the AIDS crisis in New York City in the early 1980s, much as the incident on the Bridge is modeled on one Delany reports seeing at the Port Authority Bus Terminal. A black teenager attempts to vex a tired, middle-aged white couple—"Hey, white folks! . . . Where you goin'? . . . Don't worry, I ain't gonna hurt you! . . . What's the matter? You afraid I'm gonna rob you? I'm gonna mug you?" (*Flight* 277)—until a young black man interrupts. Delany, like the smuggler, goes to find a urinal and returns to see the teenager harassing "a tall, rather refined looking white man, with silver hair and an expensive gray suit, his overcoat over one arm and carrying an attaché case" until an older black teenager breaks up the routine—"Nigger, why you acting like such a fool!" (*Flight* 278)—and escorts the provocateur away, in a headlock. Moreover, as has been the case with people of African descent in America, "barbarians in positions of power were not popular with the people" of Delany's fictional empire (*Tales* 68, *Return* 259).

Nevèrÿon's racial dynamics have evident correspondences with those operating in United States and world history. By making people of color the masters of a predominately white "barbaric" slave community, Delany playfully inverts America's racial hierarchy. But unlike Robert A. Heinlein's *Farnham's Freehold* (1964), in which a nuclear explosion blasts a white family into a future where blacks dominate, it avoids racial stereotypes of either group in its critique of vertical readings of racial difference. By associating the fictional Culhar' Text, one of the oldest narratives known to mankind, with what appears to be a black civilization, Delany can even be seen as making arguments for the African creation of civilization itself, comparable to those of Martin Bernal's *Black Athena*. Placing the series' events in Africa or Asia, however, also supports observations by scholars such as Orlando Patterson that despite (or, rather, as part of) their development of civilization, certain pre-colonial African and Asian societies demonstrated a high dependence on slave labor.[24]

This chapter's emphasis of the racial aspects of Nevèrÿon's inhabitants and their society seeks not only to indicate their relevance to African American Studies in general but also to identify discrepancies between the content of the *Return to Nevèrÿon* series and the way it has been marketed to the reading public. With so many black and/or non-white characters in these stories, a reader might reasonably expect to see some representation of them on the books' covers. Cover art is especially significant to the paraliterary cultures of SF and sword-and-sorcery, not only for the assistance they provide the reader in imagining fantastic events, characters, and settings, but also because the cover art often goes on to have an artistic and commercial life of its own apart from the text as it is reproduced in the form of calendars, posters, and so on. But when *Tales, Neveryóna*, and *Flight* were originally published by Bantam Books in the 1980s, no people of color were to be found on the covers. A painting by acclaimed SF and fantasy artist Rowena Morrill for a Bantam edition of *Tales* features renderings of (left to right) the masked swordswoman Raven, a male figure, and the red-headed storyteller Norema, perhaps during the women's ill-fated trip to find Lord Aldamir (figure 4). But the male figure looks nothing like Bayle, the "strong, stocky lad, with an inch of nappy black beard" and a "curly head" (*Tales* 165) accompanying Raven and Norema in *Tales*' "The Tale of Potters and Dragons." Although the item around the male figure's neck resembles Gorgik's astrolabe, and his side-braid suggests that, like the Liberator, he has fought in the imperial army, there is no sign of the collar that Gorgik wears for personal and political reasons. This figure resembles the text's descriptions of the Liberator as much, or as little, as the one staring at the dragon Gauine and the titular city in Morrill's painting on the Bantam edition of *Neveryóna* (figure 5), another white male figure who, other than the iron collar at his neck, does not correspond to descriptions of Gorgik. The seated female looks little like the round, brown teenager Pryn is supposed to be. Morrill's painting on the cover of the Bantam edition of *Flight* (figure 6) features a perhaps more accurate picture of the smuggler, Pryn's love interest in *Neveryóna* and a major character in *Flight*'s "The Tale of Fog and Granite" and "The Mummer's Tale," leading his ox and cart through Nevèrÿon while the Amnewor, an Elder God, watches from the woods.[25] There is no question of Morrill's artistic ability or of the beauty of the images she produces. And, of course, literal interpretations of the stories' events may be too much to expect. But at the risk of judging books by their covers, these specific inaccuracies, including the prominence of both monsters and scantily clad women, and particularly the substitution of white characters for people of color, suggest that Bantam was trying to make these volumes look like more traditional sword-and-sorcery commodities in order to market them to a specific audience: heterosexual white male adolescents. Such obfuscations were quite evidently based on—and contributed to—the misconceptions that black Americans do not read SF and that SF/sword-and-sorcery culture and black culture have nothing in common.[26] Wesleyan University Press has avoided these issues altogether

Fig. 4 "Tales of Nevèrÿon" © Rowena Morrill.

by opting for beautiful, if ambiguous, photographs by Jon Gilbert Fox, suggestive perhaps of Nevèrÿon's landscape. Wesleyan's cross-listing of the series suggests that the series is now aimed at a broader audience. Both presses, however, missed an opportunity to broaden that target audience further by acknowledging the series' black characters or its relevance to African American Studies on the covers.

If the racial makeup of the characters in Delany's sword-and-sorcery series is insufficient to classify the series as African American Literature, there is the author's own identity as a black American to consider. In a 1983 interview with *Science Fiction Studies,* he notes how his racial heritage is one that includes the legacy of race-based slavery in America:

> Three of my grandparents were children of at least one parent born in slavery. And my father's father was born a slave in Georgia. Manumitted when she was eight, my great-grandmother Fitzgerald still told *my* grandmother stories about slavery times, as did my grandmother's grandparents, with whom my grandmother stayed in summer when she was a little girl in Virginia—stories which my grandmother, who was alive till only last year (she died when she was 102), told to me.[27]

Fig. 5 "Neveryóna" © Rowena Morrill.

Slavery in America, so significant to the history of both sides of Delany's family, continues to be a one of the most vital areas of current intellectual inquiry.[28] In *Neveryóna* (329) the Earl Jue-Grutn tells Pryn, "It *is* hard to keep the past organized. And when the past is disorganized, the present is . . . well, as you see it: all barbaric splendor and misery," suggesting a relationship between history and present reality comparable to Arna Bontemps's observation in *Black Thunder* (1936) that "time is a pendulum."[29] An understanding of the history of slavery is therefore vital to a comprehension of the functions of race in contemporary America and throughout American literature and history. In their introduction to *Slavery and the Literary Imagination* (1989) Deborah McDowell and Arnold Rampersad identify slavery as "the central intellectual challenge, other than the Constitution itself, to those who would understand the meaning of America" and note its importance in landmark literary works such as Mark Twain's *The Adventures of Huckleberry Finn* (1884) and William Faulkner's *Absalom, Absalom!* (1936), "the most influential" and "the finest," respectively, of American novels.[30] Hazel Carby explains that "slavery haunts the literary imagination because its material conditions and social relations are frequently reproduced in fiction as historically dynamic; they continue to influence society long after emancipation."[31]

The *Return to Nevèrÿon* series is an example of contemporary African

Fig. 6 "Flight from Nevèrÿon" © Rowena Morrill.

American fictions that are similarly "haunted" by slavery. But the series is by no means a transparent allegory of race-based slavery that occurred in antebellum America. Slavery in Nevèrÿon, as just noted, is not exclusively race-based as it was in America. Although "the economics of as much as a third of the nation had once been based" on slavery (*Return* 169), there's nothing of the plantation systems that dominated American slave labor industries to be found in Nevèrÿon. Mining, brewing, administrative, sexual, and domestic labor are the only contexts in which the reader sees slaves at work, though road and agricultural slaves are also mentioned. Delany's own comments clearly differentiate slavery in America from slavery in Nevèrÿon. In *Plagues and Carnivals* the author explains, "The Nevèrÿon series is, from first tale to last, a document of our times, thank you very much. And a carefully prepared one, too" (*Flight* 245); and in "Closures and Openings," the Appendix to *Return*, he states, "clearly the Nevèrÿon series is a model of late twentieth-century (mostly urban) America . . . rich, eristic, and contestatory (as *well* as documentary)" (*Return* 286), a significant distortion of the present as opposed to a symbolic representation of the antebellum South. In his 1983 *Science Fiction Studies* interview, Delany differentiates what he sees as the series' playful speculations on alternative systems of the world and the subjects operating within them from a literary project that would attempt a more "realistic" representation of "the peculiar institution":

> In imaginary Nevèrÿon, slavery is an economic reality (fast fading into a historical memory) but also a persistent fantasy. The historic imaginative space, plus the paraliterary object priority S&S [sword-and-sorcery] shares here and there with SF (which allows it to be read for what it is), lets me play with notions about how things-in-the-world, *including* the socially contoured organization of people's psyches, may be functioning in such correspondences.[32]

The *Return to Nevèrÿon* series is paraliterary sword-and-sorcery fiction; these books are *not* historical novels about slavery in America. As important as such disclaimers are to keep in mind, however, it is impossible to ignore the centrality of the subject of slavery to the overall narrative, especially when this topic is placed front and center in "The Tale of Gorgik," which describes the hero's earliest encounters with slavery as a child. Gorgik is initially described as being haunted by a "double memory" consisting first of slaves and their sale in a warehouse on a Kolhari street called the Old Pavē:

> . . . leaving a room where a lot of coins, some stacked, some scattered, lay on sheets of written-over parchment, to enter the storage room at the back of the warehouse his father worked in—but instead of bolts of hide and bales of hemp, he saw some two-dozen, cross-legged on the gritty flooring, a few leaning against the earthen wall, three asleep in the corner, and one making water astraddle the trough that grooved the room's center. All were sullen, silent, naked—save the iron at their throats. As he walked through, none even looked at him. (*Tales* 27–28, *Return* 217–18)

The second part of the double memory is of the slaves' collars, the legal emblems of their enslaved status. But unfastened and detached from the slaves' bodies, the collars begin to signify differently for Gorgik than before:

> An hour, or two hours, or four hours later, he walked into that storage room again: empty. About the floor lay two dozen collars hinged open. From each a chain coiled the pitted grit to hang from a plank set in the wall to which the last, oversized links were pegged. The air was cool and fetid. In another room coins clinked. Had he been six? Or seven? Or five . . . ? (*Tales* 28, *Return* 218)

At another time, the young Gorgik stumbles upon a dirty teenage boy in the yard in front of a cistern wall. The collar around the teenager's neck triggers a profound physiological reaction:

> When he saw the iron collar around the boy's neck, Gorgik stopped— walking, thinking, breathing. There was a thud, thud, thud, in his chest. For moments, he was dizzy. The shock was as intense as heat or cold.
> When his vision cleared, the next thing Gorgik saw were the scars.
> They were thick as his fingers and wormed around the boy's soiled flanks. Here the welts were brown, there darker than the surrounding skin—he knew what they were, though he had never seen anyone bearing them before. At least not from this close. They were from a flogging. In provincial villages, he knew, whipping was used to punish criminals. And, of course, slaves. (*Tales* 32, *Return* 222)

Observing this same teenager, presumably an escaped slave, unhinge his collar, remove it from his neck, and throw it over a wall, produces chills all over Gorgik's body, as well as a considerable amount of confusion. Gorgik's initial reactions may appear to be simply the result of shock at the cruelty the enslaved teenager has endured; however, the second part of his "double memory" suggests that there is another way in which his chills, pounding heart, and dizziness should be read. Such memories and other experiences, both as a slave and as a free man, contribute to the transformation of Gorgik the slave into Gorgik the Liberator. The *Return to Nevèrÿon* series, therefore, further justifies McDowell and Rampersad's claim about the significance of slavery to American and African American literature. Moreover, it features representations of slavery as not only an economic phenomenon, but as an institution with social and cultural meanings as well. The sophistication of the series' representation of slavery can be illustrated by way of identifying its correspondences with African American slave narratives and with historical and sociological scholarship on slavery.

African American slave narratives allowed black ex-slaves to "write themselves into being,"[33] to fill in the gaps left by slavery's attempts at erasing the slave's African heritage and the fundamental role blacks had in shaping America and its history. Orlando Patterson observes that slaves "were not allowed freely to integrate the experience of their ancestors into their lives, to inform their understanding of social reality with the inherited meanings of their natural forebears, or to anchor the living present in any conscious community of memory."[34] Knowledge of this persistent attack on the heritage of the African diaspora in America informs at least part of the meaning of an oft-quoted passage from "The Necessity of Tomorrows," Delany's 1978 Studio Museum of Harlem speech: "We need images of tomorrow, and our people need them more than most."[35] As he explains in a 1993 interview,

> The historical reason that we've been so impoverished in terms of future images is because, until fairly recently, as a people we were systematically forbidden any images of our past. I have no idea where, in Africa, my black ancestors came from because, when they reached the slave markets of New Orleans, records of such things were systematically destroyed. If they spoke their own languages, they were beaten or killed. The slave pens in which they were stored by lots were set up so that no two slaves from the same area were allowed to be together. Children were regularly sold away from their parents. And every effort conceivable was made to destroy all vestiges of what might endure as African social consciousness. When, indeed, we say that this country was founded on slavery, we must remember that we mean, specifically, that it was founded on the systematic, conscientious, and massive destruction of African cultural remnants. That some musical rhythms endured, that certain religious attitudes and structures seem to have persisted, is quite astonishing, when you study the efforts of the white, slave-importing machinery to wipe them out.[36]

After his campaign to end slavery succeeds, Gorgik the Liberator reflects and makes a similar observation about what Delany identifies as slavery's effect of "massive cultural destruction" on the slaves of Nevèrÿon's obsidian mines in *Return*'s "The Game of Time and Pain":

> 'I was young when I first learned that, while the incidents that can befall a man or a woman are as numberless as sunlit flashes flickering on the sea, what the same man or woman can say of them is as limited as the repertoire on the platform of some particularly uninventive mummer's troupe. Indeed, it *is* that repertoire. Our history had been denied us as systematically as we had been denied the knowledge of our burial place, or as we had been denied sight of the guards' house or any hint that, whatever its apparatus of oppression, that house had once been ours.' (*Return* 74)

As Henry Louis Gates Jr. explains, African American slave narratives were a key toward reconstructing black history: "Accused of lacking a formal and collective history, blacks published individual histories which, taken together, were intended to narrate, in segments, the larger yet fragmented history of blacks in Africa, then dispersed throughout a cold New World." Many scholars have asserted the fundamental role slave narratives have played in the African American literary tradition, including Gates, who claims that "a black intertextual or signifying relationship" with slave narratives must be the basis for "any meaningful formal [African American] literary history."[37] Of these autobiographies of ex-slaves, none has a higher standing than the 1845 *Narrative of the Life of Frederick Douglass,* generally understood as "the greatest of the slave narratives and the most representative."[38] In the introduction to his own autobiography, *The Motion of Light in Water* (1988), Delany identifies Douglass's *Narrative* as one of his many favorite autobiographical works.[39] Like *Motion,* the *Return to Nevèrÿon* series engages in the intertextual relationship with Douglass's text upon which Gates insists.

Douglass's *Narrative* perhaps most importantly illustrates the relationship between literacy and freedom in slave narratives, "an aesthetic and rhetorical principle" on which, according to Robert Stepto, the study of African American literature can be based.[40] Douglass's description of teaching fellow slaves and "creating in them a strong desire to learn how to read"[41] supports V. P. Franklin's observation that literacy was "a communal, political act of resistance" that "helped slaves survive in a hostile environment."[42] Douglass's writing ability enables him to forge a number of "protections" for himself and others as part of his first unsuccessful plan to escape to Baltimore. "The slave who learned to read and write," Gates observes, "was the first to run away."[43] However, white slave owners were often aware of the relationship between literacy and freedom as well, and Chapter VI of Douglass's *Narrative* provides representative white arguments against teaching slaves to read and write. When Mrs. Auld "commence[s] to teaching [the young Douglass] the A, B, C," her husband launches a harangue about the ostensible dangers of such an enterprise:

> ". . . if you teach that nigger (speaking of myself [Douglass]) how to read, there would be no keeping him. It would forever unfit him to be a slave. He would at once become unmanageable, and of no value to his master. As to himself, it could do him no good, but a great deal of harm. It would make him discontented and unhappy."[44]

In Nevèrÿon, very few people know how to read and write, though more are learning every day. In *Neveryóna,* Madame Keyne is surprised at the literacy of a girl from the northern mountains such as Pryn: "Not only do you know your own name, you know how to write it. . . . That *does* make you exceptional!" (*Neveryóna* 95). But Pryn later learns that Nevèrÿon's aristocracy is decidedly less enthusiastic about slaves who demonstrate such abilities. In a passage that parallels Mr. Auld's protestations in Douglass's *Narrative,* the Earl Jue-Grutn tells his own wife, in front of Pryn, why literacy and alcohol are forbidden to slaves: "Two things slaves are never allowed to do: learn to write—and drink. Both inflame the imagination. With slaves, that's to be avoided" (*Neveryóna* 297). In a sense,

Mr. Auld wants to prevent literacy from inflaming Douglass's imagination with ideas of freedom. The most important insights on literacy and freedom in Delany's series, however, involve Gorgik. The story of how the child who would become the Liberator learned to read and write is told in "The Game of Time and Pain," in part, by an elderly Myrgot to her maid, Larla, whom the Vizirine speaks to as if she were her former slave. Myrgot recounts to "Gorgik" how he "had spent enough time in the warehouses where [his] father worked to pick up the rudiments of that old, crude, commercial script" (*Return* 101). Gorgik's rudimentary literacy can be seen as a causative factor of the rest of his life's significant events. Although his literacy does not impel escape from the obsidian mines, it keeps him alive there. Knowing how to read and write enables Gorgik to acquire a position as a foreman in the mines, "which meant that, with only a little stealing, he could get enough food so that instead of the wiry muscles that tightened along the bony frames of most miners, his arms and thighs and neck and chest swelled, high-veined and heavy, on his already heavy bones" (*Tales* 37, *Return* 227). Literacy enhances his storytelling abilities, which impress Myrgot, convincing her that "that man is wasted in the mines" (*Tales* 41, *Return* 231) and prompting her to take him with her to the High Court of Eagles. It is there that Gorgik, during a party from which he and Myrgot have been purposefully excluded, gains the Child Empress Ynelgo's favor, initiating the long process that transforms him into one of the most powerful men in the empire. Myrgot was wily enough to interpret—using what can truly be called "the semiology of silence"—the importance of literacy in Gorgik's life, by noting the absence of its mention in the Liberator's own life narratives:

> 'Your literacy—certainly one of the things *I* noticed about you when I decided to buy you from the mines—is not usually what you mention, unless asked. And more than once, my friend, my creation, my mirror, I have thought your suppression of that fact from the general narrative you tell and retell of your life is the sign of its indubitable core import'. (*Return* 101)

The only comment Gorgik himself makes about the importance of literacy to his freedom and that of all Nevèrÿon occurs in *Flight*'s "The Tale of Fog and Granite" where he and his lieutenant/lover Noyeed confront the smuggler, who asks the Liberator about the uses to which he puts writing. Gorgik explains that he uses writing to remember: "Memory often plays tricks on you even minutes after your thoughts have settled somewhere else. . . . With writing, you are free to use your thinking in other ways. I can observe clearly and carefully what I have to—but I do not have to worry about recalling it later if it is written down" (*Flight* 123). Gorgik sees the smuggler's own struggles with literacy as evidence of a larger social change concomitant with his campaign to end slavery: "Like everyone in this country . . . slowly he is learning to read and write" (*Flight* 122–23). The importance of literacy to freedom, and the series' dialogue with African American slave narratives, are unmistakable.

Apart from the literacy/freedom paradigm, Douglass's *Narrative* and Delany's series share specific rhetorical strategies as part of their renderings of slavery as a certain type of social order. The rhetorical power of the sentence in the 1845 *Narrative* that introduces Douglass's violent confrontation with the "slave-breaker" Covey—"You have seen how a man was made a slave; you shall see how a slave was made a man"[45]—has been identified by scholars such as Gates and Olney[46] as residing in the sentence's chiastic form. A similar symmetrical form and reversal of order of key words is evident in a near-paraphrase of Douglass made by Clodon the Bandit, who impersonates the Liberator in order to take advantage of the smuggler. The latter believes he is listening to the words of "the greatest man in Nevèrÿon" (*Flight* 43): "If a man's a slave, then he's not a man. If he was once a slave, well then, the better man he is for rising above it" (*Flight* 85). Clodon's saying does not introduce a climactic battle upon which the larger narrative turns as in Douglass's text, although it does precede the bandit's savage attack on the smuggler and his subsequent thrashing by the masked, twin-bladed sword-wielding adventurer called Raven and her sister warriors from the Western Crevasse. More importantly, however, the congruence of the two passages is evidence of the stylistic influence of Douglass's *Narrative* on Delany's own work.

Evidence of an intertextual communication on a more advanced thematic level can be found in Douglass's and Delany's representations of the carnivalesque, a concept attributed to Mikhail Bakhtin. In *Rabelais and His World* (1968), Bakhtin conceived of carnival as a celebratory spectacle in which a community participated.[47] During carnival, dominant social paradigms were put on hold, or even reversed:

> [O]ne might say that carnival celebrated temporary celebration from the prevailing truth and from the established order; it marked the suspension of all hierarchical rank, privileges, norms and prohibitions. Carnival was the true feast of time, the feast of becoming, change, and renewal. It was hostile to all that was immortalized and completed.[48]

Bakhtin identified numerous examples of expressions of speech and gesture informed by this carnivalesque suspension of hierarchy in Rabelaisian fiction. In *Tales'* "The Tale of Old Venn," a similar disruption of order and suspension of hierarchy is presented in Venn's description of the "naven," a festival of the Rulvyn, a tribal people located in the interiors of the Ulvayn Islands. In *Flight's Plagues and Carnivals*, Venn's former student, Norema the storyteller, reflects on these celebrations:

> [E]veryone dressed up in everyone else's clothes, the chief hunters and the head wives pretending they were beggars and outcasts, while the social pariahs were obeyed like queens and kings for the day. Women pretended to be men; men dressed as women. Parents made obeisance to their children, and children strutted like adults. It was a wonderfully healing practice. (*Flight* 229)

Some contemporary critical theorists have embraced the concept of the carnivalesque as the ultimate form of subversion and resistance. In their introduction to *The Politics and Poetics of Transgression*, Peter Stallybrass and Allon White state that "the main importance of [Bakhtin's] study is its broad development of the 'carnivalesque' into a potent, populist, critical inversion of *all* official words and hierarchies in a way that has implications far beyond the specific realm of Rabelais studies."[49] Douglass provided an example of such a dynamic fifty years before Bakhtin was even born in his description of Christmas at Mr. Covey's: "The days between Christmas and New Years [were] allowed as holidays," Douglass explains; whereas some of the slaves spent the time off tending to their homes or hunting for food, "by far the larger part engaged in such sports and merriments as playing ball, wrestling, running foot-races, fiddling, dancing and drinking whisky."[50] A similar scene occurs in *Neveryóna* during the day of the Labor Festival at Rorkar's brewery, "the area's most important holiday of the summer and held on the longest day of the year" (*Neveryóna* 361). This is the only day of the year on which slaves can drink, and it is a time for the slaves to sing, dance, and enjoy performances by traveling mummers. Neither at Covey's nor at the brewery is the hierarchy completely inverted; the slave owners do not perform as slaves or slaves as masters. Rather, the dominated group is temporarily granted a few token freedoms. Both Douglass and Delany, however, present the institutionalization of such merriment as a sinister reinforcement of slavery's social order. Close attention to Bakhtin's insistence on the "temporary" nature of the carnivalesque has suggested to some scholars that it is a transient moment of transgression already built into the dominant order to allow those beneath it to let off a little steam. For example, Karen Hohne and Helen Wussow claim that "carnival is a controlled period of subversion and inversion, of heteroglossia that happens on limited occasions during the year with the approval of the society that it ostensibly subverts. Instead of smashing social frameworks, carnival reinscribes them by being contained within them."[51] Douglass comes to this conclusion about the Christmas holidays being used to encourage slaves to get drunk and reinforce slavery's hold:

> From what I know of the effect of these holidays upon the slave, I believe them to be among the most effective means in the hands of the slaveholder in keeping down the spirit of insurrection. Were the slaveholders at once to abandon this practice, I have not the slightest doubt it would lead to an immediate insurrection among the slaves. These holidays serve as conductors, or safety-valves, to carry off the rebellious spirit of enslaved humanity. . . . Their object seems to be, to disgust slaves with freedom, by plunging them into the lowest depths of dissipation.[52]

Dissipation is rampant among the slaves at the Labor Day Festival at Rorkar's brewery. Juni, the kitchen girl at Rorkar's tavern, expresses to Pryn her disgust for the slaves' excesses while simultaneously acknowledging the Festival's near-irresistible appeal:

> 'Oh, even some of these good people around us now will behave quite disgracefully before the day's over. That's why I go home early. I mean when everybody's sick and falling over the beach, I can tell you *I'm* ready to leave! I'll stay for the first *three* fights. After that, I'm gone—though I'm always back an hour later!' She giggled. (*Neveryóna* 362)

Pryn learns that Jue-Grutn ordered the whipping of the old slave woman Bruka, ostensibly because she drank from his mug the day before, but perhaps in search of information about Pryn herself, whom he suspected of spying. The beating took place in the back of the brewery while the rest of the slaves were out front for the Festival; therefore, the Labor Festival diverts the attention of Rorkar's slaves away from a specific instance of slavery's inhumanity. A similar event occurs in *Plagues and Carnivals* when it is announced that Gorgik has accepted the Child Empress Ynelgo's offer to make him a minister and that a week-long carnival will be held in the Liberator's honor. Although this turn of events is the beginning of "the betterment of the nation and the alleviation of the suffering of all classes, high and low, slave and freeman" (*Flight* 224), Ynelgo's ministers have an ulterior motive for making the announcement: to "get their [the people's] minds off this unbearable plague!" (*Flight* 224). Both Delany and Douglass, therefore, demonstrate acute critical abilities in their depictions of the sociocultural maneuvers through which a dominant order seeks to tighten its grip on those living under it.

As Bruka's beating suggests, more immediate and brutal tactics have been used to maintain slavery's social order. Orlando Patterson notes Karl

Marx's awareness of "the peculiar role of violence in creating and maintaining" slavery as a "relation of domination."[53] Patterson quotes historian George Rawick's characterization of whipping as "a conscious device to impress upon slaves that they were slaves" and "a crucial form of social control."[54] Both Delany's fiction and Douglass's life narrative address the cruelties and violences inflicted upon slaves. No more vivid example of this exists in Douglass's *Narrative* than the beating of Douglass's Aunt Hester at the hands of a slaveholder who rips off Aunt Hester's clothes, ties her hands to a hook in a joist in the kitchen, and inflicts lashes and curses upon her despite her screams and bleeding. Douglass, just a child at this point, watches from a hiding space in a nearby closet. Even as fictive fantasy, Delany's Nevèrÿon stories have no scene as frightfully bizarre as this. The series instead, opts for showing the material aftereffects of such violences. In *Neveryóna*, Pryn has a close encounter with a former victim of slavery-enforced and enforcing violence when she gets a ride to Kolhari with three riders: the Red Badger, the Southern Fox, and the Western Wolf. The riders, who plan on joining Gorgik's campaign, suspect that Pryn is a spy and refer to her as "the Blue Heron." "Slavery is an evil at least two of us know first hand" the Wolf tells her (*Neveryóna* 35). Pryn shares a horse with the Fox, sitting in front of him until she objects to the placement of his hand on her breast. As they change positions, Pryn puzzles over the rider's shoulders, "one smooth and one scarred" (*Neveryóna* 35):

> Those scars? A mountain girl living in harsh times, Pryn had seen women and men with wounds from injury and accident. What was before her, though, suggested greater violence than the mishandling of plowhead or hunting knife. She put her hands on the rider's flanks. His flesh was hard and hot. She could feel one scar, knobby and ropy, under her hand's heel.
> Slavery? (*Neveryóna* 35)

This example of the use of force applied to the slave's body is the first of Pryn's many lessons in how people use power, and how power works on people, in Nevèrÿon.

In order to demonstrate the *Return to Nevèrÿon* series' insights on the subject of slavery I have focused on the series' intertextual relationship with Douglass's *Narrative*. As fundamental as literary forms such as the slave narrative are to the study of slavery, any discussion of the subject requires an interdisciplinary approach. The series' representations of slavery as a mode of production and as a specific type of social order can therefore be further illustrated by identifying its examples of Orlando Patterson's concept of slavery as social death. The stated goal of Patterson's *Slavery and Social Death: A Comparative Study* (1982)—"to understand the universal features of the internal structure of slavery"[55]—may initially seem antithetical to my overall project, which emphasizes specificity and difference. But although Patterson attempts a narrative about the common features of slave societies from throughout history and around the globe, he is as specific about the differences between these societies as he is about the similarities. And given the unspecified, ahistorical setting of the series—"the most accurate placement is, after all," Steiner notes, "a happy accident of the advertising copy on the back of one of the paperbacks in which some of the tales were first published, putting it at 'the borderland of history'"—a discussion of the universal characteristics of slavery is appropriate.[56]

Patterson defines slavery as "the permanent, violent domination of natally alienated and generally dishonored persons." "Natal alienation" is the process through which slaves suffer a social death. It is "the cultural aspect of the relation" of domination between the slave and master in which the slave experiences a "secular excommunication," an alienation from "all rights or claims of birth." According to Patterson, "the slave had no socially recognized existence outside of his master; he became a social nonperson." Patterson presents two modes of social death, intrusive and extrusive. "In the intrusive mode the slave was conceived of as someone who did not belong because he was an outsider," he explains, "while in the extrusive mode the slave became an outsider because he did not (or no longer) belonged."[57] The extrusive and intrusive models of social death correspond to the representations of the slave experiences of Gorgik and Small Sarg, respectively, in the Nevèrÿon books.

Gorgik fits the extrusive model of the "internally fallen" slave. The tale named for him explains that "five weeks before Gorgik turned sixteen, the Child Empress Ynelgo, whose coming was just and generous, seized power" (*Tales* 37, *Return* 227). This change in political power brought cultural changes, such as the official renaming of his home as "Kolhari": "It was no longer Neveryóna—which is what the last, dragon-bred residents of the High Court of Eagles had officially, but ineffectually, renamed it twenty years before" (*Tales* 37, *Return* 227). More drastic changes in his life would follow: "That night several wealthy importers were assassinated, their homes sacked, their employees murdered— among them Gorgik's father. The employees' families were taken as slaves" (*Tales* 37, *Return* 227). As the son of the employee of a merchant who grew wealthy under the old political order, Gorgik had no social standing under Ynelgo's reign and ended up a slave in the Empire's obsidian mines for five years. "When I was fifteen," Gorgik the Minister reflects, "my life swerved" (*Return* 33). The trajectory of his early years is an example of Patterson's observation of how some slaves "entered the [master/slave] relationship as a substitute for death." In fact, "the most distinctive attribute of the slave's powerlessness," according to Patterson, "was that it always originated (or was conceived of as having originated) as a substitute for death, usually violent death."[58] According to Myrgot, who became Vizirine when her cousin Ynelgo became Child Empress, the difference between slavery's social death and a violent, permanent, material one for Gorgik was a combination of geography, Ynelgo's decree that the children were to be spared, and the significant fact that he could read and write:

> 'The nameless gods alone know which Imperial captain, slipping on strewn entrails and sliding on bloody tiles, carried her [Ynelgo's] command outside. And on the waterfront, because of it, you, Gorgik, who had spent enough time in the warehouses where your father worked to pick up the rudiments of that old, crude, commercial script, were not tested, drugged, and slaughtered an hour after your parents, as you would have been in the south. You were never led into a room among a dozen others, where various legends had been scrawled over the walls, among them, "Freedom only to those who linger, silent, in this room when others have gone to their labors." Nor were all told to leave through the door, and the ones who stayed congratulated with a celebratory drink (heavily drugged), then killed.
>
> 'You were simply made a slave.' (*Return* 101)

As a slave, Gorgik has "no socially recognized existence." Even after he becomes Myrgot's catamite at the High Court of Eagles, the narrative makes a point of emphasizing Gorgik's natal alienation:

> Gorgik—no more than a potter's boy—*had* no place . . . if we use "to have" other than in that mythical and mystifying sense in which both a slave *has* a master and good people *have* certain rights, but rather in the sense of possession that implies some way (either through power or convention) of enforcing that possession, if not to the necessary extent, at least to a visible one. (*Tales* 48, *Return* 239)

A slave enduring the extrusive mode of social death, Gorgik escaped physical death only to find himself, literally, without a place in society. As a belonging, he had ceased to belong.

Gorgik's companion, Small Sarg, experiences Patterson's intrusive mode of slavery. In the first section of *Tales*' "The Tale of Small Sarg," the title character is introduced as "a real barbarian prince," a member of the Crow Clan (*Tales* 141), all of which signifies his possession of a definite place in his tribe's social and political structures. But strangers come and take Sarg away, and the reader next sees him in a slaver's custody, squatting in the market town of Ellamon, rubbing away at his chains with a leaf. When Gorgik comes by to take a look at Sarg, the slaver explains that the youth is "new captured from some raid in the south. A barbarian from the jungles just below the Vygernangx" (*Tales* 146). Sarg's dehumanization is the result of being, to quote from Patterson's summary of French sociologist Claude Meillasoux's framework, "violently uprooted from his milieu." Forcefully detached from his barbarian tribe, he suffers what Patterson identifies as an "alienation . . . from all formal, legally enforceable ties of 'blood,' and from any attachment to groups or localities other than those chosen for him by the master."[59] Most significant is Sarg's own interpretation of his enslavement as "death." After he has purchased the barbarian, Gorgik inquires as to why he rubs at his chains with a leaf. "I am dead, yes?" Sarg replies, "so I do my death task" (*Tales* 151). When Gorgik notes that to buy a dead slave would be a waste of money, Sarg offers a more detailed interpretation of his present circumstances:

'I am chain in a place where there is no night and there is no day; and if I rub a single leaf against my chain for a length of time equal to as many lifetimes as there are leaves on a catalpa tree three times the height of a man, my chain will wear away, I shall be free, and I can go to the fork in the river where there will always be full fruit trees and easy game . . .' (*Tales* 151–52)

Unfortunately for Sarg, he is repeatedly placed in new chains and has to start his "death-task" over again each time. When Gorgik reveals that he bought the former barbarian prince for sexual purposes, Sarg expresses bewilderment at "civilized" behavior and resignation toward his "death": "You people, here in the land of death, you are really crazy, yes? . . . Every time I think I am wearing one chain, I find you have changed it for another" (*Tales* 154). Sarg's understanding of the civilized, slaveholding empire of Nevèrÿon as "the land of death" and of enslavement itself as "death" is an example of his attempt to hold onto the native traditions and systems of meaning from which he has been taken, but they also resonate with Patterson's intrusive model of a disdained outsider brought into a community via the machinery of slavery and turned into a non-being.

Gorgik's purchase of Sarg raises an important, inevitable question: how could Gorgik, himself a survivor of slavery and its processes of dehumanization, enslave another human being and simultaneously proclaim himself to be Nevèrÿon's "Liberator," vowing not to rest until all slaves are free? As we shall see, Gorgik and Sarg's relationship is more complex than it may at first seem, but what appears to be a contradiction between ideals and practices suggests some of Patterson's other comments. He notes that many scholars have been troubled by what they see as a paradoxical simultaneity of the development of slavery and the development of democracy in ancient Greece and Rome and, most immediately, in the United States. For Patterson, this paradox is a product of an uncritical allegiance to the ideals of the Enlightenment. "For all who look to Enlightenment Europe and revolutionary America as the source of their most cherished political values," he observes, slavery "is not the peculiar institution but the embarrassing institution." The paradox also stems from a false assumption, "that slavery should have nothing to do with freedom; that a man who holds freedom dearly should not hold slaves without discomfort; that a culture which invented democracy or produced a Jefferson should not be based on slavery." Patterson, however, argues that "slavery and freedom are intimately connected" and that "it is indeed reasonable that those who most denied freedom, as well as those to whom it was most denied, were the very persons most alive to it."[60] This comment is, obviously, not a justification of slavery, but rather, the revelation of the projects of Enlightenment in general, and of American democracy specifically, to be thoroughly implicated in practices that have furthered the interests of the powerful rather than objectively advancing the cause of all humanity. Simply put, Patterson makes the logical, and historically proven, point that wanting freedom for oneself does not necessarily prevent one from taking it away from others.

Nor does having one's freedom taken away prevent one from taking it back, which helps to explain how Gorgik and Sarg could overcome the dehumanization concomitant with enslavement to become heroic antislavery adventurers. "There is absolutely no evidence from the long and dismal annals of slavery" Patterson states, "to suggest that any group of slaves ever internalized the concept of degradation held by their masters." The slave that survived what Hegel called slavery's "trial by death" came away from that trial "as a person afire with the knowledge of and the need for dignity and honor."[61] Such a need can be seen to have informed, in large part, Gorgik's quest to end slavery in Nevèrÿon.

The Liberator's campaign is notable for its double-pronged attack on slavery. Although he has become a state minister by the time of *Return*'s "The Game of Time and Pain," Gorgik's early anti-slavery efforts are as something like those of a guerrilla commando, not unlike Gabriel Prosser or John Brown. *Tales*' "The Tale of Dragons and Dreamers," illustrates the stratagem that Gorgik and Sarg employ on their two-man raid on the southern castle of the Suzerain of Strethi. Gorgik has been captured by the castle's guards; usually one of the pair present themselves as an adversary to be captured, but, significantly, Strethi's men ambush them, calling out Gorgik by name. The Liberator is taken to a dungeon, where Strethi tortures him while Myrgot looks on. While Strethi is preoccupied, Sarg, "looking like a filthy field slave" (*Tales* 222), lays siege to the castle, killing every guard and freeing every slave [except for those who resist liberation, whom Sarg also kills] therein. Before long Sarg explodes into the dungeon to free his comrade/lover. Outside the castle, the duo runs into the warrior known as Raven, and Norema, a storyteller from the Ulvayn Islands formerly employed by Madame Keyne as her secretary and emissary, to whom Sarg explains that Strethi's was the seventh castle they have sieged this way. Gorgik's paramilitary actions do not end slavery in Nevèrÿon by themselves, but neither do they hinder his transformation into one of the empire's most important political figures. This process begins years earlier at the Court of High Eagles, where a starving Gorgik, whom Myrgot has left behind for five days without any food, stumbles upon a party and accidentally falls into a conversation with the Child Empress Ynelgo, quickly gaining her favor and putting him in danger of the wrath of Ynelgo's protector, Lord Krodar. Myrgot sends Gorgik off to train as a warrior with Master Narbu, after which he becomes an officer in the Imperial Army, and later a free citizen who buys Sarg and begins his attacks on slaveholding castles. In the second volume, *Neveryóna*, Gorgik has parlayed the Empress's favor into a meeting with Lord Krodar himself that he announces to a large following of anti-slavery advocates. Years later, in *Flight*'s *Plagues and Carnivals*, Gorgik—operating in a mode more like that of abolitionists such as Frederick Douglass or William Lloyd Garrison—is made the lead minister on Ynelgo's council to end slavery. In *Return*'s "The Game of Time of Pain," Gorgik has been a minister for ten years; Lord Krodar, Gorgik's greatest political enemy and teacher, is dead, and the Child Empress's edict abolishing slavery is six years old. It is significant that Gorgik's approach toward ending slavery in Nevèrÿon, which employs both paramilitary and political means, echoes the history of the relationship between slave revolts and national abolitionist movements in nineteenth-century America. In *American Negro Slave Revolts* (1943), Herbert Aptheker is careful to make the point that slave rebellions such as those led by Nat Turner and Gabriel Prosser were impelled by slaves' own agency and were not the mere orchestrations of Northern abolitionists, thus refuting arguments made by southern slaveholders that misguidedly and simplistically blamed slave insurrections on "abolitionist propaganda."[62] In *Abolitionism* (1989), however, Aptheker portrays the campaign to end slavery in America as "the second successful revolutionary movement in the history of the United States," emphasizing both its "revolutionary nature" and its "extensive organization." The movement was revolutionary because its goal was the emancipation of slaves, "the termination of the base of (Southern) power" and the resultant "overthrow of the propertied ruling class," that is, the southern slaveholding aristocracy.[63]

Aptheker identifies a class component to American abolitionism which is important to Gorgik's campaign as well. In both scenarios, the ideology of slavery, which imposes social death on a conspicuously marked group of human beings, is used by the dominant social order to mitigate class tensions between aristocrats and free laborers. Historian Edmund S. Morgan, for example, has demonstrated how, in seventeenth-century Virginia, race-based slavery "provided a solution to antagonistic class relations among white landowners, large and small, by creating a readily identifiable black underclass that yeomen and gentry alike had a common racial interest in suppressing."[64] Such an ideology operates in Nevèrÿon as well, as is evidenced by the relationship between Madame Keyne, whose name approximates that of economist John Maynard Keynes, and her workers.[65] In *Neveryóna*, Pryn escapes Sarg's raid on Gorgik's lair only to be found by a "gaunt, pale-haired murderess" (*Neveryóna* 89) called the Wild Ini, who takes Pryn to Madame Keyne, whose dwelling is located in Sallese, a suburb of Kolhari, and next door to the mansion that serves as Gorgik's false headquarters. Pryn asks her host if she knows her neighbor. "Know him? Know this Liberator all the city talks of?" Madame Keyne replies; "I'm terrified of him!" (*Neveryóna* 93). Her meaning is made more clear when she takes Pryn to the site of the construction of the New Market, which she plans to rent out to merchants. In town, the two women meet with a man who has a plan for "liquidating [the] Liberator" that "will require twelve gold coins and five iron ones" (*Neveryóna* 128). Madame Keyne gives the would-be assassin less than half of what he needs to finance his plot. When Pryn hesitantly asks her if she really wants Gorgik dead, and wonders why so little was paid if so, Madame Keyne shrugs and explains that the scheme was by no means overpriced:

'I'm afraid that if I gave him his full twelve and five, our Liberator *would* be dead—it really *was* a fine plan. But I have not yet decided whether that's what I want. The little fellow [the assassin]'s terribly well motivated, in that way which only conservative fanatics can be. With six and two, I have no doubt that in desperation he will mount his plan anyway—under-equipped, under-manned. Which means there's a good chance he will fail. But it will give the Liberator some trouble, which, at this point, is all I am prepared to do.' (*Neveryóna* 129)

Whether Madame Keyne decides to do more than cause Gorgik "some trouble" depends upon the yet unknown breadth of his emancipatory campaign. Kolhari provides Pryn with her first encounter with urban poverty: "This was the first time she had ever seen so *many* poor people, and men at that, amassed at a single center. . . . the street seemed filled with poverty itself" (*Neveryóna* 130). Madame Keyne is not oblivious to

Kolhari's poor; rather, she is acutely aware of them. She takes Pryn to the construction site of the New Market, where she plans to rent out market space to shopkeepers. As they enter the construction site's fence, one of the crowd of barbarians outside the fence throws a clod of mud—or worse—at Madame Keyne, which is why, she explains to Pryn, she dislikes the Liberator:

> '[A] growing number of those men over there, including some of the clod throwers, think the Liberator is here for them. . . . Slaves are men and women who labor for no pay. Over there are men who do no labor for no pay. The similarity is enough so that they might make the mistake themselves. If the Liberator makes the same mistake, I may well have reason to pay out a full twelve and six to the next fanatic who asks.' (*Neveryóna* 134)

Those laborers employed by Madame Keyne have a different opinion on the Liberator from slaves and the unemployed, but one based on similar assumptions. "The men who work over here find the idea of the Liberator mildly uncomfortable," Madame Keyne says, "no doubt because they make the same mistake as the men outside" (*Neveryóna* 135). Ergi, the foreman at the site, proves Madame Keyne's analysis correct: "If the Liberator is for the unemployed," he concludes, "then he can't very well be for the employed, too" (*Neveryóna* 135). With Ergi and his workers, the ideology outlined by Morgan is clearly at work.

Patterson notes, however, that slavery can just as likely have a different effect on workers such as Ergi. "The free laborer became dangerously radicalized by the presence of slavery," Patterson observes, because slavery "*exposed* the demeaning nature" of labor for no or little pay (34). Madame Keyne, perceptive woman that she is, worries about this same possibility:

> 'Just as a man who has no work and gets no money for it may think himself a slave, so a man who has work and gets only very little money for it may think himself the same. And that—I have no illusions about it, girl— is very much the workers, men and women, on *this* side of the fence.' (*Neveryóna* 136)

And it is this concern that informs her fears of Gorgik's campaign:

> 'I want to know: when he runs out of slaves to liberate, will he choose the men on my side or on the far side of the fence as his next cause? Whatever his political program, the Liberator's is an image in our city both sincere and seductive. Whichever side he chooses, he may well succeed.' (*Neveryóna* 144)

Madame Keyne's distress over Gorgik's rise to power illustrates that, as Patterson puts it, "when the ideological camouflage is stripped from slavery, a crisis is created for the capitalist class."[66] The impact of the success of Gorgik's campaign on Nevèrÿon's upper classes is summarized by Myrgot in "The Game of Time and Pain": "What you have done, my Gorgik, by ending slavery, is to reduce the distance between the highest and the lowest by an entire social class. Thus we, who were the highest, are, thanks to you, nowhere near as high as we were" (*Return* 100). The *Return to Nevèrÿon* series is, therefore, African American fiction that represents "the peculiar institution" as a socioeconomic as well as a cultural and political phenomenon. Given this engagement as well as the demonstrated significance of the racial identities of the series' author and characters, why has the "African American" dimension of the series been ignored? Aside from the marketing issues discussed earlier, one answer might be that although slavery may reside at the series' conceptual center, another subject—semiotics—permeates every aspect of the texts and eclipses other approaches to these stories.

The Empire of Signs

> The subject matter of linguistics comprises all manifestations of human speech,
> whether that of savages or civilized nations, of archaic, classical or decadent
> periods.
> —Ferdinand de Saussure, *Course in General Linguistics*[67]

In *Neveryóna*'s Appendix B, Delany directly addresses the issue of how readers expecting more conventional sword-and-sorcery fare might react to the novel's intellectual content. Acknowledging the text's debts to "Albee, Bédier, Kafka, Balzac, [and] Baudrillard," the author states that it would be a shame if readers were scared off by such references; instead, those readers should simply ignore the above names. He adds, "any reader who normally skips footnotes may skip the headnotes with which various chapters begin with—certainly—no greater loss" (*Neveryóna* 399). Delany then makes an attempt to diminish the significance of these aforementioned epigraphs from works of critical theory:

> They only attempt to begin, by assertion, what Diderot attempted to begin by denial when he entitled a story *Ceci n'est pas un conte,* or what Magritte attempted when he entitled a picture of an upright brier *Ceci n'est pas une pipe,* or—indeed—what Guilden attempted when he made a colored poster in which scarlet letters proclaimed across a rose field (after having made one in jade and kelly portraying the same text) *This Is Not a Green Sign.* (*Neveryóna* 399)

This dismissive gesture, of course, serves only to emphasize the importance of critical theory to Delany's work. It also raises the question of just what the texts and illustrations cited are in fact denying and what they have to do with *Neveryóna*. For some answers, consider Delany's example of Magritte's painting, also known as *The Treachery of Images* (1926), a rendering of what most definitely looks like a tobacco pipe above a scripted denial. What the painting announces by way of that denial, of course, is its status as a representation of a pipe as opposed to a "real" pipe. What does this have to do with Delany's sword-and-sorcery stories? Michel Foucault provides a clue in an essay about the painting, *Ceci n'est pas un pipe* (1968), which refers to the initial "inevitability of connecting the text to the drawing" as "sorcery."[68] It is a similar metaphysical connection between slaves and slaveholders and their respective social roles of submission and domination that abolitionists, real and fictitious, have sought to expose and dismiss. The interrogation of such connections is related to and can be furthered by investigations into the relationship between words and things, in which both Delany's series and Magritte's painting engage, a mode of inquiry generally referred to as semiotics.

In the compilation of his own and his students' notes entitled *Course in General Linguistics,* Ferdinand de Saussure asserted the social aspect of language, distinguishing between the innate abilities of human speech and language making from language itself, which is "something acquired and conventional." Central to Saussure's theories was his conception of a linguistic unit, the linguistic sign, a "double-entity" formed by the association of two parts, a concept and a sound-image, renamed "signified" and "signifier" respectively. Although the two parts are "intimately united," the bond between them is arbitrary. For example, there is no innate link between the concept of a sister and the sounds *s-ö-r* [sœur] that serve as its signifier in French. With the sign thus theorized, Saussure conceived of "semiology" as "*a science that studies the life of signs within society*" and proposed that it would "show what constitutes signs [and] what laws govern them."[69]

Whereas Saussure's grounding in linguistics helped to formulate semiotics, the theories of another groundbreaking semiotician, American philosopher Charles Sanders Peirce, did not lead to a similar development in the United States. According to Jonathan Culler, "Peirce's insistence that everything is a sign did little to help found a discipline"; today, however, Peirce's claims seem not so far-fetched.[70] Delany himself has expressed similar opinions on the world as a language or "code": "what we called 'the real world' seems to be nothing *but* codes, codic systems and complexes, and the codic terms used to designate one part of one system, complex, or another."[71] The *Return to Nevèrÿon* series, which the author has described as "a child's garden of semiotics,"[72] demonstrates the influence of Saussure and Peirce, often to the point where the books read as textbooks for a graduate seminar in critical theory as much as sword-and-sorcery.

Given that the relationship between the signifier and the signified is arbitrary, a signifier is not limited to one act of signification; the Nevèrÿon stories supply numerous examples of a signifier with multiple signifieds. In *Neveryóna*, for example, Norema explains a change in her writing system to Pryn. The tale-teller has developed a "squiggle" to differentiate the names of people from things that share the same signified:

> 'My friend, for example, was called Raven. Now there are ravens that caw and fly—much more efficiently than dragons. And there's my friend, Raven. Since she left, I find that now, more and more, both will enter my stories. The distinction marks a certain convenience, a sort of stability. Besides, I like distinguishing people from things in and of the land. It makes tale-telling make a lot more sense.' (*Neveryóna* 19)

"Ini" is another multiply meaningful signifier, which can indicate the poisonous white flower that Baron *Ini*ge—a botanist and Gorgik's most trustworthy acquaintance at Court—uses to commit suicide, Madame Keyne's similarly pretty and deadly assassin, "a hopelessly mad and poisonous little white gillyflower of a girl" (*Neveryóna* 163), or a slur among the "dark-robed northern men" (*Tales* 29, *Return* 219) whom Gorgik observed as a youth on the streets of Kolhari. Radiant Jade, Madame Keyne's secretary, informs Pryn that "*nivu*" is a barbarian term for a woman's refusal to cook for a man, which in Kolhari refers more generally to female objection to male assertion: "In our own land, it is one of the most powerful of women's words—and here in yours, it has become one of the most trivial" (*Neveryóna* 109). The narrative's most playful act of signification lies in the word "gorgi," the term that the Rulvyn, a people who inhabit the innermost parts of the Ulvayn islands, use to indicate male or female genitalia. Quite obviously, it is also, but for one letter, the name of the series' hero. This similarity produces a humorous exchange in *Flight*'s "The Tale of Fog and Granite" when the smuggler gives a Kolhari student named Kenton a ride out of town:

> (Once the smuggler had asked him [Kenton] if he had any thoughts on the Liberator, Gorgik, to which the student frowned and said, 'Gorgi? I've heard the word. It's a foreign term, from the Ulvayn Islands, no?' which, by now, was an answer the smuggler had gotten enough times so that, for him, it was the sign that more questions would be pointless about his chosen topic. Today, he never pursued his inquiries beyond such an answer.) (*Flight* 64–65)

The ambiguity of the meaning of "gorgi" allows Delany the opportunity to construct a playful but significant pun on Gorgik's sexuality. As the Rulvyn word indicates the genitalia of both sexes, Gorgik's sexuality—despite his preference for barbarian men—includes an ability to perform sexually with either men or women.[73]

As a correlative to the arbitrary nature of the sign, Saussure posits its differential nature. "The linguistic signifier," is "constituted . . . by the differences that separate its sound-image from all others."[74] The differential operation of a sign within a system is represented in Delany's series by an astrolabe, which works within a vast system of signs throughout Nevèrÿon's history and geography. The astrolabe in question is a "verdigrised disk" (Tales 69, Return 259), a parting gift from Myrgot to Gorgik after she frees him and they both realize that having earned the Child Empress's favor and [therefore] Lord Krodar's enmity, the ex-slave can no longer stay at Court. With the astrolabe, Myrgot offers a cryptic warning to avoid specific sites in the Empire's southernmost areas:

> '—and as you value your freedom and your life, never set foot on the Garth Peninsula. And if the Vygernangx Monastery ever thrusts so much as the tiny tip of one tower over the treetops within the circle of your vision, you will turn yourself directly around and ride, run, crawl, away as fast and as far as you can go.' (Tales 69, Return 260)

The reasons for Myrgot's admonition become somewhat more clear after reading Tales' subsequent stories. "The Tale of Old Venn" reveals that the title character's friend Belham, a famous barbarian inventor with a tendency to drink too much who devised the lock and key system that is used, among other things, to fasten slave collars, had "taken [Venn's] navigation system and used it for a series of metal disks—rhet, scales, and map, which, today, sailors and travelers called an astrolabe" (Tales 83). The reader learns exactly where the astrolabe was manufactured in "The Tale of Small Sarg" when the slaver selling Sarg sees the device hanging from Gorgik's neck as a pendant and notes that the barbarian ex-prince is "from the jungles just below the Vygernangx . . . where [Gorgik's] astrolabe comes from" (Tales 146). In "The Tale of Potters and Dragons," a youth by the name of Bayle is sent by Old Zwon the potter, as Norema is sent by Madame Keyne and Raven by Lord Krodar, to travel to the Garth to find Lord Aldamir. Bayle and Norema's employers are competing for a contract to import Aldamir's rubber balls to Kolhari, where children play with them in a musical game that alludes to different characters in the empire's history. But it is Myrgot who receives the travelers and apologizes for the Lord's absence while putting them up in the Vygergangx Monastery, where the monks attempt to kill Norema after she decides to seek out Aldamir. Raven, who had left after announcing that she was hired to kill Aldamir, rescues Norema, and the two of them, with a young girl named Juni [who becomes the young woman Pryn meets at Rorkar's Tavern in *Neveryóna*], travel to the absent Lord's castle, where they hypothesize that Aldamir is a fiction maintained in order to serve the interests of certain scheming aristocrats. In "The Tale of Dragons and Dreamers" the reader learns just how far Myrgot will go to protect such secrets, when she instructs the Suzerain of Strethi, one of her ex-lovers from decades earlier as noted in "The Tale of Gorgik," to use the means in his possession to interrogate Gorgik about the extent of his knowledge of the secret of Aldamir, without inflicting too much bodily damage. Old Zwon's comments to Bayle and Madame Keyne suggest that it may have been Gorgik, perhaps following instructions from Myrgot, who was the messenger delivering "Aldamir's" importation plan to the elderly potter. However, Gorgik denies ever meeting the Southern Lord despite the astrolabe on his chest and the Suzerain's expertise at, and delight in, torture, referred to as "the game of time and pain" (*Tales* 232). After Sarg rescues Gorgik and they escape the castle, the duo meet and compare notes with Raven and Norema, who have had adventures of their own involving Lord Krodar, the Vygernangx, and—to borrow Steiner's formulation—those "mysterious rubber balls."[75] Gorgik reflects on the sight of a slave woman in Strethi's castle whom he almost recognizes as Myrgot in disguise and then realizes that he, like the astrolabe around his neck, has been caught in an intricate web of signification:

> 'It is as though—' Gorgik held up the verdigrised disk with its barbarous chasings—'all these things would come together in a logical pattern, immensely complex and greatly beautiful, tying together slave and empress, commoner and lord—even gods and demons—to show how all are related in a negotiable pattern, like some sailor's knot, not yet pulled taut, but laid out on the dock in loose loops, so that simply to see it in such form were to comprehend it even when yanked tight. And yet . . .' He turned the astrolabe over. '. . . they will *not* clear in my mind to any such pattern!' (*Tales* 242)

In *Neveryóna*, more secrets of the astrolabe are revealed as it completes another eventful segment of its circuit throughout Nevèrÿon. Fed up with being fondled, threatened, attacked, manipulated, and accused in Kolhari, Pryn tells Gorgik that she is leaving the fascinating but frustrating city. Gorgik offers the mountain girl his astrolabe as a parting gift, as Myrgot offered it to him, but he does not give her the same warning about the South, saying only, "If you knew the trouble this has guided me through, you might not take it" (*Neveryóna* 187). Pryn is wearing the astrolabe toward the end of the novel, when she is working at Old Rorkar's brewery on the Garth Peninsula, using her writing abilities to do exactly what Venn feared writing would be used for, to keep track of the productivity of slaves. The brewery slaves are frightened by the astrolabe, which they call "Mad Olin's circle" (*Neveryóna* 264). When the Earl Jue-Grutn, a powerful southern lord, visits the brewery, he notices the disk around Pryn's neck and invites her to his castle with specific instructions cloaked in welcoming mannerisms: "Wear one piece of jewelry, one bit of gold or jade more than that bronze pendant you have on now, and we shall consider you frightfully overdressed" (*Neveryóna* 262). The next evening, the Earl, with his family, tells Pryn of how Venn and Belham once visited his father and developed a way to approximate the numerical value of pi [π]. Jue-Grutn reveals that his father hired the two ingenious inventors for the task of creating an engine that would raise the ancient southern city of Neveryóna from the sea. "Building the engine, of course, was a job they never completed," Jue-Grutn admits, "But Venn finally did invent a sort of engine—another approximating engine. It's been working, now, for quite a while. It included a story, and a magic astrolabe . . ." (*Neveryóna* 320).

Pryn realizes that she bears both parts of Venn's "engine": Gorgik has given her the astrolabe, and, at the beginning of the novel, she is told the story of Mad Queen Olin, whom she resembles, by Norema, who must have learned it from her former teacher, Venn. Earlier in the novel, at the end of a ride on a wild dragon that takes her far away from her home outside the mountain city of Ellamon, Pryn encountered Norema, who told how Olin was captured and imprisoned, along with her retinue of servants, by the monks of the Vygernangx. Olin's servants, however, demonstrated their loyalty by devising a remarkably selfless plan for their mistress's escape. One of them would pretend to agree to kill Olin for the monks in exchange for one gold piece on the condition that if the assassination failed, the monks would hire another servant for the deed at double the price and on the same terms. One after another, Olin's servants appeared to her in the night, voluntarily offering her both their lives and geometrically increasing amounts of gold. Norema explained that this sequence of events took a toll on the young monarch's psyche:

'[I]n less than a year she had stabbed, strangled, bashed out the brains, poisoned, beheaded, and done even worse to twenty-two of her most faithful bondsmen and bondswomen, who were the closest things she'd had to friends. After that she began to act very strangely and behave quite oddly. On and off, she behaved oddly the rest of her life—even for a queen. And in those days queens were expected to be eccentric. Often, after that, she was known as Mad Olin.' (*Neveryóna* 22)

Though now deranged, Olin had virtually all of the Vygernangx's wealth, and the monks gradually left, diminished in power. Soon after, she was rescued by the last servant, an uncle, who read to her the numerical sequence by which she had gained the monks' gold—1, 2, 4, 8, 16, 32, 64, 128— after which she had a vision of a city in Nevèrÿon's southern waters. The uncle gave Olin "a circle of different stars" (*Neveryóna* 24), followed by a sumptuous dinner and a poisoned drink. Olin did not die; instead she entered a trance after which she summoned the ancient city of Neveryóna and its guardian Gauine, the Great Dragon, with whom she hid her gold before returning North.

Pryn realizes that being on the receiving end of both the astrolabe and the story of Olin, she herself has been caught up in the machinery of Venn's "engine": "The engine . . . was this astrolabe, and the tale-teller's story, and the old tales of Olin's wealth and madness, the rumors among the slaves, all the signs around Nevèrÿon that bring heroes to this spot in the Garth . . ." in search of Olin's treasure (*Neveryóna* 320). Jue-Grutn tells her, "the astrolabe is a tool to *bring* people here. But once it, itself, *is* here, it has finished its job—until it is recirculated abroad" (*Neveryóna* 321); and he describes the astrolabe as an element, a sign, in a vast and complex semiotic system:

> 'Your astrolabe is a sign in a system of signs. It has a meaning, yes, but that meaning is supplied by the rest of the system, which includes not only tales of history, madness, and invention, but the similar instruments sailors use to orient themselves at sea, the play of power in the land, and the language by which they can all of them be—systematically—described.' (*Neveryóna* 322)

The astrolabe operates within Venn's engine as the linguistic sign does: differentially. For example, the signifier "cat" indicates the signified furry feline in part by differentiating itself from other signifiers such as "cap," "cad," "bat," and so on.[76] The signifier, therefore, does its signifying work not only by indexing a signified, but also by engaging in a play of differences with other signifiers within the system. As Terry Eagleton neatly puts it, "Meaning is the spin-off of a potentially endless play of signifiers, rather than a concept tied firmly to the tail of a particular signifier."[77] This kind of play is part of what is suggested by the Derridean term "*différance*: the possibility of conceptuality, of a conceptual process and system in general."[78] Pryn's astrolabe is shown to work similarly by Jue-Grutn and his family. They indicate to Pryn the map of a coastline etched on the device's surface. The astrolabe is rimmed with Belham's signs for the geometrical number system he invented, which Venn incorporated into the tale of Olin. And with a twist, holes in the disk create a light pattern that represents the constellation of Gauine the Great Dragon. The map, according to Jue-Grutn's family, is not of the Garth's—or of any "real"—coastline, the numbers have no other particular significance, and the constellation is in fact, nonexistent. "That's why these stars are 'different'" (*Neveryóna* 325). The astrolabe is but "a sign in a system of signs . . . a map of a nonexistent coast under an imaginary constellation on an impossible sky in . . . the middle of a ring of meaningless numbers" (*Neveryóna* 326). Jue-Grutn emphasizes that the astrolabe serves only to perpetuate the legends of the old city of Neveryóna, to raise it from the sea, and to bring adventurers to the Garth. The astrolabe does this by playing against other indexes of meaning (map, code, constellation), by *not* being the things it initially appears to be:

> 'Now I hope you see . . . what your astrolabe is *not:* It is not a tool to perform a job; it is not a key to open a lock; it is not a map to guide you to treasure; it is not a coded message to be deciphered; it is not a container of secret meanings that can be opened and revealed by some other, different tool, different key, different code, different map. It's an artfully constructed part of an artfully constructed engine that, by the maneuvering of meanings, holds open a space from which certain meanings are forever excluded, forever absent. That alone is what allows it to function—to work, if you insist on the language of the brewery—in the greater system.' (*Neveryóna* 326–27)

Echoing one of Venn's lessons to Norema about language, Jue-Grutn and his family compare the astrolabe's syntagmatic exclusions and paradigmatic possibilities to those of other signs in other systems:

> 'Your astrolabe functions in the system in its particular way . . . because that is the way, finally, all signs function. . . . Take Belham's sign "one." Excluded from what it can mean are "two," "three," "four," "five," "six," or "twenty-two-divided-by-seven" . . .'
> 'Whereas it *can* mean an apple, a pear, a kumquat, a great castle, a lord, or even one other number. . . . They're not excluded.'
> 'What *is* excluded from it—what it is empty *of,* alone, is what makes it meaningful.' (*Neveryóna* 327)

The astrolabe is a meaningful part of Venn's engine because of other signs and other meanings within the system, important elements of the story of Olin. Jue-Grutn's family compares the astrolabe's practice of "holding open a space" to Lord Aldamir's empty castle and to the empty Vygernangx Monastery. The rest of Nevèrÿon remains fascinated by these places, caught up in their legends. The Empire perceives these places as sites of power and conceives of possibilities within them. Unfortunately for Pryn, she understands all too well, and compares the astrolabe, Alda-mir's castle, and Vygernangx to Gorgik's false headquarters on the Kolhari/Sallese border, a statement that evokes a frown of disapproval from the Earl, a descendant of Mad Olin's uncle. Jue-Grutn gives her a goblet of a poisoned drink, which leads not to Pryn's death, but her summoning and vision of Neveryóna and its gold treasure rising out of the sea with Gauine the great dragon. Norema's story then, serves as a model, for Pryn's own experiences in the Empire's south.

Once it is understood that the relationship between signifier and signi-fied is not a simple one-to-one correspondence, the very distinction be-tween the two terms becomes destabilized. The play of differences within a language has other consequences at which Saussure only hints when he states that "all definitions of words are made in vain; starting from words in defining things is a bad procedure."[79] What Saussure might mean by this is illustrated by the dictionary, to which one refers in order to dis-cover the definition (signified) of a word (signifier). However, that defini-tion consists of more words, whose definitions can be looked up in turn, and so on. Terry Eagleton describes this process as "not only in theory infinite but somehow circular: signifiers keep transforming into signifieds and vice versa, and you will never arrive at a final signified which is not a signifier in itself."[80] Such observations inform Jacques Derrida's decon-structive critique of Saussure's conception of the sign and inform the notion of another kind of *différance*, or rather, a "deference" or deferral of mean-ing. In *Of Grammatology* (1967) Derrida analyzes "the problematic op-position of speech [*parole*] and language [*langue*]" as well as the signified/signifier binary, noting that "there is not a single signified that escapes . . . the play of signifying references that constitute language."[81] Every signi-fied operates as a signifier, and every signifier is the signified of another signifier.

Delany has referred to Derrida's idea of the "signifier of the signifier" as an emblem of "the margin of the margin," the conceptual space on the margins of literature's always already marginal sociocultural enterprise where he locates his own "paraliterary" work.[82] In *Tales* he provides an illustration of the endless play of signification in a lesson taught by Norema's teacher, Old Venn. In the tale named for her, Venn is engaged in teaching some of the children of the Ulvayn Islands about language and writing. One day she declares, "I know something. I know how to tell you *about* it, but I don't know how to tell you *what* it is. I can show you what it does, but I cannot show you the 'what' itself" (*Tales* 86–87), a statement that further illustrates the distance between language and that which it represents. She gathers the children around her and asks the young Norema to read a message Venn has written on a sheet of red vegetable-fiber:

[Norema] held it up. The red marks across the paper, left to right, were Venn's special signs for: a three-horned beetle, three horned lizards, and two crested parrots. Red meant she had observed them before noon. (*Tales* 87)

Venn next holds the paper up to the mirror on the belly of one of the boys—"(All the boys, for the last month, had taken to wearing the mirrored stomach plates)" (*Tales* 87)—and asks Norema to read the reflection. The young girl produces a different reading from the first:

'Um . . . crested parrots two, horned lizards . . . four . . . eh . . . no, three . . . a green . . . *fish!*' Norema laughed. 'But that's because the sign for green fish is just the sign for horned beetle written reversed. That's why I hesitated over the others . . . I think.' (*Tales* 88)

Finally, Venn has another boy face the first and asks Norema what she sees in the second boy's belly:

'But I . . .' Norema, of course, had expected to see the message put back left to right, its signs in proper order. But what, in the frame within a frame, she looked at was the back of her own head. And on the paper, held up beside it, written in black charcoal:
'That great star clears the horizon two cups of water after the eighth hour.' Norema stood up, laughed, and turned the paper over. What she had read in the second mirror had been written on the paper's back. 'I didn't even know that was there,' she said.
'Which is the point,' Venn said. (*Tales* 88)

Venn had written another message on the back of the paper to show her students that the paper, its reflection, and the second reflection each have different readings. The reflection of the reflection does not necessarily lead to the original text, but to something else entirely. We can translate Venn's lesson in the following semiotic fashion: Venn's paper bears a written sequence (signifier) that has a particular translation (signified). The first mirror bears a reflection (a signifier) of the paper, turning the paper into a signified. That first reflection can in turn be reflected in a second mirror, thus turning the first reflection from a signifier to a signified. Each reflection/signification produces not the same image/meaning but something different. The process can be repeated, as Derrida and Eagleton suggest, ad infinitum. Delany has claimed that "this constant reflection of one pattern by another is the central conceit running through the tales in *Return to Nevèrÿon*'s four books—with the added factor that a reflection reverses the structure of the elements it reflects."[83]

Along with Derrida's deconstructive response to Saussure, Jonathan Culler identifies certain developments in Marxist critical theory as part of the "Saussurian Legacy" of semiotics.[84] In addressing commodity fetishism, Marx noted that "a commodity appears, at first sight, a very trivial thing, and quite easily understood"—not unlike Magritte's pipe apart from its text—but when a product of labor "steps forth as a commodity, it is changed into something transcendent." Marx however endeavored to investigate beneath the surface of the commodity and made an important distinction between a commodity's use value, which is realized when the commodity is used, and its exchange value, which is realized only when the commodity is exchanged in units that equalize all types of labor—that is, money. The exchange value has nothing to do with the use value, and therefore, commodity exchange is not enabled by an innate link to use value, but by simple convention. As Foucault identifies the traditional understanding that binds words and things together as "sorcery," Marx states that use value and exchange value are bound by "the magic and necromancy that surrounds the products of labour as long as they take the form of commodities."[85] In *For a Critique of the Political Economy of the Sign* (1972) and *The Mirror of Production* (1975), Jean Baudrillard explicitly bases the structure of the commodity on that of Saussure's structure of the linguistic sign. Reinterpreting Saussure to illuminate Marx, Baudrillard conceives of the relationship between exchange value and use value as similar to that between signifier and signified respectively. Old Venn teaches her students a similar revision of semiotics, transferring a discussion of signs from the realm of language proper to that of commodities in an effort to further identify the thing she can tell them "about," but not "*what* it is."

Venn explains that just as multiple mirrors produce successive reflections, each with different meanings, so do successive narrations of a tale. She tells her students of the time she battled "a sea monster" (*Tales* 89) and barely escaped with her life, after which she made her way to an inn on the shore where she described what happened to the hosts and guests there. That night, she was haunted, not by the monster, but by her tale: "Another time I would have said I thought about what happened to me. But it wasn't that. I thought about what I *said* had happened to me" (*Tales* 90). In the morning, other travelers arriving at the inn heard her tale, but Venn realized that the adversary of which she now spoke was "an entirely different monster" (*Tales* 91) because it was a second narrative of her battle, a reflection of the reflection of the monster.

Venn follows this example with an observation about the Rulvyn tribes that live in the Ulvayns' hills, "like an island within our island" (*Tales* 92), who have specified tasks according to gender:

'The men hunt geese and wild goats; the women provide the bulk of the food by growing turnips and other roots, fruits, and a few leaf vegetables . . . the women do far and above more work than the men toward keeping the tribe alive. But because they do not come much to the sea and they have no fish, meat is an important food to them. Because it is an important food, the hunting men are looked upon as rather prestigious creatures. Groups of women share a single hunter, who goes out with a group of hunters and brings back meat for the women.' (*Tales* 91–92)

Recently, the Rulvyn have gone from a barter economy to a money economy, a transition that Delany has identified as characteristic of the sword-and-sorcery sub-genre:[86]

'Up till a few years ago, the Rulvyn were tribes who lived entirely by their women exchanging goods and work with other women for whatever goods and work they needed. Even if meat were part of the exchange, the men would bring it to the women, who would then do the actual bartering. . . .
'But our people, here at the shore, with our bigger and bigger boats, for three generations now have been using the coins that come from Nevèrÿon to make our exchanges with. And as more and more of us went back into the hills to trade with the Rulvyn, the Rulvyn began to acquire money; and finally began to use money among themselves in order to make their exchanges.' (*Tales* 92)

Norema later hypothesizes that money is only "the first mirror," prompting Venn to imagine "a model of money without being money" (*Tales* 102); that is, a system of banking and credit, a kind of economy the transition to which Delany sees as characteristic of SF.[87] Whereas Rulvyn women had been in charge of intratribal trade, the men had traditionally been in charge of extratribal trade. As a result, Rulvyn men tended to handle money matters:

'Because money was exotic as well as part of the prestige of trading with foreigners, money went primarily to the men of the society; and indeed both the men and women of the tribe at first agreed that money *ought* to be the province of men, just as hunting was.' (*Tales* 92–93)

In language that reverberates with Marx's assertion of how commodification "surrounds" products of labor, Venn describes how money, like language and mirrors, constructs a representation of a product's value:

'Now money, when it moves into a new tribe, very quickly creates an image of the food, craft, and work there: it gathers around them, molds to them, stays away from the places where none are to be found, and clots near positions where much wealth occurs.' (*Tales* 93)

But because money is a unit of exchange value only, its representation is just that, a representation, an inadequate rendition that lacks the dimensions of the labor it reflects. "The image in the mirror . . . *looks* real, and deep, and as full of space as the real," one of Venn's students realizes, "But it's flat—really. There's nothing *behind* the mirror—but my belly" (*Tales* 101). Therefore, Venn explains, money cannot substitute for the products and labor; it merely gestures toward it:

'Yet, like a mirror image, it [money] is reversed just as surely as the writing on a piece of paper is reversed when you read its reflection on a boy's belly. For both in time and space, where money is, food work, and craft are not: where money is, food work, and craft either will shortly be, or in the recent past were. But the actual place where the coin sits is a place where wealth may just have passed from or may soon pass into, but where it cannot be now—by the whole purpose of money as an exchange object.' (*Tales* 93)

In *Capital I,* Marx states that "whenever, by an exchange, we equate as values our different products, by that very act, we also equate, as human labour, the different kinds of labour expended upon them. We are not aware of this, nevertheless we do it."[88] Venn explains that the Rulvyn learned this practice of bringing all labor down to the same system of measurement from the Ulvayn, who practice it, literally, as she speaks:

'Your parents pay me to talk to you every morning; I am happy they do. But they pay the same money to Blen's and Holi's father and uncle who are so skilled with stone they can build a stone wall in a day: and the same money goes to Crey, who is a hulking halfwit, but is lucky enough to have a back and arm strong enough to dig shit-ditches. The same money goes to your mother for a string of her sea trout as goes to your father for a boat to go catch sea trout of one's own from. So much time and thought goes into trying to figure out what the comparative worth of all these skills and labors are. But the problem begins with trying to reduce them all to the same measure of coin in the first place: skilled time, unskilled time, the talk of a clever woman, nature's gifts of fish and fruit, the invention of a craftsman, the strength of a laboring woman—one simply cannot measure weight, coldness, the passage of time, and the brightness of fire all on the same scale.' (*Tales* 101)

Now that the Rulvyn have money, however, they have begun to measure different types of labor on the same scale, thus producing troubling economic changes for the Rulvyn women,

'When money came among the Rulvyn, something very strange happened: Before money came, a woman with strength, skills or goods could exchange

them directly with another woman for whatever she needed. She who did
the most work and did it the best was the most powerful woman. Now, the
same woman had to go to someone with money, frequently a man, exchange her goods for money, and then exchange the money for what she
needed. But if there was no money available, all her strength and skill and
goods gave her no power at all—and she might as well not have had them.'
(Tales 93)

as well as social and cultural changes for all:

'Among the Rulvyn before money, a strong woman married a prestigious
hunter, then another strong woman would join them in marriage—frequently
her friend—and the family would grow. Now that money has come, a prestigious hunter must first amass money—for what woman would marry a
man in such a system who did *not* have money—and then go looking for
good, strong workers to marry . . . for that is the only way *he* can amass
more money.' (Tales 93)

"What emerges in money's wake," Kathleen Spencer observes, "is nothing less familiar than the classic pattern of patriarchy."[89] A thorough
analysis of the series' investigation of gender, from its deconstruction of
penis envy among the Rulvyn to Raven's feminist/chauvinist creation myth
story, deserves its own separate chapter. For the purposes of this study, it
is important to note that although it may be oversimplifying the matter
to suggest that capitalism has *caused* patriarchy amongst the Rulvyn, it is
clear that their adoption of a money economy has had its effects not only
on their economy but on their cultural practices, social structures, and interpersonal relations: "When last I was there," Venn says, "a woman still
married a man with the same rituals and prayers, feast-foods, and flowers;
but the look in her eyes has changed. So has the look in his" (Tales 95).
    Venn's gloomy account of the Rulvyn is not *Tales'* last word on money
and commodity exchange, however. "The Tale of Potters and Dragons"
opens with a lecture by Old Zwon, a Kolhari potter, to his apprentice
Bayle. Enthusiastic about the possibility of importing the mysterious
Lord Aldamir's rubber balls from the south to the north for sale in Kolhari, Zwon tells Bayle, his emissary to the southern Dragon Lord, that
money enables social contact across the various economic classes:

'Think of the people it connects! It makes all of us one, as if we were fingers
a-jut off a single palm: myself, a common pot spinner, a drudger forty years
in this poor waterfront shop in this poor port city; a noble gentleman like
Lord Aldamir, once an intimate, you may be sure, of the Child Empress herself (whose reign)—' The knuckles came up from knee to forehead, and the

wrinkled eyes dropped to the shards about the floor—'is fine and fecund); and even that taciturn giant of a messenger who approached me with that distant lord's ingenuous plan; and the children who will buy the little treasures, bounce them, prattle over them, trade and treasure them. It is as though we are all rendered heart, bone, liver, and lights of a single creature.' (*Tales* 163)

Zwon's rhetoric recalls the "net" or "web" that admits only certain kinds of contact between the races in "The Necessity of Tomorrows." It also echoes Booker T. Washington's Cotton States Exposition Address delivered in Atlanta in 1895, which placated whites by emphasizing the need for black vocational and economic development over social justice and political equality: "In all things that are purely social we can be separate as the fingers, yet one as the hand in all things essential to mutual progress."[90] The congruence of Washington's statement to Zwon's opening metaphor suggests that although money ties different classes of people together, those connections, about which Zwon is so thrilled, do not necessarily guarantee equal social and political standing. Nevertheless, Zwon tells Bayle that the invention of a money economy is "an entirely good thing" (*Tales* 163), in part because he realizes that commodification has the potential for liberating people from a trade economy's relatively fixed methods of exchange:

'Ah, my boy, I can remember back when it was all trade. A pot went out; eggs came in. Another pot; barley this time. Another pot; goat's milk. But suppose I wanted cheese when there was only butter available? Suppose someone with butter needed grain but had more than enough pots? Oh, those were perilous times—and perilous in ways that money, which can be saved, stored, spent wisely or foolishly, and doesn't go bad like eggs or butter, has abolished. But that was fifty years ago and need not worry a young head like yours . . .' (*Tales* 163)

But Madame Keyne, Zwon's rival for Lord Aldamir's franchise, has a different opinion, at least in this early stage of the series. "I have my serious doubts," she tells her assistant, Venn's former student Norema, "about whether money is a good thing" (*Tales* 170). Madame Keyne observes that money is a step away from—a reflection of—the labor that produces goods and services and that it thereby alienates the laborer from his or her products: "Each of us, with money, gets further and further away from those moments where the hand pulls the beet root from the soil, shakes the fish from the net into the basket" (*Tales* 171). Furthermore, Nevèrÿon's new economy threatens to submit all relations, including social relations, to a matter of market value, thus dividing people instead of connecting them: "not to mention the way it separates us from one another, so that when enough money comes between people, they lie apart like parts of a chicken hacked up for stewing" (*Tales* 171). But when Old Zwon and Madame Keyne meet at the end of the tale to discuss a joint financial venture, each has reversed their position. Zwon has attributed Bayle's disappearance in the south to a felt disrespect he now believes inherent to wage labor, and Madame Keyne has adopted the proto-capitalist perspective that informs the views toward Gorgik, her laborers, and the unemployed that she expresses in *Neveryóna*. The series' ruminations on money and commodification should not be seen as randomly selected subject matter, however; they are part of, and are illuminated by, Delany's general discussion of the linguistic sign.

Money and commodification are members of a vast set of social practices that Jonathan Culler identifies as objects of semiotic inquiry. These practices may not seem to have much in common with communicative languages, Culler states, but they are "highly codified" like languages, and they "employ a whole series of distinctions in order to create meaning."[91] Roland Barthes's *Mythologies* (1957) illustrates how practices such as etiquette, clothing, and sports operate through and as languages. Gorgik engages in a comparable study of social practices out of necessity in his "Tale" when he arrives at court with Vizirine Myrgot: "Gorgik, who had survived on the waterfront and survived in the mine, survived at the High Court of Eagles. To do it, he had to learn a great deal" (*Tales* 49, *Return* 239). Learning how one must comport oneself at Court, as in the obsidian mine, is like learning a new language: "The social hierarchy and patterns of deference to be learned here were as complex as those that had to be mastered—even by a foreman—on moving into a new slave barracks in the mine" (*Tales* 52, *Return* 243). Gorgik receives a sort of tutelage in this system from Baron Inige. Constrained by this system from approaching Myrgot directly, Gorgik learns that because "there was hardly one person at court who was not, practically speaking, in a similar position with at least one other person—if not whole groups" (*Tales* 49, *Return* 239), certain arcane combinations of guests were required at different Court functions:

> The Thane of Sallese could be invited to the same gathering as Lord Ekoris *unless* the Countess Esulla was to be present—however, in such cases Curly (the Baron Inige's nickname) would be excused. No one known as a friend of Lord Aldamir (who had not been at Court now for many years, though everyone seemed to remember him with fondness) should be seated next to, or across from, any relative, unto the second cousins, of the Baronine Jeu-Forsi . . . (*Tales* 49, *Return* 239–40)

The only thing that could "generate such complexity," Gorgik reasons, is "servitude itself" (*Tales* 52, *Return* 243). The Empire's aristocracy, he concludes are, ironically, enslaved to "power, pure, raw, and obsessive" (*Tales* 52, *Return* 243).

The cultural criticism in which Barthes and Delany (by way of Gorgik) engage is informed by what Barthes calls "a feeling of impatience at the sight of the 'naturalness'" that is ascribed to structures that are "undoubtedly determined by history."[92] The arbitrary relationship between the signifier and the signified produces a language system that is no "truer" than any other. By extension, social systems, which operate like languages, are similarly arbitrary. "Every means of expression used in society is based, in principle, on collective behavior or—what amounts to the same thing—on convention," Saussure states; "it is this rule and not intrinsic value of the gestures that obliges one to use them."[93] Semiotics, therefore, enables the important work of analyzing a range of social practices—from language to etiquette—and interpreting them as constructed systems as opposed to natural, eternal, phenomena. This is also difficult work because it involves challenging the ideological status quo. "Signs frequently seem natural—endowed with inherent meaning—to those who use them," Culler observes. "People are inclined to insist that their own behavior is governed by practical rather than symbolic considerations."[94] But it is a short step from characterizing such considerations as "practical" to naturalizing them to the point where they can become the *only* considerations. Terry Eagleton summarizes Barthes's argument:

> Signs which pass themselves off as natural, which offer themselves as the only conceivable way of viewing the world, are by that token authoritarian and ideological. It is one of the functions of ideology to "naturalize" social reality, to make it seem as innocent and unchangeable as Nature itself. Ideology seeks to convert culture into Nature, and the "natural" sign is one of its weapons."[95]

The naturalization of social signs is a metaphysical and essentializing process, which accounts in part for Foucault's use of "sorcery" to describe the bond between words and things and Marx's identification of "magic and necromancy" as the agent that seeks to link exchange value to use value in the commodity. It is appropriate, therefore, that in Nevèrÿon, the ability to manipulate signs is equated with "magic." Earl Jue-Grutn's collection of numerous written languages and his ability to read all of them in largely preliterate Nevèrÿon, contribute to his reputation as someone who is "insane, a sorcerer, or both" (*Tales* 50, *Return* 241). In *Neveryóna,* Madame Keyne defines magic as power that operates in a semiotic system. "Do you know what magic is?" she asks Pryn; "It is power. But power only functions in the context of other powers—which is the secret of magic" (*Neveryóna* 97). It is during their later conversation about Gorgik at the construction site of the New Market that Madame Keyne teaches Pryn about the ideological structures that naturalize the location of power among Nevèrÿon's elite. When Madame Keyne worries that her position in Kolhari's society is not so strong that she can hire more women and barbarians as she would like, Pryn exclaims "But you *are* a powerful woman!" (*Neveryóna* 139), after which she wonders how Madame Keyne got that way. "How did you become so?" Pryn asks, " I mean, how did you ever . . . ?" (*Neveryóna* 139). The narrative breaks out of itself to address the reader and suggest how Pryn's interrogation of how the powerful obtain power is the acme of impertinence. But because she is fond of Pryn, Madame Keyne, in her own way, obliges:

'You know, girl, there's something I've been more or less aware of since I was a child: If events ever struck me from the position of affluence and prestige that, certainly, my family secured for me far more than I did, as long as the world in general and the city in particular are organized along the lines they are today I could climb back, simply because I know *where* the ladders' feet are located—' (*Neveryóna* 140)

Madame Keyne realizes that in the unlikely event that she ever loses the socioeconomic power she wields in Kolhari she would be able to regain it because she fully comprehends Nevèrÿon's socioeconomic structure. The possibility of alternative structures, however, trouble her:

'As I've grown older, however, I've had my anxious moments. The anxiety arrives along with a kind of alternative dream, the vision of a world arranged very differently, without any such ladders at all, where no privileges such as mine exist, nor such hardship as theirs [the unemployed]: rather it is a dream of an equitable division of goods and services into which all would be born, within which all would be raised, and the paths from one point to the other would be set out by like and dislike, temperament and desire, rather than inscribed on a mystified map whose blotted and improperly marked directions are all plotted between poverty and power, wealth and weakness.' (*Neveryóna* 141)

Madame Keyne's characterization of the present system of distribution of Nevèrÿon's wealth and power as a "mystified map" identifies the imaginary, metaphysical forces that supply the alibi (to use Barthes's term) for the status quo. As discussed earlier, Gorgik is the cause of Madame Keyne's anxiety and of the intense, if conflicting, feelings among Kolhari's unemployed and working poor and her loyal employees. But according to Madame Keyne, Nevèrÿon's masses make the mistake of targeting the empire as the source of their problems: "They think the enemy is Nevèrÿon, and that Nevèrÿon *is* the system of privileges and powers such as mine that supports it, or the privileges and powers such as the Child Empress's (whose reign is, after all, benign and bureaucratic) which rule it" (*Neveryóna* 141). What the workers should attack, however, is not the state necessarily, nor power itself, but the ideology that naturalizes the state's inequitable distribution of wealth and power:

> 'As long as they do not realize that the true enemy is what holds those privileges—and the ladders of power to them—in place, that at once anchors them on all sides, keeps the rungs clear, yet assures their bottoms will remain invisible from anywhere other than their tops, then my position in the system is, if not secure, at least always accessible should I, personally, become dislodged.' (*Neveryóna* 141)

Pryn is not exactly sure about the identity of this "true enemy," and Madame Keyne will not tell her—"You really ask me that, girl?" Madame Keyne laughed sharply. "You actually want me to name it—now? here?" (*Neveryóna* 141)—but the merchant does demonstrate its pervasiveness by throwing up a gold coin that lands in front of a laborer named Kudyuk, who returns the coin. Madame Keyne offers an iron one in exchange, which the laborer is only too grateful to receive:

> 'Well, Madame Keyne, Kudyuk will work for you any day! Kudyuk, that's me! . . . Yes, I'll certainly work for you!' His fist closed on the small iron. Bobbing his bearded head and without ever really standing erect, he dropped back over the embankment and went for his shovel. 'Yes, Madame Keyne,' he called up, 'I certainly will!' (*Neveryóna* 142)

Pryn wonders where Kudyuk will put his money—"he was one of the workers who had already given up all clothing in his pursuit of labor" (*Neveryóna* 142)—and why Madame Keyne gave money away: "you *lost* money in that transaction!" she says, "Money went out—and you had to pay to get it back!" (*Neveryóna* 143). However, the iron coin, produced from the melted-down collars of ex-slaves and stamped with the image of an anonymous Nevèrÿon official, represents the money Madame Keyne pays the people who work for her. The gold coin, which Delany signals as important by having it "flash and glimmer" (*Neveryóna* 142), is stamped with the likeness of Child Empress Ynelgo, and it signifies Madame Keyne's credit, collateral, and capital—in Venn's terms—a reflection of her vast amounts of money:

> 'Here,' Madame Keyne said, holding out the gold for Pryn to examine, 'is the money with which I finance my projects—the money against which I make my loans, the money that brings me in its interest, the money I cite when I bargain over lands, the money I have at my beck and call when I arrange prices for materials and labor, the money those who know I am a wealthy woman know I possess.' (*Neveryóna* 139)

The bond between the coin and the wealth it signifies is established and sealed by the image of the transcendent (literally and figuratively untouchable) Child Empress. Madame Keyne uses her iron coin to conspicuously demonstrate her economic power, as well as, in effect, to buy Kudyuk's loyalty and servitude, thereby reinforcing—naturalizing—the connection between the hierarchical relationship between the wealthy merchant and the barbarian laborer, as well as between herself and her wealth. "If you think I *lost* in that transaction, then you do not know what the enemy is, nor, I doubt, will you ever," Madame Keyne tells Pryn, "But if you can see the real gain on my part, then—perhaps!—you have seen your enemy and may yet again recognize her glittering features" (*Neveryóna* 143). Culler notes that "the more powerful a culture, the more it succeeds in having its signs taken as natural," and it is significant that Madame Keyne equates power with magic.[96] It is these types of "illusions" that Myrgot calls "the very constitution of power" (*Return* 100). The aristocracy's success in convincing people like Kudyuk that economic power naturally and magically resides in the hands of those who have it, legitimizing the hierarchy symbolized by the Child Empress's image, is what Madame Keyne demonstrates to Pryn.

Delany's series, therefore, engages in numerous types of "play." It is a "ludic endeavor," purposefully playful sword-and-sorcery that is read for its fantastic (and un-"scholarly") content. Despite its paraliterary status, however, the quality of the series' prose and the fecundity of its conceptual terrain transports it into a realm of literary art; but it is art engaged in a play against and across discourses, blurring the lines between literature and critical theory. As we have seen, the series consistently engages in a semiotic theory intent on, among other things, identifying the meanings produced by the play of differences within language systems. But if semiotics is a pervasive intellectual approach in these texts, and slavery is the series' central subject, what do these two discourses have to say to each other? We shall find that in the *Return to Nevèrÿon* series, slavery and semiotics intersect at the site of one of the most consistent, and consistently interesting, subjects in Delany's work: sexuality.

> We can now say that all true freedom is dark, and infallibly identified with sexual
> freedom which is also dark, although we do not know why.
> —Antonin Artaud, *The Theater and Its Double* [97]

Orlando Patterson describes slavery as "a highly symbolized domain of human experience." As such, the authority of "those who exercise power" in slaveholding societies, the slaveholding class, is located in that class's "control over symbolic instruments." [98] In the *Return to Nevèrÿon* series, the slave collar is presented as the symbol of its wearer's enslavement. Through the eyes of the youthful Gorgik, the reader sees that all slaves in Nevèrÿon, regardless of their gender, the social caste of their masters, or their treatment by those masters, wear the collar:

> . . . among them all [the populace of Kolhari] the male and female slaves, those of aristocratic masters dressed more elegantly than many merchants, while others were so ragged and dirty their sex was indistinguishable, yet all with the hinged iron collars above fine or frayed shirt necks or bony shoulders, loose or tight around stringy or fleshy necks. (*Tales* 27, *Return* 217)

In Nevèrÿon, domestic and industrial slaves do different types of work, not unlike the "house" and "field" slaves, respectively, on the plantations of the American South. Domestic slaves are distinguished by the "jeweled pieces of damasked cloth" (*Tales* 27, *Return* 217) that cover their collars, each of which is so vivid a symbol of its wearer's enslavement that Sarg, as he engages in his one-man siege of the Suzerain of Strethi's castle, instructs himself to "see only the collars" (*Tales* 227) in order to efficiently differentiate between whom he should liberate and whom he should kill.

In characterizing the slave collar as a "symbol" of slavery, it is important to understand the term in its most precise sense. A symbol tends to maintain a one-to-one relationship with that which it represents. Justice, for example, is symbolized by scales; it cannot, Saussure instructs us, be as easily represented by, for example, a chariot. [99] The relationship between a symbol and its referent is strongly enforced by social convention. In "The Tale of Gorgik," slavery and the slave collar initially appear to have a tightly focused and enforced symbolic relationship. A linguistic sign, on the other hand, is a contextualized linguistic unit. Derrida has posited that in order for a sign to serve a communicative function it must be iterable, that is, able to be repeated; if a sign is iterable, it can be repeated in a different context, as a writer does by citing another individual by using quotation marks. [100] "Iteration alters," Derrida claims, "something new takes place" because "the structure of iteration . . . implies *both* identity *and* difference."[101] Again, consider how epithets such as "nigger" and "queer" have recently been rearticulated by some segments of African American and gay communities, respectively, as signs of community and purposeful transgression. It appears, therefore, that it does not take much to get from Derridean iterability to something like James Snead's theory of repetition as a figure of black culture, in which repetition means transformation. A sign "must maintain a certain consistency across [different] situations in order to be an identifiable sign at all," Eagleton explains, but "because its context is always different it is never *absolutely* the same, never quite identical with itself."[102]

As *Tales* progresses, it becomes increasingly evident that the slave collar is less a symbol, limited to representing enslavement, than it is a radically contextualized sign. In a strictly social context, it signifies its wearer's status as chattel. Gorgik, however, a free man since he left Court, wears the collar as a sign of his campaign against slavery, thus shifting the site of the collar's operation from a strictly social context to a political context. "I've sworn that while a man or woman wears the iron collar in Nevèrÿon," the Liberator tells Pryn, "I shall not take the one I wear from my neck" (*Neveryóna* 65). Such a rearticulation of the collar does not proceed without meeting resistance or causing some tumult. *Flight*'s "The Tale of Fog and Granite" reveals that Gorgik's practice of wearing the collar, an act which shifted its status from symbol to sign, was felt by the Empire's conservatives to be more unsettling than the campaign it represented:

> [I]t was not the radicalness of [Gorgik's] program that had so upset the country. . . . Rather it was the radicalness of his appearance that had bothered the nobles, merchants, and their conservative employees—not the Liberator's practice so much as his potential; for appearances are signs of possibilities, at least when one remembers that what appears may be a sign by masking as easily as by manifesting. (*Flight* 19)

In other words, changing the meaning of the collar is almost as radical a move as abolishing slavery. Gorgik's rearticulation of the collar also generates the potential for confusion. When Gorgik saves Pryn from the clutches of a brutal pimp named Nynx on the Bridge of Lost Desire, the mountain girl thinks her rescuer a slave. But Gorgik is characteristically able to use such confusion to his advantage, deferring the revelation to Pryn of his revolutionary identity and mission as he escorts her through Kolhari and its Old Market. As the stories progress and Gorgik's campaign grows in size and strength, the collar he wears becomes more recognizable as a sign of the movement to begin the end of slavery in Nevèrÿon.

As radical as Gorgik's political recontextualization of the collar is, the Liberator engages in an even more drastic shift in its meaning. In "The

Tale of Small Sarg," it quickly becomes apparent that Gorgik has bought the barbarian for sexual purposes. Sarg, who initially has little choice in the matter, submits to Gorgik's wishes but asks to have his slave collar removed first. Gorgik refuses this request: "You see . . . if one of us does not wear it, *I* will not be able to . . . do anything," he tells Sarg, "And right now, I do not feel like wearing it . . . at least tonight" (*Tales* 154). The slave collar, Gorgik reveals, is an erotically charged emblem that allows him to function sexually: "There are people I have met in my travels who cannot eat food unless it has been held long over fire; and there are others, like me, who cannot love without some mark of possession" (*Tales* 154). If the reader makes the return to "The Tale of Gorgik," suggested by the repetition of that inaugural tale at the end of the series' final volume, Gorgik's encounter with the collared slave boy—revealed in *Return*'s "The Tale of Rumor and Desire," to be not a slave at all, but a young Clodon the Bandit, bearing the scars of a public flogging he received in his home village for thievery, and masquerading as a slave as part of the experimental scheme of a Kolhari mortician—takes on a different, erotic significance. Indeed, after seeing Clodon remove his collar and throw it away, Gorgik comes close to guessing the truth of the masquerade: "Was this some criminal only pretending to be a slave?" (*Tales* 35, *Return* 225). The split between Gorgik's double memory—of collars that bind and dehumanize slaves, of collars unfastened and detached—is the split between social and sexual contexts. In addition to—for the structure of iteration implies both identity and difference—producing in Gorgik a feeling of shock at the cruelty of slavery, the collared boy also triggers a physically overwhelming erotic response. But whereas the social and the sexual present themselves at once during this formative encounter with the collar, the two meanings are significantly differentiated from each other afterward. After he and Gorgik have sex, Sarg wakes to find his collar lying on the ground and catches a young girl, the same one who saw Gorgik buy Sarg, voyeuristically observing them. "You may have once been a slave," she tells Sarg, "But you are not a slave now" (*Tales* 158). What the girl suggests is that Gorgik has freed Sarg, and the Liberator's sexual use of the collar is wholly apart from their society's use of it as a sign of slavery.

Some readers of the *Return to Nevèrÿon* series no doubt recognize the slave collar, especially when presented as an erotic emblem, as approximating part of the paraphernalia of sadomasochism (popularly known as "S/M" or "S&M"), a name for a category of sexual acts centered around the staging of domination and submission, relations of power. The eroticization of such relations, a practice in which Gorgik appears to be at least tangentially engaging in *Tales* and in which Noyeed more explicitly engages in *Flight*, may strike some readers as at best merely bizarre and at worst indecently profane. It is a common assumption that S/M perverts the history of unjust power relations that Africans in America and other groups were forced to endure to a base sexual practice.[103] But Delany has explicitly argued the opposite:

> To assume a session of "sexual torture" between two consenting adults requires only minimal reorganization of what goes on in an actual session of political torture—and in any way manifests the same "power relations"— signs only gross ignorance of the context *and* the substance of *both* situations![104]

Return's "The Game of Time and Pain" demonstrates the principle guiding Delany's logic in its brief narration of the story of the barbarian youth Udrog, an orphan who was cruelly chained and beaten by his guardian. Afterward, he was adopted by a woman who had many children, two of whom would take Udrog into the woods for sexual games that included bondage and the pretense of cruelty and beatings:

> —Perhaps the older children's early lives had been similar to Udrog's. But reducing to play what once had been true torture gave them—the two girls and the younger boy—a power over the mists of pain that was all memory had left (at least to Udrog) of childhood. (*Return* 22)

Udrog recognizes his sexual interests—bondage, collars, rough sex—as "one of the more common perversions in a Nevèrÿon so recently awakened from a troubling dream of slaves" (*Return* 24) as if the Empire seeks to reclaim the humanity it lost during slavery through this "perverse" sexual practice.

It can therefore be argued that the trust and sympathy Patterson correctly asserts was absent in slave societies' relations of domination are present, even necessary, in the S/M scenario. Such sexual "play" consists not of the reinforcement of relations of domination, but rather their denaturalization. Anne McClintock, for example, convincingly characterizes S/M as "an organized subculture shaped around the ritual exercise of social risk and social transformation" and that "to argue that in S/M 'whoever is the 'master' has power and whoever is the 'slave' has not,' is to read theater for reality," because consensual S/M's "exaggerated emphasis on costumery, script and scene" mark it as a "theater of transformation."[105]

McClintock's characterization of S/M as "theater" is apt given "The Tale of Fog and Granite"'s description of the top/bottom sex act between, respectively, the smuggler and Noyeed as a "miming of submission and domination" (*Flight* 49). It is also fundamental toward understanding the semiotic denaturalization of the social relations that such sexual practices mimic. In his study of Bertolt Brecht, Terry Eagleton notes that the dramatist made use of an "alienation effect" produced by acting that stripped everyday human actions and gestures of their "natural"-ness and revealed them to be socially determined matters of artifice: "Brechtian theatre," Eagleton states, "deconstructs social processes into rhetoric, which is to say reveals them as social *practices*"; theater, therefore, displays the constructed character of the most "natural"-seeming of human affairs, or, as Eagleton wittily puts it, "the function of theater is to show that all the world's a stage."[106] McClintock interprets S/M as similarly "self-consciously *antinature*": S/M is less about inflicting or receiving pain than it is a "theatrical organization of social risk" that operates "with the utmost artifice and levity." What Brechtian theater does to human social gestures, S/M does to the relation of domination inherent to slavery; it reveals such a relation as "sanctioned, neither by nature, fate nor God, but by artifice and convention and thus as radically open to historical change." Therefore, if, as McClintock puts it, "S/M is a theater of signs,"[107] then Gorgik's engagement in such behavior does not contradict his campaign against slavery; rather, we will see that his sexual desires actually inform his desire to transform Nevèrÿon's sociopolitical landscape.

This is not how Raven and Norema see it, however, when they meet Gorgik and Sarg after the men liberate the slaves—and themselves—from the castle of the Suzerain of Strethi toward the end of "The Tale of Dragons and Dreamers." When Raven sees Gorgik and Sarg together, with Gorgik wearing the collar, she assumes, logically but incorrectly, that Gorgik is Sarg's slave. With remarkable candor, Gorgik explains that for Sarg the collar represents their "mutual affection [and] mutual protection," whereas for himself "it is sexual—a necessary part in the pattern that allows both action and orgasm to manifest themselves within the single circle of desire" (*Tales* 238). The collar has shifted out of the social context in which it signified subordination and submission: "For neither of us is its meaning social" Gorgik says, "save that it shocks, offends, or deceives" (*Tales* 238). For this reason Sarg can earnestly utter a statement as seemingly paradoxical as "My master and I are free" (*Tales* 239). The apparent contradiction provokes laughter from Raven, who believes that she and Norema have stumbled upon "two jesters" (*Tales* 239). However, Gorgik and Sarg, respectively, do their best to explain that for them, the collar functions in an erotic context: "We are lovers, and for one of us the symbolic distinction between slave and master is necessary to desire's consummation"—and a political context: "We are avengers who fight the institution of slavery wherever we find it, in whatever way we can, and for both of us it is symbolic of our time in servitude and our bond to all men and women still so bound" (*Tales* 239). But Norema still sees the men's sexual behavior and political mission as being at cross-purposes:

"You love as master and slave and you fight the institution of slavery?" she asks, "The contradiction seems as sad to me as it seemed amusing to my friend" (*Tales* 239). It is at this point that Gorgik puts his semiotic understanding of the slave collar, which sees it as a radically contextualized linguistic sign, into terms that Norema understands:

'As one word uttered in three different situations may mean three entirely different things, so the collar worn in different situations may mean three different things. They are not the same: sex, affection, and society . . . Sex and society relate like an object and its image in a reflecting glass. One reverses the other—are you familiar with the phenomenon, for these *are* primitive times, and mirrors are rare—' (*Tales* 239)

Years ago, Norema learned a similar lesson about the nature of the sign from Venn's example of the mirrors. She now comes to understand Gorgik's point, and her subsequent silence on the matter suggests that she recognizes the strength of his argument.

As important as the contextuality of the collar is to both Gorgik and Sarg in *Tales,* such an understanding apparently breaks down for Sarg by the time in which *Neveryóna* is set, which is why he interrupts the gathering of Gorgik's followers in their subterranean headquarters. Reproaching the gathered anti-slavery forces, Sarg accuses the Liberator of despotism—"You think you have a Liberator before you? Can't you hear the voice of a tyrant in the making?" (*Neveryóna* 74)—and of vile perversion. "Before you sits a man whose every word and act is impelled by lusts as depraved as any in the nation, who would make a slave of all and anyone to satisfy them, calling such satisfaction freedom!" (*Neveryóna* 74). And perhaps worst of all, he accuses Gorgik of hypocrisy:

'If you can't see what's in front of you, then look behind you! Look at Small Sarg—Sarg the barbarian! A prince in my land, I came to yours a slave! The man you call "Liberator" bought me as a slave—and, true, he told me I was free; and, true, for three years we fought together against slavery throughout Nevèrÿon. But when he was finished with me, he *sold* me! Sold me as a slave! To traders on their way to the western desert—thinking that he would never see me again! But I have escaped! I have returned from slavery. And as I love my freedom, so I have sworn his death!' (*Neveryóna* 74)

Sarg attacks Gorgik, but is in turn attacked and slain by Noyeed, a one-eyed slave-turned-bandit who was raped by other slaves, including Gorgik, in the Faltha obsidian mines and who later succeeds the barbarian prince as the Liberator's lieutenant and lover. A melée between Gorgik and Sarg's minions ensues, and Pryn, who has come to the gathering as

Gorgik's guest, barely escapes. After her episode with Madame Keyne, Pryn goes to Gorgik's false headquarters outside of Sallese, where she is surprised to find the Liberator and asks him to respond to Sarg's accusations. Although he suspects that Pryn is a spy, Gorgik explains to her that "there are as many ways to read the iron collar, the chain, and the whip as there are to read the words a woman or a man whispers under the tent's shadow with the moonlight outside" (*Neveryóna* 179), and proceeds to refute Sarg's charges by explaining the collar's contextuality. Citing the example of the camel drivers in Kolhari's markets who routinely engage in the practice of "cursing their beasts, one another, and the whole inconvenient and crowded world of commerce through which they must drive their herd" (*Neveryóna* 179), Gorgik explains that the very same curses have different meanings in an erotic context:

> 'Are you too young to have heard, little Heron, that some of these same men, alone in their tents at night with their women, may implore, plead, beg their mistresses to whisper these same phrases to them, or plead to be allowed to whisper them back, phrases which now, instead of conveying ire and frustration, transport them, and sometimes the women, too, to heights of pleasure?' (*Neveryóna* 179)

Although the curses signify differently according to context, Gorgik is aware that many people are inclined to seek some sort of associative bond between the different meanings, a practice that only serves to pathologize the sexual meaning, and sexual activity itself:

> 'Now there are some, who, wishing to see the world more unified than common sense suggests it could possibly be, say that to use terms of anger and rage in the throes of desire indicates some great malaise, not only of camel drivers but of the whole world; that desire itself must be a form of anger and is thus invalid as an adjunct to love . . .' (*Neveryóna* 180)

Pryn notes how Gorgik's example privileges the camel driver's curse over the term of endearment, and she seeks to invert the hierarchy: "*I* would say . . . the sickness is in using terms of desire in the throes of anger and rage. Most curses are just words for women's genitals, men's excreta, and cooking implements joined up in preposterous ways" (*Neveryóna* 180). Although Gorgik finds merit in Pryn's argument, he notes that it is the privileging of either signification, labeling one "appropriate" and the other "inappropriate," that causes the problem, producing a situation where "the inappropriate signs do not enrich the reading" but instead "pollute it" (*Neveryóna* 180). The Liberator suggests the absurdity of such misreadings when he jokes "Even the most foul-mouthed camel driver knows a curse from a kiss, whatever signs accompany it" (*Neveryóna* 180). The slave collar, like the camel driver's curse, has a social significance—specifically as "a sign of social oppression"—and an erotic significance, as "an adjunct of pleasure" (*Neveryóna* 181). The difference between Sarg and Gorgik is that whereas the Liberator could easily distinguish the two acts of signification, the barbarian apparently found it increasingly difficult to do so: "My little barbarian prince, while we fought and loved together, was very much one out to have the world more unified," Gorgik explains, "while I, in such matters, am . . . a camel driver" (*Neveryóna* 181). Gorgik reveals that as their relationship and their campaign progressed, Sarg increasingly declined to wear the slave collar at night, but insisted on wearing it during the day as part of their infiltration and destruction of slavery networks. As the barbarian did so, his behavior became increasingly reckless and dangerous to the safety of the duo and the success of their missions. Ultimately, the Liberator had to abandon his partner after he had "sold" him to slavers, because Sarg was about to blow their cover. Pryn hypothesizes that Sarg felt the same erotic charge of the slave collar but became unable to accept that fact. If such was indeed the case, then Sarg's inability to come to terms with his sexuality, and his inability to distinguish his sexual behavior with Gorgik from slavery itself, began the chain of events that culminate in his tragic and violent death. But the Liberator also hypothesizes that the collar never had the same meaning for Sarg as it did for himself:

'Sarg said he felt no lust within the iron. I say I do. Why should I assume he spoke any less truly of his feelings than I speak of mine? If such a sign can shift so easily from oppression to desire, it can shift in other ways—toward power, perhaps, and aggression, toward the bitterness of misjudged freedoms by one who must work outside civil structure.' (*Neveryóna* 185)

In the *Return to Nevèrÿon* series, therefore, Delany is making a similar critique of the model of "a platonically ideal sex act after which all social relations must be formed in order to partake of the good" as he outlines in "Of Sex, Objects, Signs, Systems, Sales, SF and Other Things" and as he has dramatized in *Dhalgren*. Gorgik and Sarg play at slavery as George and June play at rape. In the Nevèrÿon books, however, with their nods to Lacanian psychoanalysis and feminist theorizations of gender and sexual identity, the target is more specifically orthodox Freudian psychoanalysis, which privileges male heterosexuality as a norm on which a society is based.[108] In remarkably straightforward language, "Sex, Objects" asserts the point that the sword-and-sorcery tales develop by way of semiotic inquiry: "Sex is sex, pleasure is pleasure, anger is anger, sadness is sadness, and fear is fear," Delany claims, "all of them, and all the paths between, are affected by the material universe we live in"; however, "to use the sex-produces-society model as a mapping tool (rather than society-contours-sex) in any sort of narrative fictions (science or otherwise) foredooms us to losing our way, both practically and ethically, once we turn back to the world."[109] One of the *Return to Nevèrÿon* series' goals, therefore, is to interrogate and denaturalize the assumption of causal relationship between the sexual and social.

Small Sarg's increasing discomfort with his relationship[s] with Gorgik, as well as Raven's amusement and Norema's skepticism toward it, plus Gorgik's rape of the enslaved Noyeed in the obsidian mines, raise questions—and shows Delany raising questions—about the degree to which social structures are transformed in a sexual context. Even as a radically contextual sign, does the slave collar ever free itself from the contamination of the history of slavery? Does a residue of slavery remain attached to the collar even after the context has shifted? Does any of that history remain untransformed? If so, does it problematize the playful sexual performance of relations of dominance and submission, especially for people in whose lives a history of slavery and of social, political, and economic submission loom horrifically large, such as Sarg or Americans of African descent? Answers to such questions must be multiple and complex, and Delany raises them further and more forcefully in later works such as *The Mad Man*.

In *Tales of Nevèrÿon* and *Neveryóna* a semiotic analysis of the slave collar enables Gorgik's sexual behavior to coexist with his political mission. However, in the series' fourth and final volume, eponymously entitled *Return to Nevèrÿon*, it is revealed that such an analysis inspired his campaign against slavery in the first place. In *Neveryóna*, Gorgik realizes that for some, as Sarg came to be, the collar operates in only one context: "For Sarg, the collar *was* social oppression, as well as all asocial freedom," he tells Pryn, "Nothing in our lives, save my anger, challenged that meaning for him. And my anger was a lover's anger, which too often feels to the loved one as oppressive as a parent's" (*Neveryóna* 186). But whereas Sarg became unwilling to shift the collar contextually, Nevèrÿon's slaves were generally unable to do so. This is the specific situation Gorgik's campaign seeks to redress. In *Return*'s "The Game of Time and Pain," slavery has been abolished for six years, and Gorgik is now a state minister of ten years who stops on the way to Lord Krodar's funeral at Aldamir's castle. The castle is deserted but not empty; it houses a bearded barbarian teenager named Udrog, who, upon seeing Gorgik's collar, wants to have sex with him. Gorgik is willing to comply, but he ultimately does more talking than fornicating, to Udrog's disappointment. The Liberator tells Udrog the story of an encounter he had with Nevèrÿon's aristocracy that shaped his destiny and that of the Empire. In this tale, which dates from his life as a slave in the obsidian mines, Gorgik is one of seven slaves selected to perform lethal entertainment for a caravan of eastward-traveling nobles: Lord Anuron, Count Jeu-Forsi, the Lesser Lady Esulla and an anonymous, but very tall, lord. It becomes evident to Gorgik that Anuron and Jeu-Forsi are competing for Esulla's attention and affection, and that he and the other slaves have a part to play in that competition. During his labors Gorgik sees Jeu-Forsi drunkenly coercing a barbarian slave named Namyuk into allowing the Count to fondle the slave's penis while he exclaims "I just don't understand why all of you have such *big* ones—even those of you who weren't born to servitude" (*Return* 39). Namyuk silently endures the Count's pawing, which Gorgik initially finds amusing: "So, this was the noble sot who was wooing the mysterious Lesser Lady" (*Return* 40). This molestation combines with another incident to illustrate to Gorgik the degree of power nobles held over the slaves. In an attempt to impress Esulla, Anuron challenges a large slave named Vrach to hand-to-hand combat, vowing to set Vrach free if the slave wins. Vrach and the other slaves are horrified at the challenge because they understand that for a slave to raise his hand against a lord means certain death. While Vrach stands stunned at the challenge itself, Anuron attacks him. The caravan guards cheer the battle on, but Gorgik and the other slaves watch in horror as Vrach holds back and Anuron proceeds to pummel him mercilessly: "[Anuron] barreled forward. What he did next was to bring his knee up, hard, between Vrach's legs and, at the same time, bring both fists down, like dropped rocks, on Vrach's shoulders" (*Return* 45). Vrach's injuries lead to his slow and painful death, and Gorgik realizes that his life and those of his fellows slaves are subject to the whims of the aristocracy:

'. . . [T]hese nobles were free, free to do anything, anything to us. They were free to summon us or send us away. They were free to speak to us as equals one moment, and free to call us disgusting fools the next. They were free to caress us in any way they wished, and free to strike or maim us in any other. They were free to promise us freedom, and free to thrust a blade in our livers as we looked up in joy.' (*Return* 44)

Anuron's violent display does nothing for Esulla, and it disgusts the tall lord, who befriends Gorgik and Namyuk and does his best to nurse Vrach back to health that night. Anuron finds the lord's habit of "talking to people in collars" (*Return* 49) a "tiresome" and "silly" effrontery to the other nobles (*Return* 50). In defiant response, the tall lord does the near-unthinkable; he removes the slaves' collars:

'He listened through Anuron's speech. Then he reached around into his cloak, brought out something that, in the torchlight, I didn't recognize—I had not seen one in over a year. He turned to Vrach, reached down for the blinking miner's neck, and inserted the metal bar into the locking mechanism that held the collar closed, twisted, then pulled open the hinged iron. With one hand again under Vrach's head, he pulled away the metal, turned forward again and, with a gesture of astonishing violence, hurled the collar in among the hangings over the pavillion's entrance. It disappeared inside with such a billowing of cloth I expected all sounds inside to cease. When they didn't, I imagined the collar itself, somehow, vanishing from the world before such power!' (*Return* 50)

Gorgik's identification of this act as a display of the tall lord's "power" proves to be apt. The lords leave Vrach in the slaves' care. When Vrach's condition worsens, Gorgik rushes for help and finds both the tall lord and the "vanished" collar:

'The tall lord stood beside his rumpled bed; he was turned a bit away, so that he did not see me. He was naked—as naked as you, Udrog, or as I. He held something, which he stared at with a fascination that, over the seconds I watched, was clear as much from his stillness as from the fragment of his expression I could see in the shadowy light. He held one of the iron collars, a semicircle of it in each fist.' (*Return* 52)

In a passage that mirrors (i.e., both resembles and differs significantly from) his voyeuristic spying on the "slave boy" in *Tales*, Gorgik watches the tall lord use the collar to enter a realm of sexual desire and feels himself drawn there with him:

'Then—and when he began the gesture I felt my body overcome with an excitement that meant I had already realized, had already recognized, had already known what you, certainly, would have known in my place—he raised the collar to his neck and closed the semicircles on it, without taking his hands away, as if afraid, once having donned it, he might not be able to doff it again. I recognized it as a sexual gesture with an intensity enough to stun me and make all my joints go weak.' (*Return* 53)

But the tall lord turns and catches Gorgik watching him, and although the two men stand before each other naked, the tall lord reacts with embarrassment and anger. Gorgik then explains that Vrach is dying, prompting the tall lord to apologize and gather himself. Before he leaves his tent, however, he decides to recollar Gorgik: "I think it's time to have these on again—for tomorrow. So they'll let you back in the mines" (*Return* 54). It is a "poor joke" (*Return* 54) that Gorgik would later repeat when taken from the obsidian mines to Myrgot's tent as noted in the "Tale" named for him, but more pertinently, the aristocrat's refastening of Gorgik's collar suddenly sends both of them into a social relation of domination and submission:

> 'And just as I had recognized the sexual in his placing of it about his own neck, I knew that, though lust still reeled in his body and still staggered in mine, this gesture was as empty of the sexual as it is possible for a human gesture to be. He was only a frightened man, recollaring a slave whom he had let, briefly and unwisely, pretend awhile to be free.' (*Return* 54)

Gorgik realizes that the power displayed in Jeu-Forsi's molestation of Namyuk, in Anuron's ruthless battering of Vrach, and in the tall lord's removal of the collar from Gorgik and its subsequent replacement, is concomitant with the power the tall lord invokes to use the slave collar for his own sexual purposes. As a slave, however, Gorgik had neither the power to remove the collar, nor the freedom to use it sexually:

> 'Now I coveted that future freedom, that further power I had witnessed in the master's tent: however vaguely, however foggily, as I drifted off to sleep, I knew I would not be content till I had seized that freedom and power for myself, even though I knew I had to seize the former for every slave in Nevèrÿon—before I could truly hold the latter.' (*Return* 55)

Thus, Gorgik the Liberator was born. Gorgik became a revolutionary who sought to attain for himself and all slaves in Nevèrÿon the power to wrest symbolic control of the slave collar from the aristocracy and the freedom to shift the significance of the collar from one context to another:

> 'What I wanted was the power to remove the collar from the necks of the oppressed, including my own. But I knew, at least for me, that the power to remove the collar was wholly involved with the freedom to place it there when I wished.' (*Return* 57)

In its very foundations, therefore, Gorgik's campaign to abolish slavery is enabled by a semiotic understanding of slavery's relations of submission and domination, relations that are exposed as artificial social roles instead of "natural" social positions when performed in a sexual context.[110]

"The Tale of Old Venn" characterizes the difference between critical analysis of the structures of the world and passive acceptance of those structures as the difference between, respectively, an adult and a child:

Childhood is that time in which we never question the fact that every adult act is not only an autonomous occurrence in the universe, but that it is also filled, packed, overflowing with meaning, whether that meaning works for ill or good, whether the ill or good is or is not comprehended.

Adulthood is that time in which we see that all human actions follow forms, whether well or badly, and it is the perseverance of the forms that is, whether for better or worse, their meaning. (*Tales* 128–29)

Interestingly, Terry Eagleton reverses this sort of characterization, portraying the child as the interrogator of the status quo and the adult as its passive supporter: "The revolutionary questioner sees the world with the astonishment of a child ['Where does capitalism come from, Mummy?'], and refuses to be fobbed off by the adults' customary Wittgensteinian justifications of their practices: 'This is just what we do, dear.'"[111] Although their analogies differ, Delany clearly values the act of questioning "reality," and sees SF—and by extension, his particular brand of semiotic sword-and-sorcery—as tools that allow the reader to see the world through the eyes of a revolutionary child. "The SF writer's overarching theme," Delany states, "is likely to be the discovery that the world itself is negotiable."[112] The series' semiotic analyses of language, commodification, cultural practices, and, most significantly, the relations of domination on which slavery has been based reveal such systems to be structured conventions as opposed to eternal truths of nature. Therefore, the *Return to Nevèrÿon* series represents, somewhat paradoxically perhaps, sword-and-sorcery dedicated to demystification.

4

THE WINDOW OF AUTOBIOGRAPHY

THE MOTION OF LIGHT IN WATER

The Negro, and especially, later, the Negro writer, has always known who he is.
—Saunders Redding, "The Problems of the Negro Writer"[1]

> A black man . . . ?
> A gay man . . . ?
> A writer . . . ?
> —Samuel R. Delany, *The Motion of Light in Water*[2]

The formal characteristics and thematic content of Samuel R. Delany's autobiography, *The Motion of Light in Water* (1988), mark it as a text that explicitly involves itself in postmodern culture. Consider, for example, the author's observation that "For a number of historians the year Marilyn [Hacker] and I entered high school, 1956, marks the transition from America's 'Industrial Period' to its 'Postindustrial Period'" (183). *Motion* provides several examples of the cultural logic made manifest in the years following that socioeconomic shift. The instability of the boundaries between "high" and "low" art and culture is implied in the autobiography's narration of Delany's dinner-party assertion that "there really was certain American popular music you could hear on any ordinary radio, which strictly from a musical point of view, was as interesting as any classical music being written in the country" (287), an argument inspired by the example of Martha and the Vandellas' "Heat Wave." Although those claims merely "produced incomprehension at the dinner table, and once it was understood, a fair amount of disbelieving laughter," Delany associates the memory with "a beginning to a period of change . . . because enough such moments followed it, in music, formal and popular, in art, on gallery walls and on comic book pages, in behavior, on the street and in private, long enough, frequently enough, and all with equal excitement, till it became undeniable that change was actually occurring"

(287). An example of that change in the world of visual arts is in *Motion*'s anecdote about a "happening," in which Delany takes his cousin Boyd, a medical student, to see Allan Kaprow's *Eighteen Happenings in Six Parts* in New York City's East Village during the summer of 1960. In *Modern/Postmodern,* art historian Silvio Gaggi identifies the "happening" as a forerunner to what is now commonly called "performance art," which often combines the visual arts (painting, sculpture) and performing arts (theater, dance).[3] *Motion* describes Kaprow's *Happenings* as "about as characteristic a work as one might choose in which to experience the clash that begins our reading" of what Delany calls "the hugely arbitrary postmodern" (190). Delany and Boyd go to a Cooper Union apartment where polyethylene walls divide the space into six chambers. Several female assistants walk about and one male assistant runs the overhead lighting while Kaprow himself observes from the periphery. At Boyd's behest, Delany stays with his cousin in one chamber. Delany describes an assistant entering to set up a small wind-up toy "which ran down faster than was expected, and so had to be wound up and set going again, several times, through the twenty minutes or so of the work's duration" (186). Delany and Boyd do not know what takes place in the other chambers, but the sounds of laughter and a tambourine come through the walls as inanimate objects such as a dish of water and a ball of string are carried through their chamber. Another assistant mistakenly enters with yet another toy and quickly leaves. When one of the female assistants signals the end of the show, the audience thinks that she is just another part of the performance, and Kaprow himself has to get up to tell people to go home. Delany admits to being perplexed as to the work's organizational principles: "I, of course, had expected the 'six parts' to be chronologically successive, like acts in a play or parts in a novel—not spatially deployed, separate, and simultaneous, like rooms in a hotel or galleries in a museum" (188–89). He later realizes that the performance is purposefully engaged in a "subversion of expectations about the 'proper' aesthetic employment of time, space, presence, absence, wholeness, and fragmentation" (189), a technique similar to that which Delany has applied in his own works, most notably *Dhalgren* and, to a certain extent, *Motion* itself. Boyd's response to Kaprow's *Happenings* appears to be equal parts confusion and annoyance. "Did you understand that?" he asks; "I mean could you explain to me what that was supposed to be about?" (187). Delany replies, "you're just supposed to experience it" (186), and then, in order to extract himself from what he interprets as "the embarrassment—or the superiority [i.e., Boyd's]—prompting [his] cousin's question," he turns to a—presumably—white woman nearby and says "That was kind of fun" (187), which triggers an exchange that demonstrates racialized assumptions about how such a work as Kaprow's would be received:

"Oh," she said, "did you think so? How did you come here?"

"I saw it advertised on a poster taped up on the side of a mailbox. It sounded interesting. So we just came by."

"You did?" she asked, a bit incredulously. I'd already noted that Boyd and I were probably the only two black people in the audience. Today I also suspect we were two of the very few there that evening unknown to the others, at least by sight. "You liked it?" And she smiled. "How unusual."

This was, remember, 1960. (187)

Motion's narration of Delany's experience at Kaprow's *Happenings* is multiply emblematic: the woman's surprise at the fact that—whom she, at least, has no trouble determining are—two black men could be interested in the performance and even find it entertaining, or at least worth puzzling over, represents a perceived gap between discussions of postmodernism and African American life and culture. And Delany and Boyd's reactions to the happening are equally significant. Although Delany found it "kind of fun," Kaprow's piece either had nothing to offer Boyd or failed to subvert any preconceptions about art he may have brought to the performance. The story of Kaprow's *Happenings,* then, efficiently represents an African American ambivalence toward the postmodern in a cultural context.

A black ambivalence toward the social and political meanings of "postmodernism" is articulated in the essay "Postmodern Blackness" by bell hooks, whose "suspicion" toward the subject causes her to consider claims that "this stuff [i.e., postmodernism] does not relate in any way to what's happening with black people."[4] However, hooks also responds to presumptions similar to those of the white woman at the *Happenings:* "The idea that there is no meaningful connection between black experience and critical thinking about aesthetics or culture," hooks says, "must be continually interrogated."[5] Ross Posnock, citing hooks's statement in *Color and Culture,* contends that the blame for the cultural "segregation" that hooks critiques lies with "postmodern identity politics," a "contemporary reductionism [that] incarnates the logic of an older one known as cultural pluralism."[6] When read within the context of the rest of her essay, however, hooks's general assertion can more accurately be seen as a validation of postmodern conceptions of "identity." The essay argues for an inter- and intraracial politics of difference, declaring that people of African descent "have too long had imposed upon us from both the outside and the inside a narrow, constricting notion of blackness." It engages in a critique of racial essentialism that "allows us to affirm multiple black identities, varied black experience" and challenges "colonial imperialist paradigms of black identity which represent blackness one-dimensionally in ways that reinforce and sustain white supremacy." Although hooks ultimately, and appropriately, dismisses claims that the "postmodern" critique of identity is necessarily counterproductive to the ongoing struggle for racial justice and equality, she takes such claims very seriously, so much so that she opens the essay by describing an occasion of her own articulation of them. "We cannot cavalierly dismiss a concern with identity politics," she wisely states, adding, "it never surprises me when black folks respond to the critique of essentialism, especially when it denies the validity of identity politics by saying, 'Yeah, it's easy to give up an identity, when you got one.'"[7] The achievement of an identity, a sense of self one can take pride in and organize around, has been a goal toward which people of African descent have struggled for the entirety of our history in America; it has been a social and political necessity. Saunders Redding argues that black writers have been faced less with a "problem of identity" than with the problem of whether to identify with American culture and society or whether American society will identify with them. African American writers have always known who they are because they have been subjected to what he calls "the fantasy construct of the slave," an identity that was "imposed upon the Negro—with all its shame-inducing particulars: shiftlessness, stupidity, bestiality, and so forth—to relieve the conscience of those who had enslaved him," an imposed identity that did not disappear with emancipation, nor, we might add, with the Civil Rights Movement. Thus, according to Redding, African American literature has served as a refutation of this fantasy construct and as an "exaltation of the Negro self." Black writing that "glor[ies in] and sometimes glorifies Negro identity" has been a common feature of the African American literary tradition.[8]

In recent years however, "the politics of representation in black culture" have been in a process of transformation. Stuart Hall explains that this change is evidence of encounters between black culture and critical theory—"post-structuralism, post-modernism, psychoanalysis, and feminism" as well as "'the end of innocence,' or the end of the innocent notion of the essential black subject." This end of innocence involves an understanding of "race" as a concept whose meanings are political and cultural, but have no natural reality. "'Black' is essentially a politically and culturally *constructed* category," Hall explains, "which cannot be grounded in a set of fixed transcultural or transcendental racial categories and which has no guarantees in nature."[9] It also involves the acknowledgment that "blackness" has its limits in terms of what it tells us of the political valences of the text in which it is articulated. Just because a cultural text is produced by a black person or deals with "the black experience" does not make it "good" politically; its class, gender, and sexual politics (for starters) must be evaluated as well. And mere reversals of racist binary oppositions in which black = good/white = bad are no longer persuasive. "The notion of essential forms of identity," Hall states, "is no longer tenable."[10] The "end of innocence," therefore, radically destabilizes previous conceptions of what it means to be black, and therefore "may seem to threaten the collapse of an entire political world."[11]

In African American literary criticism, the perception of a potential threat behind the move to understand "blackness" as a semiotic sign and/ or "identity" as a product of language has informed responses against critical theory by some prominent African American intellectuals. Perhaps best-known are those of Joyce Ann Joyce, published as part of what was entitled—with some understatement—"A Discussion" with Henry Louis Gates Jr. and Houston A. Baker in a 1987 issue of *New Literary History*. Responding to the literary criticism of Gates and Baker, Joyce makes a number of statements about the threat that poststructuralist "emphases on fragmentation, plurality of meaning, selflessness, and indeterminacy" pose to black identity.[12] "It is insidious for the Black literary critic to adopt any kind of strategy that diminishes or in this case— through an allusion to binary oppositions—negates his blackness. . . . The 'poststructuralist sensibility' does not aptly apply to Black American literature."[13] Joyce continues, "I do not understand how a Black critic aware of the implications of racist structures in the consciousness of Blacks and whites could accept poststructuralist ideas and practices."[14] Diana Fuss accurately captures the thrust of Joyce's argument and others like it: "Joyce holds the opinion that for Gates, Baker, or any other Afro-American critic to deconstruct 'race' as a dominant conceptual category amounts to turning their backs on Afro-American culture, denying not merely their literary tradition but their very identity as black. . . . to deconstruct 'race' is to abdicate, negate, or destroy black identity."[15]

With all of the preceding in mind, then, what does it mean to call *The Motion of Light in Water* a postmodern African American autobiography? Is such a designation a blessing or a curse? Does the convergence of postmodernism and the African American autobiographical tradition that the text represents produce insights as to the operations within and mobilization of black identity, or is it merely disruptive of an African American sense of self? As vital throughout history as the cultural responses such as those that Redding describes have been to confronting and overcoming race-based social, political, and economic oppression in America, understanding identity as a construct dependent on and operating as a language problematizes the project of pitting one identity formation against another. Delany articulates such an understanding when he explains his own difficulty with "constructing something so rigid as an identity, an identity in which there has to be a fixed and immobile core, a core that is structured to hold inviolate such a complete biological fantasy as race—whether white or black."[16] Delany provides a sound critique of "identity" and "race" here, and it is on the basis of such statements that he has been characterized by Posnock as one of the most recent participants in a supposed tradition of "cosmopolitan" African American *anti-race race men*" and as a "skeptic of identity politics."[17] Posnock reads *Motion* as a text that bypasses what he sees as a limiting preoccupation with identity politics, particularly those based on race.

What neither criticisms like Joyce's nor readings such as Posnock's adequately acknowledge, however, is that, as Fuss makes clear, "the deconstruction of identity . . . is not necessarily a *disavowal* of identity."[18] And this is the reality that *Motion* ultimately demonstrates; it neither essentializes nor annihilates identity, whether racial, sexual, or otherwise. Consider, for example, *Motion*'s insights on Delany's dyslexia that went undiagnosed as a child, causing his teachers "to consider the possibility that [he] might be deeply disturbed" (331), as well as his own embarrassment and frustration. This condition, however, prompted a tutor to tell Delany's parents, that "he must write and write and write—as much as he can. Eventually he will improve" (331), a suggestion that contributed to the author's childhood love for, and near-nonstop practice of, writing—across genres—as well as his cultivation of techniques for managing spelling and handwriting errors. Delany himself does not even have a word for his condition until after marrying Marilyn Hacker, who inquires about it; according to *Motion,* as with "black" and "gay," the word "dyslexic" and the identity it signified did not yet exist popularly in the early 1960s (364). During his stay at Mt. Sinai's Day/Night Center, Delany meditates on a dialectics of dyslexia, on the liberation and limitations concomitant with this new word and its identity:

> What would have been the differences in me, I wondered, there in the hospital, if I'd grown up thinking of myself as having a learning disability from the beginning? Would I have become a writer? Would I have become a science fiction writer?
> What might the word have given me?
> What might it have taken away? (332)

That "dyslexic," as identity formation, can *both* give and take away—though not necessarily to equal degrees or in symmetrical patterns—is key here. "Identity is about binding," Cornel West explains, "and it means, on the one hand, that you can be bound—parochialist, narrow, xenophobic. But it also means that you can be held together in the face of the terrors of nature, the cruelties of fate, and the need for some compensation for unjustified suffering."[19] This dual vision of identity—as a discourse to be problematized, exploded, refracted, as well as a commonality that makes politics possible and life bearable and pleasurable—

is sustained in *Motion*. Delany's autobiography challenges and revises the notion of black identity by asserting difference within blackness, but it does not shatter identity—racial or otherwise—into meaningless fragments as much as it acknowledges identity's myriad facets. Through its title image, the autobiography offers a figure for both the distinctiveness of these different narratives of identity as well as their connectedness, a figure that substitutes permeability for rigidity. Like Donna Haraway's "Cyborg Manifesto," then, *Motion* operates as both "an argument for *pleasure* in the confusion of boundaries and for *responsibility* in their construction."[20]

Life "Sentences"

Stuart Hall's "Ethnicity: Identity and Difference" provides useful insights on the impact of poststructuralist critical theory, and what he identifies as "the postmodern condition," on the concept of "identity." "Identity is a narrative of the self," Hall states, "It's the story we tell about the self in order to know who we are."[21] By calling identity a "narrative" and a "story," Hall suggests that any identity is always mediated through language. It is this view, which sees identity as—to borrow Diana Fuss's formulation—"an effect not of essence, but of language,"[22] that I wish to pursue here. As, to reinterpret the Greek roots of the term, the "life" of the "self" in the form of "writing," an autobiography represents the rendering of its author's identity in language. In a sense, "postmodern autobiography" doubly asserts the construction of identity through language. Despite its generic status as "nonfiction," Delany's autobiography, like any autobiography, is as much a narrative construct as a work of fiction is shaped according to the motives, both aesthetic and personal, of the author; in a very real sense it is a fiction of identity.

SF author Thomas Disch calls *Motion*'s fiction of identity "self-mythologization"; commenting on the book's "cool-to-mellow" tone (surprising, perhaps, for the autobiography of a gay, black man living in a homophobic, racist society), Disch wonders, "isn't it the stuff legends are made of?" Disch sees *Motion* as a creative act of self-celebration and self-invention: "Chip [Delany's nickname] can't help creating legends and elaborating myths. Indeed, it's his forté, the open secret of his success as an SF writer." Therefore, he contends, Delany is perfectly suited to the autobiographical task, adding that "self-mythologization is what memoirs are about."[23] There is much in *Motion* to support these claims. Citing Oscar Wilde's witticism that "the only true talent is precocity" (71), Delany tells his readers just how precocious he was as a youth. At the beginning of his career at the Bronx High School of Science, "a city public school . . . of megacephalic reputation" (51), Delany is already reading the novels of Faulkner and Camus and starting to write his own. During his high school years, he spends summers at the Breadloaf Writers' Conferences, working with writers such as X. J. Kennedy, John Ciardi, and Robert Frost. He publishes his first novel, *The Jewels of Aptor,* at age 20, and completes the first volume of *The Fall of the Towers* series soon after. As Delany develops as an artist and an intellectual, a concomitant sexual precocity manifests itself. Although he claims to be concerned that *Motion* might be "mistaken for an elaboration of endless and unmitigated [sexual] prowess" (422), it is all too easy to, indeed, "mistake" the book in this way. According to the autobiography, Delany's forays into "anonymous" gay sex began in Autumn of 1960 at age 18; in the following four years he had had hundreds of such encounters. Apparently, from time to time, several women found him attractive as well. At the end of his description of the events leading up to and during his marriage to Marilyn Hacker, Delany feels compelled to share with his readers an admission of desire from one of Hacker's two closest friends: "When you were 17, 18, you were simply a dish. You were smart. And you were nice. We knew you were queer . . . but what did that mean back then? When we were 17, the three of us used to spend hours talking about how we were going to get you into bed. Marilyn just won" (104). Delany apparently inspired a folksinger named Ana to make a sexual proposition to him and Hacker, and to drop by later when Hacker was out of town for "a return engagement" (242). When Ana's boyfriend turns up looking for her at Delany's apartment while they are having sex, he answers the door naked and evades inquiries by pretending that he has a male lover waiting for him in the bedroom. Delany expresses no anxiety about describing this event but expresses a felt difficulty over telling the story of a heterosexual couple that stops by for dinner and to inquire about the sexual details of Delany and Hacker's relationship with a wanderer named Bob Folsom, a relationship that influenced the representations of the triadic relationship of Kid, Lanya, and Denny in *Dhalgren* and of the starship pilots in Delany's Nebula Award–winning novel *Babel-17* (1966). (The novel is dedicated to "Bob, to explain just a little of the past year," and its protagonist is Rydra Wong, a poet who was once in a three-way relationship with "Fobo Lombs" and the science fiction author from *Empire Star* "Muels Aranlyde," men whose names are anagrams of those of Hacker's lovers.) Gradually, Hacker, Bob, and the reader realize that this conspicuously libidinous couple are interested not in an orgy but in a threesome, with Delany specifically. Delany agrees to this encounter, "to assuage their curiosity—and [his own]," but concludes, "I don't think of [that encounter] as sexually very successful" (421) and announces his ambivalences about transcribing this particular encounter: "Of all the incidents and anecdotes that remain with me from the time the three of us [Delany, Hacker, and Folsom] spent together, this is the hardest to write" (419). This willingness to explore sexual experiences, those pleasurable as well as those not "successful," is demonstrated throughout the book. Although Delany later justifies *Motion*'s straightforward description of his sexual experiences as part of a specific political project, the thorough, cool, and candid delivery of those descriptions invests his persona with an experienced, worldly, "legendary," quality.

Perhaps nothing cultivates the image of Delany as a SF legend as much as his acquaintances with other cultural legends. *Motion* portrays a man who was acquainted with musician José Feliciano, spent a morning in his high school's detention office with Black Power activist-to-be Stokely Carmichael, served W. H. Auden and Chester Kallman a shrimp curry dinner, and once, as a child, sailed a model boat with Albert Einstein. One of the more amusing stories of this sort is about one of Delany's musical performances at his friend Billy's café. For a short period in his life, Delany was earning his living mostly by playing folk music. His chosen mode of expression—folk, as opposed to, say, blues or jazz—might signal a "universalist" detachment from race-specific cultural traditions, that is, until the contributions of artists such as Odetta and Richie Havens, for starters, as well as folk music's own roots in the blues and spirituals are acknowledged. Delany describes the placard that announces his show with an "aw, shucks" modesty that is immediately displaced when he explains how Billy "squatted in front of the placard and, with two bits of scotch tape, below [Delany's] grandly lettered name, added the piece of paper on which, from maybe three feet away, you could make out: AND BOB DYLAN" (273). Soon after, Dylan enters and immediately starts playing so as to keep another appointment. Billy interrupts, an argument ensues, and Dylan storms out. This incident occurred before Dylan emerged as a major figure in the music world, but it is exactly the type of story that contributes to Delany's legend.

What keeps such stories from reading as pompous self-aggrandizement is Delany's conspicuously self-conscious approach to autobiography. Like *Dhalgren, Motion*'s "Sentences: An Introduction" addresses contending narratives of the "true" and the "real." In an autobiographical context, however, the "true" and the "real" manifest themselves as memory and fact, respectively. Delany reserves the right to base *Motion* on what he feels is the "truth" of events as he remembers them despite its disjunctions with historical, verifiable, "real," facts. "Sentences" begins with the midautumn death of Delany's father, with whom the writer had a troubled relationship. It is not surprising that this event looms in the background throughout the rest of the book and becomes one of the narrative's chief points of reference. The introduction describes Delany's father spending his final days at home, "listening to programs of eclectic classical music (Penderecki, Kodaly's *Sonata for Unaccompanied Cello*) on WBAI-FM" (3). "For most of my life, if it came up," Delany says, "I would tell you: 'My father died of lung cancer in 1958 when I was seventeen.'" (4). One would expect Delany to remember clearly the date of his own father's death; however in 1978, Robert Bravard and Michael Peplow, Delany's bibliographers at Lock Haven State College, explained to Delany that if he was born on April Fool's Day in 1942, he would have been *sixteen* in October of 1958. "Certainly my father didn't die when I was fifteen or sixteen . . . ?" (6), Delany wonders. Peplow and Bravard also revealed that the music Delany remembered his father enjoying was not available in 1958 and that WBAI did not go on the air until 1960. An old newspaper article ultimately shows that Delany's father died in 1960, when Delany was eighteen years old. This incongruity between historical fact and memory prompts Delany to close "Sentences" with an eloquent vindication of the narrative of his father's death that the author remembers:

> But bear in mind two sentences:
> "My father died of lung cancer in 1958 when I was seventeen."
> "My father died of lung cancer in 1960 when I was eighteen."
> The first is incorrect, the second correct.
>
> I am as concerned with truth as anyone—otherwise I would not be going so far to split such hairs. In no way do I feel the incorrect sentence is privileged over the correct one. Yet, even with what I know now, a decade after the letter from Pennsylvania, the wrong sentence still *feels* to me righter than the right one.
>
> Now a biography or a memoir that contained only the first sentence would *be* incorrect. But one that omitted it, or did not at least suggest its relation to the second on several informal levels, would be incomplete. (15)

Delany is not scrambling to cover up his own inaccuracies here; rather, he is making an important point about memory's role in autobiography. In grappling with the difference between the "true" narrative of memory represented in one sentence and the "real," factual, narrative represented in the other, Delany is managing what Roy Pascal identifies as the autobiographer's chief dilemma, "the conflict between the two truths" of fact and feeling.[24] The difference between the two sentences has ramifications for how Delany interprets the events that follow his father's death. After noting the discovery of the correct date of death, Delany reconstructs "a pretty accurate chronology" of his life from the summer before October 1960 until Autumn of 1961. The chronology's entries include Delany's high school graduation, the Newport Folk Festival, the Breadloaf Writers' Conference, September classes at the College of the City of New York, moving in with his friend Bob, translating Brecht, an affectionate sexual encounter with a college companion, directing a play, meeting SF author Judith Merril, dropping out of college, writing an article on jazz for *Seventeen* magazine, and marrying poet Marilyn Hacker. A second tragedy then erupts within his life: "in October, almost a exactly a year after [Delany's] father's death, Marilyn miscarried" (12). About a week later Delany started what would be his first published novel, *The Jewels of Aptor* (1962). Delany realizes that this chronology appears to present "a fairly clear emotional story":

> My father's death, my subsequent dropping out of school, and my hasty marriage speak of a young man interested in writing and music, but still under fair emotional strain. With the facts that I was black and Marilyn was white, that I was gay and both of us knew it, the implication of strain— for both of us—only strengthens. (12–13)

Delany explains, however, that this is not necessarily the story that he remembers. Although the chronology contains events that feature "the texture of the real" for him, its coordination of those events "are wholly a product of research" (13), not of his memory. He does not deny the pressures that inhere in his particular racial and sexual subject positions; rather, the narrative his memory composes does not foreground those factors. The point Delany is making is less about a disinterest in identity politics than the malleability and factual fallibility of memory. Delany's earlier "incorrect" sentence is "an emblem of the displacements and elisions committed upon [the chronology's] more objective narrative" (13). He states that despite vivid memories of his first few classes at City College one month before his father died, "there's no connection between those memories and those of [his] father's death in [his] mind" (13). Delany has equally vivid memories of Hacker's miscarriage and the composition of *The Jewels of Aptor.* "Still," he claims, "I have no sense that the book began within the month or so of the miscarriage: only the chronology tells me that. In memory, the two seem months, many months, from one another" (14). Delany cannot ignore the temporal relationship between either his father's death or Hacker's miscarriage and later developments in his career. Nor can he evade the very real possibility that each tragedy was a shaping force on the rest of his life. However, he simply does not remember these tragedies coloring his life's later events in such a fashion. As such, *Motion* presents a narrative that does not conform to the shape a reader my expect from the facts listed in the chronology alone.

"Sentences" also provides a list of Delany's favorite autobiographical works, including Frederick Douglass's *Narrative of the Life of an Ameri-*

can Slave and Roland Barthes's *Barthes* (14). Claiming these works as models, Delany continues to state what can be taken as *Motion*'s *ars poetica*:

> The autobiographer cannot replace the formal biographer. Nor am I even going to try. I hope instead to sketch, as honestly and as effectively as I can, something I can recognize as my own, aware as I do so that even as I work after honesty and accuracy, memory will make this only one possible fiction among the myriad—many in open conflict—anyone might write of any of us, as convinced as any other that what he or she wrote was the truth. (14)

Delany does not subscribe to what Pascal calls the "naive notion" of early writers such as Rousseau or Gibbon, who cited an internal "chain of feeling" which justified the memory-based content of their autobiographies; rather, he articulates a more "skeptical" outlook that is aware that one's self-knowledge may be incomplete or illusory. On the other hand, Delany's pledge to "work after honesty and accuracy," at least momentarily, works against his efforts to validate his memory's narratives; as Pascal notes, all an autobiography has to do to call its veracity into question is to claim veracity as its goal. Delany's insistence on the narrative of his life that his memory provides is ultimately justifiable, however. Pascal argues that memory is a valid basis for one's life story because autobiography is as creative, is as much a product of artifice, as an act as fiction; it "is not just reconstruction of the past, but interpretation." Facts do not make an autobiography until, and/or unless, they are filtered through the autobiographer's consciousness. Pascal describes memory as performing a "sifting process . . . shaping the past according to the will of the writer," and he concludes that although "truth" is of great importance in autobiography, "we have to define what sort of truth is meant, and this we can discover only in relation to the author's general intention."[25] Delany's stated attempt to create what he calls a "narrative he can recognize as his own" suggests a desire to liberate himself and the meaning of his life from the burdensome memories of his father's death and Hacker's miscarriage. In order to make its points about identity—public and private, racial and sexual—*Motion* must free itself from the narrative generated by the chronology, subverting the expectation that those events will operate as the central organizing force in the autobiography.

As Pascal suggests, the ever-present tension between fact and feeling has always been part of the autobiographer's dilemma. What distinguishes *Motion* as a "postmodern" autobiography is that it conspicuously and repeatedly grapples with this dilemma. For example, *Motion* tells the story of how a young Delany reads an essay by his older cousin Nanny that was published in *Dynamo,* the Bronx High School of Science literary magazine. Nanny's essay describes her discovery of the corpse of a beautiful woman in the funeral parlor run by Delany's father, who is described as a *"tall, mild-mannered, and quite the opposite of Scrooge or any stereotyped mortician"* (51). "How could she have described my father as 'mild-mannered?'" Delany wonders; "To me he had always been an angry, anxious man. Perhaps, I thought, because he might read it, she'd had to say something nice" (52). However, Delany also notices that Nanny's description of the layout of the building "committed a fundamental distortion of the architecture" (52). He claims that "you would have to have been at least nine or even ten feet tall to stand on the bottom step and lean forward far enough to see around the jamb and through the door into the other room" (53). And whereas Nanny's story was of finding "a beautiful brown-skinned young woman with a rose in her hair, lying in one of the satin-lined caskets" (53) the young Delany remembered a similar discovery of his own involving the naked corpse of a young black man on the embalming table whose hand he held, thereby triggering an erection. "Surely somewhere a reality lay behind Nanny's account—an account that, indeed, presented itself as real," Delany concludes, "But whatever that reality was, it had been sealed outside of, and by, the text. . . . Whatever had actually happened was held, in some other time and place, safely outside any language that I could bring myself to initiate, or that anyone else even thought to" (53). This disjunction between Nanny's narrative, Delany's own, and what he at that moment understood as an objective "reality" teaches Delany "the power of writing": "To hold sway over memory, making it public, keeping it private, possibly, even, keeping it secret from oneself" (53). Delany concludes that Nanny may have felt about her "distortion of the architecture" the same as he does about his "incorrect" sentence about his father's death (53).

An uncritical obedience to "the facts" can not only impede a rhetorical goal, but also conflict with a text's aesthetics. *Motion* cites Hacker's poem "Nights of 1962: The River Merchant's Wife," which reflects on her life with Delany after they had settled down in their East Village apartment:

From Avenue C west to Sixth Avenue
and Eighth Street, I'd aim for the all-night Whelan's,
eat solo ham and eggs. The night sky paled, sands
into the river's timer. One more day:
jeans switched for dark dress, tight shoes; the subway
to work at Altman's. Five months short of twenty,
I knocked back whatever the river sent. He
was gone two days: might bring back, on the third

some kind of night music I'd never heard:
Sonny the burglar, paunched with breakfast beers;
olive-skinned Simon, who made fake Vermeers;
the card-sharp who worked clubcars down the coast . . . (213)

Delany, however, remembers some of the poem's details differently: "Does it matter that it was Shirley who made the 'Vermeers,' not Simon? Or that it was Bigelow's half a block north, with its all-night breakfast counter—not Whelan's (which served no food)? Or that I have no memory at all of the card-sharp I might have brought home?" (214). But "Bigelow's," of course, does not rhyme with "sands" as "Whelan's" does. "Are these matters of meter or memory," Delany wonders, "and what is their intricate connection?" (214). Ultimately he concludes that despite the apparent disjunction in memory, the poem bears its own truth: "Such points do not matter for the poem. I have no problem recognizing it" (214).

Motion in general, and "Sentences" in particular, display what Larry McCaffery calls "the postmodern emphasis on subjectivity, language, and fiction (or narrative)-making."[26] Despite its generic status as nonfiction, the autobiography acknowledges its own artifice, its constructedness. *Motion*'s ambivalence toward mimesis as an aesthetic goal, as well as its self-consciousness regarding its own comfort with the often "incorrect" narrative of memory as an alternative, are, like some of the text's other formal traits, recognizable as characteristics of postmodern literature. Like Kaprow's *Eighteen Happenings in Six Parts*, *Motion*'s surface suggests a linear structure, dividing the text into sixty-one numbered sections, many of which are further subdivided into discrete events and passages (39.1, 39.2, 39.3, etc.). Like Kaprow's *Happenings*, however, *Motion* subverts expectations about its use of space and time. The events of Delany's life are not presented in a straight linear chronological progression from childhood to adult. *Motion* begins in 1961, with Delany and Hacker as newlyweds, and moves forward through time. When Delany starts to reflect upon why he and Hacker married, he finds himself pondering over their respective identities:

> But who were we, this Jew from the Bronx, this black from Harlem?
> In many ways, neither of us was typical of the image the preceding sentence evokes—yet the truth it tells, under its bipartite interrogation, is necessary for any understanding. (30)

Although the second paragraph may, as Posnock states, "mock" the "bipartite interrogation" of the first,[27] it does not mean that racial and identity politics do not play a role in the story of Hacker and Delany's relationship. This passage also triggers the narrative's temporal redoubling on itself, going back in time to when Delany was a child in order to begin to answer these questions. The narrative then progresses forward until it catches up with Delany's life as a young man in the East Village.

In postmodern fashion, characteristic for Delany, *Motion* confounds generic boundaries, operating in a number of rhetorical modes simultaneously. Arguments could be made for labeling it autobiography, critical theory, erotica, or perhaps most accurately, all of these. In "The Law of Genre" Jacques Derrida problematizes the very notion of genre by arguing that the mark of a text's participation in a specific genre does not itself belong in that genre. Moreover "a text would not *belong* to any genre," Derrida states; "every text *participates* in one or several genres, there is no genreless text, there is always a genre and genres, yet such a participation never amounts to belonging."[28] This hypothesis would seem to apply to *Motion;* however, it is important to understand Delany's text specifically, even if only provisionally, as "autobiography" in order to more substantively connect it to a larger tradition of African American autobiographical writing and thereby bring to bear upon it a critical discussion on the interplay of memory, desire, and identity. Pascal identifies six types of autobiography: the autobiography of childhood, the acquisition of an outlook, the story of a calling, the autobiography of the poet, "man in all the truth of nature," and the autobiographical novel. Although *Motion* initially appears to fall into the category of the story of the life of a "poet," Pascal's term for "all imaginative writers," I want to argue that *Motion* is rather the story of "the acquisition of an outlook," which Pascal identifies as "that class of autobiography where the author's range of interest and relevance is defined not only by the actual form of his life but also consciously, deliberately, by the formulation of a philosophy."[29] To this end, *Motion* presents the theorization of a postmodern perspective on identity in general and on black identity in particular while it dramatizes Delany's education in what political identity means. The autobiography's theoretical underpinnings inform, and are informed by, its key aesthetic features: the formal structure of the autobiography and the shimmering image presented in its title.

Alternate Realities

In his introduction to *Dhalgren,* Jean Mark Gawron explains that the novel's critics were interested in reading the multifaceted novel as a single unified narrative and against a single set of expectations. But "all the phenomena of Bellona can not be encompassed in a single system," he writes, "there must be different fictive levels, fictions within fictions without end."[30] Similarly, *Motion* refuses to privilege a single narrative of its author's life. Instead of presenting a unified narrative told from one perspective, Delany asks his readers to imagine the story of his life as being told in two distinct, parallel columns of text. Since age five, Delany claims, his dyslexia has enabled him to "take any comic book page, any book illustration, any column of print—even without knowing what it said—and double it" (327). Posnock is correct when he characterizes Delany as a writer who "not merely accept[s] but relish[es] the poetics of division and 'double consciousness' that in earlier figures reflected ambivalences and conflict."[31] Delany has construed this doubling phenomenon as a "wonderful ability" (327) that he attempts to cultivate conceptually among his readers. The "second column" is invoked early in the autobiography after Delany interrupts descriptions of childhood summers spent productively and pleasantly at Camp Woodland to describe three specific psychological and physiological phenomena that he experienced during the same time of his life: the sensation of a sudden recession, as if "observing the stairwell or the backyard or the street through a hollow tube from a paper roll," convulsions strong enough to "shock" Delany awake and shake him out of bed, and a "heart-pounding panic" at the thought of the inevitability of his own death (43, 44). Delany explicitly asks the reader to envision the narration of these unusual occurrences, along with those of other regularly repeating physiological events, as occupying a second column, apart from his narrative of summer camp:

> [C]onsider these three things inscribed again and again, page by page, in a second column of type that doubles the one that makes up this book, a parallel column devoted only to those elements that are repeated and repeated throughout any day, any life, incidents that constitute at once the basal and quotidian—waking up, breakfast, lunch, dinner, washing, elimination, drifting off to sleep—as well as the endlessly repeated risings and fallings of desire. (45)

Although Delany has distinguished the sequence of physiological phenomena comprising this second column from the narrative of other events of his life that *Motion* provides, it is particularly important to him that the reader understand the temporal proximity of the events in the two columns:

> There is almost nothing I will write of—or have written of—here that is more than four minutes or four hours (and certainly no more than fourteen) from one or, often, all three. (45)

The relationship between the two columns of narrative is even more important in *Motion*'s next chapter, in which Delany describes his entry into the Bronx High School of Science. This moment is full of transitions: from Harlem to the Bronx, and from elementary school to high school, for example. Envisioning himself as "Someone Who Could Make Friends Easily" (59), Delany proceeds to do just that. Chapter 6 tells the story of becoming friends with two other teenagers, Chuck and Danny. Delany had another close friend at Science named Joe, but as he introduces the story of this friendship he assigns it to a second, parallel column:

> One other friendship I must speak about formed in that same time. Elements of it coalesced during the same minutes as those I've already written of. It was probably more important, at least to me as a writer, than those with Chuck or Danny. Reviewing it, however, what strikes me is how quickly the written narrative closes it out—puts it outside of language. Reading over what I've already written of that first day, searching for a margin in which to inscribe it, within and round what's already written, I suspect it might well be printed in a column parallel with the above, rather than as a consecutive report—certainly that's the way I experienced it. (64)

Delany was attracted to Joe, who had "a large hand—on which the broad nails were gnawed back behind a line of adolescent grime" (64). Large, rough, or dirty hands and/or bitten fingernails are particularly attractive to Delany; it is a fetish, which, *Motion* reveals, may have its origins in a childhood incident at the Washington Market, where he was rescued from an oncoming "loaded dolly" by a workman "looking like a young Burt Lancaster—or maybe Kirk Douglas" with "fingers broad as broom handles and dirt gray, with knuckles big as walnuts" and "badly bitten" nails (38). Joe becomes the model for the protagonist of one of Delany's earliest attempts at novel-length fiction. Two pages later, the author admits that he looked at Joe's hands every chance he got (66). Reflecting on "the double narrative, in its parallel columns" (67), Delany observes the juxtaposition of the story of his friendships with Chuck and Danny and that of his friendship with Joe, and notices that a traditional interpretation of these stories would isolate them from each other and would use the latter to interrogate the former:

> Within the two (or more . . .) tales printed as they are, consecutively and not parallel at all, a romantic code hierarchizes them: the second account— full of guilt, silence, desire, and subterfuge—displaces the first—overt, positive, rich, and social—at once discrediting it and at the same time presumably revealing its truth. (68)

Delany refutes this interpretation, however:

> Yet reread closely.
>
> Nothing in the first is in any way *explained* by the second, so that this "truth" that the second is presumed to provide is mostly an expectation, a convention, a trope—rather than a real explanatory force. (68)

Delany identifies an "older—and conservative—code" which generated "the Romantic questioning, distrust, and uneasiness" toward the public articulation of erotic feelings (68). "It holds," he claims, "that, in day to day occurrences, the desire- and deceit-laden narrative *always* develops alongside the 'socially acceptable' one" (68). This code demands that these feelings be relegated to the realm of the "private," that is, hidden and silenced (68). Delany, however, is interested in challenging the exclusion of narratives of sexual desire from public articulation. He concludes that the space between the two columns is not just an emptiness; rather, it is the point of contact, crossover, and intermingling of the two narratives. It is in this place, where private narrative and public narrative meet, that subjectivity resides: "It *is* the split . . . that constitutes the subject" (69). The opposition of that which is publicly "legitimate" and that which is "illegitimate" and "should be kept private" is a product of the received code of interpretation: "It is only after the Romantic inflation of the private into the subjective that such a split can even be located" (69). Delany asserts that it is language that enables what he sees as his necessary project of articulating what has traditionally been conceived of as part of "the private self" publicly: "That locus, that margin, that split itself first allows, then demands the appropriation of language—now spoken, now written—in both directions, over the gap" (69).

The commingling of narratives that have been previously understood as publicly "legitimate" or illegitimate and therefore "private" is figured again in the image of the spiral notebook Delany used at Bronx High School of Science. "Generally I wrote down impressions, journal entries, or jottings on occasional projects (along with a fair amount of homework) in the front of the book," Delany explains (78). But he reserved the back of the notebook for writing "masturbation fantasies" from the back page forward (78). Over time, the two sets of writing converged:

> The entries in the back and the front of the book, over a period of four to six weeks, would move closer and closer together, like complex graphic parentheses, eating from both sides the diminishing central sheaf of blank, blue-lined white—till, sometimes, they interpenetrated. (78)

"One could distinguish memoir from reminiscence," Pascal notes, "by saying that memoir concerns itself with public events, reminiscence with private";[32] however, it is this very distinction between "public" and "private" that Delany's notebook and *Motion*'s title image reveal to be permeable, or as translucent as a sheet of glass.

The Window of Autobiography

[T]he study of autobiography in America clearly cannot be confined to studies of masterpieces any more than the study of domestic architecture can be confined to the work of Louis Sullivan or Frank Lloyd Wright. . . . The "American book"—be it novel, poem, or autobiography—builds an ideal house (like Thoreau's), a house of fiction (like James's) that is an improvement on the shabby, imitative, or mundane houses in which we are born. The autobiography is, or can be, that second house into which we are reborn, carried by our own creative power. We make it ourselves, then remake it—make it new.

—Robert F. Sayre, "Autobiography and the Making of America"[33]

Images of light and its reflection and/or refraction, such as the optic chain in *Dhalgren*, have already been identified as trademark formal features of Delany's work, and as its title suggests, Delany's autobiography is representative in this regard. However, the "motion" in the title does not suggest the "fluidity" of meaning or identity that Posnock prioritizes as much as it figures a connection, an interpenetration by distinct entities previously thought to be separate, as with the text's dual columns.[34] The image of the motion of light in water first appears when Delany reflects on the first month of married life with Hacker in their East Village apartment:

> 1961's was a hot September. Outside, among the domino games on the sagging bridge tables at the sidewalk's edge, grubby kids without shirts, in shorts and sneakers, opened both ends of empty beer cans (this was pre-poptop; this was when some women carried a "church key" [a pocket can opener] to rip the necks of muggers or sexual assailants) and used them to deflects arcs from the spuming hydrants up through the harsh purple light of the newly installed vapor street lamps, high enough to splatter our second-story windows with bright drops. . . (112)

On this particular day, Delany pursues activities both literary and quotidian, that is, writing a one-act play and cooking dinner. But the "bright drops" on the window hold a particular fascination for him:

Every once in a while I would get up to wander into the kitchen to stir the skillet full of spaghetti sauce I'd done from a recipe on the back of the small white-and-green cardboard box of oregano leaves, the counter still flaked with bits of onion and three fugitive pieces of tomato. Or I'd wander into the front bedroom—just as another arc from the hydrant below broke between the black fire escape slats to sing across the glass, and five hundred purple crescents would gem and drool the pane, while I stood watching the motion of light in water. (112)

Given Robert Sayre's comparison of American autobiography to American architecture, it is significant that the image of "the motion of light in water" first appears when Delany is looking at and through a window in his apartment. Thomas Keenan's "Windows: of vulnerability," an essay that is numerically divided and decimally subdivided in the same manner as Delany's autobiography, presents the window as a figure for both the boundary between public and private spheres—the "distinctions between inside and outside, private and public, self and other, on which the house of the human is built"—and the penetrability of that boundary. Keenan asserts that "in every understanding of the window is an interpretation of architecture and of politics." Transgressing traditional boundaries of "public" and "private" is not without risks, however. The window can be understood as that which enables the subject to see out into the world, or as that which admits light, not in a benign act of "illumination," but rather in a violent act of invasion: "The more light, the less sight, and the less there is in the interior that allows 'man' to find comfort and protection, to find a ground from which to look," Keenan states; "[light] disrupts the space of looking. . . . The window can breach, tear open, the 'protection' that is the human subject." Keenan uses the subject's [over-]exposure to critique the ideal of discrete public and private spheres and of the possibility of the subject's unproblematic transit between them: "The public is not the realm of the subject, but of others, of all that is other to—and in—the subject itself. . . . Publicity tears us from our selves, exposes us to and involves us with others, denies us the security of that window behind which we might install ourselves to gaze." Any representation of one's identity, in or to the public, puts that identity at risk because identity is a narrative; it is always within language, and it is language that "opens up a window to the self."[35]

Delany's autobiography both figures and dramatizes the risk to the self inherent in its representation, to the public, in the form of language. *Motion*'s publication has enabled the dissection of the author's identity in which this chapter—and other extant criticism on the text—engages. The autobiography also tells the story of a particularly frustrating attempt by the author to represent his *self* to other people in public. After experiencing a range of mental health problems including acute acrophobia and a profound fear of subway trains—the latter obviously affects one's mobility in New York City—Delany checks himself into Mount Sinai hospital where he receives treatment that includes his participation in a therapy group. His presentation of himself and his sexuality to the group is hindered by the inability of language to provide transparent access to the self. The expression "gay," the social and political positions indicated by it, and the cultural signifieds to which it refers were not yet in existence. Delany's self-representation to the group is made even more difficult by his worries about a particularly insensitive patient named Hank. Nevertheless, he gives it his best shot:

> So Monday morning, when the eighteen of us were seated around on our aluminum folding chairs, I launched in: as I recall, it was the most abject of confessions. I explained the whole thing, looking fixedly at the white-and-black vinyl floor tile. I had this problem—I was homosexual, but I was really "working on it." I was sure that, with help, I could "get better." (368–69)

After some reflection Delany realizes that his "confession" was a product of his exposure to a discourse comprised of psychological and literary texts that separately and collectively pathologized homosexuality, and that his representation of himself in therapy group had only made him vulnerable:

> When you talk about something openly for the first time—and that, certainly, was the first time I'd talked to a public group about being gay—for better or worse, you use public language you've been given. It's only later, alone in the night, that language reflects your experience. And that night I realized that language had done nothing but betray me.
>
> For all their "faggot" jokes, the Hanks of this world just weren't interested in my abjection and apologies, one way or the other. They'd been a waste of time. They only wounded my soul—and misinformed anyone who actually bothered to listen. (371)

That Delany describes his vulnerability resulting from the publicity of his sexuality as inflicting a "wound" upon his "soul" is particularly meaningful considering that, as Keenan's "Windows" reminds us, "vulnerable" derives from the Latin root *vulnerare*, meaning "to wound."[36] But although this passage demonstrates Delany's awareness of the problems attendant to articulating the self in public space, Delany's chief project, like Keenan's, is to generally analyze and interrogate distinctions between the public and the private.

The interpenetration of the public and private can therefore be a turbulent encounter that leaves the subject betrayed and invaded. But *Motion* also demonstrates that this interpenetration is a crossing that must be attempted; it cannot *not* happen. The violence with which public light, via the window of language, enters the house which holds the private, human self only emphasizes the fragility of the distinction between "public" and "private," a fragility that "the motion of light in water"—which Delany perceives by standing at his own literal and figurative window—represents.

This luminescent image appears again after Delany's description of going to the Apollo Theatre at age seventeen to see the Jewel Box Review, a multiracial troupe of singing and dancing female impersonators led by their tuxedoed master of ceremonies, "Stormy." "I committed myself to seeing the show," Delany explains, "with the same desperation with which I had sought out Gide's *Corydon* and *The Immoralist* . . . Tellier's *The Twilight Men*, Vidal's *The City and the Pillar*, and Baldwin's *Giovanni's Room*" (94). Billing themselves as "Twenty-Five Men and a Girl," the Review would have its audiences guessing who the "real" woman was until the very end of the show, when "Stormy" is revealed to be a woman impersonating a man. Years later, Delany overhears his mother and a neighbor in the kitchen discussing the Review, revealing yet another surprising fact about "Stormy": she was a counselor at Camp Woodland, where Delany went to summer camp as a child. In that moment the "legitimate" world of his camp experiences and the "illegitimate" world of his own and others' sexuality collide. *Motion* presents this collision as, again, the interpenetration of narratives in parallel columns presumed to be segregated from each other but revealed to be separated only by the most fragile of boundaries:

> And for a moment (and only a moment), it was as if a gap between two absolute and unquestionably separated columns or encampments of the world had suddenly revealed itself as illusory; that what I had assumed two was really one; and that the glacial solidity of the boundary I'd been sure existed between them was as permeable as shimmering water, as shifting light. (96)

Delany takes pains to point out that the philosophical tendency to divide human phenomena into realms of either desire or materiality only provides part of the picture, because those realms—or columns—are in contact, penetrating, and interfacing with each other:

That the two columns must be the Marxist and the Freudian—the material column and the column of desire—is only a modernist prejudice. The autonomy of each is subverted by the same excesses, just as severely. (326)

In a typically self-conscious maneuver, Delany reasserts the connectedness of these narratives through the example of his own autobiography:

> Consider two accounts of a life.
> They seem as if they take place on different planets.
> Yet the narrator, through all that surrounds them both, insists the parallel columns write of one person . . . (326)

It is at this point that Delany re-emphasizes *Motion*'s most interesting theoretical arguments by suggesting that the space between public and private narratives of the self is characterized by the permeability suggested by the autobiography's title image, and that because it is the place of contact between the narratives, it is the site of subjectivity:

> the gap between them, the split, the flickering correlations between, as evanescent as light shot water, as insubstantial as moon-shot cloud, are really all that constitutes the subject: not the content, if you will, but the relationships that can be drawn out of that content, and which finally that content can be analyzed down into. (326)

Delany goes on to suggest again that the division of the self into separate "public" and "private" categories is an artificial one, that the two narratives converge and articulate themselves:

> But read them carefully. Neither is pure. Both suffer their anacolutha, their parataxes, their syllepses, their catachreses, the rhetoric that joins each to an excess that, if it begin in the reader's eye as supplemental, under closer examination is ultimately revealed as constitutive, a rhetoric that joins each—however tenuously—to the other. (326–27)

Aside from functioning as autobiography, then, *Motion* makes complex arguments about the interconnectedness of public and private spheres. But to what end? What do such arguments accomplish for Delany? An answer is suggested by Delany's assertion of the story of his crush on Joe and is related to the autobiography's candor regarding its author's sexual activities.

Why Must a Black Writer Write About Sex?[37]

If Audre Lorde is correct in identifying the erotic as "a measure between the beginnings of our sense of self and the chaos of our strongest feelings,"[38] the erotic would seem to be ideally suitable material for autobiography. Delany apparently thinks so. Some critics of *Motion* have disagreed, however. Gerald Jonas's review in the *New York Times Book Review* offered high praise for *Motion* in general, but criticized the book for being "excessively frank about [Delany's] sexual experiments," which, Jonas worried, may "limit the book's appeal."[39] This kind of criticism of the book's sexual candor might be dismissed as mere prudery, except that, as Delany himself admits, "When we come upon [the sexual] in a place, context, or simply a mode we don't expect, the sexual always frightens" (375). Jonas's review does make the very correct observation, however, that the degree of sex in *Motion* alters the way one reads the text. Similarly, Phillipe Lejeune's concept of "the autobiographical pact" demonstrates that a book's front matter matters, and attention to *Motion*'s front matter reveals that although it was originally published in 1988 by Arbor House, an unabridged version was first published in 1993 by Richard Kasak, one of the world's largest publishers of erotica and sexually explicit reading material. All of which means that a reader cognizant of this information might approach Delany's autobiography with slightly different expectations than they would approach, say, Benjamin Franklin's. *Motion* provides a window through which the reader views a range of sex acts in which its author has participated, the very publication of which transgresses traditionally understood public/private boundaries. The autobiography discusses childhood events, such as Delany's masturbation notebooks, and adolescent sexual exploration with other boys during summer camp and in locker room showers. His forays into "anonymous sex"—which are distinguished from "social sex" (i.e., sex with friends or lovers)—comprise most of the text's sexual material and begin shortly after his father's death. Delany explains that by November of 1964, "[he]'d had many hundreds of sexual encounters . . . a hundred of them probably in the previous six months" (289). These sexual acts—traditionally understood as behaviors conducted "in private"—often take place in "public" places such as public restrooms and pornographic movie houses. The autobiography also describes sexual experiments with women, including, and other than, Delany's wife. Toward its conclusion, *Motion* provides illuminating details on the sexual and emotional mechanics of Delany and Hacker's relationship with Bob Folsom and chronicles the author's sexual adventures on a hitch-hiking trip to Texas. Most impressive for their candor, as well as shocking for their representations of cruelty, are the book's reports of Delany's experiences of being assaulted sexually.

Motion's considerable amount of sexual content is often presented matter-of-factly–for example, "After some necking, I blew him. Then he blew me" (289)—in keeping with the text's overall cool-to-mellow tone and its stated aim of presenting thorough and accurate representations of sex. Delany's initial argument for the permeability of public and private spheres is a refutation of the following imagined arguments for keeping sexual material "private":

> Why speak of what's uncomfortable to speak of?
> What damage might it do to women, children, the temperamentally more refined, the socially ignorant, the less well educated, those with a barely controlled tendency toward the perverse?
> Since publishing it in most cases explains little or nothing of the public narrative, why not let it remain privy, personal, privileged—outside of language? (68–69)

Delany is most interested in cultivating frank and conspicuous sexual discourse, however. Noting that *Motion*'s accounts of frequent, unprotected, and anonymous sex might seem to be out of step with today's "safe sex" zeitgeist, he explains that the autobiography is a small step in a sexual liberation movement that is fundamental toward combating HIV/AIDS:

> What is the reason, anyone might ask, for writing such a book as this half a dozen years into the era of AIDS? Is it simply nostalgia for a medically unfeasible libertinism? Not at all. If I may indulge in my one piece of science fiction for this memoir, it is my firm suspicion, my conviction, and my hope that once the AIDS crisis is brought under control, the West will see a sexual revolution to make a laughing stock of any social movement that till now has borne the name. That revolution will come precisely because of the infiltration of clear and articulate language into the marginal areas of human sexual exploration, such as this book from time to time describes, and of which it is only the most modest example. (269–70)

Delany's more purposefully AIDS-related writing will be addressed in a later chapter. It is clear, however, that social justice for gay men and lesbians is a necessary step on the way toward the ideal that this passage describes, and *Motion* is at its most interesting in its documentation of the emergence, for Delany, of a gay identity politics. Posnock claims that racial identity is "displace[d]" by sexuality in *Motion,* and goes on to say that "Delany distrusts 'Gay Identity,' regarding it as a policing device when it is anything more than a 'provisional strategic reality.'"[40] *Motion* does demonstrate Delany's understanding of gay identity as a construct, not as an essence. For example, the memory of a gay friend named Fred—

who, like *Dhalgren*'s Tak, prefers a dash of Worcestershire sauce added to his scrambled eggs—introduces a sequence in which Delany theorizes "gay identity" as both an index to valued experiences and qualities in his life as well as a fiction located entirely in the superstructural realm not completely congruent with his own life's experiences:

> I've often pondered on the terms "gay culture," "gay society," "gay sensibility." The hard-headed Marxist in me knows that we must be talking about behavior, mediated through psychology, that responds to a whole set of social and economic forces that it would have been as easy to locate under Fred's life as under mine. But at the intuitive level (i.e., that level *wholly* culture bound), where we feel as if, somehow, there is such a thing as culture apart from infrastructural realities, gay society has always seemed to me an accretion of dozens on dozens of such minutiae, a whole rhetoric of behavior—how to twist the skin off a clove of garlic, how to open the doors to the unsold box seats at Carnegie Hall with a dime, the shifting, protein [sic] and liquid knowledge of where sex is to be found in the city, this season, or Worcestershire sauce in your eggs—that together make up a life texture I was at once wholly appreciative of, and at the same time felt almost wholly estranged from: as if it were a myth that I could never quite reach.
>
> But perhaps (though today I *still* like Worcestershire sauce in my eggs) any "identity"—semantic, generic, personal, or cultural—is always such an accretive, associative, but finally disjunctive illusion. (211)

Part of what informs this critique of gay identity here is an awareness of the ways in which imposed identities—racial and/or sexual—can be limiting. Delany's brief essay "The 'Gay' Writer/'Gay Writing' . . . ?" addresses "the problems accruing to the production of writings perceived to be gay"; for example, historian Martin Duberman gets pigeonholed as a "gay writer" and is relegated to reviewing books on gay topics only, even though much of his scholarly expertise is in other areas.[41] But thinking critically about "gay identity" is not the same as dismissing it in its entirety. Delany's comments about identity as an "illusion" stand in stark contrast to the perspective from which he remembers Harlem Renaissance icon Bruce Nugent in an interview with Joseph Beam:

> Bruce of course was sixty back in 1965. And it was very easy to see the gay activism of the late sixties and the early seventies as leaving men like Bruce (and Bernie [Kay, a close friend of Delany's]) behind. A number of times I heard Bruce say, in passing, "I just don't see why everyone has to be labeled. I just don't think words like homosexual—or gay—*do* anything for anybody." And I would hold my counsel and rack it up to age.[42]

The two different attitudes toward identity that these passages represent do not indicate self-contradiction as much as a double-conscious, or multiplex view of, identity. Indeed, if we return to "Aversion/Perversion/Diversion," a work that Posnock cites as demonstrating Delany's skepticism toward "gay identity," and pay attention to the context in which the citation was originally stated, we find that Delany adds the following caveat:

> In terms of gay rights, Gay Identity represents one strategy by which some of the people oppressed by heterosexism may come together, talk, and join forces to fight for the equality that certain egalitarian philosophies claim is due us all. . . . In those terms, Gay Identity is a strategy I approve of wholly, even if, at a theoretical level, I question the existence of that identity as having anything beyond a provisional or strategic reality.[43]

The terms Delany ponders in *Motion* are understood in "Aversion" to be what Diana Fuss calls "indices of the emergence of a long-repressed collective identity"[44] necessary to sustaining a sense of community and to the numerous manifestations of gay political activism.

Even if sexuality displaces race in *Motion*—which, we will see, it does not *entirely* do—the status of "identity" is still a matter for inquiry; it is just as much of a contested terrain in terms of queer theory and politics as it is in a racial context. Diana Fuss describes "the question of whether 'gay identity' is empirical fact or political fiction" as one of the most "divisive and . . . simultaneously energizing" in gay and lesbian studies.[45] Steven Seidman's comments, however, suggest that the debate has long outlived its usefulness: "The arcane polemics between constructionists and essentialists has evolved into a sterile metaphysical debate devoid of moral and political import. . . . I sense the battle over identity politics beginning to grow tiresome." Seidman calls for "an analysis that embeds the self in institutional and cultural practices" and "a politics of resistance that is guided by a transformative and affirmative social vision."[46] It would seem that both these kinds of projects are enabled by the insights of Eve Kosofsky Sedgwick's *Epistemology of the Closet,* which suggests abandoning the constructivist/essentialist debate for two reasons; first, the intractable "deadlock" between the two sides, which has already compromised the efficacy of any "theoretical tool(s)" of "adjudication," and second, a desire to move away from discourses of "ontogeny," of origins or "causes" of homosexuality, which have been contaminated by their proximity to and deployment by anti-gay and anti-lesbian sociopolitical agendas. "I am very dubious," Sedgwick writes, "about the ability of even the most scrupulously gay-affirmative thinkers to divorce these terms . . . from the essentially gay-genocidal nexuses of thought through which they have developed."[47] (I must acknowledge that Sedgwick's comment is congruent with Delany's claim in "Racism and Science Fiction" that "the discourse of race is so involved and embraided with the discourse of racism that I would defy anyone ultimately and authoritatively to distinguish them in any absolute manner once and for all."[48]) As alternative frameworks for theorizing gay identity, Sedgwick promotes viewpoints known as minoritizing, "seeing homo/heterosexual definition on the one hand as an issue of active importance primarily for a small, distinct, relatively fixed homosexual minority," and universalizing, "seeing it on the other hand as an issue of continuing, determinative importance in the lives of people across the spectrum of sexualities"[49] (which should not be confused with the "universalism" championed by Posnock and others).

To the extent that the universalizing viewpoint asserts that, to quote Cindy Patton, "people are polymorphously perverse or queer in different ways and by degrees," and "leads to politics that diminish sharp lines between forms of sexuality,"[50] it is a mode in which Delany's autobiography frequently represents homosexuality. Consider that the sexual exploits recorded in *Motion* include Delany picking up or getting picked by various individual men, sex with many men simultaneously, as well as sex with women, including the woman who would become his wife. A month after the death of Delany's father, Hacker comes over to his apartment while his roommate is gone, "and made it clear we were to go to bed" (99):

> In Bob's back room I discovered (and was, I confess, pleased about it) I
> *could* perform heterosexually—but, while I enjoyed the laughing and the
> play, as well as the orgasms and the affection, I knew this just wasn't what
> I was interested in, save intellectually. There was nothing particularly un-
> pleasant about it. But there was a whole positive aspect, somewhere in the
> hard-to-define area between the emotions and the physical that I knew
> from my experiences with other men was missing. (I certainly had no feel-
> ing that the experience "cured" me in any way.) (100)

Motion also details Delany's experiences with his wife and another woman, and with his wife and Bob Folsom. His heterosexual activity, as the above passage indicates, does not make him any less "gay" as much as it demonstrates the breadth of sexual possibilities that exist and to which he is open. Similar deviations from a supposedly normative heterosexuality are illustrated in Delany's hitch-hiking trip from New York City to the Gulf shore of Texas. The first driver to give him a ride does not take long to broach the topic of oral sex: "Man, I tell you, I like my pussy. I got an ol' lady waitin' for me in Tennessee and we're as good as married. But I'll be up front with you . . . I sure like to get my dick sucked, too" (438). Delany ultimately obliges, and "seven rides and three hundred miles later"

(441), another driver picks him up, eventually giving him the same line. Some of Delany's other works that incorporate autobiographical material sustain this universalizing view. *Heavenly Breakfast,* a book-length essay about the commune/folk-rock group of the same name of which Delany was a part from late 1967 through early 1968, describes the sex that occurred there in terms almost identical to Patton's, "perpetual, seldom private, and polymorphous if not perverse," and instructs that "in a communal situation bisexuality has to be of at least passing interest to everyone. (That's assuming both sexes are represented.)"[51] Similarly, in one of 1984's letters to Robert S. Bravard, Delany describes seeing for the first time in years one "of the minuscule number (eight?) women I have been to bed with in my life," who triggers feelings of desire in him: "Really, I was quite charmed with myself and I wish all heterosexuals could from time to time have similar gay stirrings as untroubled and as pleasing. (Actually, I suspect most—however rarely—do.)"[52]

This universalizing conception of human sexuality as a continuum of desires and interests—distinct from each other, yet with permeable borders—exists side by side with and spills over into a minoritizing view of homosexuality in Delany's autobiography. *Motion* reveals that its author engaged in anonymous gay sex in the back of trucks parked by the docks at the end of Christopher Street. On his way there one night he witnesses the police raiding the trucks and is shocked at "the sheer number" of gay men who are flushed out: "That night at the docks policemen arrested maybe eight or nine men. The number, however, who fled across the street to be absorbed into the city was ninety, a hundred and fifty, perhaps as many as two hundred" (268). A significantly similar kind of perception occurs on Delany's first trip to the St. Mark's Baths, a locus for gay male sexual activity in New York City. After clumsily wandering around in the dimly lit building for a few minutes, he enters "a gym-sized room" with blue lights where "maybe a hundred twenty-five" people make up "an undulating mass of naked male bodies, spread wall to wall" (267). Both of these instances produce "a kind of heart-thudding astonishment, very close to fear" (267), which was the product of a disjunction between contesting narratives. Delany explains that during the 1950s and into the 1960s, "before the 'sexual revolution' of the sixties had even begun to articulate itself" (269), a popular narrative said that homosexuality "was a solitary perversion" that "before and above all, it isolated you" (268).[53] But Delany's experience, and the narrative of it embodied in *Motion,* tells a different story:

> What the exodus from the trucks made graphically clear, what the orgy at the baths pictured with frightening range and intensity, was a fact that flew in the face of that whole fifties image.
>
> And it was the contradiction with what we "knew" that was fearful. (268)

The sight of numerous gay men—a veritable "community"—at each event triggers a political consciousness in Delany. "Whether male, female, working or middle class," he explains, "the first direct sense of political power comes from the apprehension of massed bodies" (268). Delany's experiences at the baths and at the trucks provide him with an empowering sense of community and history:

> [W]hat *this* experience said was that there was a population—not of individual homosexuals, some of whom one now and then encountered, or that those encounters could be human and fulfilling in their way—not of hundreds, not of thousands, but rather of millions of gay men, and that history had, actively and already, created for us whole galleries of institutions, good and bad, to accommodate our sex. (269)

Motion presents a narrative that contests the "fifties image" of homosexuality; it militates against forces that would keep the stories of gays and the issues important to them "private," silent, and therefore marginalized. This kind of minoritizing representation, to quote Patton, "leads to civil rights . . . [and] stabilize[s] the mark of difference in order to demonstrate and historicize harm and clearly distinguish those who should be protected or given a remedy."[54] Moreover, Delany demonstrates an investment—no matter how strategic or provisional—in a "gay identity" that coexists with his critical perspective on identity as well as his "universalizing" representations of sexuality.

"The expressed desire to live as one would choose, as far as possible; and the tacit or explicit criticism of external national conditions that, also as far as possible, work to ensure that one's freedom of choice is delimited or nonexistent" could be associated with the writings of gay and lesbian writers who seek freedom from discrimination and equal protection under the law, and militate against the largely homophobic disposition of American society.[55] However, this is Roger Rosenblatt's description of the features common to African American autobiography.[56] *Motion,* the autobiography of a writer who is both black and gay, offers an opportunity to understand the difference race makes to sexuality, and that sexuality makes to race, a project that may identify cultural, political, and ideological threads common to both black and gay communities.

Postmodern Blackness

Numerous scholars have demonstrated that autobiography is central to the tradition of African American literature. William Andrews writes that "autobiography holds a position of priority, indeed pre-eminence, among the narrative traditions of black America."[57] The reasons for the genre's importance to African American culture have to do with the its unique characteristics and the need to create and maintain black history. James Olney explains that autobiography is "the story of a distinctive culture written in individual characters and from within" and provides "a privileged access to an experience . . . that no other variety of writing can offer."[58] John Blassingame points out that autobiography has served to "preserve" black history due to its exclusion from "standard" narratives of American history.[59] Autobiography and autobiographical fiction have been vehicles through which many African American writers have made their entry into, and/or mark upon, the literary world, greatly influencing the shape of African American fiction. Robert Stepto's *From Behind the Veil: A Study of Afro-American Narrative* identifies a "call-and-response" relationship between African American slave narratives and modern African American narratives, including novels such as James Weldon Johnson's *The Autobiography of an Ex-Colored Man* and Ralph Ellison's *Invisible Man,* which imitate the forms of autobiography. *Motion* announces its participation in the tradition of African American autobiography by citing Frederick Douglass's *Narrative of the Life of an American Slave* (1845) among its many influences in "Sentences" (18) and by employing a selection from the first paragraph of *The Interesting Narrative of the Life of Olaudah Equiano* (1789)—Douglass's "silent second text"[60]—as its epigraph:

> If, then, the following narrative does not appear sufficiently interesting to engage general attention, let my motive be some excuse for its publication. I am not so foolishly vain as to expect from it either immortality or literary reputation. If it affords any satisfaction to my numerous friends, at whose request it has been written, or in the smallest degree promotes the interests of humanity, the ends for which it was undertaken will be fully attained, and every wish of my heart gratified. Let it therefore be remembered that, in wishing to avoid censure, I do not aspire to praise.[61]

Quoting this epigraph may be slightly disingenuous on Delany's part. In 1967, after the accidental incineration of a large envelope of correspondences and other writings—including the only uncut manuscript of his 1968 SF short story "We, in Some Strange Power's Employ, Move on a Rigorous Line" and letters from Hacker, Bob Folsom, and others—Delany had despaired that his life would never be studied the way that lives of great literary figures are and had given up "hopes for a certain kind of writing celebrity."[62] He had clearly overcome this feeling by the time he started to compose *Motion,* which nevertheless gave him the opportunity to tell the story of his life, a story he once thought would never be told.

More significantly, however, the epigraph demonstrates that *Motion* is in dialogue with autobiographies by black Americans that preceded it.

The inverse relationship between the humility of Equiano's introductory gesture and Delany's own youthful aspirations for a certain degree of literary fame suggests that *Motion* acknowledges the themes and tropes of the tradition of African American autobiography—or at the very least, of Equiano's narrative—if only to reflect, or reverse or refract, or recontextualize them. As part of his argument for the privileging of the "fluidity" of meaning in *Motion*, Posnock paraphrases Roland Barthes, stating that "one reason Delany's meanings remain fluid is that they are unconstrained by the grimly weighted signifieds of black autobiography." *Motion*'s allusions to Douglass's *Narrative*, according to Posnock, serve only to set up expectations about African American autobiography that are subsequently subverted, as with Kaprow's *Happenings*: "Delany . . . initially announces Douglass's text as a precursor, but then (characteristically) suspends his presence, letting Douglass cast a shadow by virtue of remaining a silent witness. [Douglass] is a ghostly presence here,"[63] as is James Baldwin, who despite also being a black gay writer from Harlem, appears only briefly toward the autobiography's end as party to a "nonconversation" (513) between the two writers about an encounter they never have. I want to suggest, however, that, as with the previous chapter's illustration of an intertextual relationship between Douglass's *Narrative* and Delany's *Return to Nevèrÿon* series, there is a more substantive relationship—with connections made both through and around race—between *Motion* and slave narratives than Posnock allows. For example, Equiano's *Interesting Narrative* is notable for its multiple voices: Henry Louis Gates identifies "two voices [that] were meant to distinguish, in language, the simple wonder with which the young Equiano approached the New World of his captors, and the more sophisticated vision, captured in a more eloquently articulated voice, of the author's 'present.'"[64] Werner Sollors also identifies two voices, "both that of 'the African' (as the title page of his book promises) and that of a European." These readings offer avenues for dialogue between Equiano's "double-voiced" narrative and Du Bois's concept of "double-consciousness." Both tropes are refigured in *Motion*'s double columns of contiguous and commingling narratives. Equiano's slave narrative is also suffused with "the language of the sea,"[65] which must have appealed to the author of *Babel-17*—either before or after the novel's composition—"a novel about" (among other things) "a crew working on a spaceship" (485). Delany went to work on the shrimp boats in the Texas Gulf in part to "pick up insights that could lend [his] book verisimilitude" (485), which he could have found with Equiano as well. The 1814 edition of Equiano's *Interest-*

ing Narrative features a version of the emblem of the Society for Effecting the Abolition of the Slave Trade emblem, an illustration of a chained black slave and a question aimed at its predominantly white readers— "AM I NOT A MAN AND BROTHER?"—that a number of black gay intellectuals, including Delany, are, in effect, turning toward black heterosexuals in their interrogations of the language of racial authenticity.[66] Consider also that both Equiano and Delany represent remarkably well-read polymaths. Moreover, we will see that the "literacy and freedom" paradigm exemplified in Douglass's *Narrative* manifests itself in *Motion*'s representation of difference within identity.

Posnock is correct, however, in seeing *Motion* as qualitatively different from the characterization of African American autobiography offered by Roger Rosenblatt, who argues that "there are discernible patterns within black autobiographies that tie them together" and that "the outer world apprehended by black autobiographies is consistent and unique, if dreadful." Rosenblatt describes blackness, as represented in these autobiographies, as "a variation of fate," the guaranteed encounter with "violence, unfairness, poverty, a quashing of aspiration, denial of beauty, ridicule, [and] often death itself." In texts where the likelihood of the assault of race-based oppression is almost, as Rosenblatt states, a "divine inevitability,"[67] Saunders Redding's statement that black writers have always known who they were, because they were defined by a racist society or reacting against those definitions, is persuasive. But these insights apply more to an earlier generation of black autobiographies, what Posnock identifies as the "tropes of anguish, self-hatred, victimization, redemption, and uplift" are simply not to be found in Delany's autobiography.[68] It is true that *Motion* is not the "typical" narrative a reader might expect from "a black from Harlem," because its thematics are not centrally located in its protagonist's struggles against racism.

This is not to say, however, that such struggles are nowhere to be found in *Motion*. Delany's autobiography includes several stories about his encounters with racism, most of them related to his marriage to Marilyn Hacker. The two writers were friends and then lovers in high school, from which Delany graduated in 1960 and Hacker the year before. It was during this time that Delany's father let him know about the risk involved in being with a white woman after he finds his son in the company of the mother of a schoolmate:

> [W]hen I was sixteen, my father stood under the street lamp on Amsterdam Avenue at one in the morning, his coat bowing wide, shouting at me: "No, I will *not* go up and meet her! I will not! A white woman, old enough to be your mother? And now you tell me that she's drunk? Don't you understand, you are a little *black* boy!" Now he practically hissed, in that epoch when

to call someone "black" was precisely as insulting as calling them a nigger. "Suppose she took it into her head to say you *did* something? Just suppose? You could be hauled into court for rape! You could be killed—" (342–43)

The young Delany finds this suggestion "shocking . . . because it at once floodlit the chasm separating the worlds we lived in" (343). Delany and his father provide a prime example of "the generation gap," though the young writer must have known that the rape-charge scenario his father described was not an impossibility. Judging from *Dhalgren*, Delany was aware of such stereotypes about black male sexuality and became interested in interrogating them. The "separate worlds" that Delany claims existed, could therefore refer to different evaluations of the *possibility* of civil interracial contact across genders, despite society's proscriptions, between father and son.

Given his father's attitude toward interracial relationships, it is not surprising that Delany married Hacker after his father's death. *Motion* tells the story of Hacker, in June of 1961, showing up at Delany's apartment on the Upper West Side with scratches and bruises from a physical fight with her mother. Delany comforts her, but he really wants her to leave. Instead they end up going into Central Park where they have sex. Weeks later, when Hacker tells him that she is pregnant, he suggests an abortion, but neither of them are comfortable with the idea since, as he explains, in 1961 "abortions were illegal and generally presumed to be dangerous" (102–3). Despite Delany's sexual inclinations, the idea of marriage appeals to Hacker, and because fatherhood appeals to Delany, they decide to marry and have the child. But it is not easy for the teen-age, interracial couple to get married. "Because of different age-of-consent laws for men and women, not to mention miscegenation laws, there were only two states in the union where we could legally wed," Delany explains, "The closest one was Michigan" (22). So Delany and Hacker must take a bus to Detroit, marry, and return to New York to move into a filthy apartment across from a "shooting gallery," a colloquialism for "an apartment where neighborhood addicts dropped in to shoot up" (20). The apartment is in a tenement on East Fifth Street, in "which the land-lord, who owned a goodly number of apartment houses in the neighborhood, just *happened* to put all the interracial couples who came to his dim, store-front office out on Avenue B, looking for a place to live" (20). Delany's mother offers the couple congratulations and support after some preliminary worries, but it is safe to say that Hacker's mother, Hilda, hates her new son-in-law. Delany describes Hilda as making "adjustments to having a married daughter" (106), but her statements to him suggest great discomfort with her daughter having married a man who is both black and gay, demonstrating that as with multiple subjectivities, multiple bigotries can coexist and combine with one another. At dinner "[Hilda] would lean over to her daughter and whisper loudly behind her hand 'He's a homosexualist, isn't he?'" (28). When Hilda takes her brother Abe with her to the East Village apartment to bring Marilyn back home they find Delany mopping the floor. While Hilda is frantically searching and asking for Marilyn, who is out, Abe tries to settle her down, saying "you know the kids are married. You said they've both got jobs," to which Hilda replies, "Oh, I don't believe he's got a job" (106). Delany's reaction to these insults is to laugh at them because he does not feel threatened by Hilda, but although he states that his relationship with Hilda troubled him more than his problems with Marilyn (106–7), the former certainly did not help to improve the latter.

These and other representations of Delany's encounters with racism, however, are not *Motion*'s most interesting link to other black autobiographies. Both Saunders Redding and Roger Rosenblatt identify an endless quest for self-definition in the African American literary tradition. "Every autobiographer, black or otherwise, must find a guise or voice with which to come to terms with himself and his world," says Rosenblatt. "If he is candid, he will admit to a number of voices and guises that he will adopt as his mind and world enlarge."[69] These comments apply to *Motion* as well, which is structured by interrogative subheadings that comprise what has been called "the memoir's anthem":[70] "A black man . . . ? A gay man . . . ? A writer . . . ?" (327), which represent neither uncertainty about the author's authenticity in any of these categories nor skepticism toward the identities that they signify but rather the critical reading of these identities and their relations. One of *Motion*'s most significant accomplishments is that it demonstrates that Delany's identity has sexual and writerly dimensions as well as a racial dimension. Joan Scott's reading of *Motion* explains that by themselves "the available social categories aren't sufficient for Delany's story. It is difficult, if not impossible to use a single narrative to account for his experience."[71] Even more interesting are the ways in which these identities make contact with and inflect each other. Delany is fond of pointing out that "genres are never pure," that like *Motion*'s dual columns, "the splits between them, while always noticeable, always oppressively there, are most important, most valuable by virtue of what they allow to cross over."[72] The same goes for the multiple "columns" or "genres" of his own identity in *Motion*: Delany's identity as a black man puts a different spin, a spin of difference, on his identity as a gay man and as a writer, and his gay and writerly identities put their own spins on his blackness. For example, sexual identity inflects racial identity at Camp Woodland, where the young Delany has "an official girlfriend" (59). A young black girl pursues him for PG-rated sexual contact with what Delany calls the "interesting, if strange" understanding "that because we were *the* two black campers in that age group, we *had* to go together" (59). Meanwhile, Delany "wanted to be [his friend] Johnny's 'best friend all the time,'" (59). Although the situation is somewhat comic, it was clearly frustrating for Delany who admits "I was somewhat relieved to go home" (59). This anecdote suggests that there is some merit to Posnock's assertion that sexuality displaces race in *Motion,* as it is Delany's homosexuality that thwarts the female black camper's advances, which are informed by a rather arbitrary racial logic.

Race and sexuality, however, are more often identities that intersect rather than oppose each other in *Motion.* The autobiography, for example, tells of Herman, a "brown, round, irrepressibly effeminate man" (334) who was the organist at Delany's father's funeral home. In the section of *Motion* that begins by combining two question-marked-identities— "A black man . . . ? A gay man . . . ?"—Herman is described as "flamboyant in every phrase and gesture" (334). Delany observes how Herman "camps" or playfully flirts with a delivery man. Herman's antics are met with differing levels of tolerance by men, including Delany's father, but completely vanish in the presence of women, especially his mother. After Herman dies of a diabetes-related illness, a sexually maturing Delany wonders if the late organist's sexual outlets were limited to "the touch teased from some workman" (337), or incidental contact between the two of them on the piano bench. "Herman had a place in our social scheme," he realizes, "but by no means an acceptable place, and certainly not a place [Delany] wanted to fill" (336). Herman represents the difference that gay sexuality makes to African American double-consciousness, what Essex Hemphill identifies as an unwillingness "to be disconnected from [the] institutions of the black family and black community," but also a "willing[ness] to create and accept dysfunctional roles in them, roles of caricature, silence, and illusion."[73] Although that role allowed room for his flamboyant behavior, it did not allow space for him to openly declare his homosexuality. Delany admires Herman's "outrageous and defiant freedom to say absolutely anything," but notes that the one thing Herman could not say was, "I *am* queer, and I like men sexually better than women" (338). The quality and character of both Delany's racialized experience at Camp Woodland and Herman's position within the black community are what they are due to each subject's sexuality.

Herman's relatively unrestrained personality provides Delany with an example of how the meaning and expression of sexuality is different for black gay men than for white gay men. The author observes "that some blacks were more open about their homosexuality than many whites," hypothesizing that "because we had less to begin with, in the end we had less to lose" (338). The personal narratives of other writers suggest, however, that blackness provides no necessary immunity to the anxieties associated with coming or being "out" as a gay man. Keith Boykin, for example, suggests that "for black lesbians and gays, coming out is often more difficult than for whites" because "blacks must contend with issues of racism that compound their struggles with homophobia, and most blacks are already so obviously identified by their race that they are reluctant or unwilling to identify themselves further by their sexual orientation."[74] As for Delany, *Motion* subverts readerly expectations of a gay autobiography in that it features no great conflict about "coming out," in either the pre-Stonewall—and therefore contemporaneous with the historical setting of *Motion*—sense of "'coming out *into*' gay society: [by] having your first homosexual experience," or the post-Stonewall sense of "'coming out' *of* 'the closet,'"[75] a conspicuous assertion of one's homosexuality to family, friends, and/or the larger, (i.e., mostly non-gay) public. *Motion* does not really explain why coming out was not an issue in the author's life, but other of Delany's texts provide more information. In one interview he says, "Possibly because I had an extremely supportive and wide-ranging extended black family, I've rarely felt myself the odd man out in any group I've entered—though I probably was."[76] Although he admits, "I didn't come out sexually to my family at all when I was a youngster, and would have been scared to death to,"[77] the short essay "Coming/Out" reveals that Delany decided to "have the by-now-fabled 'coming out' talk with Mom" during the composition of *Motion*. Unfortunately, his mother's stroke prevented such a conversation from ever occurring, but for Delany, "it's not a major regret," largely because he assumes that she must have known for years given his identification as a "gay writer" in the press, their trip to see William M. Hoffman's AIDS drama, *As Is*, together, and her good-natured inquiries about the men accompanying her son.[78]

"Racism," writes Martin Duberman, "has always been alive and well in the gay world,"[79] which makes the absence of any sustained representation or critique of racism among white gays during the convergences of race and sexuality in *Motion* perhaps more surprising than the lack of a "coming out" story. Other artistic works by black gay men in the 1980s responded forcefully to black exclusion from gay social spaces. The lyrics of Blackberri's song "Beautiful Blackman," published in *In the Life* (1986) and featured in Isaac Julien's film *Looking for Langston* (1989), dramatize the discrimination black gay men have faced. It is a narrative affirmed by the experiences described in an article entitled "Gay Racism" in the anthology *Black Men/White Men* (1983), in which black men in Philadelphia recount their experiences with being carded at gay clubs, rejected in bathhouses, and feared as potential thieves after going home with white men. "Contrary to popular belief," the volume's white editor points out, "bedding down with Blacks doesn't necessarily make one less racist."[80] The proof of that statement lies also in the fact that black men encounter racial fetishism and racist stereotypes about their sexuality in a gay cultural context as well as in the straight world.

Robert Reid-Pharr identifies Delany as one of several "Black queer" writers who have "paid considerable attention to the questions engendered when one 'sleeps with the enemy,'" including the myths that non-blacks buy into.[81] This appraisal is quite accurate, as we will see in a subsequent chapter on Delany's pornographic novel, *The Mad Man*. As for representations of such myths in *Motion*, consider Bob Folsom, who enters the story toward the end of the book as Delany's and Hacker's live-in lover. When Folsom discovers, after the three have sex, that the light-complexioned Delany is "really black," his reaction is shock—"So I'm doin' this shit with a nigger?"—followed by unabashed enthusiasm: "Well I ain't gonna lie about it. Niggers always did turn me on. 'Specially with white women" (393). Bob's language does not alienate Delany; rather, the trio grows even closer afterward. But unless Delany is simply repressing any sense of racial self-respect here, this moment can only be seen as the "play"-ful rearticulation of social relations internalized and transformed—repeated with a difference—in a sexual context, a concept introduced in *Dhalgren*, developed in *Return to Nevèrÿon*, and amplified in *The Mad Man*. However, some of Delany's other autobiographical writings have more specifically illustrated the awkwardnesses and dangers he has experienced because of stereotypes of black male sexuality. "A Bend in the Road" (1994) is an autobiographical essay that describes events that occurred on the 1965 trip to Europe for which Delany leaves at the end of *Motion*. In Greece he picks up a young man who, like Bob, asks "Are you really black?" after they have sex. When Delany explains that he is indeed black, the young Greek gets very excited and initiates more sex, "which merely confirmed what I'd already learned really, in France and Italy: that the racial myths of sexuality were, if anything, even more alive in European urban centers than they were in the cities of the United States."[82] Apparently, you do not have to be white to fetishize American blackness, as is illustrated when a Kenyan asks him the same question as the Greek and gets the same answer, producing the same results. This phenomenon is repeated, with a difference, in "Citre et Trans" (1991) a brief autobiographical story in which Delany tells of being raped by a pair of Greek sailors. The day after, the roommate who brought home the soldiers says, "I really thought, because you were colored, they weren't going to bother you and isn't *that* . . . the dumbest thing I could possibly have said this morning!"[83] The roommate's comment is "dumb" because blackness in and of itself is no shield against such assaults and because of the worldwide circulation of myths of black sexuality as part and parcel of the American cultural imperialism that "A Bend in the Road" comments on.

Fascinating though these meditations on the difference race makes to gay sex and sexuality are, it is clear that *Motion* does not address the black exclusion from predominantly white gay social spaces about which Hemphill, Beam, Boykin, and others have commented. Either the autobiography represents the author's decision to not report the racism in gay bars, at the St. Mark's Baths, or in the dockside trucks, or Delany simply did not encounter racism in those spaces to any appreciable degree. A factor in the latter scenario is that, at least to some extent, he was passing for white. Delany describes himself as "a young black man, light-skinned enough so that four out of five people who met me, of whatever race, assumed I was white. (Some figured I was Italian or possibly Spanish)" (102). Both of his parents were "light enough to pass for white . . . though both were adamant about never doing so" (31). Such attitudes toward passing as his parents' have informed, and been informed by, what Gayle Wald identifies as "cultural representations of 'black' racial passing . . . as morally reprehensible, racially inauthentic, and destructive of bonds of family and community."[84] Wald argues that "racial passing also reveals the pressures to maintain and/or secure sexual and gender 'respectability,' as a means of *racial* self-assertion," developing arguments found in Phillip Brian Harper's work, which has uncovered the masculinisms of narratives of racial authenticity.[85] It should come as no surprise, then, that when Delany transgresses the boundaries of "respectable" (i.e., heteronormative) sexuality in *Motion* by engaging in "anonymous" gay sex, he simultaneously demonstrates what Wald calls the "failure of race to impose stable definitions of identity, or to manifest itself in a reliable, permanent, and/or visible manner."[86] For example, Delany is disappointed at the brevity of the entry that Phil, with whom he had fallen in love, records in his personal sex journal, an entry that reveals a difficulty in fixing him racially:

> Met a kid on the docks last night, twenty or twenty-one. He sucked me. I sucked him. Went for a beer afterwards. Name was Chip. He's Negro— maybe Spanish. Exchanged numbers. Then went home. (384)

As for Bob Folsom, he asks Delany to confirm his racial identity only *after* getting into bed with him and Hacker. As with Clare Kendry's husband in *Passing* (1929), "it appears," to borrow from Judith Butler's reading of Nella Larsen's novel, "that the uncertain border between black and white is precisely what [Bob] eroticizes." The second driver to pick up Delany on his hitch-hiking trip to Texas tries—and fails—to initiate sex with him through a story about watching a white "truckdriver" fellate a "nigger kid" and remarking, "You look like you could have some colored blood in you, too, huh?" (442). Again, what Butler says of *Passing* applies to *Motion* as well: "The question of what can and cannot be spoken, what can and cannot be publicly exposed, is raised throughout . . . and it is linked with the larger question of the dangers of public exposure of both color and desire."[87]

Not all of Delany's passing occurs in a sexual context, however. For example, en route to Texas, the young author stops in Louisiana where he encounters a restaurant's unmarked entrance and another with a sign that reads, "COLORED ENTRANCE" (459). "It was," the Harlem-born-and-raised writer explains, "the first segregated eating establishment I'd ever found myself about to enter" (459). Delany's hunger makes him unsure about whether he should "make a statement" (459) and about which entrance he should use to make it. Realizing that his light complexion makes it difficult for some people to classify him racially, he enters the unmarked entrance, takes a seat and is served food by the "redheaded waitress" (459) without incident. Later, looking for work on a boat on the Aransas Pass waterfront, Delany is surprised when a white man named Jake tells him that "the nigger boats [is] down at the other end." "I didn't know if that meant I should try them or avoid them," Delany says, "but I figured this probably wasn't the time either to make a stand or [find] out" (460). He eventually gets a job on a shrimp boat as a header—"the third man in the three-man crew, who pulls heads off the shrimp" (466)—and later, cook. The boat is run by a "Captain Elmer," whom Delany politely calls "Sir."[88] Elmer's response to this mode of address reveals his racism as well as Delany's ability to pass:

> "You gotta quite [sic] this 'Sir' shit, boy, even if you *are* from the north! You ain't no nigger! So I don't want you talking to me like a nigger. You a nigger, you can call me 'Sir.' But you a white man, you can call me by my name!"
>
> "Yes, sir . . ." I began, surprised, scared, and at a loss for what to say. (473)

Confronted with white inability or disinterest in fixing his racial identity as "black," Delany repeatedly responds not with indignation so much as a combination of surprise, fear, bemusement, and a willingness to take advantage of the situation, particularly so that he can eat and gain employment. The humor of these anecdotes, significantly—and perhaps more clearly than in, say, Mapplethorpe's "Man in Polyester Suit"—is at the expense of white racism. It is also significant that he does not choose or intend to pass for white. The Delany of *Motion* is comparable to Clare Kendry and Irene Redfield in that they all enact what Butler calls a "dissociation from blackness . . . through silence"; like Larsen's characters, he passes by "refus[ing] to introduce . . . blackness into conversation . . . withholding the conversational marker which would counter the hegemonic presumption that [he] is white, and enter[ing] conversations which presume whiteness as the norm without contesting that assumption."[89] Posnock attempts to demonstrate that *Motion* defeats the race-centered expectations and thematic antecedents associated with African American autobiography. But at the location where race and sexual desire intersect in the narrative, where passing presents itself as a topic, *Motion* reveals itself to be in evident dialogue with passing narratives in the tradition of African American literature; this is because the desire, opportunity, and decision to evade certain racial definitions are themselves raced, specific to African American experiences. Moreover, Delany's willingness to pass should not be misconstrued as "anti-black" or as evidence of a lack of "race pride." According to Wald, there is no reason that the "[critique] of the black/white binary" implicit in passing "cannot contribute to the erosion of the authority of race, and hence to conditions that might allow us to live in a more just and equitable society." Wald parts company with arguments like Posnock's, however, when it comes to what passing does for and to the concept of race: passing narratives "ask contemporary readers to consider their own political, theoretical, or ideological interests in race as a site of identification and political or cultural investment"; however, passing ultimately represents "not racial transcendence, but rather struggles for control over racial representation in a context of the radical unreliability of embodied appearances."[90] *Motion* represents its author as an "anti-race race man" in the best (i.e., racially just, politically astute) sense of Posnock's term: a black intellectual who exploits the artificiality and instability of racist racial boundaries even as he draws on and responds to a cultural heritage defined in terms of race.

Race and sexuality are not the only dimensions of Delany's identity that permeate each other. His persona as "a writer," that is, an intellectual, almost keeps him from writing about the Jack and Jill of America, a "black social club which middle-class black parents joined to provide monthly programs for their younger children and seasonal affairs for the older ones" (81). According to Delany, participation in the Jack and Jill was both loathed and lusted after by many black parents. The intellectual identity Delany had adopted in high school brought with it a certain attitude toward such organizations, "a value that said that dances, that dating (and dating the right children of the right parents), indeed, that the whole conservative social machinery through which the Jack and Jill both existed and managed to wield its considerable social power, were, in themselves, beneath contempt for intellectuals" (81). He admits, however, that these functions "had still filled up [his] childhood, and continued to, up through the first high school years" (81–82). In such passages Delany articulates what Cornel West calls "the dilemma of the black intellectual," a dilemma that is most clearly stated when, after reading LeRoi Jones's *The System of Dante's Hell,* the young writer wonders "if there was something wrong with me that so many of my friends were white, that so few were black" (344). As his intellectual identity makes a difference to his racial experience, race reciprocates when in the fall of 1957, Delany hears news stories about the launching of Sputnik and the harassments endured by the Little Rock Nine as they entered school. His written message to a Danish camper—"It's both astonishing and tragic that these should happen on the same day" (75)—speaks to the incongruities of technological and social evolution and symbolizes the way racial realities and the amazing alternatives that technological culture make posssible and imaginable are always attendant on each other, contiguous and interconnected like *Motion*'s double columns.

The significance of *Motion*'s insights into the dimensions of Delany's identity is articulated by Stuart Hall in "New Ethnicities." Hall, among others, has asserted that any "question of the black subject" that does not in some manner acknowledge "dimensions of class, gender, sexuality, and ethnicity" is incomplete. *Motion,* however, is a text that does acknowledge these dimensions and revises earlier understandings of blackness. In fact, it goes even further, for Hall notes that "black radical politics has frequently been stabilized around particular conceptions of black masculinity, which are only now being put into question by black women and black gay men."[91] *Motion*'s project of showing not only that the black subject can be a gay subject but that these subjectivities pervade each other is part of the critical movement Hall describes. The split between "public" and "private" is not the only boundary with a penetrability suggested by "the motion of light in water;" the boundaries between Delany's identities as a black man, a gay man, and a writer, are similarly permeable.

Disbelief of Suspension

Understanding that one's "blackness" in particular or "race" in general are constructed narratives does not require that they be dismissed as meaningless concepts. All fictions are by definition "made up," though most fictions mean something. (Isn't *that* the object of and reason for literary criticism?) "Fictions of identity," Diana Fuss reminds, "importantly, are no less powerful for being fictions."[92] It is exactly this understanding of identity that *Motion* promotes. In "The Style of Autobiography," Jean Starobinski remarks that "one would hardly have sufficient motive to write an autobiography had not some radical change occurred in his life."[93] Delany goes through many changes in *Motion,* but one of the most interesting of these is his transformation from a fledgling artist with a politically naive conception of his identity to an experienced artist with an understanding of the political significance of his subject positions. After he and Hacker make love in Central Park, Delany takes his future wife to make a phone call home and then to the subway train that takes her back to the Bronx. Delany returns to the park, sits on a bench and is faced with "glimmer[ing]" questions: "What was I doing? . . . I'd begun what I'd since planned out as a huge novel. Why wasn't I working on it? . . . Just who was I? . . . Where was I going"? (102). The answers the nineteen-year-old comes up with reveal a willingness and a desire to discard his racial, sexual, and artistic identities altogether:

> I was a young black man, light-skinned enough so that four out of five people who met me, of whatever race, assumed I was white. (Some figured I was Italian or possibly Spanish.) I was a homosexual who now knew he could function heterosexually.
> And I was a young writer whose early attempts had already gotten him a handful of prizes, a few scholarships, most of which Marilyn had already won for her own writing a year before I had.
> I spread my arms out on the back of the bench.
> So, I thought, you are neither black nor white.
> You are neither male nor female.
> And you are that most ambiguous of citizens, the writer.
> There was something at once very satisfying and very sad, placing myself at this pivotal suspension. It seemed, in the park at dawn, a kind of revelation—a kind of center, formed of a play of ambiguities, from which I might move in any direction. (102)

Here Delany appears to have momentarily settled into an identity as a "universal human being" similar to Michael Dyson's description of "king of pop" Michael Jackson as "a Promethean allperson who traverses traditional boundaries that separate, categorize, and define differences."[94] On the Central Park bench, Delany decides that he exists outside of positions that are generally understood to be in binary opposition to another—"black/white," "male/female," "gay/straight"—and can therefore invoke any of them at will, or none of them at all. He momentarily finds "suspension," not committing himself to any position, "very satisfying," in part because of the absence of commitment but also because he feels he can "move in any direction" to occupy any position. The significance of this moment to Delany's life is made explicit in his 1984 letter to bibliographer Robert Bravard, which presents this incident as a benchmark against which Delany measures "one of the most important moments of his life."[95]

This quasi-epiphany is also central to Posnock's interpretation of *Motion* as a "cosmopolitan collage" that "frustrate[s] the demand of identity . . . anticipate[s] . . . the current decline of identity politics" and represents "a post-ethnic embrace of simultaneity." Posnock takes the "suspension" described in this passage to be Delany's "master-trope" and argues that it informs the "neutrality" of *Motion*'s cool and calm tone.[96] "The Neutral" comes from Roland Barthes, whose autobiography Delany identifies as another of his favorites, and represents the incessant and irrepressible "fluidity" of meaning, the evasion of what Barthes, in his autobiography, calls "the definitive form of a sign grimly weighted by a signified."[97] The problems with such a reading of *Motion*, however, are several. Most importantly, it omits the fact that *Motion* dramatizes Delany's re-evaluation of his Central Park revelation, during which he discovers what makes this construction of himself as a "suspended" universal human being so "very sad." This re-evaluation begins when he enters the Day/Night program at Mount Sinai Hospital in November of 1964 for treatment of his mental health problems, and "Dr. G." asks him why he has come to the hospital. "Well," Delany begins, "I'm homosexual. I'm married. I've written and sold five novels in three years. I've got this thing about subways: and I feel kind of like I'm coming apart at the seams . . ." (310). Dr. G.'s response—"Then you obviously like to tell stories . . ." (310)—indicates a degree of incredulity toward the notion of a twenty-three-year-old, black, gay, published science fiction novelist, a concern that Delany might be "really" crazy, and a subliminal awareness of the importance of narrative to identity. When Delany brings copies of his books to the hospital the next day, Dr. G. all but admits that he thought his patient was lying or even more disturbed than he initially thought. Without the books to prove that the black man before him had written five novels, the doctor tells him, "I'd have had a very different picture of you than I have now" (310).

Delany's time at Mount Sinai triggers a sequence of memories which represent a kind of reckoning, a taking stock of the dimensions of his identity. "It's hard to go into a hospital situation," Delany writes, "and not spend a good deal of time wondering what exactly brought you there, figuring out who you are, or why this is where you've ended up, reflecting on the select elements of the past that led to this particular present" (311). What follows are scenarios from his childhood, for example, the memory of accidentally drowning a pet baby chick, which he associates with his own feeling of "suffocating, choking, drowning" and with his father's bizarre electric chicken plucker (313–14). He also reflects on his mother, her efforts to broaden her children's cultural horizons, and her quite human, but still startling, capacities for rage and cruelty. The memories include Delany's father's "destruction" of his son's imaginary friend "Octopus" and the betrayal of a grade school friend who lies to escape a harsher punishment that awaits him. This part of *Motion* also provides the history of Delany's personal experiences with dyslexia, a disability that he did not even know had a name until Hacker told him months before he went to Mount Sinai. In the midst of these reflections, Dr. G. tells Delany that "change is a very frightening thing" and that his life has been filled with changes over the past three-and-a half years (333). The doctor hypothesizes that this has something to do with Delany's fear of subways because of the disjunction between the world that the subway passenger leaves to "submerge" himself underground and the world he emerges into at the other end, as well as the sheer speed at which this transformation occurs. Armed with the instructions to "concentrate on [his] destination," Delany's experiences on the subway become "a *whole* lot better" (333).

Delany's reflection on his past continues with each memory fitted under a variation of *Motion*'s interrogative anthem of identity. "A black man . . . ? A gay man . . . ?" precedes memories of Herman. "A black man . . . ?" precedes memories of Delany's parents introducing their eight-year-old son to Matthew Henson, the discoverer of the North Pole and an example of the greatness that a black man could achieve. Delany reflects on a range of cultural experiences, many of which are specifically black cultural events or address race, such as watching Miriam Makeba sing on television, seeing Sidney Poitier in the 1957 film *Edge of the City*, and listening to jazz pianist Thelonious Monk. He also describes meeting his cousin's white boyfriend and his father's anger over his son's social contact with an older white woman. These various memories represent Delany's explorations of his own "black experience." Delany is mapping out associations he has made between blackness and his family, and his culture. He is understanding his racial identity through what Stuart Hall calls "an act of cultural recovery."[98]

A process of what might be called "gay cultural recovery" is dramatized in a set of memories that present Delany's reflections on his sexuality. In 1960, Delany composes an opera with a black musician and actor named Cranford. Though aware that Cranford has a crush on him, Delany is not prepared for what amounts to a sexual assault. The next year, Delany goes home with a white man named Peter. After they have sex once, Delany finds it impossible to get Peter to do it again. The "(near) rape" by Cranford and the "(almost) rejection" by Peter (359) influence Delany's preference for "anonymous" sex, which he finds "quietly calmer, physically more satisfactory, and—nine times out of ten—far more friendlier in its air and attitude" than what Delany calls "social sex" (350). Delany further explains this preference by recounting one of his first experiences with it. Another black man picks him up and takes him back to the Endicott Hotel. Throughout the journey to the hotel room, Delany fears that he may be with some murderous lunatic.[99] But when the sexual activity between the two men takes place safely, if somewhat perfunctorily, Delany concludes that "there were not *enough* psychotic maniacs running around to justify the total avoidance of sexual pursuits with strangers" (364). In a fashion similar to that in the preceding set of memories of African American culture, Delany's reflection on these sexual events represents a conscious investigation and construction of his sexual identity.

The next section of *Motion* marks a significant change in Delany's understanding of his own identity. The dimensions of Delany's identity—"A black man. A gay man. A writer" (364), now punctuated with periods instead of question marks—figure Delany's rethinking of his earlier conception of his identity as a set of what he now calls "romantic ambiguities" (364). His time at Mount Sinai has given him the opportunity to reflect on that evening on the Central Park bench: "Now I began to see," Delany says, "that what I'd taken as a play of freedom and mystical possibility had actually meant something quite different" (364). Delany realizes that he had been trying to escape the very real social, political, and economic burdens and responsibilities concomitant with being a black, gay, and male writer:

> In my exhaustion, what I'd been experiencing was the comfort of—for those few moments—shrugging off the social pressures I felt from being black, from being gay, indeed, from being a citizen who made art. (Above all, perhaps, from being male). (364)

At least some of his earlier naïveté was a matter of language and history. As with "dyslexia," there was no adequate language yet available to Delany with which he could construct an identity, let alone an identity politics, around race or sexuality:

> But at that time, the words "black" and "gay"—for openers—didn't exist with their current meanings, usage, history. 1961 had still been, really, part of the fifties. The political consciousness that was to form by the end of the sixties had not been part of my world. There were only Negroes and homosexuals, both of whom—along with artists—were hugely devalued in the social hierarchy. It's even hard to speak of that world. (364)

However, Delany recognizes that his adoption of a philosophy of ambiguity was chiefly due to political forces that seek to avoid acknowledgment of racial or sexual difference on an ideological level, thus inhibiting political action aimed at redressing racial or sexual inequality:

But looking back on that morning and the mystical ambiguities that seemed so important to it, I saw that such moments were themselves largely social and psychological illusions—unless you realized that what they meant was that forces both social and psychological were at work to pull you toward the *most* conservative position you might inhabit, however poorly you might be suited for it. (364)

Ultimately, Delany interprets the revelation about his "suspended" subject position, or lack thereof, as a dangerous lapse in political awareness and uses the incident to emphasize once more the interplay between, the connectedness of, public and private spheres:

The mystic experience was a psychological sign that you'd reached a cul de sac where it was too exhausting to separate the personal from the social on the most conservative level. It was an exhortation to vigilance against this muddying phenomenon, for which I suspect, a few years later, the radical slogan, "The Personal *is* the Political" was formulated. (364–65)

According to Stephen Butterfield, "The appeal of black autobiographies is in their political awareness." *Motion,* therefore, may not engage itself in what Stephen Butterfield calls the "Search for the Unified Self," but in its recovery of multiple selves, it articulates and satisfies what Butterfield identifies as the autobiographer's desire "to discover who I am."[100] *Motion* can be seen, then as recontextualizing the "literacy and freedom" trope of the slave narratives in its portrayal of how a critical literacy of the self frees Delany, not in the form of what Jane Gallop identifies in *The Daughter's Seduction* as "some sort of liberation from identity," but as a freedom from what Gallop calls "another form of paralysis—the oceanic passivity of undifferentiation."[101]

In *Motion* Delany learns the value of claiming the identity of a black, gay, writer and the political positions that go with it. "What we've learned about the theory of enunciation," Stuart Hall states, "is that there is no enunciation without positionality. You have to position yourself *somewhere* to say anything at all."[102] The silence to which his "suspended" identity relegated him is figured in his dream of Snake, the boy who inspires and appears in Delany's first published novel *The Jewels of Aptor.* Delany sees Snake as being "of the same racial makeup" as himself (90) and as "some version of [him]self, who both doubled [Delany] and split something off from [him], as though [his] self (itself) had been split by an astonishing gap" (91). Snake, however, is mute: "Bad people had cut his tongue out" (90). Shortly after Hacker's miscarriage, Delany decides to imitate Snake in public. Unfortunately, in the Staten Island subway terminal, a depraved fifty-year-old running a flower booth mistakes him for "one of them stupid kids" (127) and clumsily forces himself sexually on Delany. The lesson is clear; if you have no position, you have no voice. Without a voice, you cannot protect yourself from victimization or violation.[103]

As for Posnock's preoccupation with "the Neutral," the Barthian "thrill"[104] of the radical fluidity of meaning, I would like to reread Derrida's statement on genre in order to suggest that the assertion of (an) identity does not necessarily freeze or limit the subject's ability to move between identities. Derek Attridge reminds readers that "The Law of Genre," is relevant not only to discussions of "literary genre but also to gender, genus, and taxonomy (classification) more generally."[105] Derrida's insights into literary genres therefore apply to the categories that are the bases of human identity: to paraphrase, it is not that there is no identity, but rather, that an individual subjectivity participates in several identities simultaneously. There is always an identity and identities, yet such participation never amounts to belonging/fixing. To make it plain, invoking a racial, sexual, or artistic subject position does not lock the subject into that position and out of all others for eternity. Neither the "motion" nor the "water" in the title of Delany's autobiography are figures for mere "fluidity." Again, the glimmering, refracting, title image is a figure for the *multiplexity* of identity and for the interactions between those multiple meanings. Consider how a single signifier has numerous signifieds—all equally, simultaneously, potentially meaningful—each one activated by a certain context. That moment of signification does not lock the signifier within that context, to that signified, for all time. We can say that meaning is multiple, but we cannot say that meaning is permanently suspended, that it is fluid to the extent that no signified ultimately matters, that no meaning can be identified. Moreover, consider how the signifieds differ from each other—as when a word's denotative and connotative meanings shade into and/or against each other—a difference that also models the interplay of identities in *Motion*. In his introduction to *Dhalgren*, Gawron reminds readers that "a science of semiology presupposes, that we 'read' the relations between signs rather than their references,"[106] which is the kind of reading that *Motion* enables and the reason Posnock's investment in a suspension above identities—outside of sign systems—misses the point. Race is one of many signs—perhaps not central, but hardly irrelevant—interacting with each other in Delany's autobiography. Therefore, a double-conscious critical perspective—anti-essentialist *and* politically astute, emphasizing *both* specificity and multiplicity—is central to understanding *Motion*'s unique exploration of African American identity.

This interpretation of *Motion* as the narrative of discrete but intermingling identity formations might be critiqued as incomplete or not going far enough, however. Diana Fuss finds accounts of identity that "argue that each subject is composed of multiple identities which often compete and conflict with one another" to be slightly inadequate to the task of responding to concepts that boil identity down to an "essence." Describing this conception of the subject as "a highly charged electronic field with multiple identity particles bouncing off each other, combining and recombining," Fuss argues that a poststructuralist view that locates difference in "the spaces *between* [a subject's] identities" is not as radical as that which "locates difference *within* identity." Fuss prefers to deconstructively see "identity *as* difference"; that is, within every singular identity there is a "not-identity" against which it defines itself. Although I am interested in identifying discrete narratives of each of Delany's subject positions, I am not interested in interpreting those identities as necessarily separate, or as competing or conflicting. Rather, for the purposes of this study, I am interested in these narratives' interaction, the points at which they cross over. Conceiving multiple interior identities as not separate, but rather, intersecting with each other provides a model to be applied toward the practice of what Fuss identifies as a sorely needed "coalition politics" among progressive movements within groups with their own investments in their own public identities.[107] More simply put, "the black experience," "the gay experience," and "the portrait of the artist" are not mutually exclusive narratives. And "the motion of light in water" figures the interpenetrations between these different narratives of identity. Robert F. Sayre tries to divert the burden of representation from the genre of autobiography when he claims that "the amassed diversity and prodigious energy of modern America should not be seen exclusively through the window of autobiography anymore than through the steel doorway of a bank vault."[108] But *The Motion of Light in Water* demonstrates that it is through the window of autobiography that the diversity of the individual identity can be seen.

5

MAGIC, MEMORY, AND MIGRATION

ATLANTIS: MODEL 1924

> The Boulevard is sleek in asphalt, and, with arc-lights and limousines, aglow.
> Dry leaves scamper behind the whir of cars. The scent of exploded gasoline that
> mingles with them is faintly sweet. Mellow stone mansions overshadow clap-
> board homes which now resemble Negro shanties in some southern alley.
> —Jean Toomer, "Bona and Paul," *Cane*[1]
>
> A city, Sam thought, turning over, that was everywhere and nowhere, where
> we all come from, where we all go . . .
> —Samuel R. Delany, *Atlantis: Model 1924*[2]

Atlantis: Model 1924 (1995) represents a departure for Samuel R. Delany, from paraliterature to a more traditional, though highly experimental, form of literary fiction, or what some SF readers might call "mundane" fiction. It is a departure paralleled by that of the novella's protagonist, a young man named Sam, who has left his home outside of Raleigh, North Carolina, and has arrived in New York City. Sam's story is based on the experiences of Delany's father, Samuel Ray Delany Sr., who migrated to New York to make a life for himself. Upon arrival, Sam, the youngest of ten children, moves into a Harlem apartment with his older brother Hubert, who is a law student at New York University. The character of Hubert is based on the author's uncle, Hubert T. Delany, who would later become an active leader in the NAACP and an assistant U.S. Attorney and domestic relations court justice. Sam also reunites with his sisters Elsie and Corey, characters based on Sarah and Elizabeth (a.k.a. Sadie and Bessie) Delany, the pioneering professional women who gained celebrity as co-authors of the best-selling memoir, *Having Our Say* (1993). The novella explores and expresses Sam's fascination with New York, which for him represents another Atlantis, "a truly wonder-filled city."[3] The subway, skyscrapers, lights, and bridges—particularly the Brooklyn Bridge, perhaps the model for the bridges to some of Delany's other cities

such as Bellona in *Dhalgren* and Kolhari in the *Return to Nevèrÿon* series—make the city a place of magic for Sam. The novella also conveys
sophisticated insights into the mechanics of memory in a graceful, almost
effortless style reminiscent of the poetry of Rita Dove, which is not to say
that it lacks the hallmarks of Delany's other texts. Henry Louis Gates Jr.'s
cover blurb, for example, claims that *Atlantis* "is to post-modernism
what Jean Toomer's *Cane* (1923) was to modernism." For proof, readers
can turn to just about any page and note the story's multiple columns, a
formal characteristic that Delany deploys in *Dhalgren* and suggests that
the readers of his autobiography *The Motion of Light in Water* imagine.
The typography serves to connect the "pastiche" or patchwork of rhetorical and narrative styles—history, biography, memoir, bildungsroman, and
other miscellaneous fragments of relevant information that appear in parallel columns—that fill the novella's pages.

Despite its focus on the author's family as opposed to, say, an alien language system or a journey to the farthest reaches of the galaxy, one review
of this innovative tale suggests that the racial authenticity of Delany's
work is still in question. Although the *Review of Contemporary Fiction*
states that "*Atlantis* has much to recommend it,"[4] Rose Kernochan's *New
York Times Book Review* piece describes *Atlantis*'s Harlem as "a neighborhood washed in a mild, innocent light, a place where racism seems
alarming but remote, like an ugly rumor or a hurricane delayed on business farther south" and characterizes the Delany family as "so contentedly
white-collar, so warm and unflappable, that it seems to have stepped off
the set of some jazz age *Cosby Show*,"[5] all of which reads like an attempt
to damn with faint praise. The implications are clear: for Kernochan,
Atlantis is insufficiently "racial" in content.

There are plenty of ways to challenge such evaluations of Delany's
book, however. Hubert, Elsie, and Corey are, respectively, a law student,
educator, and dentist as well as the children of administrators at a black
college, based on St. Augustine's in Raleigh, North Carolina. They are indeed "contentedly white-collar," and as such they represent a new black
identity that was part of the zeitgeist that captured black America in the
1920s, which Alain Locke heralded in his 1925 classic, *The New Negro*.
This new black identity entailed what Locke called "a spiritual emancipation . . . a new vision of opportunity, of social and economic freedom,
of a spirit to seize, even in the face of an extortionate and heavy toll, a
chance for the improvement of conditions"; it also included a casting
away of previous black identities based on an understanding of African
Americans as "a social problem."[6] That anti-black racism is not central
to a story set during the emergence of "the New Negro," therefore, is not
necessarily surprising. To make the point more plainly, although racism
has been an all-too common part of African American experiences, black

writers have the ability and the right to write about other subjects, a right to which the novella's conclusion stakes it claim. But Delany's decision to emphasize a celebration of black lives and experiences instead representing blackness as being in constant reactive opposition to white racism does not mean that the novella exists "suspended" above cultural traditions and specificity. On the contrary, *Atlantis* is Delany's most conspicuous example of drawing from and recasting specifically African American literary forms and themes.

The contention that *Atlantis* does not address anti-black racism, for example, is simply incorrect. Sam takes a train from North Carolina to New York, but he has to ride the Jim Crow car as far as Washington, D.C. In Harlem, Sam notices the "black and yellow and tan and brown faces" of customers at the post office, as well as the white faces of all of the postal clerks; "he'd just expected, well . . . maybe *some* dark faces behind the squared brass bars" (30). It is at the post office that Sam meets a group of black children, each of whom has been disfigured in some horrific accident or another, who, because of their race and poverty, are housed at the Manhattan Hospital for the Insane. Even so, Sam finds the children—including one whose name, "Ella Ablir," suggests some kind of anagram or a name from Delany's early SF—to be the most wondrous of beings, "like wounded angels or emissaries from another world" (34). Sam's encounter with these girls is emblematic of the way in which his enjoyment of the wonders of life in New York is qualified by realities of race and racism. He unexpectedly encounters a picture of the Ku Klux Klan in the basement of a black veteran of the American Civil War while digging around for pulp adventure magazines. A false thumb—"painted a luminous pink"(60)—dampens his enjoyment of a set of dime-store magic tricks as do memories of being forbidden by his racially proud parents to see Harry Houdini perform in Raleigh's segregated Jackson Theater. Elsie and Corey tell Sam about the presentation of *Birth of a Nation* in New York, which they disrupted by tearing down the theater's movie screen. Cataloguing *Atlantis*'s explicit treatment of racism refutes readings such as Kernochan's; however, to focus solely on this aspect of the novella would be to ignore one of its most significant features, its representation of the memory at work.

Memory Triggers

Atlantis's revelation that Boni and Liveright published Sigmund Freud's *Beyond the Pleasure Principle* and Toomer's *Cane*, the literary hallmark of the Harlem Renaissance, within a year of each other (88), provides an extratextual connection between theories of the unconscious and modern

African American culture in general and its representation in *Atlantis* in particular. The significance of memory in Delany's tale is further suggested by the "green-covered magazine" that Sam finds in Corey and Elsie's bathroom, "one of Corey's journals from the time of her language pursuits" (23) entitled *Mnemosyne*, which Delany has called as "a recondite classics journal."[7] In *Civilization and Its Discontents* Freud makes a claim about memory and the unconscious that parallels Albert Einstein's theory of relativity. Just as the formula $E = mc^2$ suggests that matter cannot be destroyed, only changed, Freud asserts that memories are never lost: they exist to be excavated from the unconscious:

> Since we overcame the error of supposing that the forgetting we are familiar with signified a destruction of the memory-trace—that is, its annihilation—we have been inclined to take the opposite view, that in mental life nothing which has once been formed can perish—that everything is somehow preserved and that in suitable circumstances . . . it can be brought to light.[8]

Freud then compares the unconscious to the concentric layers of development of Rome, which he calls "the eternal city":

> Historians tell us that the oldest Rome was the *Roma Quadrata,* a fenced settlement on the Palatine. Then followed the phase of the *Septimontium,* a federation of these settlements on the different hills; after that came the city bounded by the Servian wall; and later still, after all the transformations during the periods of the republic and the early Caesars, the city which the Emperor Aurelian surrounded with his walls. . . . we will ask ourselves how much a visitor, whom we will suppose to be equipped with the most complete historical and topographical knowledge, may still find left of these early stages in the Rome of to-day. Except for a few gaps, he will see the wall of Aurelian almost unchanged. In some places he will be able to find sections of the Servian wall where they have been excavated and brought to light. If he knows enough . . . he may be able to trace out in a plan of the city the whole course of that wall and the outline of the *Roma Quadrata.*[9]

For Freud, "the past is preserved in historical sites like Rome" and similarly in the human unconscious; it does not take too much of "a flight of imagination" for Freud to "suppose that

> Rome is not a human habitation but a psychical entity with a similarly long and copious past—an entity, that is to say, in which nothing that has once come into existence will have passed away and all the earlier phases of development continue to exist alongside the latest one.[10]

Delany's novella compares Atlantis, another "eternal city," to the New York of 1924, whose subway system and stations Sam perceives as a "buried city" (16). As Hubert rapidly leads Sam from Grand Central Station to his Harlem apartment, the young man reflects on his psyche's capacity to retain all that he sees:

> Following Hubert through resonant tunnels, considering his trajectory, like a bullet through a beehive, Sam wondered which of the enclosed images he'd recall in a day, in a decade. (16)

In *Atlantis*, New York City is the setting for an exploration of memories and their triggering devices in the perceived world. For example, the sound of the train that brings Sam to New York triggers a memory: "'. . . tut-tut-tut-tut-tut . . .' just like the song" (4). Twelve pages later, the song in question is revealed to be "Billy Rose and Ernest Hare singing Harry Von Tilzer's 'In Old King Tutankhamen's Day,' with its infectious refrain: 'Old King Tut-tut-tut-tut-tut-tut-tut . . .'" (26). Sam associates this memory with his father's purchase of a "Diamond Disc Official Laboratory Model" (25) Edison record player specifically, and the life he has left behind in North Carolina more generally. Later, the conductor brings a "poor-white family . . . barefoot . . . with their twine-tied boxes and traveling baskets" (5) into the Jim Crow car, including a boy who notices Sam: "the littlest stared at all the car's dark faces, to fix finally—pink lips lax in a thoughtless 'o'—on Sam, four seats behind and across the aisle, as if Sam, and not they, were the anomaly here" (5). Sam is then puzzled by the way that the child's gaze triggers a memory from just before his departure from North Carolina:

> But why did that make him remember, how many days before, Lewy, arguing with—well discussing with—Mama, in an extraordinarily grown-up manner, how going north would be good for him—while Sam sat silent, impressed, across the kitchen table, listening to them go on earnestly for fifteen minutes, as though he wasn't there. (5–6)

Both the child's gaze and being spoken of as if he were not present have made Sam feel uncomfortable and out of place. This example, in which a sensory experience triggers a memory, recalls Marcel Proust's *Remembrance of Things Past*, particularly Part One of *Swann's Way*, in which a spoonful of tea with crumbs from a "petite madeleine" evokes memories for the narrator. One may well ask: if Sam's moments of remembrance are Proustian, what is so "postmodern" about them, especially if, as Margaret Gray notes, "few writers are so confidently cited as high modernist" as Proust?[11] First, it is important to understand postmodernism not as "anti-modernism," but rather, as a revisiting, a rethinking, or a "rewriting" of modernism.[12] Larry McCaffery convincingly argues that in terms of cultural characteristics, "there is no sharp demarcation line between what constitutes modernism and postmodernism." Both "modern" and "postmodern" literary texts feature, for example, "heightening of artifice, a delight in verbal play and formal manipulation of fictive elements, [and] the widespread use of fantasy and surrealism." Therefore, McCaffery concludes, "the differences between the two periods, then, is finally one of degree—the degree to which contemporary writers have turned to these strategies."[13] Although *Atlantis* may engage in a modernist, Proustian representation of the retrieval of memory it does so in a radical, postmodern fashion that resembles the dynamics of a pinball machine, nuclear fission, or more precisely, what I call "the unlimited semiosis of memory," a phrase I derive from Jacques Lacan's dictum, "the unconscious is structured like a language," from the "unlimited semiosis" alluded to in the title of the thirteenth chapter of Delany's *Neveryóna* (itself derived from the work of Charles Saunders Peirce), and from Sam's reflection on memory prior to his arrival in New York City:

> Watching the dawnscape, still iceless, flip along, he contemplated for the thousandth time the astonishing process by which the seamless and inexorable progression of the present slipped away to pack the past with memories, like numbered stanzas in a song, like cells in a comb, like cakes in a carton, to be called back (though he'd ascertained, most he'd never recall) in whatever surprising, associative order. (5)

In "The Agency of the Letter in the Unconscious," Lacan claims that "what the psychoanalytic experience discovers in the unconscious is the whole structure of language."[14] More importantly, a sign system predates the subject, so that "language and its structure exist prior to the moment at which each subject at a certain point in his mental development makes his entry into it."[15] In *Freud, Proust, Lacan: Theory as Fiction,* Malcolm Bowie explains that since the only access one has to the unconscious is language, for all intents and purposes, "there is no point in speculating about a possible 'pure,' pre-linguistic state of the unconscious," indeed, "language creates the unconscious." In making such claims, Lacan "draws upon [Ferdinand de] Saussure's binomial definition of the linguistic sign—signifier [or sound image] and signified [or concept] in arbitrary association."[16] Lacan's concept of the Symbolic, one of three cognitive orders including the Imaginary and the Real, stems from such structuralist insights.

I want to suggest a reading of *Atlantis*'s representation of memory that relies on the dynamics of Saussure's linguistic sign. Such a reading would interpret sensory experiences—that is, the sound of the train, the gaze of the white child—as something like sound images or signifiers that indicate, gesture toward—in a surprisingly associative fashion—memories, or signifieds. Therefore, the "tut-tut-tut-tut-tut" of the train operates as a signifier and the memory of the Von Tilzer song is its signified (or one of them). The white child's gaze is a signifier and the memory of the conversation between Lewy and Mama is its signified. However, considering Jacques Derrida's assertion that "there is not a single signified that escapes . . . the play of signifying references that constitute language,"[17] we should be aware that every signified also operates as a signifier. Again, consider the example of the dictionary, to which one refers in order to discover the definition (signified) of a word (signifier). However, that definition (signified) consists of more words (signifiers), whose definitions (signifieds) can be looked up in turn. "The process we are discussing is not only in theory infinite but somehow circular," to quote Terry Eagleton, "signifiers keep transforming into signifieds and vice versa, and you will never arrive at a final signified which is not a signifier in itself."[18] This understanding allows us to see that the retrieval of Sam's memories does not represent the end of the process; rather, those memories become triggers for other memories. Arriving at Grand Central Station, for example, Sam marvels at the blue-tiled arched ceiling as well as the "great clock," a "multi-faced spherical time keeper" (11). Of special interest to Sam are the clock's hands:

> Curlicued arrows at their tips, oar-long hands lay a diametric certainty across its face, a horizon ruled on the rising moon, on the setting sun. Short hand lower at the left and long hand higher at the right told Sam it was within seconds, one way or the other, of eleven past eight— (11)

The clock hands cause Sam to reflect not only on his journey but also on a memory of his friend John imitating a fighter plane in North Carolina:

> a slant horizon forward of the dark prow of his trip, lifting and listing from spurious waters, if not the pointer on some turn and bank indicator of the sort Sperry had been putting into aeroplanes since the war's close, an artificial horizon unknown to him a year ago, when he'd watched John, shirtless in the field, with his rusty hair and freckled skin the hue of a tobacco leaf, play at being a bomber, dancing like a deranged Indian over red earth, feet—blam! blam!—on the earth's red flesh, running into waves of hip-high grass, holding one hand aloft, thumb and little finger spread apart from the others, swooping left, turning right, blood remembering some aeronautic invasion, crying Vrummmmmmmmmmmmmm, while Sam and Lewy stood at the field's edge, laughing, clapping, celebrating fantastic catastrophes. (11–12)

The same page features one of *Atlantis*'s parallel columns, which contains a memory of Sam's mother threatening to "skin [John] alive" (12) if his mule eats any of her Swiss chard. But what has triggered this memory of Mama and John's mule? The parallel column provides a possible answer: "(Sam had heard [Mama] swear like that maybe twice in his life. That's probably why he remembered it)" (12). The rarity with which Sam's mother's swore may be the reason the memory has been retained, but it may not be the reason for the excavation of this particular memory from the depths of his unconscious at this particular moment; the parallel column continues to narrate the conclusion of the episode with John's mule:

> The mule jerked to the side—and John slipped right to the ground. Then Mama started laughing. Splayed on the grass, John was laughing too.
> "Get up . . . from there John—" Mama called, between hysteric eruptions. "And get him . . . out of here!" While the mule wandered over to the porch steps and ate a hollyhock. (12)

The real trigger for the parallel memory was the memory of John imitating a fighter plane and evoking the kind of laughter that ends the memory of Mama and John's mule. The first memory, a signified indicated by the clock, in turn becomes a signifier of the second, parallel memory of John's mule. Some of the novella's other dual columns appear to operate similarly, whereas the association between some is of an entirely different order.

Just as a signified can operate as a signifier, so can a signifier be the signified of other signifiers. But does the same follow for memories and their triggers? Can a sensory experience pass over into the realm of memory? *Atlantis* demonstrates that once a sensory experience has occurred and ended, this is exactly what happens. Sam's experience with the poor white family on the train triggered memories of Mama and Lewy in North Carolina, but he never sees the family again after that:

> [A]pparently the family for whom there'd been no room in the white cars had gotten off at some prior local stop, so that, Sam realized, with all the myriad details that were his train trip north, they too had sunk into yesterday's consuming sea. (10)

Sam's experiences in New York City become submerged in memory, in the unconscious, as Atlantis was consumed by the sea.

Just as "signifier" and "signified" are unstable categories, so are experience and memory in *Atlantis*. So much so, in fact, that Sam often gets confused about whether sensory experience triggers memory, or vice versa. For example, walking home one early April night after working late as a stockboy in a 117th Street haberdashery, he is struck, seemingly out of the blue, by the following insight into the workings of desire in both politics and the arts:

> It was the powerless who produced most of the myths of power, as it was the poor who articulated the most staggering fantasies of wealth—in the same way it was probably the Philistines and illiterates who perpetrated the soaring images of art and poetry which, once they came loose from the Edgar Guests, from the Courier [*sic*]-and-Ives, the rest of the world was seduced by; and real poets and artists doubtless exhausted their lives trying to make them happen. And so desire fueled the engines of the world. (42)

Nothing signals the reader or Sam that this fascinating theory is coming. And Sam forgets it as suddenly as it came to him. However, toward the novella's conclusion, yet another page with a parallel column reveals this idea to be a variation on part of Sam's memories of a summertime conversation with John and Lewy back in North Carolina that precedes John's "bombing run." Lewy, commenting on what Delany has described elsewhere as American slavery's "systematic, conscientious, and massive destruction of African cultural remnants,"[19] suggests, "I think it's those deprived of history who create the world's great histories" (115). This recollection prompts Sam to recall his winter walk home and to question whether his sudden insight triggered this late-blooming North Carolina memory, or if the memory of Lewy's words—buried in the unconscious— actually triggered the revelation:

> Was this prior summer's amble the origin of that peripatetic revelation? Or had the winter evening's revelation been the origin of this memory of summer, which, without it, would never have returned? (116–17)

Sam cannot remember which operated as a signifier/trigger first. And before he can make up his mind about it, he forgets and falls asleep. Indeed, as much as *Atlantis* revels in the play of remembering, it also reveals the depths of "the chasm of [Sam's] forgetfulness" (102). For example, Sam feels guilty about how quickly he forgets about his acquaintance Mr. Poonkin, a black Civil War veteran, after the old man dies of pneumonia. Sam also, quite typically, misremembers the titles of the Paul Robeson performances he sees, as well as the frequency with which he sees them. Chapter "c" opens by noting the ease with which people remember incidents "that tell of a certain strength" and just as easily forget those "confirming our own weaknesses" (57). As Robert Hayden describes "the dark ships" that brought captured Africans through the Middle Passage as "shuttles in the rocking loom of history," the narrative comments on how memory uses "imagination's intricate loom" (57) to change a remembered weakness into a strength or vice versa.

Atlantis represents memory as a semiotic system through experimental narrative and typographical techniques. As the preceding examples demonstrate, Sam's memories, the experiences that trigger/signify those memories, or both, involve matters of race. Moreover, the novella's use of epigraphs that include excerpts from Hayden's poem "Middle Passage" (1962) suggests that the novella is in dialogue with larger traditions of African American literature and history. The wonder that Sam finds in New York City is an example of the "life on these shores" achieved by a people that has persevered through a veritable "voyage through death," centuries of enslavement and oppression, and demographic changes of immense proportions.

Song of the Son

> But I am in the very way at last
> To find the long-lost broken golden thread
> Which reunites my present with my past,
> —James Thomson, "The City of Dreadful Night"[20]

Atlantis is an example of, as well as a variation on, the African American migration narrative. In the early part of the twentieth century thousands of African Americans seeking access to economic opportunity and refuge from racist violence relocated themselves, from rural areas to urban centers, from the South to the North. This demographic shift, also known as the "The Great Migration," was an important factor in the New Negro movement and the black cultural phenomenon known as the Harlem Renaissance; it was central to the modern African American experience. As such, migration is a key subject in much twentieth-century African American literature. In her definitive study of such texts, *"Who Set You Flowin'?"* Farah Jasmine Griffin describes the African American migration narrative as follows:

> Most often, migration narratives portray the movement of a major character or the text itself from a provincial (not necessarily rural) Southern or Midwestern site . . . to a more cosmopolitan, metropolitan area. Within the migration narrative the protagonist or central figure who most influences the protagonist is a migrant.[21]

Delany has treated the topic of migration in his earlier works of science fiction and fantasy. In *The Einstein Intersection,* Lo Lobey's pursuit of

Kid Death takes him from his rural community to the city of Branning-at-Sea. *Flight from Nevèrÿon*'s *The Tale of Plagues and Carnivals* explains that the disposition of longtime barbarian residents of the capital city of Kolhari toward their newly arrived kinsmen was not always welcoming: "Zadyuk's parents' life in Kolhari predated the coming of the Child Empress to the High Court of Eagles, and they clearly had mixed feelings about the most recent influx of southerners."[22] This attitude is comparable to that of some northern and/or urban African Americans toward newly arrived black migrants from rural areas and/or the South. Of Delany's fictions, however, *Atlantis: Model 1924* is the work that most purposefully explores this topic. The protagonist moves from rural North Carolina to New York City, and if 1920s-era Raleigh, North Carolina, is not "provincial," Sam himself certainly is. Griffin explains that migration narratives tend to be marked by four pivotal moments: 1) an event that propels the action northward; 2) a detailed representation of the migrant's initial confrontation with the urban landscape; 3) an illustration of the migrant's attempt to negotiate that landscape and his or her resistance to the effects of urbanization; and 4) a vision of the possibilities or limitations of the northern, western, or midwestern city, and the South. Although many migration narratives present these moments in this particular order, Griffin adds that they "may occur in any given order within the context of the narrative. . . . It is not necessary that there be a straightforward linear progression from the South to a vision of the consequences of migration."[23] This is particularly important to keep in mind when reading a migration narrative penned by Delany, an author famous for nonlinear SF narratives like *Empire Star* and *Dhalgren*. With its multiple columns and frequent flashbacks, *Atlantis* defies a conventional "beginning, middle, end" plot structure. The elements that Griffin identifies all appear in *Atlantis*, but with significant variations, and in a different sequence.

The first phase of the migration experience that *Atlantis* presents is Sam's initial encounter with New York City's urban landscape. The novella begins with Sam on the train, and the first chapter chronicles his impressions of the city. Griffin notes that in most migration narratives, the migrant initially experiences alienation stemming from his or her confrontation with new systems of racial relations, as well as bewildering differences in the value and conceptualization of time and space. In addition, the level of technology that the migrant finds in the urban site is often more advanced than that with which he or she is familiar. Most significant for Griffin, are the subtle, sophisticated, and often indirect ways in which power works to change, oppress, or victimize the black migrant. Bigger Thomas, in Richard Wright's *Native Son* (1940), is the classic example of a migrant hounded by a seemingly omnipresent but intangible force, who understands the forces of white power allied against him as a blizzard.[24]

Whereas alienation is central to many migrant encounters with the city, Sam's initial encounter with New York City is characterized by wonder. He enters New York City already knowing not only that the Woolworth Building is the world's tallest, but also that "counting basements and sub-basements, the Woolworth had exactly sixty stories" (3). Everything about New York City suggests something magical to Sam. As he gets off the train he meets "a stately Negro woman" (9) known as Mrs. Callista Arkady, whose names suggest the celestial and the utopian. Grand Central Station greets Sam not only with the multi-faced clock, but also its high-arched ceiling done in blue tile, the watery color of which suggests the submerged city of Atlantis, set with lights and filigreed with gold images of the zodiac. The sight forces Sam to "set down his case . . . [pull] his cap from his pocket and, still gazing up, [position] it on his head" (11). Sam clearly encounters what are for him new levels of technology in New York City, but again they provoke fascination, not alienation. For example, it takes him a while to realize "that the 'sub' in 'subway' . . . was short for 'subterranean'" (16–17). Hubert takes him to the front of the subway car to show him where the engineer sits, and Sam naively asks "This is the *engine?*" (14) When Hubert jokingly claims that some subway trains run above ground and even into the sky, Sam is genuinely and charmingly awestruck:

> Cities underground . . . ? Cities in the air . . . ? With subterranean and super-terranean ways between? And all were among New York's honied algebra of miracles? Hurrying after Hubert, a-grin at the mystery of it, Sam tried to fathom it and keep from laughing. All this—*and* skyscrapers? (17)

The initial view of the city's skyscrapers also has a most astounding impact. On the night of his younger brother's arrival, Hubert and his girlfriend Clarice take Sam to Mount Morris Park, where they climb the high rocks for a wondrous sight reminiscent of Pryn's vision of an ancient city rising up and out of the sea in *Neveryóna:*

> Far away, specular and portentous, they glimmered behind haze-hung night. (It felt as if it might rain any moment.) Sam seemed to be looking across some black and insubstantial river to another city altogether—a city come apart from New York, drifting in fog, in air, in darkness, and wholly ephemeral: the idea of a city—with no more substance than his memory of his memories on the train. (27)

Griffin notes that the moment of the migrant's initial confrontation with the urban landscape focuses primarily on the migrant's psyche.[25] The glimmering imagery seen in the distance represents not only Sam's own experience of a kind of sense of wonder, but also the semiotic mechanics of his psyche: the idea of a city, and the city itself, distinct from, but linked to each other, like memories and their referential triggers. On top of that, weeks later, Sam spends three hours in a magic shop named Cathay and buys an astrology pamphlet on the Transit of Mercury. Therefore, like other black migrants, Sam enters a brave new world different from anything he has experienced before. But absent from *Atlantis*—at least at this stage in the narrative—is any example of power operating over Sam and forcing him to act according to written and unwritten racial expectations, which may partly explain Kernochan's criticisms. For that, we must turn to the next phase of *Atlantis*'s migration narrative: Sam's navigation through his new material and psychic environment.

If the urban environment does not completely transform Sam, he represents the arrival of something different to that environment. In identifying migration as a significant theme in African American literature, Griffin cites Hazel Carby, whose essay "Policing the Black Woman's Body" suggests the differences that class, region, and gender make to modern black experience: "For Carby, the 1920s marked a time when established black Northern intellectuals were confronted with large numbers of migrants who challenged earlier notions of sexuality, leadership, and any sense of a monolithic black culture."[26] Sam brings a raw—both unmitigated and unrefined—sexuality with him to New York City. When it comes to human sexuality, Sam is [as many teenagers are] both naïve and curious. On the train to the city, his left nipple catches "on a thread or fold in his shirt / pulling till it cut" (4) in a passage reminiscent of more unabashedly erotic moments in *Dhalgren* or *The Mad Man*. Sam then "glance[s] around the car—especially at the women in their seats, black and white" (4), and reflects on the erotics of railway travel:

> Five times now he'd noticed, first with distress, then with curiosity, and finally with indifference, that if he sat on the rumbling plush, relaxed, and let his knees fall wide, through loose wool the train's joggling gave him an erection. (4)

Upon meeting a Scottish woman who lives in Brooklyn, Sam "look[s] down at the flounce on her skirt, to see if he could glimpse an ankle" (7). This image may not seem very racy to readers at the dawn of the twenty-first century, but in *Having Our Say* the Delany sisters explain that in the 1920s "you [could] get in enough trouble just with a little ankle showing."[27] The same Scottish Brooklynite later catches Sam bringing his mouth to the nightlight at the end of the aisle, as if to kiss it. Upon arrival, Sam's "genitals, buttocks, nipples, tongue all seem so insistently present" (8) as he leaves the train. He later reflects on the pleasant shape of Clarice's body, wondering if his brother ever allows his own sexuality to manifest itself long enough to kiss her. Sam could be compared to the women of the first section of *Cane*, who, according to Darwin Turner, generally "respond naturally and instinctively to their urges."[28] There is a touch of the transgressive about Sam, particularly when he takes pleasure in Paul Robeson's performance of a progressively backsliding preacher in Nan Stevens's *Roseanne:*

> [T]he glee, the wild joy with which he embraced his sins—drinking, crap shooting, shirking his Sunday sermons, and finally falling into the arms of a no-account Negro woman and getting her with child—made those weaknesses seem almost like some socially rebellious strength. (38)

Atlantis's focus on Sam's sexuality avoids the stereotypical representation of a black man as oversexed black beast; rather, these insights into his desires contribute to his complexity, his humanity, as a character. However, desire is met with a harsh, disciplining force in *Atlantis* from an unexpected source.

"Urban power," Griffin states, "sustains a discourse around race, sex, and desire" that "separates and categorizes individuals." The source of this categorization in *Atlantis* is the black bourgeoisise, represented by Sam's brother Hubert. Griffin notes that in the 1920s "the established black middle class began to do the work of Southern black colleges as outlined by Booker T. Washington in his autobiography and as parodied by Ralph Ellison and Nella Larsen in their novels," *Invisible Man* (1965) and *Quicksand* (1928) respectively.[29] Instructing newly arrived black migrants on the appropriateness of attire, address, and behavior were frequent topics in northern black periodicals such as the *Chicago Defender* and *Opportunity*. Hubert's girlfriend Clarice is an avid reader of the latter journal and of the *Messenger* and, characteristically, she never splits infinitives, dutifully corrects Sam's own Southern speech patterns, and disapproves of his smoking. Hubert himself has had plenty of experience in disciplining black youth. "One of three colored teachers recently hired to teach first grade in the colored all-boys public school" (20), Hubert had written Sam and the rest of the family in North Carolina about how he had adopted another teacher's technique for preventing unruly student behavior, which involved breaking a baseball bat against a curb, displaying it by his classroom desk, and telling the students that he broke it during his most recent administration of corporal punishment. When Sam asks Hubert if "he really did that thing with the baseball bat" (21), Hubert replies affirmatively, but notes that whereas his predecessor taught "big, rough, country boys—field hands right in from pickin' cotton" (21), his own students were younger, city kids who perhaps did not require such a harsh admonition. Hubert's didacticism extends to his younger brother; his criticisms of Sam are often the "playful, hopelessly damning, inescapable sibling judgment" of statements such as, "Boy, you a *real* country nigger, ain't you!" (18). When Sam is late for his 4:00 p.m. birthday dinner at Elsie and Corey's apartment, Hubert comments that his brother has arrived at 4:00 p.m. "CPT," or "Colored People's Time"— which Clarice, either in an attempt to protect Sam from what she may perceive to be a coarse expression or to apply a humorous turn of the screw, calls "*country* people's time" (104), with hilarious results.

More serious, however, and more disturbing, are Hubert's warnings to Sam about sexual behavior. He warns him not to ride the front car of the subway during rush hour "'Cause things can happen to you in there. . . People can do things to you" (15). When Sam, incredulous, asks for more details, Hubert slaps his brother's legs, saying "You got to watch out for yourself, that's all. . . . You just have to remember that this is New York" (15). This cryptic bit of information is embellished slightly when Hubert later criticizes Sam for smoking. He begins by separating and categorizing the kind of black laborers with whom he worked in the tobacco fields of Connecticut: "By and large, it's a pretty ordinary sort of Negro you find there . . . you got hardworking Negroes. You got lazy Negroes. Then you got no-accounts. . . . But you got another kind you're going to run into up here—only thing to call 'em is animals" (55). These men are "animals" because an animal "makes water or does his business" (55) wherever it happens to be at the time, which is what these workers did. Hubert's abjection and the name he calls these workers recall Julia Kristeva's observation that "the abject confronts us . . . with those fragile states where man strays on the territories of *animal*."[30] But Hubert reveals that some workers went even further:

> "And at least ten times or more I come across some feller doing a lot worse than making water or his business—grinning and telling you he's gotta do it now 'cause there ain't much more to life but that and getting drunk and he's just *got* to do it! Right on top of what you're putting in your mouth and sucking into your body! They know white people going to be smoking them things—they think it's funny." (55–56)

Sam wonders "What's a lot worse" (56) than making water and doing one's business. But he is sharp enough to notice that "the veiled suggestions went immediately with the things that could happen to you in the vestibules of subway cars" (56). Sam does not stop smoking, nor do his desires curb themselves in any significant way. For example, he is continually captivated by a black woman's silhouette—"Body of shadow, body of light" (43)—in a window across the street from his bedroom, whose disappearance literally brings him to his knees with a "thudding chest" (43), the sign of arousal and desire from the *Return to Nevèrÿon* series. However, his brother's story does give Sam and the reader an opportunity to pause and consider the reasons for Hubert's tirade and his willingness to describe other black Americans as "animals." The answers lie in Sam and Hubert's recent family history, and the reasons for Hubert's own migration.

According to Griffin's framework, most migration narratives begin with an event that propels the action northward. Many Southern blacks moved in search of employment opportunities in the industrialized North. Sam's reasons for relocating to New York City seem to be primarily economic and educational. Since "he was the one among the ten [children] who hadn't finished high school," Mama and Papa decided "when he'd worked awhile in New York and grown more serious, the older ones could settle him into night school and help him toward a diploma" (5). More often, however, migration narratives tend to focus on the desire to escape "Southern power . . . inflicted on black bodies in the form of lynching, beating, and rape." "If social scientists stress economic factors," Griffin states, "then artists emphasize violence as a cause of migration."[31] Such may initially appear to be the case with *Atlantis*. Elsie and Corey's story of their protest against the showing of *Birth of a Nation* triggers Sam's childhood memory of seeing the mutilated bodies of his cousin and her husband "brought, in a creaking wagon, back through the evening trees" (48). This fictional memory is based on historical fact. In a 1983 interview, Delany vividly recalls his father telling him the entire story:

I was seven when, with quivering rage, my father told me—because of some racial incident at my New York private school—how, sometime in the 'teens or '20s, a cousin of his had been stopped with her husband by a gang of white men; she was perhaps eight months pregnant. Substantially darker than she, her husband was lynched, and she was dragged to a tree, hung up, her belly slit open, and, in my father's words, "her unborn baby was allowed to drop out on the ground"—because the men assumed she was a white woman and would not believe otherwise. My father was there when their bodies were brought back to the campus of the black southern college where his father and mother were vice-chancellor and dean of women. My father, I gather, was about the age I was when he told me . . .[32]

This lynching very likely became the basis of a story that became a key tool for anti-lynching activists such as the NAACP's Walter White. A variation of this horrific tale appears in the "Kabnis" section of Jean Toomer's *Cane,* and it is echoed in Mouse's story of the massacre of his gypsy family in *Nova.* The transportation of lynched black bodies onto the campus of St. Augustine's, and *Having Our Say*'s brief mention of Bessie Delany's near-lynching as she traveled to teach in Georgia,[33] suggest that there are limits to Ross Posnock's characterization of the Negro college as "a model" of a "'kingdom of culture,' somehow off-limits to lynch mobs."[34] The sisters' memoir also makes a point of explaining that "despite their privileged status, they suffered the insult of Jim Crow when it first became law."[35] *Atlantis* appears to support Griffin's claim that lynching is the dominant literary image of the cause for migration, but it also illustrates that the sources of Southern violence are many. Griffin notes that Gloria Naylor's *The Women of Brewster Place*, in which Mattie Michael suffers physical abuse from her father, as well as Toomer's "Kabnis," in which Southern blacks throw a stone though a window to scare away the northerner Lewis, feature examples of "the black community repeat[ing] codes of violence enacted upon them by whites."[36] *Atlantis* features a comparable moment that manifests itself as yet another of Sam's southern memories. As he washes up in Hubert's apartment after his railroad journey, Sam glances up from the corner sink at his big brother, the sight of whom triggers two separate memories. First Sam remembers the pleasure his family in North Carolina took in reading a letter from Hubert on Thanksgiving day. The second memory is of a wholly different tone and character:

> Sam hopped, and shook quickly from his mind another memory (". . . an *animal* . . . !" The crate's slats smithereened across Hubert's shoulder, and dragging the chain across the gravel where the grass had worn from around the pump, Hubert cowered back: "*Papa! No . . . !*" He remembered his father's grunts, precise and ugly). (21)

Not only does Papa repeat the South's codes of violence by chaining Hubert to a water pump and beating him soundly with an orange crate, he also repeats its rhetoric, denouncing him as a subhuman "animal," the same language Hubert used himself to categorize the masturbating tobacco workers. The memory of Papa beating Hubert later intrudes on Sam's imaginary visit to Mr. Poonkin, who contracted pneumonia a week earlier and perhaps has already died by the time Sam hears about the old man's illness. The exclusion from membership in the community of "rational" humanity that accompanies Papa and Hubert's judgmental inflictions of the label "animal" upon others resonates with that accompanying what Michel Foucault identifies as animalistic representations of madness at the dawn of the Renaissance: "the beast [that] is set free . . . the animal that will stalk man, capture him, and reveal him to his own truth." The social function of exclusion that Foucault sees manifesting itself in the stigma that madness inherits from leprosy after the latter's eradication in the Middle Ages and in seventeenth-century Europe's Great Confinement, "which seemed to assign the same homeland to the poor, to the unemployed, to prisoners, and to the insane,"[37] is repeated in the geographical and social isolation of the ill and/or destitute, such as Mr. Poonkin and the disfigured impoverished children from the Post Office, to the Hospital for the Insane on Ward's Island.

In *The Motion of Light in Water,* Delany recalls hearing his aunts and uncles' stories about Hubert's beating, noting that "despite the levity with which [they] remembered it, they could not recall the nature of the particular infraction."[38] Whereas Sam's reasons for migration are matter-of-factly laid out early in *Atlantis,* the relationship between Hubert's beating at the hands of Papa, his reluctance to discuss sexual matters, and the reason for his migration articulate themselves more gradually over the course of the story. Toward the end of the novella, Sam broaches the topic of sexuality with his brother by noting how back in Raleigh he and his adolescent friends would watch women board a trolley car and nudge each other as their skirts would swing up, revealing their ankles. In New York in 1924, skirts were rising well above a woman's ankle. Hubert's response to such conversation is telling:

> "Sam, why do you want to talk about things like that? . . . Like you said, skirts are up now—and in ten or fifteen years, *everybody's* going to have forgotten it. You should forget it too. Stuff like that's nasty, Sam! . . . Boy, you a country nigger to your soul. You better think about gettin' civilized— that's what coming up here was supposed to do for you!" (112)

Two weeks later, after a nightmare in which he is trapped in a "subterranean chamber . . . descending into the sea" (115), Sam wakes to find Hubert standing above him, asking if he is all right. Sam reveals his feelings about the beating, and Hubert reveals why Papa chained and beat him:

> "It was just stuff . . . with a girl. . . . You remember Alina, Reverend Fitzgarn's daughter? . . . I stole some of Papa's money, to go out and get a bottle and be with her. And then Reverend Fitzgarn caught the two of us, doing it—or, least ways, just *about* doing it." (117)

Hubert also explains how, after venting his rage, Papa talked to him:

> "Papa didn't let me stay outside all night, you know. He turned me loose— after he wore himself and that orange crate out. He made me come inside and sit in his study—my nose was bleeding, my arm was sore—and he talked to me. . . . He said we had to call a truce, him and me. He said we had to call

a truce between us—that if we didn't, he was going to kill me or I was going to kill him. If I didn't drive him to his grave with shame and sorrow. . . . 'You want to go to New York,' he said, 'with Hap and Corey'?" (118)

Darwin Turner suggests that in focusing on "Southern women isolated or destroyed because they have ignored society's restrictions on sexual behavior," the first part of *Cane* conveys a "sympathetic awareness that tragedy eventuates as long as society itself erects taboos," an awareness also communicated to the reader by Hubert's beating.[39] Based on his aunts' and uncles' descriptions of the incident, the image of the family home in North Carolina in the mind of the young Chip Delany was that of "a house of an extraordinary violence and rigid order."[40] Yet in *Atlantis,* Hubert says that his father really loves all his children, which is why he sent his "strong-willed" children north. After this revelation, Hubert expresses a willingness to talk about the incident, which the reader can now recognize as the root of his impulse to categorize black migrant workers and discipline his migrant brother, with Sam in the future.

The last segment of Griffin's migration narrative blueprint is a final vision in which the migrant realizes the possibilities and limitations of life in the North and/or South. Griffin illustrates that the sentiment generated by such a vision can range from an appreciation of the South—as in Toni Morrison's *Song of Solomon* (1977), in which Milkman ultimately "wonder[s] why black people had ever left the South"—to its complete renunciation, as in Nella Larsen's *Quicksand* (1928), in which Helga Crane thinks "The South. Naxos. Negro Education. Suddenly she hated them all." It can range, Griffin explains, from a realization of the complexity of life in either region such as that articulated by the characters in Richard Wright's *Lawd Today!* (1963), who exclaim "'Boy the South's good . . . and bad!' 'It's Heaven . . . and Hell . . . all rolled into one!'" Or it can suggest the possibility of a reconciliation or spiritual synthesis such as that articulated by the speaker of Toomer's "Song of the Son,"[41] or by the arcs that punctuate each section of *Cane.* There are two final visions that greet Sam in *Atlantis,* neither of which apparently has much to do with his attitude toward the North or the South. For him New York is a city of limitless magic and wonder, despite the racial realities that confront him as a black man in the 1920s. The visions are distinctly Northern and Southern in their settings however, and each teaches Sam a valuable racial lesson: the first about Sam's attitudes toward another group of people, the second about Sam's own racial identity.

The attitudes of African Americans toward Jews is a topic that surfaces repeatedly throughout *Atlantis.* In one of the story's early parallel memories, Sam remembers Lewy showing him and John his elaborately encoded journal, with "two columns, one barely comprehensible, the other *complete* nonsense" (8). The cryptography is intended to keep the journal safe from the prying eyes of Sam and of John, who claims that Lewy's system is not foolproof: "'You don't want none of them jewboys to get hold of this,' John said. 'They could figure it out on you'" (8).[42] Eight pages later, another, shorter, parallel column suggests that Lewy does not take John's suggestion seriously; but perhaps Sam does. The following March in New York, Sam listens to his sisters Elsie and Corey justify their decision to tear down the movie screen at the presentation of *Birth of a Nation*. "Not a man or woman, black or white, Christian or Jew with free-thinking ideas and care for his fellows," Corey says, "was safe anywhere in the country while that movie was on" (51). Sam experiences a severe case of cognitive dissonance at these words, and unfortunately attempts to articulate it:

> "Jews?" Sam said. "They don't lynch Jews." Back home, John and his brother had told Sam that, because Jews had all the money, everybody was afraid to cross them and that's why they were taking control of just everything. "They got too much money." (51)

Sam is, of course, badly misinformed, and his big sister Corey is more than willing to let him know about it:

> "Don't lynch *Jews?*" Dr. Corey declared. "And just what makes you think they don't, boy? That poor Jew, Mr. Frank,[43] he was lynched down in Georgia, right near where Papa was born, the very summer that movie was showing. Don't lynch Jews? Where have you been, boy? Back when the Jim Crow laws came in, *everybody* was getting lynched. That was the crime of it, see? That's what taking the law into your own hands is all about. Anybody they didn't like, got lynched—for any reason. You think they didn't lynch Jews? They lynched white people, they lynched black people—they lynched women, children, *and* Jews. Don't let me hear you talkin' nonsense like that anymore, Sam. Sometimes I think you don't know anything!" (51–52)

Although Elsie makes her sister concede that most lynching victims have been black, Sam acknowledges the strength of Corey's argument, though it does not change his mind: "though Corey probably had her point, John was pretty smart, and Sam was not yet ready to dismiss completely John's judgment of the Jews . . ." (52). Unfortunately, this attitude affects his relations with Jews he meets in New York. When Hubert suggests to Sam that he return the magic trick with its luminous pink thumb and ask the magic store's owner for his money back, Sam demurs; "though he liked Mr. Horstein [the store owner], he was still a little afraid of him (he *was* a Jew, after all)" (60–61).

What Corey's chastisement cannot accomplish, however, perhaps an encounter on the Brooklyn Bridge does. The following Saturday, on his birthday, Sam goes on a solo trip across the Bridge (repeating, with a difference, *Motion*'s description of Delany's trip with Marilyn Hacker across its wooden walkway thirty-six years later) which will provide him with the truest vision of the city, according to Clarice, who claims "that's the way to really see New York" (27). On the walkway, Sam has "the disorienting experience of being suspended more than a hundred feet in mid-air above glass-green water" (66), similar to what the acrophobic Delany experienced on his own bridge-walk with Marilyn Hacker in *Motion*.[44] Noting the gap between each of the walkway's planks, Sam figures out that his quick pace "let the light from the river glitter up through the spaces, creating the illusion that the walkway had vanished—or at least had gone largely transparent! Green as trolley sparks, the water—thousands of millions of drops of it—flowed below" (66). Not only does this image trigger a parallel memory of Lewy's invention of a water clock inscribed with the signs of the zodiac and Hebrew letters, it also signals the importance of this moment in the story. Light and its emission, reflection, and refraction are frequent images in Delany's fiction, signifying the displacement of "unitary images," validating "fragmentation and multiplicity," and serving as "a metaphor for analysis, brilliance, and pluralism."[45] The next thing Sam knows, he has literally run into a man who walks on by but returns to ask, "Excuse me . . . But you're a Negro, aren't you?" (73). The stranger, introducing himself as "Sebastian Melmoth" (78), notes Sam's light complexion and resemblance to Jean Toomer before revealing his true identity as Hart Crane, the poet who would write *The Bridge* (1930), which concludes with a section entitled "Atlantis." Crane explains that he has been using the pseudonym Oscar Wilde used after his release from prison and during his residence in France. Sam is familiar with Wilde from seeing a performance of *The Importance of Being Earnest* at his father's school, but Crane laughs at the suggestion of Wilde performed "in blackface" or "as a minstrel" show (78–79). Crane's momentary dismissal of such a performance suggests that cultural exchange across the color line has not flowed as evenly or as equitably in *Atlantis* as Posnock seems to suggest. When he asks if "they only used the lighter-skinned students" (79), Sam sets him straight by saying that black students of all complexions auditioned for and performed the parts, forcing Crane to admit, "I wouldn't be surprised if it's the sort of thing that *all* white people should be made to see—Shakespeare and Wilde and Ibsen, with Negro actors of all colors, taking whichever parts. It would probably do us some good!" (79). But the poet has a lesson to teach Sam as well. Among the many topics the poet discusses with Sam is the life and work of poet Samuel Bernhard Greenberg, who died at age twenty-three of tuberculosis in the Manhattan Hospital for the Destitute on Ward's Island. The excerpt from Percy Bysshe Shelley's *Adonaïs* that serves as an epigraph to this chapter of the novella speaks to both Greenberg's untimely death and Crane's own in 1932. When Crane states that the namesakes have a lot in common, Sam exclaims "He [Greenberg] was a jewboy!" to which the poet laughs, "Yes, he was, my young, high-yellow, towering little whippersnapper!" (87). Startled by this language, Sam does not know if he should take offense and wonders whether Crane is Jewish. But significantly, Sam's anti-Semitic thoughts and comments cease from this point onward. This northern vision is completed when Crane manages to summon Atlantis itself for Sam to see:

> [T]he city had changed, astonishingly, while they'd been sitting. The sunlight, in lowering, had smelted its copper among the towers, to splash the windows of the southernmost skyscrapers, there the Pulitzer, in the distance the Fuller, there the Woolworth Building itself.
> "Risen from the sea, just off the Pillars of Hercules—that's Atlantis, boy—a truly wonder-filled city, far more so than any you've ever visited yet, or certainly ever lived in." (92)

Although Sam's experience on the bridge is an important moment both in Sam's appreciation of New York City and in his racial education, his contact with Crane generates as much confusion as understanding. Crane invokes racial stereotypes when he tries to pick Sam up: "Do you want to come back to the place with me—have a drink? We could be alone. I'm a good man to get soused with, if you like to get soused—and what self-respecting Negro doesn't?" (97). As with Hubert's reference to masturbation, Sam is too naive to realize that the meaning here is sexual, although he is also preoccupied with the thought that a boater below may have committed suicide by jumping into the river, an eerie parallel to Crane's suicidal leap from a ship into the Gulf of Mexico. When Sam decides to get a police officer, Crane misinterprets the move as an attempt to get the law to crack down on a homosexual. They leave each other, Crane losing an object of desire at the bridge and believing Sam to be a sexual bigot, and Sam thinking Crane a fool. Later at Elsie and Corey's, Sam incorrectly deduces that Crane was scared off by the thought of the police because he had offered Sam a drink during Prohibiton. Despite its symbolic setting on a bridge, his meeting with Crane produces only an imperfect connection and an incomplete Northern vision.

The episode on the bridge does feature its own parallel memory, however, the continuation of—or rather, a prelude to—Sam's conversation with John and Lewy back in Raleigh. Two weeks later the memory is associated by way of a parallel column with Sam's nightmare of being swallowed by the sea. In this memory, Sam, John, and Lewy, who has been studying Jewish mysticism, play a little make-believe:

> "John, you can be the White Devil," Lewy explained. "And Sam. . . will be the Dark Lord. And I'll be the Ancient Rabbi who understands the Cabala's secrets and can speak them backwards." (113)

John asks, "Why you always want to take things back to the Jews, Lewy? Why you do that? Take 'em back to somewhere else, now—Egypt. Or Africa. You should take 'em back to Africa. . . . You don't really want to originate with the Jews do you?" (113). Lewy, whose inclusion of Hebrew letters on the dial of his water clock also informs John's protest, cleverly responds by saying, "I think, with Christianity we already do" (113). Lewy then provides an eloquent explanation of his right to lay claim not only to the cultures of his African ancestors, but to those of other groups with which he comes into contact as well:

> "Now, me—I'm going to originate everywhere . . . from now on. I've made up my mind to it. . . . From now on, I come from all times before me—and all my origins will feed me. Some in Africa I get through my daddy. And my momma. And my stepdaddy. Some in Europe I get through the library: Greece and Rome, China and India—I suck my origins through my feet from the paths beneath them that tie me to the land, from my hands opened in high celebration of the air, from my eyes lifted among the stars . . . and I'll go on originating, all through my life, too. . . . Every time I read a new book, every time I hear something new about history, every time I make a new friend, see a new color in the oil slicked over a puddle in the mud, a new origin joins me to make me what I am to be—what I am always becoming. The whole of my life is origin—nowhere and everywhere. You just watch me now!" (114–15)

Lewy's words suggest Whitman here, but more specifically, his contention that he "sucks his origins through his feet" recalls the Georgia soil that provided Jean Toomer with the setting and the cultural nutrients that enabled him to create the "everlasting song, a singing tree" of Southern black folk culture that is *Cane*.[46] Toomer initially credited his immersion in southern black folk culture with enabling his writing, unlike the title character of his short story crossed-with-drama "Kabnis," a black northerner whom the narrative compares to Antaeus and is described as "*suspended* a few feet above the [Southern] soil whose touch would resurrect him" [emphasis added].[47] (Darwin Turner reads this passage as suggesting that "although Kabnis has come to the South, he cannot gain strength by rooting himself in the culture of that region." But whether this situation is the result of a failing on the part of Kabnis, or evidence that the attempt at cultural immersion itself was doomed, is unclear and perhaps a matter of debate.) However, neither enfeebling suspension nor a rootedness to a single place of identity is sufficient for Lewy, whose multiplex sensibility prompts him not to opt out of positionality altogether, but to be rooted in his blackness in a manner that does not amount to a fixing as much as it is a base to return to after drawing sustenance from other cultural locales. There is indeed some similarity between Lewy and *Nova*'s Mouse; both are experts at the technique of collage, of creatively borrowing from diverse cultural traditions, on which Posnock places so much value. Moreover, Lewy demonstrates an understanding that his identity is not the product of some sort of racial essence; rather, it is constructed through the process that Stuart Hall identifies as "cultural recovery."[48] Lewy's claim to "originate everywhere" is central to Ross Posnock's reading of *Atlantis* as a text that "continues to meditate upon and ingeniously extend the figure of suspension so conspicuous" in *Motion*:

> Lewy's joyous commitment to ceaseless originating crowns the intricately imagined effort of *Atlantis: Model 1924* to dismantle the rhetoric and ideology of authenticity, to cast off the yoke of provincialism and the proprietary. By dispersing origin everywhere, Lewy desacralizes it, or, more precisely, bastardizes it. Thus, he deprives the logic of identity of metaphysical grounding and mitigates its capacity to foment violence.[49]

Posnock compares Lewy to Toomer, "an extravagant inventor of origins who refused to be 'limited to Negro' but instead took that as a starting point and from there 'circled out'"(292). Posnock acknowledges that "Toomer's refusal to respect (allegedly) fixed origins and his mystical urge to be in touch with cosmic ones led to obscurity," but refuses to interpret that fact as "a cautionary tale: the price of betraying one's genuine black identity."[50] It is true that this particular narrative of the consequences of some alleged racial betrayal has always seemed somewhat simplistic, or at least a *post hoc ergo propter hoc* argument. It is a narrative reproduced, if not explicitly suggested (or fictively recreated) in what appears to be correspondence from Arna Bontemps to Langston Hughes during their editing of a second edition of *The Poetry of the Negro* in another of *Atlantis*'s parallel columns. But we should not overlook the very real limits of Toomer's opinions about race, which may have had less to do with cultural freedom than social privilege. Darwin Turner suggests that the possible reasons for Toomer's sudden refusal to be identified as a "Negro" range from a belief that his grandfather P.B.S. Pinchback lied about his African ancestry in order to become governor of Louisiana during Reconstruction to longing for inclusion in Waldo Frank's literary circle. A

1930 diary entry reveals that at least temporarily, what Toomer truly desired was "to be dominant, to have freedom and power" and to live "first, as an individual," which, he states, "will not allow of my being colored."[51] Similarly, a "colored" friend of his could only conclude that the author of "The Blue Meridian," and its vision of a raceless America, was white. Whether he ever admitted it to himself or not, Toomer's decision to live "as neither black nor white," was effectively, to use Darwin Turner's language, a "decision to live as a white man."[52] Moreover, we have seen that the young Delany's desperate craving for ambiguity in *Motion* was, as he describes it in one interview, the moment when he was "most trapped by [his] identity, most paralyzed and most limited by greater society, and that is the sign one has given up, given in; that you are precisely *not* in a condition of freedom—but of entrapment." Toomer may have felt similarly trapped, paralyzed, and "wounded" by the categories of identity imposed upon him by society. But by opting out of the race game entirely, Toomer rejected the opportunity to change the significance of race, of Delany's project of making race mean differently. "Saying 'I am not a part' is *very* different from saying 'Because I *am* a part, I will not participate in *that* manner,'" according to Delany; "The first is delusion. The second is power."[53] Posnock is right to identify Toomer as a "shadowy presence [that] threads through the novel,"[54] but an association between *Atlantis*'s racial politics and Toomer's is not necessarily something to celebrate.

As with his reading of *Motion*, Posnock ignores a key passage in *Atlantis*. After Lewy's rhapsodic claim to "originate everywhere," John asks "How you gonna stay a nigger . . . if you come from so many places?" (115) Characteristically, John's chief concern is Lewy's racial authenticity as an African American. Posnock characterizes this interrogative as an attempt "to puncture Lewy's bravado"; Lewy's reply, in part because of John's use of the N-word, shifts the context of the discussion from the cultural and historic to the social and involves more than what Posnock suggests, a simple admission of his inability to stop "anybody calling me a black bastard" (115).[55] As Lewy says,

> "That don't stop anybody from calling you a nigger, calling Sam a black boy, calling me colored, calling you a redheaded African, calling Sam a negro, calling me black. And I guess we're what we're called, no matter where we're from." (115)

Lewy is saying more here than just "sticks and stones"; he is acknowledging the degree to which identities are defined from outside of the self, at least in the social world where different people (and peoples) come in contact with one another. Society will interpellate you as it will no matter how you configure your own sense of self. Lewy refuses to privilege such an interpellation over his own sense of self, downplaying the former's importance. "That's what calling means—that's all," he says, "It isn't no more important than that" (116). But Lewy's is not the last word in this discussion of race and identity. That belongs, somewhat surprisingly, to Sam: "Well," Sam said, "it's pretty important, what they call you, when it means where you got to live, got to go to school, even what you got to work at" (116). Sam understands that no matter what cultural sources Lewy taps to enrich and construct his identity, in segregated America, racial identity—defined from within or without—is central to the political issues that affect the lives of African Americans in very specific ways, like it or not, want it or not. Lewy may be able to—and should, by all rights—transcend racial distinctions when it comes to culture. But the social reality of segregation in 1920s America is more difficult to negotiate. For all of his cross-cultural explorations, the boys understand that Lewy will always be interpellated—and will identify himself—as "black." The understanding they approach is similar to that expressed by DuBois in *Dusk of Dawn* (1940): "The soul is still individual if it is free. Race is a cultural, sometimes an historical fact"; however, that spiritual freedom and the constructedness of racial identity do not change the fact that "the black man is a person who must ride 'Jim Crow' in Georgia."[56] Or as Henry Louis Gates, Jr. puts it, "You can love Mozart, Picasso, and ice hockey and still be as black as the ace of spades."[57] The silence and "closeness" (116) that follows this conversation on race signifies its importance to *Atlantis*'s theme, and it is broken only by John's sudden imitation of a bomber plane, the memory that is triggered by Grand Central Station's clock and triggers the memory of John's mule early in the story.

Lewy's theorization of a process of perpetually multiplying points of origin echoes the multiplicity and permeability of the self Delany develops in *The Motion of Light in Water* as well as the thematics and rhetoric of W. E. B. DuBois, who declared his right, on behalf of all Americans of African descent, to European culture in *The Souls of Black Folk* (1903): "I sit with Shakespeare and he winces not. Across the color line I move arm in arm with Balzac and Dumas."[58] But DuBois claims white European culture as his own not so much because "culture has no color," but because it belongs to African Americans too, by right; black Americans are heirs to the European cultural traditions as much as white Americans. DuBois stakes his claim and that of the race to a cultural heritage that white America would keep to itself. "I am related to them," DuBois says of whites on behalf of blacks in *Dusk of Dawn* (1940), "and they have much that belongs to me."[59] For Posnock, Lewy's philosophy and the "paired epigraphs at the head of [DuBois's] chapters represent the 'kingdom' [of culture] itself in miniature as a utopian realm above the Veil where sorrow songs and Swinburne dwell together 'uncolored'"; according to this argument, *Atlantis* transforms the "kingdom" of colorless culture "from a distant realm beyond the veil to a living reality, as accessible and functional as the Brooklyn Bridge: I sit with Hart Crane and he winces not."[60] But if Lewy envisions a culture "above the veil," in Sam's final vision the three friends approach a sophisticated theory of race that acknowledges the sociopolitical reality they inhabit.

Posnock's reading of *Atlantis* might seem to be supported by the novella's citations of Robert Hayden, whose "Middle Passage"(1962) provides one of two epigraphs to all but one chapter. Hayden is a key literary antecedent for Delany, the latter an avid reader and one-time acquaintance of W. H. Auden, the former citing Auden as a major literary influence. Hayden used SF–related themes and topics to great effect in poems such as "Stars," "Astronauts," "[American Journal]," and "Unidentified Flying Object." Known for his resistance to the Black Arts Movement's program of cultural nationalism, Hayden wrote poems that can be read as demonstrating a kind of universalism. The undercover alien voice of "[American Journal]" identifies the population's "varied pigmentations" as signs of "the imprecise and strangering / distinctions by which they live   by which they / justify their cruelties to one another."[61] "El-Hajj Malik El-Shabazz" is the name of Hayden's elegy for Malcolm X as well as that which the slain leader bore when "He fell upon his face before / Allah the raceless in whose blazing Oneness all / were one."[62] And "Words in the Mourning Time" speaks of "the vision of/a human world where godliness / is possible and man/is neither gook nigger honkey wop nor kike / but man //   permitted to be man."[63] According to Arnold Rampersad, Hayden "saw himself, in his central identity, as an American poet," but Rampersad's portrayal of Hayden as "a pre-eminently racial poet and as one ultimately transcending race" is perhaps more accurate.[64] With the possible exception of "El-Hajj Malik El-Shabazz," the poems just cited are more antiracist than anti-race. Claiming African American history and culture as his own did not restrict Hayden's access to or limit his appreciation of English and white American cultural traditions; these claims instead informed his belief in racial equality and thereby enabled that transcendence.[65] African American history saturates Hayden's best-known poems (e.g., "Frederick Douglass," "Runagate Runagate," "Homage to the Empress of the Blues"), which "confirm Hayden's profound commitment to the culture out of which he had come, even as he was also committed to linking the particularities of black culture to the universal concerns of the human condition."[66] "Middle Passage" features prominently in *Atlantis,* at least partly because of the poem's specificity with regard to black history and the poet's deep knowledge of that history. Prior to his 1997 public reading of Hayden's poem, Delany explained that Hart Crane had planned to include in *The Bridge* a similarly epic verse treatment of the experiences of enslaved Africans in the New World that would incorporate the rhythms of jazz, but—fortunately, according to Delany—he changed his mind:

> In the 1920s when Hart Crane was struggling with his great poem-cycle *The Bridge*, one of Crane's early ambitions was to include, among its sections, one to center on a black Pullman porter named after John Brown that would be "a history of the Negro Race." Eventually he abandoned this ambition and turned his poem to other things. The Hayden poem I shall be reading tonight always makes me realize *why* Crane couldn't do it—and how intelligent he was to leave that job to someone else.[67]

Delany's "Atlantis Rose . . . : Some Notes on Hart Crane" praises Crane for his "astute poetic tact" in making this decision.[68] It is not so much that a white writer could not ever write a poetic "history of the Negro Race," but rather, that such a project requires the author to be familiar with that history and culture, which Crane may not have been. Hayden, whom Delany describes as a man who "loved the black community, its history, its culture, as he loved the world community of art and artists,"[69] possessed just such a knowledge, not by virtue of his race, but because his race informed his pursuit of knowledge about African American history. Moreover, the pairing of lines from "Middle Passage" at the opening of *Atlantis*'s first chapter—"Voyage through death / to life upon these shores"—with an excerpt from Foucault's *Madness and Civilization*—"It is for the other world that the madman sets sail in his fools' boat; it is from the other world that he comes when he disembarks"—does not suggest a colorless kingdom of culture where the two meet. Instead, it suggests that as much as the madman on the Ship of Fools, the enslaved African fits Foucault's description of "the Passenger *par excellence*: that is, the prisoner of the passage."[70]

It is specifically the history of people of African descent in modern America that *Atlantis* celebrates. The novella has been compared to *Fatheralong* (1994), John Edgar Wideman's autobiographical meditation on African American fathers and sons, which Wideman calls "an attempt, among other things, to break out, displace, replace the paradigm of race. Teach me who I might be, who you might be—without it."[71] *Atlantis*, however, can be read as its author's attempt to teach himself about himself and his father through racial and family history. The most notable aspect of *Atlantis* is its representation of Delany's father, who in *The Motion of Light in Water* "had always been an angry, anxious man."[72] In *Atlantis*, however, Sam is smart and likable, if somewhat naive, and not unlike the author in his love for pulp adventure fiction and intellectual musings on culture and history. It is as if Delany has written out his own Oedipal complex; *Motion*'s threatening father figure gives way to *Atlantis*'s sympathetic protagonist, whose love for New York City and sensitivity to the wonders it provides resonate with the author's own.

Yet it is quite possible that throughout his career Delany has had to look to others as mentors and role models, particularly when it comes to his writing. Delany's description of meeting Harlem Renaissance figure Bruce Nugent suggests a young man who in some ways favors the writer and artist over his father:

> Bruce . . . was actually the same age as my father: Both were born in 1906. But during my adolescence and young manhood, this tall, soft-spoken, black, gay man, multi-lingual, artist and writer, so wonderfully sophisticated about dance and theater and literature, had seemed to me everything fathers were not.[73]

Hence the significance in *Atlantis* of Hart Crane. Indeed, the very title of the novella may be a variation of an article by Earnest Boyd published in the *American Mercury* that mentions Crane, entitled "Aesthete: Model 1924."[74] It is evident from "Atlantis Rose" that Delany sees the poet as kindred spirit and literary forerunner. When Delany describes Crane as the antithesis of "a common-sensical, super-average man" and "as fiercely a self-taught intellectual as a writer could be," he could very well be describing himself.[75] Moreover, in Crane Delany finds a writer who has also written about gay sexuality in a sophisticated, coded, fashion. Delany recalls the emotional force that accompanied his realization of a shared experience upon his first encounter with Crane's poetry:

> I also remember, even more forcefully, the lines that, for me—at sixteen— sent chills racing over me and, a moment later, struck me across the bridge of my nose with a pain sharp enough to make my eyes water. It came with the lines from "Harbor Dawn" that Crane the lyricist of unspeakable love had just managed to speak:
>
> > And you beside me, blessed now while sirens
> > Sing to us, stealthily weave us into day—
> > > . . . *a forest shudders in your hair*
>
> For suddenly I realized that "you" was another man![76]

In Crane's poem "Harbor Dawn," the young Delany found the "explicit lack of feminization" that would support a gay reading and contend with the straight one most readers would tend to make.[77] The shock of recognition, and the sense of community it immediately produces, is comparable to Delany's experience at the St. Mark's Baths in *Motion,* or to that described in James Thomson's "City of Dreadful Night," often alluded to in Delany's writing: "'I suffer mute and lonely, yet another / Uplifts his voice to let me know a brother / Travels the same wild paths though out of sight.'"[78] Moreover, the unwillingness of Sam's urbane siblings to confront sexual matters parallels what Delany identifies as the censoring of communiqués addressing the subject from collections of Crane's letters, and the exclusion of discussion of Toomer's affair with Waldo Frank's wife in Crane's biographies.[79]

In Delany's novella, Hart Crane recites for Sam fragments of early versions of "Atlantis," which Crane intended to be "a specifically American affirmation to counter Eliot's presumably international despair."[80] When Sam questions the morality of "tak[ing] words and phrases from somebody else's" poem for one's own, Crane refers to "The Waste Land," which he describes as "a poem by a man named Eliot . . . in *The Dial* a few Novembers back . . . [that] is nothing *but* words and phrases borrowed from other writers: Shakespeare, Webster, Wagner" (91). Crane also justifies literary allusions by way of the principles of Derridean iterability. By repeating another poet's words, Crane transforms their meaning. "I'll link Sam [Greenberg]'s words to words of mine," he says, "engulf them, digest and transform them, *make* them words of my own" (91). Posnock contributes a quite useful and accurate evaluation of this technique: "The radical originality of Crane's art arises out of the abandonment of any conventional grounds of originality. . . . creative appropriation is continual, limitless, and reciprocal. For those who are borrowing words of another are, in turn, having their words appropriated. Sovereign ownership is disowned in the kingdom of culture."[81] Just as Lewy borrows from various cultural heritages, which he transforms into the construction of his own identity, Crane's citations help to create his own, new, lyrical constructions. One could say that both Crane and Lewy are like hip-hop musicians, sampling bits of prerecorded music to construct their own compositions, or—perhaps more appropriately, given the temporal setting—jazz musicians riffing on a musical phrase from other sources or putting their own variations on established themes. The parallelism of Lewy's and Crane's lessons represents a reconciliation, a coming together of Sam's Northern and Southern visions. Sam and Crane approach a cultural realm "above the veil" but fail to sustain their connection, in part because of miscommunications stemming from their racial and sexual differences; they do not speak the same language.[82] There is, after all, a bit of wincing going on above the veil. But the bridge symbolizes exactly the type of articulation that must be built between anti-racist and anti-homophobic cultures and politics. Just as the Brooklyn Bridge links (or articulates) "city to country" (70), orderly and known Manhattan—"a grid

in which everything had its place, in which nothing could be lost" (69)—
to the relatively wild countryside of Brooklyn in 1924, which for Sam
"had become in memory a kind of field, verdant and vasty, of fronds out
of idle depths, pleasant to the eye, but in which nothing much could be
found" (69), it also links Delany's biological and literary fathers. *Atlantis*
is therefore characterized less by a politics of universalism than it is by its
attempt to connect, and connect itself to, specific African American and
gay cultural histories. In *American Literary History,* Delany has been
quoted as stating, "the writer has no existence without . . . a relationship
to [an American literary] past."[83] If Ken James is correct in identifying the
theme of Crane's *The Bridge* as "speaking across the gap . . . communi-
cating across time, space, and death,"[84] then *Atlantis* can be seen as Delany's own bridge across that gap, linking the two fathers to the author
and to each other, a linkage figured in the dual interracial epigraphs that
open three of the novella's chapters as in DuBois's *Souls.* "Father stories
are about establishing origins," according to Wideman, "and through
them legitimizing claims of ownership, of occupancy and identity."[85] Such
is Delany's purpose in *Atlantis.*

"What is 'Atlantis'?" is a question Delany confronts in his notes on
Crane and *The Bridge.*[86] Although he arrives at his own answers, another
might be found in the first part of *The Books of Magic,* a four-part
graphic novel scripted by one of Delany's favorite writers, Neil Gaiman.
In Book I, Arion, an ancient Atlantean sorcerer, says, "The true Atlantis
is *inside* you, just as it's inside *all* of us. The sunken land is lost beneath
the dark sea, lost beneath the waves of wet, black stories and myths that
break upon the shores of our minds."[87] As a reflection, refraction, and
celebration of its author's African American heritage, Delany's novella
succeeds in—as its epigraph from Hart Crane's "For the Marriage of
Faustus and Helen" suggests—"distinctly prais[ing] the years." *Atlantis:
Model 1924* unequivocally embodies acts of gay and African American
cultural recovery.

6

A REVOLUTION FROM WITHIN

PARALITERATURE AS AIDS ACTIVISM

> As long as black sexuality remains a taboo subject, we cannot acknowledge, examine, or engage these tragic psychocultural facts of American life. Furthermore, our refusal to do so limits our ability to confront the overwhelming realities of the AIDS epidemic in America in general and in black America in particular.
> —Cornel West, "Black Sexuality"[1]

> I do not have AIDS. I am surprised that I don't. I have had sex with men weekly, sometimes daily—without condoms—since my teens, though true, it's been overwhelmingly . . . no, more accurately it's been—since 1980—*all* oral, not anal.
> —Samuel R. Delany, *The Mad Man*[2]

From the recent comments of some writers, one might assume that at the dawn of the new millennium, "the AIDS crisis," as the title of a 1997 essay by sex columnist Dan Savage declares, "is over."[3] Andrew Sullivan published an essay called "When Plagues End: Notes on the Twilight of an Epidemic" in the November 10, 1996 issue of the *New York Times Magazine*. Unfortunately, there is plenty of evidence to prove that the AIDS crisis is far from being resolved. The *AIDS Epidemic Update*, produced by the Joint United Nations Programme on HIV/AIDS (UNAIDS) and the World Health Organization (WHO) reports that as of December 2002, there were 42 million people in the world living with AIDS.[4] The *Update* also reports that there were 3.1 million AIDS deaths, and 5 million people were newly infected with HIV, the virus that causes AIDS, in 2002 (3).[5] All inhabited parts of the world have been affected, but AIDS has devastated Sub-Saharan Africa, where UNAIDS/WHO reports it has accounted for an estimated 3.5 million (70 percent) of the world's new infections and 29.4 million (70 percent) of the world's population living with HIV/AIDS in 2002 (16).

In the United States, 816,149 AIDS cumulative cases and 467, 910 AIDS deaths had been reported to the Centers for Disease Control and Prevention (CDC) as of December 2001.[6] The CDC lists the number of *reported* cases of people in the U.S. living with HIV or AIDS, cumulative through December 2001, at 506,154.[7] However, the National Institute of Allergy and Infectious Diseases and the National Institutes for Health estimate that "as many as 900,000 Americans may be infected with HIV."[8] African Americans are disproportionately affected by this health crisis. The CDC calculates the cumulative number of reported AIDS cases for the category "Black, not Hispanic" as of December 2001 to be 313,180 (approximately 38 percent of all reported cases[9]); AIDS deaths for this group were 168,202 (approximately 36 percent of all reported cases).[10] According to the CDC's most recent information, approximately 73 percent of African American AIDS cases reported through December 2001 were men,[11] among whom the leading HIV exposure categories were "men who have sex with men" at 37 percent and "injecting drug use" at 33 percent.[12] "Injecting drug use" and "heterosexual contact" were the leading exposure categories for African American women, each at 39 percent.[13] The CDC's 2001 National Vital Statistics Report identifies "HIV disease" as the leading cause of death for African American women between 25 and 34 years of age and for African American men between 35 and 44.[14] The National Minority AIDS Council [NMAC] notes that "race and ethnicity are not risk factors for HIV infection; however, race and ethnicity in the U.S. are associated with key factors that determine health status such as poverty, access to quality health care, health care seeking behaviors, illicit drug use and high rates of sexually transmitted diseases."[15] Despite the positive impact of recent developments in drug treatments, HIV/AIDS continues to present a health crisis that demands the attention and action of the American and the world communities.

The continuing reality of AIDS puts pressure on academics in humanistic studies, particularly those who assume that their production and spread of knowledge matters socially and politically, to reflect on the efficacy of the responses to the crisis generated by literature, literary studies, critical theory, and cultural studies. What can such disciplines really do to improve the situation, to halt the impairment of health and the loss of life? "Against the urgency of people dying in the streets," Stuart Hall asks, "what in God's name is the point of cultural studies?"[16] Ross Chambers opens his study of AIDS diaries by noting several specific concerns about his project: that "writing criticism in the midst of an epidemic can feel uncomfortably like getting on with one's needlework while the house burns down," and that time and energy would be better spent "contributing to AIDS research" or to "working with ACT-UP, hassling congress people." With regard to the first and most general anxiety, Chambers reaches his own conclusion: "In an epidemic, rhetoric *also* plays a not insignificant part."[17] Paula Treichler's *How to Have Theory in an Epidemic* (1999), represents the best thinking and most sustained focus on the relationship between AIDS and language systems. "To speak of AIDS as a linguistic construction that acquires meaning only in relation to networks of given signifying practices may seem politically and pragmatically dubious, like philosophizing in the middle of a war zone," Treichler says, but adds, "making sense of AIDS compels us to address questions of signification and representation."[18] Susan Sontag has warned against the dangers of comprehending AIDS through figurative language—particularly the military metaphors that allow us to speak of a "war on AIDS"—as part of her effort to see it as an illness and nothing more.[19] But Treichler maintains that "illness *is* metaphor, and this semantic work—this effort to 'make sense of' AIDS—must be done," because AIDS itself "compels" us to interpret it in such a way; "hence its enormous power to generate meanings."[20] Add to that Laurie Anderson's musical reminder, cited by a number of scholars, including Treichler, that "language is a virus."[21] The second anxiety that Chambers identifies reflects the relative privilege and authority of the biomedical sciences, the "anchoring tradition" of "AIDS research." Treichler notes that in 1989, at the fifth International AIDS Conference, the program committee chair acknowledged the number of panels and papers on "social aspects of the epidemic" and that "AIDS is not simply a medical problem, but also a human drama," before claiming that "naturally, we all know that the ultimate solution will eventually come to light in a laboratory," thereby framing the humanities as "handmaiden to the biomedical sciences, [which] do their best to ease the suffering and combat ignorance until the laboratory can find the 'ultimate solution.'" Treichler has identified AIDS as not only a biological epidemic, but also as "an epidemic of signification," a phenomenon that has generated multiple meanings of itself in multiple contexts, articulated for multiple reasons.[22] Similarly, Simon Watney has argued that AIDS is not only "a medical crisis" but also "a crisis over the entire framing of knowledge about the human body and its capacities for sexual pleasure."[23] The intellectual work Treichler and Watney, among others, describe and perform should be counted as contributing to the fight against AIDS. As Phillip Brian Harper asserts, "if we are indeed facing the 'end' of AIDS, this is due not only to the 'discoveries' of medical 'science' but also to developments in the discursive field that actually make those discoveries possible."[24]

The third anxiety Chambers describes speaks to a perceived gap between the efficacy of literature and criticism on AIDS and AIDS-related political activism. But, of course, there must be an "art" to activism; any articulation of a politics must take the form of a signifying practice—

poetry, prose, speech, photography, film, and the like—that is potentially meaningful to an audience. More to the point, gay men and lesbians—the groups that started AIDS activism and have remained at its forefront—have demonstrated an impressive critical acumen, a recognition that battles for awareness, action, and dollars must include a battle over meanings. "Almost from the beginning, through intense interest and informed political activism," Treichler states, "members of the gay community have repeatedly contested the terminology, meanings, and interpretations produced by scientific inquiry," such as "whether homosexuality was to be officially classified as an illness by the APA." For example, as a result of gay activists challenging the representation of their sexuality in academic medical journals, "terms like *promiscuous* were forced to give way, at least in regularly scrutinized publications like the *Morbidity and Mortality Weekly Report (MMWR)*, to more neutral terms like *sexually active*."[25] On the other hand, art that responds to AIDS can operate as activism itself. "Within the arts," Douglas Crimp argues, "it is . . . assumed that cultural producers can respond to the epidemic in only two ways: by raising money for scientific research and service organizations or by creating works that express human suffering and loss"; however the most effective response consists of "cultural practices actively participating in the struggle against AIDS." AIDS can be more than just subject matter, Crimp explains; art about AIDS can do more than "'express feelings,' 'share experiences,' 'demonstrate the indomitability of the human spirit,' 'raise consciousness,' provide a 'human face' for the crisis, or represent that which 'lives on forever.'" Activist art is distinguished by its "engagement in lived social life."[26]

Perhaps out of modesty, Samuel R. Delany has made a distinction between his writing on AIDS and "real" AIDS activism. In response to an inquiry about what he has done "in his neighborhood or local community with respect to HIV/AIDS," Delany replies, "outside of writing and writing-related activities (lecturing to and talking with various groups, usually in colleges around the country), I've done very little."[27] It can be argued, however, that in his numerous works of fiction and nonfiction essays that address AIDS—including *Flight from Nevèrÿon*'s *The Tale of Plagues and Carnivals* (1985; the first novel-length work of fiction on AIDS from a major publisher in the United States), the short essay "Street Talk/Straight Talk" (1991), the lecture entitled "The Rhetoric of Sex/The Discourse of Desire" (1995), the letters collected in the volume entitled *1984* (2000), and most notably the "pornotopic fantasy" (ix)[28] of *The Mad Man* (1994)—Delany effects his own brand of AIDS activism. Treichler explains that "the AIDS epidemic has been articulated to a remarkable diversity of issues, perspectives, and agendas."[29] As such, no single category or identity can provide a sufficient vantage point for analysis and activism. Political scientist Cathy Cohen asserts that African Americans' response to AIDS must involve a politics of difference: "Analyzing AIDS through a singular framework, such as race, class, sexuality, or gender is unproductive and misleading. Instead, it is the intersection of multiple identities that determines how black Americans will experience this disease."[30] AIDS, therefore, would appear to necessitate a multiplex mode of analysis, one we might readily expect Delany's work to provide. This chapter interprets Delany's paraliterary and theoretical writing on AIDS as activist interventions in the epidemic. Moreover, his novel *The Mad Man* is vital to the project of recognizing sexual difference within the African American community, which is fundamental to the formation of appropriate responses—social, political, scientific, or cultural—to AIDS's impact on black lives.

How to Have Race Theory in an Epidemic

> The question of AIDS is an extremely important terrain of struggle and contestation. In addition to the people we know who are dying, or have died, or will, there are the many people dying who are never spoken of. How could we say that the question of AIDS is not also a question of who gets represented and who does not?
> —Stuart Hall, "Cultural Studies and Its Theoretical Legacies"[31]

"The Fire This Time," an article in the January 1999 issue of *POZ*, a magazine aimed at HIV-positive readers, identifies various African American leaders and organizations taking measures to combat AIDS in black communities. The article describes the efforts of organizations such as Outreach (Atlanta), the National Black Leadership Commission on AIDS (New York), the South Side Help Center (Chicago), Leading for Life at Harvard University, and the National Association of People with AIDS (D.C.), whose executive director at the time was African American. The article also recognizes the work of African American faith-based organizations such as Chicago's Trinity United Church of Christ's AIDS ministry and Balm in Gilead, based in New York City with affiliates throughout the country, which encourages black churches to address the spiritual needs of people with AIDS (PWAs), distributes HIV prevention information, and organized a national "Week of Prayer for the Healing of AIDS."[32] The efforts of these organizations—as well as of other African American and gay and lesbian organizations that formed the earliest response to AIDS in black communities[33]—led to action by the Congressional Black Caucus, chaired by Maxine Waters, which managed to secure $130 million (later increased to $156 million) "earmarked specifically to expand

HIV prevention, substance abuse programs and treatment access in African American communities" out of the 1999 federal budget. Evaluations of this development ranged from sober ("a beginning step") to ebullient ("the start of a revolution"), but most notably the funding prompted the executive director of AIDS Action in Washington, D.C., to say that "the strongest leadership in the fight against the epidemic is now coming from the black community."[34]

Whatever the truth value of such a statement is at present, it must be acknowledged that in previous years, the response of "the black community" and black leadership to AIDS had been insufficient. For years the National Association for the Advancement of Colored People (NAACP) and the National Urban League implicitly, and sometimes explicitly, sent the message that "this isn't really our issue."[35] Cathy Cohen characterizes the efforts of the NAACP and the Southern Christian Leadership Conference (SCLC) as "uneven at their best moments and neglectful in their worst" and the early responses of national black political organizations as "first denial and later a focus on service activity and distributional claims." In 1986 the National Coalition of Black Lesbians and Gays organized the "National Conference on AIDS in the Black Community" in Washington, D.C., which was co-sponsored by the NMAC and the National Conference of Black Mayors, but not by the NAACP or the Urban League. The NAACP did sponsor a Health Summit in 1992, but as Cohen notes, the document it produced "contain[ed] no language about gay men."[36] *POZ* quotes a Balm in Gilead administrator describing the response of the SCLC, "under the noble leadership of this important young man, Martin Luther King III," as "slow." And despite the great deal of attention paid to AIDS by the Nation of Islam, given the group's "controversial endorsement of the experimental drug Kemron . . . advancement of conspiracy theories . . . [and] Minister Louis Farrakhan's open homophobia," its response to the crisis can be described as, at best, "mixed."[37] Cohen characterizes African American political leadership at the national, state, and local levels as "transactional"—that is, diplomatic, deal-making—instead of "transformational," which is distinguished by "profound purpose" and an effort "to bring about social change." This is particularly true of African Americans in the U.S. Congress. Although Rep. Louis Stokes has gone on record as admitting that "AIDS is an issue that black leadership has shied away from," voting records show that "black congressional members might be considered, instead, good foot soldiers in the war against AIDS" because they have backed proposals and legislation on the issue that started with other members of Congress. But such records do not represent "efforts to redefine and transform thinking about this epidemic, especially as it raged in African American communities."[38]

What are the reasons for such a tardy and, until recently, muted black response to AIDS? In general, there has been a failure among African Americans to see AIDS as a social or political issue that "belongs" to the entire community. Cohen notes that 55 percent of PWAs are men who were infected with HIV through sex with another man, but wonders about the degree to which African Americans see this fact as a matter that directly affects their communities. The black political agenda has long been dominated by what Cohen calls consensus issues, "political issues understood or defined in ways that tap into a racial group framework, initiating feelings of linked fate and the perception of advancing the interests of the entire black community," although such issues often serve only "the most visible segments of any black political agenda." In black politics, however, AIDS is what Cohen calls a cross-cutting issue, one that has been "constructed or framed in ways that highlight not [its] relevance to the entire group but [its] limited or bounded impact on a fragment of the community." Cross-cutting issues speak to the political necessity of recognizing and valuing difference and abandoning "monolithic" or "uni-dimensional" representations of the African American community. They "arise out of the multiplicity of identities that marginal group members embody and personify the dilemmas that marginal group members face in trying to mold such intersecting identities into a strategy for survival and progress." Such difficulties are evident in the tendency for cross-cutting issues to take a back seat to consensus issues, as the history of the subordination of gender equality to the struggle for racial equality in black political organizations demonstrates. Hence, Cohen asks, "When we talk about the endangered status of black men, does that discussion include the devastation to black gay men resulting from the AIDS epidemic?"[39]

AIDS is also, as Stuart Hall contends, "a question of who gets represented and who does not"; therefore, the political agenda is shaped by, and shapes, the representation of issues in key scientific and other cultural contexts. Cohen argues that in the U.S., "AIDS began in black communities, apparently, with black gay men, black men who have sex with men, black injection drug users and their sexual partners," but these are "groups we are accustomed to ignoring."[40] Douglas Crimp has also commented on the perception that AIDS—originally known as GRID (Gay-Related Immunodeficiency)[41]—was a health issue that exclusively affected white, middle-class, gay men:

> What is now called AIDS was first *seen* in middle-class gay men in America, in part because of our access to medical care. Retrospectively, however, it appears that IV drug users—whether gay or straight—were dying of AIDS in NYC throughout the 70s and early 80s, but a class-based and racist health care system failed to notice, and an epidemiology equally skewed by class and racial bias failed to begin to look *until* 1987.[42]

Cohen's argument is similar; she demonstrates that the AIDS problem in African American communities was largely invisible to the Centers of Disease Control, to mainstream "white" media, and to black media. The CDC shaped the definition of AIDS; its 1981 *MMWR* "highlighted the common sexual identity of patients, suggesting that some aspect of their gay 'lifestyle' might be the underlying cause of the disease." It maintained an "overriding focus . . . on the gay community," thereby "possibly unwittingly, sending a message to those who take their cues from this institution . . . that this was a disease primarily, and possibly exclusively, of gay men." Cohen's analysis demonstrates "the social construction of a medical crisis" and is not intended "to deny the overwhelming numbers of gay men who suffered from this disease or to suggest that such attention was unmerited." Today, AIDS researchers are using "a model that emphasizes the parallel tracking or multiple sites of development of the epidemic among both gay men and IDUs [intravenous drug users]."[43] Whereas the CDC shaped an understanding of AIDS, the media communicated that understanding to the American people. Cohen describes the media as a "'linking institution,' transferring agency-specific information into more general ideological frames for the public's consumption." Earvin "Magic" Johnson's announcement that he was HIV-positive, for all the media coverage in garnered, did not result in subsequent stories on AIDS in African American communities. Cohen notes that "cumulatively through 1993 blacks constitute[d] 32 percent of all AIDS cases." The amount of media coverage did not correspond with these figures. For example, "from 1981 to 1993 the *New York Times* printed 4,671 stories on the AIDS epidemic. Unbelievably, only 231, or five percent, of those 4,761 stories had African Americans as their focus"; and most of those were on Johnson or Arthur Ashe. Within the same time span, the *Times* published only three stories on AIDS and gay black men. In general, black media has not done much better. The record of some scholarly journals is particularly embarrassing: "Journals like *Race and Class, Sage, The Black Scholar,* and *Africa News*—known for their attention to the struggles of people of color around the world—were noticeably absent from most discussions of AIDS in black communities." And like mainstream "white" media, black media had little to say about black homosexuality: "Only one in fifteen stories in *Ebony,* as an admittedly limited example, between 1981 and 1993 focused explicitly on a gay man with AIDS"; the rest focused on heterosexual transmission.[44]

Homophobia is certainly another reason for the slow response to the AIDS crisis in black communities, but as Cohen convincingly argues, it is hardly the sole factor. Any attempt to comprehend homophobia—"the fear or hatred of gay and lesbian people"[45]—among African Americans must include an understanding of the history of the degradation and spectacularization of black bodies throughout American history. Cornel West identifies "two hundred and forty-four years of slavery and nearly a century of institutionalized terrorism in the form of segregation, lynchings, and second-class citizenship in America" that have "left its toll in the psychic scars and personal wounds now inscribed in the souls of black folk . . . clearly etched on the canvas of black sexuality."[46] For centuries, white America has suffered from a neurotic fear of a black penis, what Frantz Fanon identifies as "Negrophobia," based on "the image of the biological-sexual-sensual-genital-nigger."[47] The fear of black masculinity as a threat to white womanhood is promoted in the racist works of Thomas Dixon, shown to have tragic consequences by Richard Wright in *Native Son* (1940), and critically analyzed in Delany's *Dhalgren*. The flipside of it, however, is the myth of black sexual superiority, which some black men have claimed—with varying degrees of sincerity—should not be debunked, even though it, to quote Kobena Mercer, "arises from the core beliefs of classical biologizing racist ideology, which held Africans to be inferior in mind, and morality also, on account of their bodies."[48] This last example demonstrates how the legacy of slavery and colonialism includes troublesome constructions of black sexuality by African Americans themselves.

The marginalization of gay men in black media coverage of AIDS in turn reflects and shapes African Americans' conceptions of themselves and their communities. African Americans, according to Cohen, are in a state of "advanced marginalization," which is characterized by "a symbolic opening of the dominant society" in strategic positions. Those "more privileged members of marginal groups" engage in a process of "secondary marginalization," the "management" or policing of other marginal group members. Among the scholarship that Cohen cites to support her claim is James R. Grossman's study of "how the Urban League in conjunction with black and white institutions worked to help black migrants 'adjust' to urban standards of behavior," an activity evident in urban Hubert's criticisms of his rural younger brother in Delany's *Atlantis: Model 1924*. Examples such as Grossman's demonstrate an African American tradition of self-image control that has often focused on sexuality. Community leaders and organizations, fighting for civil rights, equal access, and full recognition as citizens, have struggled to "clean up" the image of black sexuality in black communities.[49] Phillip Brian Harper's *Are We Not Men?* identifies contemporary efforts by "a moralistic black bourgeoisie that seeks to explode notions of black hypersexuality" by "stifling discussion of black sexuality generally" as the latest form of this kind of policing of black representations. Such efforts shape the "profound silence regarding actual sexual practices, either homosexual or heterosexual" that characterizes black responses to AIDS.[50]

Throughout American history, black masculinity has been degraded not only ideologically, but materially in white supremacist removal of "authority, familial responsibility and the ownership of property" from black men; black assertions of patriarchal values can therefore be seen as a desperate and misguided "means of survival against the repressive and violent system of subordination to which they were subjected."[51] The subordination that black men and women endured was often sexual in nature, as represented in Toni Morrison's novel *Beloved* (1987). For example, at the Sweet Home plantation, Halle is forced to watch in silence as his pregnant wife Sethe is robbed of the very milk in her breasts by schoolteacher's nephews, a sight which drives him to madness. Sixo is burned alive for daring to secure freedom for the "Thirty Mile Woman" and their unborn child. And Paul D is made to wear an iron bit in his mouth. As hesitant as he is to confront that particular memory, Paul D recalls his first morning on the chain gang in Georgia with as much, if not more, trepidation:

> Chain-up completed, they knelt down. The dew, more likely than not, was mist by then. Heavy sometimes and if the dogs were quiet and just breathing you could hear doves. Kneeling in the mist they waited for the whim of a guard, or two, or three. Or maybe all of them wanted it. Wanted it from one prisoner in particular or none—or all.
> "Breakfast? Want some breakfast, nigger?'
> "Yes, sir."
> "Hungry, nigger?"
> "Yes, sir."
> "Here you go."
> Occasionally a kneeling man chose gunshot in his head as the price, maybe, of taking a bit of foreskin with him to Jesus. Paul D did not know that then. He was looking at palsied hands, smelling the guard, listening to his soft grunts so like the doves', as he stood before the man kneeling in mist on his right. Convinced he was next, Paul D retched—vomiting up nothing at all. An observing guard smashed his shoulder with the rifle and the engaged one decided to skip the new man for the time being lest his pants and shoes got soiled by nigger puke.[52]

This passage represents white supremacist sexual degradation of black— in this case, male—sexuality, and the type of violation that numerous African Americans, men and women, had to endure. It can also be said that this is a history that informs some kinds of black homophobia. If, as Kobena Mercer suggests, the conceived range of black masculinity runs from Uncle Tom to Shaft,[53] black homosexuals and homosexual acts are often associated with the Uncle Tom side of the spectrum. Consider LeRoi Jones/Amiri Baraka's poem "Black Art" (1969), which identifies a number of moderate "negroleader[s]" and imagines "one/kneeling between the sheriff's thighs/negotiating cooly for his people,"[54] or Baraka's "CIVIL RIGHTS POEM," which begins, "Roywilkins is an eternal faggot."[55] Other homophobic formations exist throughout the Movement, such as Larry Neal's manifesto, "The Black Arts Movement," which speaks of a "homosexual hell hole" and calls lesbianism a "rejection of the body,"[56] and what Mercer identifies as Eldridge Cleaver's "remorseless attack on James Baldwin" in *Soul on Ice*.[57] As Harper suggests, "homophobia is implicated in 'Black Arts' nationalism, whose influence has long outlasted the actual aesthetic movement."[58] The proof of Harper's assertion is in recent hip-hop music, where some rappers script homophobic narratives of black authenticity. Kendall Thomas has initiated critical readings of, for example, Ice Cube's claim that "True Niggas ain't gay" and Buju Banton's incitement to anti-gay violence in "Boom Bye Bye."[59] As Mercer, among many other cultural critics, contend, anti-gay assertions of black authenticity perpetuate the misconception that homosexuality is "the white man's disease"[60]; this myth has been perhaps most [in]famously posited by Dr. Frances Cress Welsing in *The Isis Papers* (1991). Welsing makes no distinction between the consensual sexual behavior of gay black men and the forced sexual submission such as that portrayed in *Beloved*. For her, homosexuality in the black community is the result of "racist programming" geared toward transforming black men into women as part of "a strategy for destroying Black people that must be countered."[61] Talk about science fiction. To quote Ron Simmons, "There may be racist genocidal plots against the black community. Homosexuality, however, is not a part of such plots."[62]

But when it comes to AIDS among African Americans, the effects of beliefs like Welsing's are all too real. They discursively minimize the impact of AIDS on black America and enable the secondary marginalization of black gays and lesbians. As Cohen says, "We have to recognize that a gay sexual identity has been seen as mitigating one's racial identity and deflating one's community standing."[63] African Americans must also engage in a kind of self-critique, to analyze the ways in which an effective response to AIDS is hampered by bigoted attitudes toward a segment of the community that is affected by the crisis, by attitudes that refuse to recognize them not only as members of the African American community, but also as men. This is what Harper means when he says "with respect to combating AIDS among black men . . . the critical intervention must extend to an immediate and uncompromising literal revision of everything we 'know' about masculine identity, in order to ensure that what we know about HIV can be effectively communicated throughout the population."[64]

In *The Mad Man*, Delany can be seen as engaging in this very necessary project. Like works by other black gay and lesbian activists, artists, and intellectuals—including James Baldwin, Bayard Rustin, Langston Hughes, Bessie Smith, Audre Lorde, Marlon Riggs, Essex Hemphill and others—the novel demonstrates that gayness does not impede black race pride. Jumping genres as Delany's works do, *The Mad Man* is part detective novel, part academic novel, part philosophical novel, and almost entirely pornographic. The narrator and protagonist is John Marr, a black man raised in a middle-class, Staten Island family, and a Ph.D. candidate in philosophy at fictional Enoch State University. As Harper points out, being an intellectual can itself be seen as troubling one's racial authenticity: "a too-evident facility in the standard white idiom can quickly identify one not as a strong black man, but as a white-identified Uncle Tom who must also, therefore, be weak, effeminate, and probably a 'fag' . . . Simply put, within some African American communities the 'professional' or 'intellectual' black male inevitably endangers his status both as black and as male whenever he evidences a facility with Standard Received English."[65] But there is no crisis of blackness with the gay and very intellectual John Marr, who balks when his white, straight, dissertation advisor, Irving Mossman, refers to him as "boy" (12). With his good friend Pheldon, Marr maintains an important black and queer solidarity that is valuable to them both. "The fact is, John," Pheldon says, "I don't *have* a lot of black, gay, men friends. You mean a lot to me" (129). Pheldon also encourages Marr to pay attention to hip-hop "because, if nothing else, it's black art that's *verbal*" (297). They attend the Lincoln Theatre performance of Anthony Davis's opera *X: The Life and Times of Malcolm X,* which prompts Marr to compose an analysis of its audiences: "Bewildering white writers, the event filled the papers for a week before and a week after. It's an experience to see, in a theatre space like that filled with black people, all of us rise to our feet to applaud, not a political revolution, but the representation of such a revolution in the most sophisticated musical terms" (216).[66] Toni Morrison's 1993 Nobel Prize for literature and Wole Soyinka's own seven years earlier are milestones of racial pride that approximately frame the novel's events. After Sam, Mossman's soon-to-be ex-wife, outs Marr, she apologizes, saying "I didn't even know black guys *could* be gay" (13), but obviously they can, while simultaneously demonstrating a kind of race consciousness.

Given this race consciousness, then, what is the reader to make of the way race works in the novel's detailed sexual encounters? For example, Marr encounters a white homeless man who asks to be called "Piece of Shit" and agrees to let Marr fellate him under some very specific conditions. Piece of Shit claims that he is heterosexual and that he has a thing for black women in particular, so he will imagine that Marr is a woman. But first he has to teach Marr the proper technique:

"Come over here, next to me. Slide on up and lemme see you make your mouth into a cunt . . . . Yeah, bitch—there you go! Now you got a hole there that'll do for a funky black pussy just about any way. You wanna wiggle that clit a little? . . . I just close my eyes, and, man, you turn into the biggest, nastiest, dirtiest black bitch." (27, 28, 37)

You do not have to be a Black Nationalist to feel, at least upon a first reading, that there is only one way to read such passages: as yet another example of white supremacy attempting to emasculate and feminize the black man, in this case, via a homosexual act. Is there any significant difference between the violation that Paul D remembers in *Beloved* and Marr's sex act with Piece of Shit?

The answer to this question is, yes there actually is a difference, a very important one too; and given that Delany has written extensively and convincingly on fetish sexuality—so much so that bibliographer Robert S. Bravard told him, "If you can explain the fascination with licking sneakers so that I can understand it, you can probably explain anything to anybody"—it should not be too surprising that he is able to provide an apparatus with which to read sexuality in general, and Marr's in particular, critically. In "Aversion/Perversion/Diversion," Delany notes that "fetishism" is often associated with a solo sexual act: "Its assumed pathology is the fact it is thought to be non-reciprocal." When fetishism is reciprocated, "the vocabulary and analytical schema of sadomasochism takes it over; and to me this seems wholly to contravene common sense and my own experience."[67] Delany then recounts several fetishistic phenomena he has encountered or participated in:

I recount these stories not as "the strangest" things that have happened to me. Purposely I am not going into particulars, here, about the well-dressed 60-year-old gentleman in the 96th Street men's room who asked for my shit to eat, or the American tourist who picked me up in Athens who could only make love to me if I wore a wristwatch with a metal band, and that band low on the arm, or the young Italian who had me hammer his stretched scrotum to a piece of pine planking with half a dozen ten-penny nails.[68]

What is significant about these examples is that they have broadened, "however troublingly" so, the list of behaviors that Delany can understand as comprising human sexuality, thereby decentering heteronormative sexualities, which then lose their privilege and look, therefore, no less or more "perverse" than anything else human beings do for sexual pleasure:

It seems to me that when one begins to consider the range of diversities throughout the sexual landscape, then even the unquestioned "normalcy" of the heterosexual male, whose sexual fantasies are almost wholly circum-scribed by photographs of . . . female movie stars! Suddenly looks—well, I will not say "less normal." But I will say that it takes on a mode of sexual social specificity that marks it in the way every other one of these is marked, i.e. as perverse. Similarly, the heterosexual woman whose fantasies entail a man who is wholly faithful to her . . . her sexual condition seems only a particular form of a socially prescribed perversion. . . . Certainly it would be no more difficult than getting off on someone licking my sneakers . . . both strike me, as do all the other situations I have described tonight, as so-cially constituted and perverse.[69]

As further evidence of the relative "perversity" of normative sexuality, in "The Rhetoric of Sex/The Discourse of Desire," Delany mentions that many of the readers who approach him to talk about *The Motion of Light in Water* are straight white men, most of whom are seeking advice on how to, literally, get their hands on the specific type of woman they want: "The range of tales I have heard from these fellows since 1988 when my book was published is enough to make the variety of vanilla heterosexual male desire seem a seething pit of perversions quite as inter-esting as any to be found in any S & M bar, lesbian, gay, or straight."[70] The *Return to Nevèrÿon* series also provides insights along these lines. In the *Flight from Nevèrÿon* tale named for him, the Mummer recites the wise words he used to calm the smuggler, who is infuriated by the for-mer's suggestion that their sexual tastes are similar:

> —Well, whatever you do, and like, and feel, and think, you must learn to accept them all and live with whatever contradictions between them the nameless gods have overlooked in your making, like cracks in an imperfect bit of ceramic still pleasing in its overall shape. Certain strains, certain tasks, certain uses one does not impose on such pieces. But everyone has them. Learning what they are is, no doubt, why we were put here.[71]

Consider also Delany's own predilection for rough hands and bitten nails, Clodon the Bandit's fixation on women who match his vision of "a strong, young, dark-eyed creature with beautiful feet and cunning hands,"[72] or Madame Keyne's explanation, in *Neveryóna*'s fifth chapter, of why she felt compelled to "take an interest" in a "not traditionally beautiful" girl—that is, a girl who does not fit historically sedimented notions of beauty—like Pryn:

> 'But what most people mean by beauty is really a kind of aesthetic accept-ability, not so much character as a lack of it, a set of features and lineaments that hide their history, that suggest history itself does not exist. But the tem-

plate by which we recognize the features and forms in the human body that cause the heart to halt, threatening to spill us over into the silence of death—that is drawn on another part of the soul entirely. Such features are different for each of us. For one, it is the toes of the feet turned in rather than out; for another it is the fingers of the hand thick rather than thin; for still another it is the eyes set wide rather than close together. But all sing, chant, hymn the history of the body, if only because we all know how people regard bodies that deviate from the lauded and totally abnormal norm named beauty. Most of us would rather not recognize such desires in ourselves and thus avoid all contemplation of what the possession of such features means about the lives, the bodies, the histories of others, preferring instead to go on merely accepting the acceptable. But that is not who I am. That is not who I have struggled to be.'[73]

Nor is it who Delany is; the author's decentering of heteronormative sexuality by revealing its "perversity" as well as that of the myriad and multiple sexualities that exist throughout humanity in both expository and fictive prose, is clearly in step with what Sedgwick identifies as "universalizing" representations of homosexuality.

With the understanding that human sexuality encompasses a near-infinite amount of "perversions"—some socially sanctioned and others deemed "deviant" or "immoral"—Marr's predilection for dirty white men can be seen for what it is, that is, a predilection for dirty white men, as opposed to brutal sexual submission. As Darryl Towles explains in his essay "Black and Gay: One Man's Story," he is a black man "with a sexual preference for White [sic] men" who finds that "it's really no different than preferring vodka to scotch."[74] Throughout the novel, we see Marr, a self-described "snow queen" (i.e., a black man attracted to white men) consensually reciprocating the desires of white men (who may or may not identify themselves as "dinge queens")[75] like Piece of Shit, who has his own predilection: dirty black women.

Readers may criticize Marr's fetishization of the homeless as a fixation on economic class difference that does nothing to improve the objectified's condition. To put it plainly, if coarsely, do the homeless really need blow jobs as much as they need food, shelter, or employment? Are the homeless in *The Mad Man* being exploited by middle-class characters like Marr and Hasler? First, consider that the novel is primarily a work of pornography; as its opening disclaimer states, it is not an attempt to represent the day-to-day lives of people without homes who struggle to survive, in the most ironic of injustices, in the wealthiest nation in the world:

The Mad Man is not a book about the homeless of New York—or, indeed, of the country. No book could be which all-but-omits scenes of winter and does not deal with—indeed, focus on—the criminally inadequate attempts by the municipality to feed, clothe, and shelter these men, women, and children. Such a novel would have to be substantially darker than this one—which, I suspect, will be found quite dark enough. (x)

The question of whether *The Mad Man* would be a better novel, or better pornography, with the addition of such content is open to debate. Secondly, although sexual exploitation of all heinous types occurs in the world, Marr's dealings with the homeless are of a decidedly different quality; the homeless characters voluntarily make contact with him as well as Hasler and appear to be getting as much pleasure out of that contact as they do. Moreover, the novel has a palpable investment in relativizing Marr's "perverse" desire for homeless men. Responding to questions about sexual and class relations in the *Return to Nevèrÿon* series in an interview with *Camera Obscura*, Delany asks, "is anything ever eroticized *other* than class relations?" and argues that there is a class component to any sexual desire—whether for a sex partner of the same or different class—"since all human signs have their class associated aspects." In this interview, Delany asks explicitly the question that *The Mad Man* asks implicitly: "why is the eroticizing of certain class relationships egregious and always made explicit in an accusatory tone, while the eroticizing of certain others is always mystified and allowed to remain implicit by calling that process anything other than what it is?"[76] The reason, according to Delany, is that in the pursuit of satisfying the transgressive desire for the lower-classes, the desiring subject places himself or herself in a position where his or her politics might be transformed. Indeed, it is that possibility that makes such desire transgressive in the first place:

> For a middle-class man or woman to desire the lower or the marginal classes means that, whatever he or she makes of it, a middle-class man or woman spends a lot of time *listening* to what the lower or marginal classes have to say. It means that they are under that class's influence. This is, of course, dangerous to the *status quo*.[77]

Marr does indeed enter into meaningful dialogues with his homeless sex partners, especially Leaky, who becomes his lover. Desire across class lines "is real," according to Delany, and "certainly no more evil than any other mapping of desire."[78] *The Mad Man*'s guiding logic, therefore, is an extension of that established in *Dhalgren*: "Every sex act, from the most 'normal' to the most 'perverse,' is an internalization of one or another set of social parameters. Once internalized, however, they are sexual and no longer social—save in their social *effect* as sexual behavior."[79] Delany's goal, then, is to decenter "normative" sexuality and valorize the individual's "perversions," the specificity of which is as significant in *The Mad Man* as it is in some of his previous works. For the smuggler in *Flight*'s "The Tale of Fog and Granite," for example, "freckles on a male were as physically repulsive to him as they were attractive on women."[80] Comparably, Piece of Shit gets off with Marr only because he can imagine that he is having sex with his ideal (black, female) partner: "I don't need me no picture magazines. No dirty movies—though, if you got 'em, I don't mind takin' a look at 'em. But I can do it all in my head" (25–26). As for Marr, the sexual activities in which he engages with Piece of Shit include fellatio, urolanglia, anal fingering, and much more. But it is not as if he will do *anything* with the homeless man. For example, when his new friend offers the contents of his nostril, Marr sternly replies, "I will suck your dick . . . I'll drink your piss. I'll even lick out your asshole. But I will *not* eat your snot!" (36). Later, when Piece of Shit has found the girl of his dreams, Marr declines the invitation to a threesome: "You do your thing," he says, "you have to let me do mine" (75). Like Risa in *Dhalgren*, Marr is no one's sexual servant; nor is he a victim who is coerced into indiscriminately catering to other's lusts. Harper describes him as having a "willingness actually to *mobilize* [racial] identity in relation to power for the sake of maximally intense erotic effect."[81] Marr understands himself as an agent in an act of mutual sexual pleasure, who later returns home to masturbate to his memories of the encounter: "using *my* imagination, not unlike the Piece of Shit—[to] get mine" (65).

Marr's willingness to imitate female genitalia is less evidence of white supremacy's effeminization of black men than it is an example of the Lacanian dictum Delany frequently cites, "We desire the desire of the other." Delany explains in a postscript to a letter in *1984* that features a pornographic story sent to a hustler friend in prison, a former acquaintance from Forty-second Street, who is attracted to Asian women in particular: "What turns everyone on is the fact that some other person is turned on."[82] Therefore, a gay man like Marr takes the man he finds to be his *own* ideal sexual object, a homeless man by the name of Leaky Sowps, who initially identifies himself as straight, to a "heterosexual" pornographic movie. Leaky expresses a desire to reciprocate by telling Marr "I'm into anything you are" (358). The diary of Timothy Hasler, the gay Korean American philosopher whose 1973 stabbing death Marr is investigating, reveals that its author engaged in sexual experiments with homeless men for similar reasons. Hasler writes about water sports with a black homeless man, who afterward inquired as to how pleasurable the experience was. "I *kind* of liked it," Hasler responded, "but I guess that's mainly because—well, *I'm* drunk; and too, because I could tell you liked it and it was getting you off" (93).[83]

How should one read, however, Piece of Shit's use of "nigger" during sex with Marr? How is an African American reader to respond to a passage that is riddled with an insulting epithet that is often the marker of white supremacist ideology at work? Does not such toxic nomenclature mark the sexual encounter as degrading? It certainly could, as the passage from *Beloved* demonstrates. But perhaps the reader should "return" to the *Return to Nevèrÿon* series, and Gorgik's explanation to Pryn that the words camel drivers yell at their beasts of burden in a busy market during the day are the same ones they whisper to, or long to hear from, their lovers in the bedroom at night: "Even the most foul-mouthed camel driver knows a curse from a kiss, whatever signs accompany it."[84] In the *Return to Nevèrÿon* series, the sexual reverses—or at least rearticulates—the social; *The Mad Man* extends the sword-and-sorcery series' semiotic analysis. Delany is not suggesting that Marr and Piece of Shit have necessarily internalized the social dynamics of racial oppression. The situation is closer to, though not exactly like, Dany Laferrière's semi-serious explanation of mutual sexual attraction between white women and black men: "History hasn't been kind to us, but we can always use it as an aphrodisiac."[85] Another "camel driver" in *The Mad Man* is Mike Bellagio, "an incredibly pumped-up, handsome, hairy, and hung Italian undergraduate" (15) who "dies horribly" in a car wreck, almost as as a parody of the type of clichéd representations of gay men that the novel generally avoids.[86] Bellagio specifies and links his sexual and political goals when he tells Marr that he came to Enoch State "to eat out as many black assholes as I can—and do as much for Gay Liberation as I can while I'm at it" (15). When he gets Marr alone in the boiler room with Rod the maintenance man, he stops fellating only long enough to say "Fuck me, you goddam black bastards—fuck the shit out of me, you fuckin' niggers!" (21). *The Mad Man*, like the *Return to Nevèrÿon* series and *Dhalgren* represents Delany's attempt to practice what Michel Foucault suggests in "About the Beginning of the Hermeneutics of the Self": "We must get rid of the Freudian schema. You know, the schema of the interiorization of the Law through the medium of sex."[87] Indeed, this dynamic is repeated several times throughout *The Mad Man*. When it comes to racial epithets in a sexual context, Marr can give as well as receive; he calls Tony, another white homeless man with whom he regularly has sex, an "ass-eatin' lace-curtains honky punk!" (199). Tony's apparently paradoxical reply—"You're a good nigger, professor" (200)—in actuality indicates that not only does he not interpret Marr's words as a race-based insult, but also that he would address Marr differently, as "professor" (even though he is a graduate student), in a nonsexual setting. Leaky demonstrates a similar understanding as well as some good sense when he tells Marr, "Most hillbillies don't go around callin' every black fella they meet 'nigger, this,' and 'nigger, that' . . . If we did, we'd get our fuckin' heads handed to us" (400). This scenario is inverted when Marr picks up Dave, a white alcoholic carpenter and "dinge queen" (129), who finds Pheldon, "a muscular blue-black, six-foot-two, thirty-five-year-old photographic librarian for a major city newspaper" (119), to be just his type. Marr takes Dave to meet Pheldon at the Fiesta, from which they go to the Mine Shaft for a GSA (Golden Showers Association) party. Before long, Pheldon exclaims "I think I'm gonna *piss* on this honky motherfucker [i.e., Dave]! That'd really make me feel good!" (124). He does, and it does. But it is Dave who reaches the heights of sexual pleasure when a third African American man joins in, whose voice Marr characterizes by referring to a novel spectrum of black masculinity: "In a voice as deep as Darth Vader's and as country as Steppin' Fetchit's, the new guy intoned: 'Now suck that big, black dick, white boy! You got three pieces of prime nigger meat here—don't let it go to waste now!'" (125). Afterward, Vader/Fetchit makes it clear that the racial epithets said to Dave, and in reference to himself, were all in fun. Harper notes that Marr and Pheldon become better friends after this episode: "thus the black men's highly motivated, eroticized engagement with the fact of their fetish status" (and, I would add, their fetshization of white men like Dave) "actually affirms their sense of self not only as individuals but as a social entity rendered ever more cohesive through its developing consciousness regarding its minority condition."[88]

That said, in both *The Mad Man* and "the real world" it is often difficult to tell where a mere "perversion" ends and the derogation of blackness begins; the difference between a kiss and a curse is not always evident, especially where race is involved. Consider the fact that many African Americans, understandably, do not approve of the use of the *n*-word at all, even when used by other African Americans in what are generally considered to be black cultural contexts, such as hip-hop. Can *any* white use of the word, therefore, be defensible? Given that the epithets "nigger" and "queer" continue to be used as hurtful speech by the hateful and intolerant, despite the recent rearticulations of those words by urban black youth and gay activists and intellectuals respectively, can they ever be completely transformed? Because iteration implies *both* identity and difference, are they ever truly released from their histories as brutal linguistic weaponry? More specifically, the writings of James Baldwin, Essex Hemphill, Joseph Beam, Keith Boykin and other black gay writers have criticized the racism in predominantly white gay spaces, including the reduction of black men to a mythic sexuality. Although it signifies in multiple ways, the example of Robert Mapplethorpe's "Man in Polyester Suit" reminds us that the fetishization of the black male body is potentially no less problematic in a gay context than in any other. *Black Men/ White Men* editor Michael J. Smith's comment that "bedding down with Blacks doesn't necessarily make one less racist" suggests that the interracial aspect of a sex act does not necessitate a process of reciprocal "listening" or progressive race-thinking.[89] Robert Reid-Pharr notes that "if you believe the hype," every act of interracial gay or lesbian sex is a "revolutionary act," but exactly what people "think when they fuck" is not always clearly progressive, and can even be dangerously retrograde, or both simultaneously, especially when a sense of the history of race in America is absent or elided.[90]

Delany's novel, purposefully and characteristically, explores this very same border. The sexual and the social do touch, contend, and permeate each other in *The Mad Man,* and Marr is alert to the occasions on which they do. "The fetishization underlying nonwhite men's status as trade can entail an objectification that is stultifying rather than empowering," Harper notes, "the effects of fetishization are irreducibly ambiguous."[91] For example, *after* a GSA night, *outside* The Mine Shaft, Marr has to tell a white man, "Hey, Tex . . . I was just wondering . Did anybody ever tell you that you weren't suppose to call black guys 'boy'?" (109). Tex's attempt at an apology is momentarily perplexing:

> "No offense then, nigger."
> It kind of made me start. Then I laughed. "No offense, you fart-faced old toothless piss-drippin' scumbag honky!" (110)

Marr's response gets a laugh, as well as the offer of a ride home, out of Tex. In this exchange there is considerable ambiguity as to the context in which the men are making contact. It is that ambiguity that startles Marr and prompts him to gauge Tex's meaning with his own rejoinder, which is a risky maneuver if he miscalculates. Similarly, Marr finds himself educating the homeless man called Crazy Joey, who claims to be part black because of the size of his penis, eats "nigger cum" because "that's gotta be the healthiest," and urinates on his hands in an effort to make them hard, which is why he is looking for "Nigger piss . . . 'cause it's stronger, or something" (241, 244). By the end of the novel, Marr has to tell Leaky that Joey's theories are completely baseless, much to Leaky's chagrin.

It is around Leaky's, and Marr's own, particular "perversions" that the novel's best examples of how the most hurtful epithets can be veritable terms of endearment in a sexual context are located. Simply put, Leaky gets off on being told how stupid he is, which is what Marr does in language that features a racial component: "You're probably the stupidest whitey running around homeless in this fucking neighborhood. You're so fucking stupid you'd piss on a nigger in the middle of the street then let him suck your fucking dick. You fucking retard—they don't make 'em stupider than you, do they?" (302–03). The homeless man responds to words like these by telling Marr, "Nigger, you an' me gonna get along real good" (320). Although he frequently refers to his lover as "nigger," Leaky explains to the best of his ability that he has no tolerance for racism, especially the kind he witnessed in his home state of West Virginia:

> "I do not like the south though. I was born there. I been back down there a few times—Florida, Georgia, Alabama. But, you know, I can't take the way they treat black people. I'm serious. You'd think with me, gettin' off on black guys what get off on bein' called 'nigger' and stuff, that wouldn't make somebody like me blink an eye. But I can't take it. It fucking turns my stomach—not that it's much better up here—at least everybody isn't joking about lynchin' them up and cuttin' their balls off and expecting you to laugh your head off. So now I guess you *really* think I'm strange." (326)

But Marr understands him completely, and instead of summarizing "Freud's idea of perversions as the opposite of character neuroses," he interprets the concept to Leaky in a way that he can understand and that demonstrates Delany's assertion of the radical possibilities of sexual contact between classes and races:

> "You like black guys. Even if it's just to piss on . . . Anyway . . . it makes sense to me that, if you like some group sexually, and you want them to be around and happy and fuck with you a lot, you might be concerned with how they're treated socially—and politically." (326)

This conversation provides one of several lessons heterosexual readers, though they are clearly not Delany's intended or expected audience, can take from this novel. When Leaky points out that "Guys who like to fuck women . . . usually treat women like shit," Marr notes, "heterosexuals were always kind of beyond me" (326).

As constructively provocative as these aspects of the novel are, Delany pushes—and perhaps exceeds—the limits of a black reader's credulity and tolerance with Leaky's tale of his family life outside of Hagerstown, West Virginia. Leaky tells Marr that "some weird things go on, up in those mountains" (331). This is a colossal understatement. In West Virginia, Leaky lived with his father, Billy Sowps—a.k.a. "Ol' Fuck"—and his friend Big Nigg. The interracial pair were friends in reform school who masturbated together and ate each others semen. They escaped to the Sowps home and regularly had sex with Billy's mother, Sarena, who disappeared after Leaky's birth. The two men and a baby lived and slept together, very often urinating on one another. However, it is the fourth member of this happy family that truly tests the reader's limits. "Blacky" is Big Nigg's brother and Frances Cress Welsing's worst nightmare: a hunchbacked black urolangliac who fellates the rest of the household, concluding every sentence with a deferent "Suh" or "Yessuh." Leaky tries to explain, however, that Blacky was better off living with the Sowps than with his own father, who would have killed him because of sexual "perversions." Marr is not sure how much of Leaky's story about his home life is true, but he recognizes that the way he was treated skirts the boundaries of abuse. Boundaries are exactly what Delany has experience exploring, of course, and Leaky takes great exception to Marr's suggestion that such behavior was child abuse. He explains that he escaped an orphanage where he endured true physical, psychological, and sexual abuse, to return to the Sowps' residence where he felt safe and loved. Where others might see degradation, Leaky sees affection, which is affirmed upon his return home late in the novel.

After Marr and Leaky have sex several times—and, of all things, eat breakfast together—Leaky decides that he wants to formalize the relationship, and therefore asks to wear a dog collar, signifying Marr's "ownership" of him. Marr is unsure about the collar because he feels like the "bottom" in the relationship; plus it smacks a little too much of slavery. The relationship between Gorgik and Sarg in the *Return to Nevèrÿon* series—and Sarg's feelings about the meaning of the collar in that relationship—is momentarily echoed here. But with the dog collar, Leaky feels like "a fuckin' human being again what means something to somebody else—for the first time in a fuckin' *long* time" (353–54). When Marr worries that their relationship is contaminated by its apparent congruency to the bondage his ancestors endured, Leaky is quick to point out, again, the difference between the sexual and the social:

> "It would be a real head-fuck," I said, "if this is what buying and selling slaves turned out to be all about."
> "Naw," he [Leaky] said, like some kind of teacher. "That's about makin' people what don't got nothin' do all the fuckin' work. This is somethin' else." (354)

The "Yours truly" at the end of a letter from Almira Adler (an approximation of "Aldamir"?), an elderly Pulitzer-winning poet and friend of Hasler's, causes Marr to consider the "appalling connections . . . inscribed in that phatic figure . . . in a land built on slavery" (364), and the collar "as a *true* sign of belonging, of ownership, of the genitive in its possessive mode" (363). The novel later ends with the two men living happily ever after.

If Marr does behave in a way that betrays the race, it is in composing a fiction about "three black guys—they were Haitian . . . Though one of them *looked* more like he might have been Hispanic—maybe Dominican" (431) breaking into and wrecking his home, a lie told to Mossman to explain the monumentally befouled state of his apartment after being "turned out" by Leaky, Tony, Crazy Joey, Big Buck, and Mad Man Mike. It says something about Mossman that he readily believes the story, and it says something about Marr that he feels guilty about telling it: "May the spirit of Toussaint L'Ouverture," he prays, "have mercy on my soul" (432).

At the closing of a letter that takes over a month to compose and spans almost ninety of the novel's pages, Marr asks Sam (who will later divorce Mossman and enter a lesbian relationship, in that order) that his descriptions of his life, including his sexual life, not be mistaken as representative of all gay men, or all black gay men. With John Marr, and others in *The Mad Man*'s cast of characters, however, Delany has forged a representation of black gay life that interrogates anxieties about black gay masculinity and race consciousness. More importantly, John Marr gives Delany the opportunity to speak candidly about and theorize his character's sexuality as neither deviant nor degrading but simply another frequency in the vast human sexual spectrum. As such, *The Mad Man* contributes to that important first step toward African Americans' approach to the AIDS crisis. Lisa Duggan has said that "every production of 'identity' creates exclusions that reappear at the margins like ghosts to haunt identity-based politics."[92] But as Marlon Riggs's documentary film *Black Is, Black Ain't* powerfully asserts, African American communities' sense of self must be constantly re-theorized so that no member of our "family" is left out.[93] "African American social difference must be acknowledged, attended to, engaged, and interrogated," Phillip Harper argues, "rather than denied or deemed inadmissible."[94] Reed Woodhouse's review essay on *The Mad Man* concludes that "to the extent that we admit we are no different from [Marr], we widen the scope of our sexual, racial, and intellectual categories," a process he calls "the revolution from within."[95] The continuation of the struggle for African American liberation and the formation of a cogent response to AIDS among African Americans require this kind of revolution from within black America.

This kind of race theory informs a much-needed praxis. All too often white gays and straight African Americans see themselves as competing for the same fragments of political enfranchisement. Cathy Cohen cites an official at a black AIDS organization, for example, who complains that the gay (that is, white) organizations get all the funding.[96] In "Is the Rectum a Grave?" Leo Bersani upbraids white gays for their racism, yet claims that "the power of blacks *as a group* in the U.S. is much greater than that of homosexuals."[97] Although both are arguable claims that can be supported or refuted with the appropriate evidence, ultimately such arguments do not advance the politics of either group as much as they set them both up to be divided and conquered. Cindy Patton observes that "it is a mark of the intransigence of homophobia that few look to the urban gay communities for advice, communities which have an infrastructure and a track record of highly successful behavior change."[98] Similarly, Kobena Mercer notes that "the origins of the modern gay liberation movement were closely intertwined with the black liberation movements of the 1960s . . . but although white gays derived inspiration from the symbols of black liberation—Black Pride being translated into Gay Pride, for example—they failed to return the symbolic debt, as it were, as there was a lack of reciprocity and mutual exchange between racial and sexual politics in the 1970s."[99] One humbly suggested way to clear accounts and to establish a meaningful exchange between the ongoing black and gay liberation movements would be for African Americans to start and, or, continue to turn to gays and lesbians—including black gays and lesbians and their organizations—as valued allies and as knowledgeable leaders in HIV prevention and AIDS activism in order to halt the further decimation of black lives.

Criteria of Activist Art

> AIDS is the site at which not only people will die, but desire and pleasure will also
> die if certain metaphors do not survive, or survive in the wrong way.
> —Stuart Hall, "Cultural Studies and Its Theoretical Legacies"[100]

AIDS would appear to be perfect subject matter for science fiction. Paula Treichler refers to HIV as "a viral Terminator" and provides a list of thirty-eight other "characterizations of AIDS," including (no. 9) "an Andromeda strain with the transmission efficacy of the common cold," (no. 36) "Science fiction," and (no. 37) "Stranger than science fiction."[101] In Delany's *The Tale of Plagues and Carnivals*,[102] the beginning of the AIDS crisis in New York City is mirrored in, and then merges with, the crisis generated when the plague that killed Norema's people on the Ulvayn Islands starts claiming lives in the empire's capital city of Kolhari. But SF rhetoric is seen following AIDS into the realm of fantasy—sword and sorcery when Delany writes, "AIDS is like unto the Scourge of Satan, the Wrath of Khan."[103] Delany, of course, is not just any SF writer; he is a gay man who has written of gay life before and after Stonewall, and before and after the discovery of HIV. And he is an African American, a member of a racial demographic that is disproportionately affected by the syndrome. "AIDS has become," Delany says, "the largest killer among my personal circle of friends and acquaintances," which suggests the extent of his investment in the battle against AIDS.[104] But it is Delany's identity as a writer of SF, which he identifies as "paraliterature," that suggests the ways in which *The Mad Man* meets certain criteria for AIDS activist art.

In his analysis of a 1987 artwork by ACT-UP entitled "Let the Record

Show," Douglas Crimp argues that art that is engaged with the AIDS crisis on social and political levels cannot limit itself to "high culture" outlets; rather, it must make itself available to the communities that are most affected by the crisis, at what some might call a "street level." "Activist art therefore involves questions not only of the nature of cultural production," Crimp says, "but also of the location, or the means of distribution, of that production."[105] *The Mad Man* is a work of serious writing, but it is also a work of pornography, published, as was *The Motion of Light in Water,* by Richard Kasak, "one of America's leading publishers of erotica—gay, lesbian, straight, [or] S & M."[106] Although it can be found in the fiction sections of some bookstores and in some SF–comic book specialty shops, *The Mad Man* circulates in locations and among audiences that "literature" cannot or does not because of its generic, paraliterary identity and its author's identity as a renowned SF writer. It has been reviewed—positively, in general—in gay periodicals such as *Lambda Book Report, Harvard Gay & Lesbian Review,* and *Girlfriends* and listed among "the best gay smut of the last 1000 years."[107] The novel does not appear to have been reviewed as much, however, in popular or scholarly periodicals on African Americans.

As demonstrated in his SF, Delany is an expert at crossing the boundaries between literature and the marginalized paraliterary genres, whose exclusions define "literature," within a single work. A synecdochic relationship can be identified between the novel—adorned with epigraphs from Foucault, Nietzsche, Wagner, and Yeats—and Timothy Hasler's notecards. "Many of them read like Barthes's *Fragments d'un discours amoureux,*" Marr states; "and some read like rank pornography" (406). But perhaps such a synthesis or juxtaposition of "high" and "low" should not be so surprising. *The Mad Man*'s meditations on risk, "the systems of the world," and detailed descriptions of various kinds of gay male sex proves Michael Warner's point about the philosophical and moral significance of "queer" culture: "From Plato's *Symposium* to contemporary queer theory, the study of sex has generally involved such fundamental questions as the relation of ethics to pleasure, the nature of consent, and the definition of freedom. What could be better questions for humanists to ask?"[108] Moreover, Delany can be seen as selecting the genre of pornography strategically so as to exploit its specific paraliterary advantages. Despite the sexual revolution, Stonewall, and academia's acceptance and recognition of "queer theory," Delany claims that "the sexual experience is *still* largely outside language—at least as it [language] is constituted as any number of levels," and "what is accepted into language at any level is *always* a highly coded, heavily policed affair."[109] But the topics of *The Mad Man* require language at its most explicit. In writing about "things that are new to most people . . ." Delany explains, "you have to talk about such subjects as clearly and as cleanly as possible."[110] Moreover, when it comes to AIDS, he says, "information in any but the most clear, common, and comprehensible language is immoral."[111] Nothing meets Delany's requirements for candor or decenters the object of heteronormative sexuality quite as well as the paraliterary genre of pornography.

AIDS is quite obviously a subject with which many are uncomfortable, due in large part to the many complex issues to which it is related and toward which Americans tend to be particularly anxious. Nevertheless, "anyone doing work on AIDS," Crimp contends, must confront—and, one expects, transcend—"the psychic resistance to confronting sex, disease, and death in a society where those subjects are largely taboo."[112] In 1987 Leo Bersani said, "There is a big secret about sex: most people don't like it."[113] More than a decade later, that statement appears to still be true according to Michael Warner, who claims that "it might as well be admitted that sex is a disgrace." He agrees with Bersani that efforts to reclaim sex as wholesome and healthy—"as though it were simply joy, light, healing, and oneness with the universe"—often result in making sex non-sexy.[114] The dominant American moral attitude toward sex at the beginning of the new millennium is best characterized in the words of the "frelk" attracted to the unsexed spacefaring narrator of Delany's Nebula Award–winning 1967 short story "Aye, and Gomorrah . . . ," who describes her society as "still fighting [its] way up from the neo-puritan reaction to the sexual freedom of the twentieth century."[115] Warner seeks to re-envision gay sexual culture as a moral culture, which in turn questions the morality and perceptive faculties of its detractors:

> But anytime it seems necessary to explain away other people's sex in these ways, the premises of one's morality could just be flawed. What looks like crime might be harmless difference. What looks like immorality might be a rival morality. What looks like pathology might be a rival form of health, or a higher tolerance of stress.[116]

For a demonstration of Warner's point one has to look no further than *The Mad Man*, a paraliterary assertion that non-heteronormative sexualities can be both moral and sexy (or at least "dirty"). In *Motion* Delany predicts that a "sexual revolution to make a laughing stock of any social movement that till now has borne the name" will manifest itself "once the AIDS crisis is brought under control,"[117] but *The Mad Man* demonstrates that perhaps a sexual revolution—or a revolution in attitudes toward sex and sexuality—can play a part in responding to the AIDS crisis. At the root of Delany's work on sex is his conception of human sexuality as a vast range of "perversions," each enjoying or enduring its own degree or lack of social privilege. This concept is informed by a belief that "there may be as many ideal sex lives as there are different people."[118] This is one way of saying that Delany probably has few qualms with the model of "sex as sweetness and light" that Bersani and Warner criticize, though that particular model is decidedly *not* the one on which *The Mad Man* is based. There is nothing sanitized—or sanitary—about the sex in this novel at all. Marr finds certain homeless men sexually interesting because of their dirt, as did Hasler, whose interest in dirty men forces Mossman to reconsider his own work on the late philosopher:

> At this point, I'm unearthing material about Timothy Hasler that—finally, John, I confess—has upset me. . . . This biography has now become really problematic. Between April and June of '73 . . . Hasler must have been in- dulging in the most degrading—and depressing—sexual "experiments": bums on the New York City streets, destitute alcoholics in Riverside Park, white, black, or Hispanic winos lounging about on the island in the middle of upper Broadway, about whom his only criterion could have been, as far as I can make out, the dirtier the better . . . ! Really, John, I have to consider seriously whether Timothy Hasler is a man I want to be writing about. (18)

But Marr, who sees Hasler's "degrading sexual experiments" as nothing compared to his own, constructs a counternarrative—a "revision" of "Mossman's basic picture of Hasler" (94)—that represents the murdered philosopher as "a fairly ordinary gay man with an obsessive fetish for men's bare feet" (84). Marr himself initially finds Piece of Shit interesting because of his dirty hands and fingers. On the subject of dirt, Julia Kris- teva, in her "essay on abjection" *Powers of Horror,* writes that "filth is not a quality in itself, but it applies only to what relates to a *boundary* and, more particularly, represents the object jettisoned out of that bound- ary, its other side, a margin."[119] It is not surprising, then, that Delany, a master of paraliterary genres at and across the boundaries of the literary, who locates his work at "the margin of the margin,"[120] would compose a novel awash in what Mary Douglas calls "marginal stuff of the most obvious kind," that is, "matter . . . that by simply issuing forth [has] tra- versed the boundary of the body."[121] At different moments the novel fea- tures, for example, Marr swallowing ejaculates, mouthing Piece of Shit's semen-encrusted yoni rings (circular foreskin stretchers), and Tony "rim- ming" (performing oral-anal contact on) Marr. Most of the novel's char- acters engage in "water sports," particularly the appropriately named Leaky, who, as Woodhouse explains, "likes to take his leaks on John [Marr], in John, around John, it scarcely matters."[122] Kristeva concludes that "the danger of filth represents for the subject the risk to which the very symbolic order is permanently exposed, to the extent that it is a device of discriminations, of differences," of what Douglas identifies as "lines of structure, cosmic or social, [that] are clearly defined."[123] The contact between Marr and his sexual partners traverses boundaries of class, race, generation, and education. They are "contacts" in the sense that Delany describes in *Times Square Red, Times Square Blue:* "cross-class contacts in public space," which are without the competitive component he attributes to "networking."[124] Collectively they blur the distinctions between "good" heteronormative sex and "degrading" perversions. Sex in *The Mad Man* is represented as, to borrow William Haver's language, "an infinite proliferation of difference" and with "a certain impossibility of containment."[125] When Marr is "turned out" by Leaky, Mad Man Mike, and the others in his apartment, the inability or unwillingness to contain one's excrement accompanies a conversation in which the men describe every single different sexual combination possible between them, an activity that Marr can compare only to the writings of the Marquis de Sade. The bodily fluids that are generally understood to be contained in the body until they are properly disposed of in private are exchanged by Marr and company like party favors. Leaky's explanation of this to Marr demonstrates that their sexual behavior does not happen outside of moral systems, just inside an alternative one:

> "Piss, shit, spit, cum, snot, cockcheese—all that stuff: See, that's like a present, little guy. That's like a present that comes from inside you. Inside your own body. I mean: How am I gonna give somebody something more personal than my own cum, my own piss, my own spit, my own shit?" (332)

Bodily fluids flow like, well, bodily fluids in the description of Wet Night at The Mine Shaft in Marr's letter to Sam, which emphasizes feelings of comfort and pleasure as opposed to degradation:

> You know what it feels to be pissed on by nine guys at once while you lie spread-eagle on your back in a bathtub, Sam—I mean, more than anything else?
> It feels warm! (100).

This emphasis on "warmth" as a good feeling associated with water sports is repeated throughout the novel: in Crazy Joey's description of holding a Coke can filled with his own urine, and in Leaky's distinction between "piss" and the cold of the rain that falls on him and Marr when they meet for the first time. Indeed, as Reed Woodhouse's review essay asserts, *The Mad Man*'s thesis might very well be simply summarized as "sex is good for you."[126] At the beginning of the novel, Marr reflects on his realization at the beginning of graduate school that "a 500-page tome about every-thing of philosophical interest was less likely to be considered a work of serious philosophy than a self-help manual starting off: 'It's important to feel really *good* about yourself . . .'" (8). William Haver interprets the novel as Delany asking "What if . . . queer theory (or 'lesbian and gay studies') were not so much about feeling good about oneself as about feel-ing good?"[127] And it is sex that makes Marr feel good. He describes, in his letter to Sam, how he felt as he paused for a beer during GSA night at The Mine Shaft:

> I put a forearm either side of the bottle, and wondered if I should drink it. Should the urge hit, I was all set to scoot back into the john and loose more water. Finally, though, I picked up the bottle and took a swallow . . . and realized, as I set it back down, that I felt . . . good!
> Incredibly good!
> And peaceful.
> And content.
> I didn't feel the need to talk to anyone. The feeling that gets you up, look-ing for this and that, that starts you off doing one thing of the other, just to have something to do, was in abeyance—an abeyance I usually associate with tiredness; only, though it was after three in the morning, I didn't *feel* tired.
> I thought about that strangely and rarely attainable condition Heidegger called "meditative thinking" and wondered if this was it. (105)

Marr explains to Sam that this post-sexual satisfaction is for him not ec-stacy so much as simple pleasure.[128] But it is a pleasure that is socially significant in that it frees him from what Bersani and Warner identify as a culture of sexual shame:

> . . . people feel guilty about *wanting* to do stuff like this. But this is the re-ward for actually *doing* it, for finding someone who wants to do it with you: The fantasies of it may be drenched in shame, but the act culminates in the knowledge no one has been harmed, no one has been wounded, no one has been wronged. (344–45)

More than politics or philosophy, it is sexual pleasure that enables Marr to "feel good about himself" as a gay man in a homophobic society. It is what allows him to transcend the anxiety generated by a 1950s psychology textbook by Erich Fromm—practically identical to the texts by Fromm and Burgler informing Delany's "confession" in group therapy that his homosexuality was something that he was "working on" and would "get better"[129] in *Motion*—that pathologized homosexuality:

But it was only through years of doing what I was doing and looking at the people I was doing it with, many of whom seemed no less happy than anyone else, that I began to ask that most empowering of questions: Could all these people be both crazy and damned? (153)

The sense of connection to others that Marr describes here is what Michael Warner means when he identifies "sexual culture [as] a principal mode of sociability and public world making"[130] and echoes Delany's discovery of a community of gay men in *Motion*. The novel does not shy away from representing, to borrow Stephen Seidman's formulation, "eros as an aggressive, carnal, lascivious desire."[131] For example, Pheldon "breath[es] hard and hoarsely" (124) before urinating on Dave, and Marr "growl[s]" (372) his desires to Leaky and his friends. But more often than not, such encounters are commenced and concluded with an earnest gratitude and politeness, as when Big Buck tells Marr "That was real nice how you and Tony done me when I come in" (388), an "eccentric civility"[132]— to use Gorgik's terminology—that seems more characteristic of a rural small town than New York City. In his heartfelt elegy for the city's pornographic theatres, *Times Square Red, Times Square Blue*, Delany explains that this kind of "contact" represents real, meaningful relationships, "not love relationships . . . not business relationships . . . encounters whose most important aspect was that mutual pleasure was exchanged. Most were affable but brief because, beyond pleasure, these were people you had little in common with. Yet what greater field and force than pleasure can human beings share?"[133]

It is safe to say that many people find bodily fluids—despite the fact that they are merely the products of natural functions—disgusting, particularly when they exist outside of their "proper," private, bodily boundaries. This attitude is also often aimed at the kind of sex in which Marr regularly engages, that is, outside of its "proper" private space and within public locales (toilets, clubs, parks, and the like). The early discourse of AIDS also marked "bodily fluids" in general as a route for contagion, thus intensifying the abjection they provoke.[134] But again, Kristeva suggests that what makes their visible presence truly transgressive is the threat that they pose to order: "It is thus not lack of cleanliness or health that causes abjection but what disturbs identity, system, order. What does not respect borders, positions, rules." What provokes abjection speaks profoundly of life and death, but not necessarily through its association with disease: "Refuse and corpses *show me* what I permanently thrust aside in order to live," Kristeva says. "These body fluids, this defilement, this shit are what life withstands, hardly and with difficulty, on the part of death."[135] The sex acts in which Marr and his partners engage involve the permeability of borders, a theme central to other Delany texts, especially *Motion*. But it also involves embracing the matter that suggests death. When Marr asks Tony, a homeless man who has practiced co-praphagia for years, to reflect on what they do together, Tony suggests that their particular "perversions" afford them a unique perspective from which to contemplate the end of life:

> [Marr:] ". . . I was wondering. What do you think that's all about—piss and shit? Wanting to roll around in it—eat it, drink it?"
>
> "I thought about the shit part," Tony said. "A lot. I think it has something to do with death."
>
> "Huh?"
>
> "When you die, you rot—go back into ook and slime and decayed muck—before you just dry up and blow away. That's pretty grim to think about. So, I guess, somehow, getting into shit, eating it and stuff, bein' low-down and all, that's like getting close to being dead. Making it more natural, more ordinary. It's warm. Ordinary, pleasurable. It makes life easier—because it makes the idea of dying, as much as we can really think about it, easier." (289)

Other than birth, death is the only universal experience, which paradoxically, as Crimp points out, nobody likes to think or talk about. Marr and his friends' sexual interest in the abject involves not only a confrontation with death—mirrored in the Calling of the Amnewor, "a god of edges, borders, and boundaries"[136] in *Flight from Nevèrÿon*'s *The Tale of Plagues and Carnivals*—but also its transformation into something approachable as a topic for reflection and acceptable as a fact of life.

Sex is a more literal life-saving force for Timothy Hasler. Marr explains that, like Harold Brodkey, whose 1993 *New Yorker* essay announcing the author's AIDS diagnosis is ironically paraphrased in *The Mad Man*'s opening lines,[137] "Hasler was the most self-tortured of hypochondriacs" (82). Marr discovers journal entries revealing that the late scholar experienced intense fear of imminent death "sometimes four and five times a week, sometimes two or three times a day" (82). The attacks were so bad when Hasler was a teenager that he considered suicide. In other entries, however, "Hasler cites philosophy *and* the active pursuit of sex as capable of warding off—for a few hours at least—his death fears" (84). For example, the journal entries reveal Hasler's crush on Pete Darmushklowsky, an undergraduate student in the philosophy course he taught as a graduate student at Stilford University. "Given his hypochondriacal mortality terrors as well as his intense foot fetishism," Marr reminds the reader, "Timothy Hasler starts as a man—and as a philosopher—with a very different relationship to death and desire from most of us" (94). One day, Hasler saw Darmushklowsky—topless, barefoot, and jeans unbuttoned—

in the bathroom at the Student Union. Hasler's infatuation, which focused on the undergraduate's feet, triggered a severe and almost inevitable reaction: "Without even saying hello, he fled the place for his office, locked the door, and masturbated"; and although Hasler later reprimanded himself for his behavior, "it left him without a hypochondriac attack for three wonderful days" (86), which puts a new spin not only on Woodhouse's "sex is good for you," but also on the slogan "safe sex saves lives." "How much of human accomplishment," Hasler wonders, "is a simple and direct attempt to stave off such mortal terror?" (84). In this light, then, Hasler's triumph over the fear of death represents its own "revolution from within."

Not only is sex good for you in *The Mad Man,* it is there for the having. This understanding of the world was Hasler's most important lesson to Darmushklowsky, who was attracted to Asian women and befriended his half-Korean graduate instructor, in part, so he could meet some. But, partly because his father did not approve of "Orientals," Darmushklowsky's "perversion" made him feel bad about himself: "I thought I was weird," he tells Marr, "I thought I was sick. I though I was damned and would go to Hell" (184). Hasler, whom Woodhouse accurately describes as "a conflation of Foucault, Wittgenstein, and Delany himself,"[138] did two things for his friend. First, he gave the hero of the SF stories he authored, "Pete Flame" (quite evidently based on Darmushklowsky), a girlfriend by the name of Diamonda, who was "beautiful, raven-haired, violet-eyed, brilliant, [and perhaps most importantly] half-Korean" (89).[139] Diamonda was not the result of Hasler imagining a feminized version of himself as Darmushklowsky's love interest, but rather an approximation of the girl of his student's dreams. Hasler then made Darmushklowsky feel better about his "perversion" and feel as if it was obtainable:

> ". . . not only did he tell me that he'd figured it out—like I suppose, at this point, anyone could have missed it—but he also told me that it was . . . all right! And that I should go for it. And that he would help me! And that he felt the same way about my feet as I felt about Oriental girls. . . . And Tim was the first guy—hell, the first person—to sit me down and explain to me that, first, I could *have* what I wanted, and second, that the only person who was keeping me from getting what I wanted was me." (185)

Hasler's creation of Diamonda is another of Delany's examples of the "we desire the desire of the other" dictum. "[Hasler] was saying," Darmushklowsky tells Marr, "because *I* love *you,* it's all right for *you* to love somebody else . . ." (187). Such sexual/emotional configurations do not work for everyone—as Darmushklowsky's Japanese American wife makes clear—but understanding Hasler's perspective on such matters was an important educational experience. It can be said that Darmushklowsky suffered from a belief in sexual scarcity, which, within the logic of the novel, is a myth that informs the sale of sex at "hardcore hustling bar[s]" (313) like The Pit, where Hasler was stabbed. Leaky makes his own attitude toward such transactions quite clear: "That's stupid, people payin' money for stuff like that" (343). Pheron, the Kolhari weaver in *The Tale of Plagues and Carnivals*, feels similarly about the male and female prostitution at the Bridge of Lost Desire: "But, my dear, I never go anywhere *near* it! There're too many other places in the city to get what *I'm* after!"[140] According to such logic, the best things in life *are* free. Like the pre- and post-Disney incarnations of Times Square contrasted in *Times Square Red, Times Square Blue*—the former being a site where Delany did not have to pay for the sexual fun he found, the latter being a place that "reduces fun almost wholly to spending money"[141]—The Pit and Marr's apartment, where Marr is "turned out" by Leaky and his friends, are homes to two very different "systems of the world." When those systems meet, they produce what William Haver identifies as Lyotard's definition of a *différend*, "a difference so profound there is no possible common ground on which that difference might be adjudicated."[142] It is that irreconcilable difference, Marr discovers from a bartender at The Pit, that led to Hasler's death:

> "You see . . . this place is a lot of older men who think the only way they can get anything worth having sexually is to pay for it. And the kids who come here are all kids who want to get paid—need to get paid. . . . But the thing that makes this whole place possible is a belief that sex—the kind of sex that gets sold here—is scarce. Because it's scarce, it's valuable. Now suppose, one day, you had some guy come in here—twenty, twenty-one, twenty-two: young, good body, nice looking. But the thing about him was he didn't think sex was scarce at all. He thought it was all over the place. He didn't mind older guys—'cause he liked all sorts of guys, young, old, and everybody in between. As far as sex, he's one of these guys who lives his life with his hand in his pocket, playing with himself. And whipping it out and giving it to one of these . . ." He looked left and right, then leaned forward again to whisper, under his breath: ". . . old cocksuckers here, well he just thinks that's the most fun you could possibly have in an evening. Money . . . ? He'd pay *them* to suck on it, if he thought they wanted it! So what happens if one of these guys comes in and starts hanging out here, huh?"
>
> "I guess it kind of upsets the system—at least the one this place operates on."
>
> "You better *believe* it does! . . . Something like that happens, it generates a lot of hostility. Especially from the kids working here. Fast, too." (313–14)

Marr soon meets the man who accompanied Hasler to The Pit and unwittingly contributed to the hostile atmosphere that led to the philosopher's death. Leaky invites Mad Man Mike, "a towering, light-skinned black guy, with yellow, steelwool-tight hair . . . [a] large scar jagged his left pectoral" (366), who is somewhat reminiscent of *Nova*'s Lorq Von Ray and the *Return to Nevèrÿon* series' Gorgik, major characters in Delany's fiction who are also large, disfigured, black men. Mad Man Mike recognizes Marr's apartment building as the same one in which Hasler lived. He has Marr, Leaky, Tony, Crazy Joey, and Big Buck join him in a game in which participants "purchase" each other from their respective "owners," in order to have sex with them. Hasler's journal indicates that the philosopher told Mike about his reservations about such a game: "I pointed out to him in a country as historically entailed with slavery as the U.S., that was a rather dangerous position for a Negro to adhere to" (405). But Mike, a homeless chronic masturbator and refugee from a mental hospital, already the most marginal of men, does not see his race marginalizing him that much further. (Here, Posnock's contention that sexuality supplants race as a mode of identification may seem to apply; however, consider also that race and sexuality permeate each other in Mike's public identity, the stereotypes linked to each other, each reinforcing the other.) The "purchase" price is set at a penny; as such, the game parodies the commodification of sex (or human beings for sex), denying exchange value, asserting what Haver identifies as "nothing-but-use value."[143] As Tony tries to explain to Marr, the game is not about reducing a person to monetary value as much as it is to provide a sexual charge that comes from *performing* possession—as with Gorgik in the *Return to Nevèrÿon* series—and to provide some structure for the sexual free-for-all: "[Mad Man Mike] said that the thing you buy and sell, when you buy some scumbag this way, it don't got nothin' to do with what someone can *do*— I mean, how much he's *worth* out there. It just has to do with . . . I don't know. Owning" (370). Being bought and sold, in this context, is not a problem for Marr: "When it actually occurs among people of good will— and I think that's what we all were—[it] is as reassuring as a smile or a warm hand on your shoulder or a sharp, friendly smack on the ass" (391). After the conclusion of the epic sex-fest at his apartment, Marr returns to The Pit. There he learns that when Hasler and Mad Man Mike were there in 1973, joking about sex for a penny, they attracted the wrong sort of attention, that of hustler Dave Franitz—"a perfectly psychotic young man" (415)—who tried to kill Mike with a knife and fatally stabbed Hasler. History repeats itself—with a difference—when Crazy Joey, with Mad Man Mike's game on his mind and his own considerable genital endowment on display, follows Marr to The Pit, announcing that he is available for sex at the cost of a penny, payable to Marr. This time, however, it is the philosopher who survives and the homeless man who is killed. Crazy Joey's murder prompts Marr to go home, where he does "some funny things" (425), like mimicking Hasler by writing "EKPYROSIS" in excrement on his mirror.[144] It also prompts Mad Man Mike to return to the apartment, where he commits the novel's only real sexual violation— interestingly an intra-, not inter-, racial crime—by raping Marr in his mouth; it is a remarkably violent act that Marr's narrative does not describe in any detail so as to avoid the suggestion that it had any erotic component. This shocking act is even more remarkable in that it runs counter to the novel's prevailing logic, considering that up to this point in the novel, a number of characters are called or refer to themselves as "mad" or "crazy" (Mad Man Mike, Crazy Joey, Darmushklowsky, Hasler, even Marr), but the only characters who truly act insane—hustlers like Dave Franitz and Kerns (Crazy Joey's killer), and the city fathers who close down The Mine Shaft because of its safe-sex demos—are those who believe that sexual pleasure is or should be scarce.

Ellis Hanson writes that "AIDS has helped to concretize a mythical link between gay sex and death."[145] With *The Mad Man*, Delany interrogates that myth and disarticulates that particular link. Such a project, however prompts Woodhouse to ask, "But can sex really be 'good for you' during a sexually spread epidemic?"[146] Although Woodhouse declares "yes," a more accurate answer would acknowledge that it depends on the *kind* of sexual activity being discussed, and the safeguards necessary to maintain one's health.

Risk, Management, and Agency

> There's been a hundred, and that's not boasting,
> Just the ways of this world . . .
> —Kitchens of Distinction, "Prize"[147]

"AIDS intersects with and requires a critical rethinking of all culture" according to Douglas Crimp, "of language and representation, of science and medicine, of health and illness, of sex and death, of the public and private realms."[148] *The Mad Man* revises the representation of AIDS as a white gay issue and understands sex in general, as well as the sex in which Marr engages on the borders of the body and of public and private spheres, as a life-affirming activity through which issues of health and of death are confronted. As the novel represents a sexually active black gay man's negotiations with the fear of AIDS, it also performs a critical analysis of biomedical discourse on HIV/AIDS and safe-sex education. In *The Mad Man*,

Delany seems to be committed to not only validating sex and a range of specific gay sexual practices, but also rethinking the parameters of "sex" itself, which in a sexually spread epidemic, is a matter of immense importance.

As we've already seen, in *The Mad Man,* John Marr engages in a variety of sexual activities—active and passive oral sex and "scat" practices, including water sports, urolanglia, coprophagia, rimming, and so on—all without condoms, dental dams, or other prophylactics. But he does *not* engage in receptive or insertive anal intercourse, mainly because he just does not care for it. He is also fully aware that unprotected anal sex has been implicated as an HIV transmission route. When Leaky, eager to profess his affection, says, "You wanna shove it up my fuckin' asshole, man, shove it up my fuckin' asshole," Marr, offers a good-humored admonishment: "You know it as well as I do, that's the way you end up with AIDS" (437). This attitude parallels that articulated by Delany himself and by a hustler and intravenous drug user given the name "Joey" during a 1988 meeting described in the third postscript to *Flight from Nevèrÿon*'s *The Tale of Plagues and Carnivals:*

> "Joey," I said, "don't take this wrong." We stood together under the grey sky. "But how come you're still alive?"
>
> He didn't even ask me what I meant. "Cause," he said, "I don't share needles with no one, no how, no way. And I don't take it up the ass without a condom." He looked at me askance. "You?"
>
> I shrugged. "I don't use needles. And I don't take it up the ass, period."[149]

The first three postscripts to *Plagues and Carnivals*—dated 1984, 1987, and 1988—feature various safe-sex tips as well as a sobering tally of increasing AIDS cases and deaths. In the second postscript, dated "September 1987," Delany offers a most straightforward message regarding preventing HIV transmission: "Ass-fucking is your biggest risk. Don't take it or give it, to men or women, without a condom—ever!"[150] But what about unprotected oral sex, such as that in which Marr engages with multiple partners of unknown HIV status? It is on this topic that Delany's critical rethinking of science and medicine is activated.

Much of Delany's work on AIDS can be described as discursive analysis. Taking his cue from the work of Michel Foucault, he understands discourse as "an order of response, a mode of understanding,"[151] that is also a "structuring and structuating force. . . . Men and women do what they do—what they're comfortable doing," Delany says; "But the constraints on that comfort, on who does what and when, are material, educational, habitual—feel free to call them social. And where all three—material, education, and habit—are stabilized in one form or another by language, we have discourse."[152] He identifies various "rhetorical features" as "symptoms" of discourse: "Discourse and rhetoric control one another, yes—but precisely because of that control, neither is wholly at one with the other."[153] Such rhetoric is analyzed in *The Tale of Plagues and Carnivals*, which "documents *misinformation, rumor,* and *wholly untested guesses* at play through a limited social section of New York City during 1982 and 1983, mostly before the 23 April 1984 announcement of the discovery of a virus (human t-cell lymphotropic virus [HTLV-3]) as the overwhelmingly probable cause of AIDS."[154] The collection of Delany's letters in *1984* documents similar rhetoric, including the hypothesis that one population of gay men was more susceptible to AIDS than another. The structuring and structuating effects of AIDS discourse, operating at the level of "it is said," are dramatized in *The Mad Man* when Pheldon calls Marr to announce the end of Wet Nights at The Pit: "It's this AIDS stuff. The word out now is no exchanging of bodily fluids. And I don't think you can do more in the line of fluid exchange than the guys on Wet Night get into!" (141). Marr is disappointed and asks if "they really think that it can be passed by . . . pee and stuff" (141). The antecedent of "they" could be the management of The Pit, or the "it" of "it is said," the locus of discursive authority. Pheldon also tells Marr that "Kelly," a regular at The Mine Shaft, has AIDS; at this point in the novel he believes that "bodily fluids" were the mode of HIV transmission and not receptive anal sex: "Kelly told me he *almost* never gets fucked. Maybe once or twice a year—no more. And if that business about repeated sexual contacts is true, then that probably wouldn't be the way for him" (142). As with "they" in the preceding passage, "that business" possibly refers to a presumably authoritative discourse on the subject. The AIDS discourse of 1984, then, associates HIV infection with "bodily fluids" and "repeated contacts." As previously described, Marr's sexual activities have him ingesting and (almost literally) swimming in bodily fluids. As for "repeated sexual contacts," Marr admits to Sam that although he has cut back, he has "never, for more than a month at a time, been able to cut out casual sex entirely. At best, I've reduced 350-plus contacts a year to a frequency that, if I could keep it up, would still total more than a hundred a year anyway, if not two hundred, two-hundred-fifty" (154). He also dislikes condoms, telling Sam, "I've never yet sucked off a dick with a condom on it, and I'm not particularly anxious to start" (159). What enables Marr to navigate through the sexual landscape of gay New York in the era of AIDS and satisfy his particular desires is what he calls the "most mystical of mystical experiences" (152). The experience is practically identical to Delany's own, which he calls "one of the most important things in my life" in a 1984 letter to bibliographer Bravard.[155] One Saturday afternoon in November, Marr goes to the Variety Photoplays, elegized in *Times Square*

Red, Times Square Blue, which features pornography aimed at heterosexual male audiences (i.e., with heterosexual and/or lesbian sex scenes). But much of the action among the audience involves men having sex with men. In the Variety, Marr fellates three men to ejaculation, masturbates, and observes a variety of other activities. He then leaves, goes to the St. Mark's Bookstore and then to a candy store for an egg cream, concluding what he calls "kind of an average day's cruising" (152). But the day also includes a powerful "inner drama" (152) that changes his perspective on his sexuality and the AIDS crisis, what Reed Woodhouse identifies as "a revolution from within":[156]

> When I entered the Variety Photoplays Theater, I was, doubtless, like half the men there, terrified of AIDS. As I walked around the theater, doing what I did, like most of the men there, I thought about AIDS—constantly and intently and obsessively. But when I left (and in this aspect alone, perhaps my experience is—not unique—but certainly rare), I no longer had any fear of the disease.
>
>   At all. (152)

The Variety experience parallels—or repeats with a difference—Hasler's triumph over hypochondria through sex, which bestows "a New Feeling of Power and Strength" (157) upon him. More significantly, it represents Marr's necessary and, within the logic of the novel, heroic, negotiation of risk and desire. Nevertheless, because of "repeated contacts" with "bodily fluids"—almost all without condoms—Marr does find himself suffering from a fear that parallels Hasler's anxiety attacks, but it does not prevent him from seeking sex. "People who cruise with any frequency are not gambling on the possibility of avoiding it," he tells Sam. "Largely, they are gambling on what strikes them as the much higher probability that they already have it—so that in terms of their *own* eventual health, their activity makes no difference" (152–53). Therefore, after mailing his letter to Sam, Marr has a second sexual encounter with Piece of Shit—in a cardboard box, on the sidewalk—that eventually reveals purple Kaposi's Sarcoma lesions on the homeless man's leg. Although Pheldon tells him, "Some people are saying—you can't get it through oral sex. Or, at any rate, you're not very likely to" (173), Marr now fears that he has HIV; but he does not get an ELISA test, feeling a mixture of fear and outrage that he never gets to communicate to Piece of Shit, who is never seen again.[157] Sex with Tony later reveals purple marks on both men; Tony's disappear in a few days, but Marr's do not. The belief that he is now "a carrier" limits Marr's sexual adventures at first, but he eventually resumes his regular cruising routine: "That's when I learned," Marr says, "the idea of total abstinence in terms of AIDS was preposterous advice" (206), a sentiment echoed in *The Tale of Plagues and Carnivals* and *1984*. As it turns out, Marr does not have Kaposi's, but "a psoriasis-like condition" (207). His single act of performing oral sex on a penis with a condom on it is with a man who turns out to be a criminal and tries to force Marr to give him some money. Refusing to pay for sex, Marr soon finds himself running for his life out of a theatre and onto a bus, calling his assailant "a *madman*," and noting how ironic it is that attempting to practice safe sex has jeopardized his life. Marr's experiences, therefore, call the early 1980s AIDS discourse of "repeated contacts" and "bodily fluids" into question.

To discuss "AIDS discourse," according to Paula Treichler, is to engage in "an examination of the context—the entire apparatus—through which utterances about AIDS are produced and interpreted and speaking positions made possible."[158] Such is the work that *The Mad Man* performs in its interrogation and appropriation of biomedical discourse. Cohen and Patton have demonstrated the truth of Crimp's warning that "blind faith in science, as if it were entirely neutral and uncontaminated by politics is naive and dangerous."[159] According to Delany, although discourse and rhetoric "control each other," it is the "power" of the former that distinguishes it from the latter. In order "to highlight some of the structures of a given discourse," Delany offers two strategies, which "may boil down to the same thing." The first is "critical observation of what is around us, precisely while on the alert for things that contravene what we expect."[160] Marr's health, for example, contravenes the general associations of "repeated contact" and "bodily fluids" with HIV transmission, and at least some of his sexual activities are practically identical to Delany's own. The author concludes his 1991 essay "Street Talk/Straight Talk" by sketching out his own statistics on oral sexual encounters:

> A conservative estimate would be 300 (sexual encounters) a year between 1977 and 1983; that falls down to about 150 a year till I left for Massachusetts in 1988; that has been a bit more than halved, to somewhere between 40 and 65 a year since. Four months ago, on a visit to the city (New York), I availed myself of the city's HIV testing facilities. Four months ago, I was seronegative.[161]

If the number of Delany's contacts seems high, consider his July 1983 statement to a friend working at New York City's Gay Men's Health Crisis (GMHC) transcribed in *Plagues and Carnivals*:

> "You know as well as I do, you can keep up an eight-hour-a-day job, an active social life, have your three hundred contacts, and not even be late for dinner. Thousands of men in this city live that way. . . . The fact is, the straight people who're dealing with AIDS—say the ones in the media—

simply have no notion of the *amount* of sexual activity that's available to a gay male in this city!" I said: "Most straights, Peter, don't realize, when they're putting together these statistics, that a moderately good looking gay man in his twenties or thirties can have two to three contacts while he's in the subway on his way to the doctor's to see if he *has* AIDS . . ."[162]

Delany's statement is not meant to be representative of all gay men in New York. The tale features S. L. Kermit's critique of *Plagues and Carnivals* in which the gay archeologist, who does not frequent public toilets or pornographic movie houses, exclaims, "Three hundred contacts a year? Good Lord, if I've had three in the last five years, I'd consider myself drowned in a surfeit of orgiastic pleasure!"[163] But Delany's words do shape, as Marr tells Sam, "some understanding of the field and function—the range, the mechanics—of the sexual landscape AIDS had entered into" in the 1980s, which is essential to a comprehension of "what AIDS means in the gay male community" (158).

In "The Rhetoric of Sex/The Discourse of Desire," Delany states that "the only way we can obtain information about AIDS transmission vectors that can in any way be called scientific" is with what he calls "monitored studies":

In a monitored study of sexual transmission vectors for HIV, a number of people, preferably in the thousands, who test sero-negative are then monitored, in writing, at regular intervals, as to their sexual activity: from the number of times, to the number and sex of partners, to the specific acts performed, oral (active and passive), anal (insertive or receptive), vaginal (insertive or receptive), anal-oral (active and passive), and what have you. At the end of a given period, say six months or a year, the same people are tested for sero-conversion. The status of various HIV positive and HIV negative people is then statistically analyzed against their specific sexual activity.[164]

Delany has written that he knows of only two such studies. One of these, a study of 2,507 gay men originally published in *The Lancet* in 1987, is reprinted as an appendix to *The Mad Man* and reveals what Delany cites in "Rhetoric/Discourse" as "a statistical correspondence of 0 percent—not 1 percent, not 3 percent, not ½ of 1 percent—0 percent of sero-conversions to HIV positive for those (147 out of the total 2,507) gay men who restrict themselves to oral sex, unprotected, active or passive." The 1986 San Francisco Men's Health Study had similar results. *The Lancet* study also "reported eight sero-conversions to HIV positive among men who reported only a *single case* of anal-receptive intercourse for the duration of the study." Hence Kelly's seroconversion, which was most likely a result of "*almost* [as opposed to absolutely] never getting fucked" without a condom. For Delany, these facts "[render] the rhetoric of 'repeated sexual contact,' so much a part of AIDS education both before the 1987 study and since, murderous misinformation,"[165] which he condemns, in "Street Talk/Straight Talk," with his strongest language:

> And I am convinced that a later age will look back on this one and respond to these rhetorical moves that scatter so many of our texts today; it will read them with the kind of mute horror with which we read the anti-Semitic rhetoric that proliferated through Germany in particular and Europe in general all through the '30s and '40s.[166]

Delany sees the discourse of AIDS as "producing its own rhetorical array" in the inflation of statistics on seroconversion due to oral sex due to "interpretation preced[ing] perception."[167] What people say they do sexually is contoured by the dominant discourse, and therefore, incongruent with what they actually do:

> To the official question, "What has your sexual activity been for the past few years?" straight talk takes the myriad answers given by persons with AIDS, in all their discomfort or certainty . . . and the myriad answers given by men and women who often inhabit a world of borderlines, lines laid out very differently from where the straight world might place them, and conflates these answers into an official statement, "AIDS can be passed through fellatio," complete, in many cases, with statistics on the number of people who have so caught it.[168]

As Delany explains in "Street Talk/Straight Talk," this confusion produces not only an inflation of statistics, but also a mistaking—and a misrepresenting—of "unoperationalized rhetoric" for "operationalized rhetoric."[169] It is in this essay that Delany presents a second way to highlight the structure of a discourse, to "suffuse it with another."[170] The presumed "precision and sophistication" of straight talk is in opposition to—and defined by—the presumed "brutality and vulgarity" of street talk." However, each has "shadows": Straight talk can "use knowledge to hide the truth," whereas street talk's "specific vulgarity is the stuff of poetry—in the sense that good taste is the enemy of great art," which has been placed "outside the precinct of what may legitimately be articulated." Delany provides examples of contact with men he meets who have sex with men but do not identify as "gay," who will therefore inflate statistics on HIV transmission via heterosexual sex. He also scrutinizes biomedical discourse in the form of a *New York Daily News* feature on the *New En-*

gland *Journal of Medicine* (320.4, 26 Jan. 1989) reporting the first "confirmed" case of the "transmission of HIV infection from a woman to a man by oral sex," when, in fact, unoperationalized rhetoric is being taken for operationalized rhetoric. According to Delany, there is no article in that issue of the *NEJM,* but rather, a correspondence column and a four-paragraph letter to the editor that is the source of the "confirmed case."[171] This is the kind of misrepresentation for which Delany has no tolerance; moreover, it demonstrates what he identifies as the relatively superior precision of "street talk."

> [T]he conflation of discursively operationalized rhetoric with unoperationalized rhetoric, both taken as equally weighted evidence, has produced the current discourse of AIDS—provisionally, locally, and at this historical moment, a demonstrably murderous discourse, vigorously employed by the range of conservative forces promulgating the anti-sexual stance that marks so much of this era, a discourse of "high risk" and "low risk" behavior, rather than the dicta of street talk: "Don't get fucked up the ass without a condom. Don't use anyone else's works."[172]

The accuracy of nonprivileged rhetoric is modeled in *The Tale of Plagues and Carnivals* when Arly, "a one-legged barbarian," suggests to the young prince who becomes the Master of Sallese—a name that connotes articulated expertise and authority, or discursive power—that the "Venn" whose name frequently comes up at sites along their quest to follow the lifepath of Belham the inventor, was an inventor herself. The young Master and Terek, an accompanying soldier, howl with laughter at this "most preposterous suggestion,"[173] even though the barbarian is, of course, correct.

The conflation of operationalized and unoperationalized rhetoric is not indicative of "the scientific method," according to Delany, but of the absence of such a method, and of settling for a highly problematic, and ultimately dangerous, wager:

> A kind of wager far more immediate, if not more desperate, than the one Pascal so famously conceived: "If 'Don't get fucked up the ass without a condom' is safe, perhaps 'Don't do anything without a condom' is safer." But because the latter is far harder to follow, it militates instead for laxness; and to the extent that the two are perceived as somehow the same, the laxness finally infects the former.[174]

Delany provides a counterexample in the form of street talk, "a rhetorical moment from 1983" at the Variety, where he questions a man fellating other men in the audience:

"Aren't you worried about AIDS?"

"Naw," he said. "You can't get it suckin' dick—unless you got cuts in your mouth or something like that."

I grinned back. "You're probably right—'cause if you weren't, we'd both have it." And though we exchanged no more words, a minute later, he was crouched down between my knees and the back of the theater seat in front of me, his head between my legs.[175]

Delany also notes, as Marr does, how the safe-sex demonstrations at The Mine Shaft, which led to the club's closing, are incongruent with "the word on the street."[176] He again invokes the *Lancet* study, which along with "street talk" contravenes what is "known"—or more accurately what is *said*—about HIV transmission and oral sex:

> [A]ll the monitored studies strongly suggest that it is difficult or impossible to transmit AIDS orally, while perfectly learned statements flood society, all stating, equally unequivocally, that AIDS can be transmitted by any and every sexual act involving an interchange of bodily fluids—all of them based on individual, after-diagnosis requests for origins . . .[177]

In *The Mad Man*, John Marr writes to Sam that although he takes precautions to manage the risk of HIV transmission via unprotected oral sex, those precautions do not constitute a recommendation for others to follow. Given how much remains to be discovered regarding oral transmission, all sexual behavior, including no sexual behavior, is an exercise in taking and managing risk:

> Until much more is known, there is no earthly way I can, with any degree of responsibility, recommend the logic of these precautions to anyone else with any suggestion of probable safety. They are all entirely blind gambles. Still—until much more is known—any course of action is more or less a gamble—even unto cutting out sex entirely. And in such a situation every one of us must put up our own stakes and know that the outcome can be death . . . (157)

Delany closes "Street Talk/Straight Talk" by claiming his choices as his own, and not a prescription for others: "In no way am I asking anyone to change his or her behavior on the strength of ways I may or may not have behaved."[178] His argument is less that unprotected receptive oral sex is "safe," than that without the proper studies, we do not have accurate information about the risk of HIV transmission by that particular route. Delany does ask his audience to join him in calling for more monitored studies—of women and, particularly, of oral sex, without which, he acknowledges, his personal experience and example mean very little[179] and "to begin to put forward the monumental analytical effort, in whichever rhetorical mode we choose, needed not to interpret what we say, but to say what we *do*."[180] Clearly, then, these works demonstrate that Delany has engaged in what Treichler identifies as "a challenge to the 'clinical construction of culture' in which 'the natives' talk back, articulating their own interests and writing their own texts."[181]

One does not criticize the scientific discourse on AIDS and safe-sex education as Delany has without receiving some criticism of one's own. Delany has been called irresponsible and even "a murderer" because of his arguments.[182] Such hyperbolic, ad hominem attacks, obviously, help no one; and they are based on a misreading, or rather, reading one argument where a different one is stated. *The Mad Man* and Delany's essays and speeches on HIV/AIDS should not be construed as declaring unprotected oral sex to be safe; they are, respectively, discourse-critiques that argue for more research, specifically more monitored studies, and the story of a young man managing risk and his own desire. Yet it is possible to get these arguments mixed up if we over-read Delany's candor about his preference for receptive oral sex over insertive or receptive anal sex and over-estimate it as a motivation for his arguments on these issues.[183] Perhaps Delany does not believe in the remotest possibility of unprotected oral sex as a significant route for HIV infection. Even so, without the monitored studies, Delany clearly acknowledges that this belief cannot justifiably be offered to the public as advice from him or a health organization; he presents it only as part of the rationale for his and Marr's individual negotiations with risk in their real and fictional sexual landscapes.

There continue to be numerous and conflicting messages about both the degree of risk associated with unprotected oral sex and the type of recommendations that the scientific community and organizations committed to confronting the HIV/AIDS crisis should be making about oral sex. In early 2000, the Options Project, funded by the CDC at the University of California at San Francisco, reported finding that 8 (or 7.8 percent) of 102 men, a very small sample, recently diagnosed as HIV-positive, probably were infected through oral sex.[184] In 2002 the preliminary results of a study that questioned participants about their sexual behavior prior to HIV testing, in a manner similar to the monitored studies Delany calls for, were published. The study found that "the estimated probability of orally acquired HIV was 0"; however, due to the "modest sample size" (243 participants) the report's authors note that "we cannot rule out the possibility that the probability of infection is indeed greater than zero."[185] A CDC December 2000 fact sheet states that "oral sex is not considered safe sex" and acknowledges that "the exact proportion of HIV infections attributable to oral sex alone is unknown, but is likely to be very small."

The fact sheet also states that one reason that a precise numerical percentage remains elusive is that "most individuals who engage in unprotected (i.e., without a condom) oral sex also engage in unprotected anal and/or vaginal sex," which is another reason the CDC recommends "lower[ing] an already low risk of getting HIV from oral sex by using latex condoms each and every time."[186] Moreover, the CDC notes that unprotected oral sex continues to be implicated as a route for a variety of other sexually transmitted diseases (STDs) besides HIV, as the 1987 study published in *The Lancet* and reprinted in *The Mad Man* also explains:

> The relative "safety" of the sexual practices not detected as risk factors for seroconversion in this report deserves comment. Oral intercourse with ejaculate introduced into the oral cavity, anilingus, "fisting," enema/douche use, and dildo use are all potentially unsafe. HIV infection apart, many of these practices have already been associated with other sexually transmitted diseases that present a public threat to male homosexuals. These sexual practices should be considered in the light of all the infections transmissible by these means—e.g., hepatitis B, cytomegalovirus, herpes simplex virus, amoebiasis, syphilis, and gonorrhea. "Safe sex" guidelines should not apply only to prevention of HIV infection.[187]

These other STDs are known to be more easily transmissible if lesions are present, and although they may be manageable by themselves, contracting them can increase the likelihood of HIV infection.[188] Therefore, many HIV/AIDS–prevention organizations continue to recommend condom use, especially on the penis of a body whose HIV status is unknown, for oral, anal, or vaginal sex. Such would appear to be sound and necessary counsel.

That said, given that unprotected anal sex is the way HIV is most frequently transmitted sexually, clear and factual information about alternative, relatively safer sexual practices, including oral sex, as well as their concomitant risks, is vitally important. The CDC states that individuals who engage in unprotected fellatio may also engage in higher risk behaviors; however, knowledge of oral sex's lower risk may actually prevent individuals from engaging in unprotected anal or vaginal sex. According to the 2002 study described above, "If individuals believe that the risk of HIV from fellatio is high or on par with well-documented high-risk exposures such as anogenital sex, they may not feel that sexual behavior choices make a difference. Acquiring HIV through fellatio is significantly less risky than from anal sex, and therefore one's choice of sexual practices do [sic] matter."[189] As I've already noted, Delany believes that the generalism of some HIV/AIDS prevention slogans can lead to indifference instead of vigilance. "Sex involves more than slogans," according to

GMHC, "and staying safe from HIV is more complicated than just saying, 'use a condom every time.'"[190] In addition, there is the fact that some people simply do not like sucking a penis with a condom on it. Marr tells Pheldon that "a blowjob with a condom . . . sounds about as exciting as sucking off a pencil eraser" (158). Hence the value of what GMHC calls individualized harm reduction strategies, "think[ing] through the values we attach to our specific sexual practices and relationships, as well as the risks,"[191] which is what Marr does. Perhaps what the politics of difference means in this context is the recognition that different people are at differing comfort levels with the amount of risk understood to be associated with different sexual activities: "Those who don't strongly value oral sex may rely more on limiting the number of encounters they have," according to GMHC, "Those who value oral sex more may decide to continue to have it but not allow partners to cum in their mouths."[192] *The Mad Man* represents Marr as a gay man who is candid—with himself and others—about his desires, figures out the risks associated with those desires, and makes decisions accordingly. "[HIV] prevention has to start by imagining a mode of life that seems livable, and in which decisions about how much risk can be tolerated will not be distorted by shame and stigma," Michael Warner states. "Effective prevention, in other words, to some degree requires everyone to act as their own philosopher."[193] It is *The Mad Man*'s dramatization of such decisions, as much as its allusions to the great figures of Western intellectual history, that make it a philosophical novel as well as a pornographic one.

The Mad Man performs the valuable cultural work of representing sex as pleasurable, redemptive contact between bodies, militating against an anti-sex conservatism that is both unrealistic and ultimately unhealthy. Second, it represents gay sex—and sex in general—as a remarkably varied spectrum of possibilities, highlighting safer options than unprotected anal sex and "acknowledging the unpredictability of sexual variance and working toward a world in which people could live sexual lives as part of a shared world," which is where Warner suggests "the best work in HIV prevention begins."[194] Third, it demonstrates how to think critically about scientific AIDS discourse, instead of simply receiving it. Fourth, it contributes to making the necessary demands for monitored studies on HIV transmission via oral sex and other sex acts. Finally, it theorizes and represents black masculinity and sexuality in ways that embrace difference and combat stereotypes, contributing to more and better African American responses to the AIDS crisis. It is not a book for everyone; its detailed representations of certain sexual activities are sure to alienate some readers and stimulate others. But *The Mad Man* may be among Delany's most important novels.

NOTES

Introduction (pp. 1–4)

1. For more examples of Afro-diasporic SF see *Dark Matter*, ed. Sheree Thomas (New York: Warner/Aspect, 2000).
2. Quoted in *The Encyclopedia of Science Fiction*, ed. John Clute and Peter Nicholls (New York: St. Martin's Press, 1993) 316.
3. Charles Saunders, "Why Blacks Should Read (and Write) Science Fiction," *Dark Matter*, 399.
4. Ursula K. LeGuin, introduction, *The Norton Book of Science Fiction*, ed. Ursula K. Le Guin and Brian Attebery (New York: Norton, 1993) 27.
5. Delany provides an accurate brief history of SF in general and the New Wave in particular in a number of interviews gathered in *Silent Interviews* (Hanover, N.H.: UP of New England/Wesleyan UP, 1994). See "Toto, We're Back!" (67–68), and "Sword and Sorcery, S/M, and the Economics of In-adequation" (152–157).
6. See Samuel R. Delany, "Some *Real* Mothers . . . : The SF Eye Interview," 1987, *Silent Interviews*, 164–185.
7. Charles Johnson, *Being and Race* (Bloomington: Indiana UP, 1988) 68.
8. Reed Woodhouse, *Unlimited Embrace: A Canon of Gay Fiction, 1945– 1995* (Amherst: U of Massachusetts P, 1998) 213.
9. Samuel R. Delany, "Wagner/Artaud," 1988, *Longer Views* (Hanover, N.H.: UP of New England/Wesleyan UP, 1996) 2.
10. Samuel R. Delany, "Atlantis Rose . . . : Some Notes on Hart Crane," *Longer Views*, 187.
11. Robert Elliot Fox, *Conscientious Sorcerers: The Black Postmodernist Fiction of LeRoi Jones/Amiri Baraka, Ishmael Reed, and Samuel R. Delany* (Westport, Conn.: Greenwood Press, 1987) 96, 97.
12. Fox 8.
13. Robert F. Reid-Pharr, *Black Gay Man* (New York UP, 2001) 12.
14. Bill Albertini, Ben Lee, et al. "Introduction: The End of Identity Politics?" *New Literary History* 31.4 (2000): 622.
15. Samuel R. Delany, introduction, *Shade: An Anthology of Fiction by Gay Men of African Descent*, ed. Bruce Morrow and Charles H. Rowell (New York: Avon, 1996).
16. Ralph Ellison, *Invisible Man* (1952; New York: Vintage, 1989) 498.
17. Kobena Mercer, *Welcome to the Jungle: Identity and Diversity in Postmodern Politics* (New York: Routledge, 1994) 204.
18. See K. Leslie Steiner, "'The Scorpion Garden' Revisited," *The Straits of Messina* (Seattle: Serconia, 1989) 17–31.

19. Quoted in *Atlantis and Other New York Tales: Samuel R. Delany Reads at the Judson Church,* Eric Solstein, dir. DMZ/Voyant Publishing, 2001.
20. Quoted in Delany, "Wagner/Artaud" 7.
21. See, for example, Robert Elliot Fox, "The Politics of Desire in Delany's *Triton* and *The Tides of Lust,*" *Black American Literature Forum* 18.2 (Summer 1984): 49–56; and Ray Davis, "Delany's Dirt," 1995, *Ash of Stars: On the Writing of Samuel R. Delany,* ed. James Sallis (Jackson: U of Mississippi P, 1996) 162–188.

1. Dangerous and Important Differences (pp. 5–54)

1. Stephen Henderson, *Understanding the New Black Poetry* (New York: Morrow, 1973) 8.
2. Samuel R. Delany, *The Einstein Intersection* (1967; Hanover, N.H.: UP of New England/Wesleyan UP, 1998) 47.
3. David Palumbo-Liu, "Assumed Identities," *New Literary History* 31.4 (2000): 765.
4. Kobena Mercer, *Welcome to the Jungle: Identity and Diversity in Postmodern Politics* (New York: Routledge, 1994) 259.
5. Stuart Hall, "Ethnicity: Identity and Difference," *Radical America* 23.4 (Oct.-Dec. 1989) 10, 11. Subsequent citations are noted in parentheses.
6. Bill Albertini, Ben Lee, et al. "Introduction: The End of Identity Politics?" *New Literary History* 31.4 (2000): 621.
7. Diana Fuss, *Essentially Speaking* (New York: Routledge, 1989) xi.
8. Judith Butler, *Gender Trouble* (New York: Routledge, 1990) 142, 141.
9. Stuart Hall, "New Ethnicities," 1989, *Stuart Hall: Critical Dialogues in Cultural Studies,* ed. David Morley and Kuan-Hsing Chen (New York: Routledge, 1996) 443.
10. Hall, "New Ethnicities" 443, 444.
11. Butler ix.
12. Hall, "New Ethnicities" 444.
13. Palumbo-Liu 766. Two works, in particular, that are identified in this issue of *NLH* as sources for such claims are Wendy Brown, *States of Inquiry: Power and Freedom in Late Modernity* (Princeton UP, 1995) and Todd Gitlin, "Organizing Across Boundaries: Beyond Identity Politics," *Dissent* 44.4 (Fall 1997), 38–41. Palumbo-Liu also identifies critiques of identity politics in the work of Richard Rorty, David Hollinger, and Michael Tomasky.
14. Ralph Ellison, *Invisible Man* (1952; New York: Vintage, 1989) 187.
15. Frank B. Livingstone, "On the Non-existence of Human Races," 1962, in Michael Banton and Jonathan Harwood, *The Race Concept* (New York: Praeger, 1975) 13. Quoted in Lucius Outlaw, "Toward a Critical Theory of 'Race,'" *Anatomy of Racism,* ed. David Theo Goldberg (Minneapolis: U of Minnesota P, 1990) 79.
16. See Walter Benn Michaels, "Race into Culture: A Critical Genealogy of Cultural Identity," 1992, *Identities,* ed. Henry Louis Gates Jr. and Kwamé Anthony Appiah (U of Chicago P, 1995) 32–62; "Autobiography of an Ex-

White Man," *Transition: An International Review* 7.1 (73), (1998): 122–
43; *Our America* (Durham, N.C.: Duke UP, 1995); and "Political Science
Fictions," *New Literary History*, 31.4 (2000): 649–64.

17. Anthony Appiah, "The Uncompleted Argument: Du Bois and the Illusion
of Race," *"Race," Writing, and Difference*, ed. Henry Louis Gates Jr. (U of
Chicago P, 1986). 31, 21, 35–36.

18. K. Anthony Appiah and Amy Gutmann, *Color Conscious: The Political
Morality of Race* (Princeton UP, 1996) 38, 90, 105.

19. Dick Hebdige, *Hiding in the Light* (London: Routledge, 1988) 186.

20. Albertini, Lee, et al. 624.

21. Paul Gilroy, *Against Race* (Cambridge: Harvard UP, 2000) 335.

22. Gilroy 335.

23. Gilroy 334, 333.

24. Quoted in Gilroy 327.

25. Frantz Fanon, *Black Skin, White Masks* (1952; New York: Grove Press,
1967). Quoted in Gilroy 336.

26. Richard Wright, *White Man, Listen!* 1957. Quoted in Gilroy 340.

27. Gilroy 356.

28. Appiah, *Color Conscious* 105.

29. Kodwo Eshun, "Black Britain's Planetary Humanists: 4Hero and Nitin
Sawhney are charting the future of black British music," *The Fader* (Spring
2002).

30. Ross Posnock, *Color and Culture* (Cambridge: Harvard UP, 1998) 2, 7.
Subsequent citations are noted in parentheses.

31. Phil Harper makes a similar argument about the centrality of a rigid conception of masculinity to black authenticity, and the "weakness" or "ef-
feminacy"associated with black intellectualism in *Are We Not Men?: Masculine Anxiety and the Problem of African-American Identity* (New York:
Oxford UP, 1996) 11.

32. Delany, "Toto, We're Back!" 73. Quoted in Posnock 45–46.

33. Charles Johnson, *Being and Race* (Bloomington: Indiana UP, 1988) 17, 20.

34. Samuel R. Delany, "The Semiology of Silence: The *Science Fiction Studies*
Interview," 1987, *Silent Interviews* (Hanover, N.H.: UP of New England/
Wesleyan UP, 1994) 51. Quoted in Posnock 260.

35. Darko Suvin, *Metamophoses of Science Fiction* (New Haven: Yale UP,
1979) 16.

36. Suvin 7–8.

37. Samuel R. Delany, "Science Fiction and Criticism: The *Diacritics* Interview," 1986, *Silent Interviews*, 192. Delany's extensive response to what he
calls "the demand for definition" in Suvin's book and in Scott McCloud's
more recent *Understanding Comics* (1994) is featured in "The Politics of
Paraliterary Criticism," 1996, *Shorter Views* (Hanover, N.H.: UP of New
England/Wesleyan UP, 1999) 218–70.

38. Delany, "Science Fiction and Criticism" 191, 192.

39. Samuel R. Delany, "Now It's Time for Dale Peck," *Shorter Views* 386. And
"Sex, Race, and Science Fiction: The *Callaloo* Interview," 1990, *Silent Interviews* 226.

40. Delany, "Semiology" 27–28, and "The Second *Science-Fiction Studies* Interview," 1990, *Shorter Views* 317.
41. Samuel R. Delany, "An Interview with Samuel R. Delany," interview with Charles Rowell, *Callaloo* 23.1 (2000) 255.
42. Samuel R. Delany, "Coming/Out," 1997, *Shorter Views* 68, 69 73, 74.
43. Delany, "Coming/Out" 88–89.
44. Samuel R. Delany, "Aversion/Perversion/Diversion," 1995, *Longer Views: Extended Essays* (Hanover, N.H.: UP of New England/Wesleyan UP, 1996) 142, 143.
45. Delany, "Semiology" 31.
46. Samuel R. Delany, "Wagner/Artaud," 1988, *Longer Views* 40.
47. Samuel R. Delany, "Introduction: Reading and the Written Interview," *Silent Interviews* 8.
48. Samuel R. Delany, "Sex, Race, and Science Fiction" 224.
49. Delany, "Reading" 8.
50. Samuel R. Delany, "Racism and Science Fiction," 1999, *Dark Matter,* ed. Sheree R. Thomas (New York: Warner/Aspect, 2000) 396.
51. Delany, "An Interview" 250.
52. Appiah, *Color Conscious* 31.
53. Samuel R. Delany, foreword, *Black Gay Man* by Robert F. Reid-Pharr (New York UP, 2001) xvi.
54. Samuel R. Delany, "A Bend in the Road," 1994, *Shorter Views* 100.
55. Posnock 261.
56. Delany, "A Bend in the Road," 100. Delany goes into much more detail about how homosexuality is seen to pollute racial authenticity as well as the similarities of racism, sexism, and homophobia in "Some Queer Notions About Race," *Dangerous Liasons,* ed. Eric Brandt (New York: The New Press, 1999) 259–89.
57. Quoted in Michael W. Peplow and Robert S. Bravard, *Samuel R. Delany: A Primary and Secondary Bibliography, 1962–1972* (Boston: G. K. Hall, 1980) 55.
58. Joseph Beam, "Samuel R. Delany: The Possibility of Possibilities," *In the Life: A Black Gay Anthology,* ed. Joseph Beam (Boston: Alyson Publications, 1986) 202.
59. Samuel R. Delany, "The Necessity of Tomorrows," 1978, *Starboard Wine: More Notes on the Language of Science Fiction* (Pleasantville, N.Y.: Dragon Press, 1984) 24, 25. Subsequent citations are noted in parentheses.
60. Sputnik I was actually launched on October 4, 1957. It is possible that Delany is referring to a report not of the satellite's launch, but of its development.
61. Delany identifies his trilogy *The Fall of the Towers* (rev. 1966) as "a direct answer to Heinlein's *Starship Troopers*" in "The Second *Science Fiction Studies* Interview" 322.
62. Samuel R. Delany, *Nova* (1968; New York: Vintage, 2002) 220. Subsequent citations are noted in parentheses.
63. Fuss xi, xiv.
64. Outlaw 77. See also Avery Gordon and Christopher Newfeld, "White Phi-

losophy," 1994, *Identities,* ed. Kwamé Anthony Appiah and Henry Louis Gates Jr. (U of Chicago P, 1995) 380–400.
65. See Michael Omi and Howard Winant, *Racial Formation in the United States: From the 1960s to the 1990s* (New York: Routledge, 1994).
66. Outlaw 77–78.
67. Appiah, *Color Conscious* 103, 99.
68. George Lipsitz, *The Possessive Investment in Whiteness* (Philadelphia: Temple UP, 1998).
69. Albertini, Lee, et al. 622.
70. Grant Farred, "Endgame Identity? Mapping the New Left Roots of Identity Politics," *New Literary History* 31 (Autumn, 2000): 639, 640.
71. Appiah, *Color Conscious* 103–04.
72. Farred 644, 645, 631.
73. Farred 636.
74. Farred 637.
75. Ellison 292.
76. Mercer, *Welcome* 265.
77. Palumbo-Liu 766.
78. Farred 632.
79. Farred 638.
80. Robert F. Reid-Pharr, *Black Gay Man* (New York UP, 2001) 60.
81. Terry Eagleton, "Nationalism: Irony and Commitment," *Nationalism, Colonialism, and Literature,* ed. Terry Eagleton, Fredric Jameson, and Edward Said (Minneapolis: U of Minnesota P, 1990) 25. Quoted in Gordon and Newfeld 399.
82. For example, see Lisa Duggan, "Dreaming Democracy," *New Literary History* 31.4 (2000): 851–56; and Eric Lott, "After Identity, Politics: The Return of Universalism," 665–78.
83. Butler 148.
84. Reid-Pharr 8.
85. Samuel R. Delany, "The Susan Grossman Interview," *Silent Interviews* 267.
86. Samuel R. Delany, "*Dichtung und* Science Fiction," *Starboard Wine* (Pleasantville, N.Y.: Dragon Press, 1984) 176.
87. Isaac Asimov, *I, Robot* (1950, Greenwich, Conn.: Fawcett Crest, 1970) 6.
88. Delany, "Necessity" 28, 29.
89. Quoted in Mark Dery, "Black to the Future: Interviews with Samuel R. Delany, Greg Tate, and Tricia Rose," *Flame Wars: The Discourse of Cyberculture,* ed. Mark Dery (Durham: Duke UP, 1994) 195.
90. "The Situation of American Writing," *American Literary History* 11.2 (Summer, 1999): 220. Citations from Delany's response are noted in parentheses.
91. Joanna Russ, "Towards an Aesthetic of Science Fiction," 1975, *To Write Like a Woman: Essays in Feminism and Science Fiction* (Bloomington: Indiana UP, 1995) 4.
92. Peter Nicholls and Cornel Robu, "Sense of Wonder," *The Encyclopedia of Science Fiction,* eds. John Clute and Peter Nicholls (New York: St. Martin's, 1993) 1083, 1084.

93. Samuel R. Delany, Afterword to *Stars in My Pocket Like Grains of Sand,* 1984 (New York: Bantam, 1990) 380.
94. W. H. Auden, "In Memory of Sigmund Freud," *Collected Poems* (New York: Vintage, 1991) 276.
95. Damon Knight, "The Classics," *In Search of Wonder,* Second ed. (Chicago: Advent, 1967) 12–13.
96. Gary K. Wolfe, *Critical Terms for Science Fiction and Fantasy* (New York: Greenwood Press, 1986) 140.
97. Quoted in Nicholls and Robu 1083.
98. Nicholls and Robu 1085, 1084.
99. Quoted in Peplow and Bravard 50.
100. Samuel R. Delany, introduction to *Empire,* by Samuel R. Delany and Howard V. Chaykin (New York: Berkley, 1978) 1.
101. Delany, *Empire* 2.
102. Delany, *Empire* 2.
103. Suvin vii.
104. Delany, "Semiology" 32.
105. Samuel R. Delany, "The *Para • doxa* Interview," 1995, *Shorter Views* 205.
106. Delany, "*Dichtung*" 188.
107. Delany, "Semiology" 31.
108. Delany, "*Dichtung*" 188.
109. Roland Barthes, *Mythologies* (1957; New York: Noonday, 1993) 142. Quoted in Kenneth James, "Extensions: An Introduction to the Longer Views of Samuel R. Delany," Samuel R. Delany, *Longer Views* xix.
110. James xxi.
111. Delany, "Shadows," 1977, *Longer Views* 254.
112. James xx.
113. Delany, "Susan Grossman" 251.
114. Earl Jackson Jr. *Strategies of Deviance* (Bloomington: Indiana UP, 1995) 93.
115. James xxiii.
116. Ihab Hassan, "Pluralism in Postmodern Perspective," *Critical Inquiry* 12 (Spring 1986): 503–20; Dick Hebdige, *Hiding in the Light* (London: Routledge, 1988); Fredric Jameson, *Postmodernism, or the Cultural Logic of Late Capitalism* (Durham, N.C.: Duke UP, 1991); Jean-Francois Lyotard, *The Postmodern Condition: A Report on Knowledge* (1979; Minneapolis: U of Minnesota P, 1984).
117. Andrew Ross, introduction to *Universal Abandon?* ed. Andrew Ross (Minneapolis: U of Minnesota P, 1988) vii.
118. Steven Seidman, "Identity and Politics in a 'Postmodern' Gay Culture: Some Historical and Conceptual Notes," *Fear of a Queer Planet,* ed. Michael Warner (Minneapolis: U of Minnesota P, 1993) 105–42.
119. Delany, Afterword 378–380.
120. Robert Young, *White Mythologies: Writing, History, and the West* (London: Routledge, 1990) 19.
121. Young 20.
122. Quoted in Delany, Afterword, 383.
123. Delany, Afterword, 384.

124. Ross xvi.
125. Wahneema Lubiano, "Shuckin' Off the African American Native Other: What's 'Po-Mo' Got to Do with It?" *Cultural Critique* 18 (1991): 157–58.
126. Lubiano 152–53.
127. Hall, "New Ethnicities" 445–46.
128. Harper, *Are We Not Men?* ix.
129. Hall, "New Ethnicities" 444.
130. Harper xi-xii.
131. Delany, "Racism and Science Fiction," 392.
132. Delany, "Semiology" 41.
133. Farred 639.
134. Quoted in Dery 189.
135. Delany, "Semiology" 27.
136. Delany, "Shadows" 290.
137. Delany, "The Second *Science Fiction Studies* Interview" 347.
138. Delany, "Semiology" 26.
139. Samuel R. Delany, *Return to Nevèrÿon* (1987, Hanover, N.H.: UP of New England/Wesleyan UP, 1994) 243. *Tales of Nevèrÿon* (1979, Hanover, N.H.: UP of New England/Wesleyan UP, 1993) 52–53.
140. Samuel R. Delany, *Empire Star* (1966, New York: Vintage, 2001) 74–75. Subsequent citations are noted in parentheses.
141. Quoted in Dery 190.
142. Delany, *Einstein* 50. Quoted in Emerson Littlefield, "Mythologies of Race and Science in Samuel R. Delany's *The Einstein Intersection* and *Nova*," *Extrapolation* 23.3 (1982): 235–42. "Whitey" is actually a character in *Einstein*, the "non-functional" brother of Lo Easy, not an abstract representation of white authority and privilege. However, Littlefield's formulation provocatively suggests that Lobey and his people may have received racialized language as part of their cultural inheritance.
143. Robert Elliot Fox, *Conscientious Sorcerers: The Black Postmodernist Fiction of LeRoi Jones/Amiri Baraka, Ishmael Reed, and Samuel R. Delany* (Westport, Conn.: Greenwood Press, 1987) 99.
144. Samuel R. Delany, *Babel-17* (1966; New York: Vintage, 2001) 30. Subsequent citations are noted in parentheses.
145. Carl Freedman, *Critical Theory and Science Fiction* (Hanover, N.H.: UP of New England/Wesleyan UP, 2000) 158. See also Jackson 104.
146. Delany, *Tales* 180, 179, 181, 182.
147. Michel Foucault, *The Order of Things*, 1966. Quoted in Samuel R. Delany, *Trouble on Triton* (1976; Hanover, N.H.: UP of New England/Wesleyan UP, 1996) 292.
148. Tom Moylan, *Demand the Impossible* (New York: Methuen, 1986) 193.
149. Moylan 161.
150. Delany, *Trouble on Triton* 99.
151. Butler 148.
152. Moylan, 189–90.
153. Jackson 103, 104.
154. Moylan 193.

155. Jackson 103–04.
156. Edward K. Chan, "(Vulgar) Identity Politics in Outer Space: Delany's *Triton* and the Heterotopian Narrative," *Journal of Narrative Theory* 31.2 (Summer 2001): 198, 191, 205.
157. Fox 7.
158. Delany, "Science Fiction and Criticism" 203.
159. Delany, "Science Fiction and Criticism" 203.
160. Samuel R. Delany, "Critical Methods/Speculative Fiction," 1970, 1971, *The Jewel-Hinged Jaw* (New York: Berkley, 1978) 127.
161. Quoted in Beam 200.
162. Andrew Ross, *Strange Weather* (London: Verso, 1991) 143.
163. Stuart Hall, "On Postmodernism and Articulation: An Interview with Stuart Hall," ed. Lawrence Grossberg, 1986, *Stuart Hall: Critical Dialogues in Cultural Studies,* ed. David Morley and Kuan-Hsing Chen (New York: Routledge, 1996) 141.
164. Mercer, *Welcome* 264–65.
165. Kendall Thomas, "'Ain't Nothin' Like the Real Thing': Black Masculinity, Gay Sexuality, and the Jargon of Authenticity," *The House That Race Built,* ed. Wahneema Lubiano (New York: Pantheon, 1997) 116. See also Phillip Harper, *Are We Not Men?,* and Rinaldo Walcott, "Queer Texts and Performativity: Zora, Rap, and Community," *Queer Theory in Education,* ed. William F. Pinar (Mahwah, N.J.: Lawrence Erlbaum Associates, 1998) 157-71.
166. Mercer, *Welcome* 214.
167. Posnock 260.
168. Freedman 160n.
169. James Morrow, interview with Samuel R. Delany, "*Para • doxa* Interview with James Morrow: Blinded by the Enlightenment," *Para • doxa* 5.12 (1999): 147.
170. Samuel R. Delany, *Neveryóna,* 391–92.
171. Samuel R. Delany, *The Motion of Light in Water,* 1988 (New York: Kasak, 1993) 256.
172. Delany, "An Interview" 259.
173. Walter Mosley, "Black to the Future," *New York Times Magazine* 1 Nov. 1998. 32.
174. Dery 182.
175. Freedman 160n.
176. Charles R. Saunders, "Why Blacks Don't Read Science Fiction," *Brave New Universe: Testing the Values of Science in Society,* ed. Tom Henighan (Ottawa: Tecumseh, 1980) 160.
177. Robert Crossley, introduction to *Kindred* by Octavia Butler, 1979 (Boston: Beacon, 1988) xiv–xv.
178. Michael W. Peplow and Robert S. Bravard, introduction, *Samuel R. Delany: A Primary and Secondary Bibliography: 1962–1972,* Peplow and Bravard (Boston: G. K. Hall, 1980) 32. The struggle for black writers to cross SF's own version of the color line was recently dramatized in the *Star Trek: Deep Space Nine* episode, "Far Beyond the Stars." Written by Marc

Scott Zicree, the episode features Avery Brooks, who directed the episode as well, as Starfleet Capt. Benjamin Sisko, who is having visions of himself as a SF writer in 1953 writing a story about a space station called Deep Space Nine, with a black captain—that is, himself. Deep Space Nine's supporting characters appear as "Benny's" colleagues at a SF magazine, whose editor refuses to publish a story about "a Negro captain."

179. Samuel R. Delany, "The *Black Leather in Color* Interview," 1994, *Shorter Views* 116.
180. Mosley 34.
181. John Leonard, "Gravity's Rainbow," *The Nation* 15 Nov. 1993: 580.
182. Delany, "Semiology" 50. Delany's subsequent description is that of Michael W. Peplow, co-author, with Robert Bravard, of the 1980 Delany bibliography.
183. Delany, "Semiology" 50.
184. Thulani Davis, "The Future May Be Bleak, But It's Not Black," *Village Voice* 1 Feb. 1983: 19.
185. Greg Tate, "Ghetto in the Sky: Samuel Delany's Black Whole," 1985, *Flyboy in the Buttermilk* (New York: Simon & Schuster, 1992) 165.
186. Tate 166.
187. Dery 190.
188. Toni Morrison, "Unspeakable Things Unspoken: The Afro-American Presence in American Literature," 1990, *Within the Circle,* ed. Angelyn Mitchell (Durham, N.C.: Duke UP, 1994) 385.
189. Delany, "Science Fiction and Criticism" 200.
190. Laurie Anderson, "Sharkey's Night," *Mister Heartbreak,* Warner Bros. 1984. Quoted in James xxx.
191. Samuel R. Delany, *Flight from Nevèrÿon* 348. Quoted in James xxx.
192. Delany, "Reading" 2.
193. In addition to Fox, see Mary Kay Bray, "Rites of Reversal: Double Consciousness in Delany's *Dhalgren,*" *Black American Literary Forum* 18.2 (1984): 57–61; Sandra Y. Govan, "The Insistent Presence of Black Folk in the Novels of Samuel R. Delany," *Black American Literature Forum* 18.2 (1984): 43–48; and Jane Branham Weedman, *Samuel R. Delany* (Mercer Island, Wash.: Starmont House, 1982).
194. Fox, *Conscientious Sorcerers* ix.
195. Audre Lorde, "Age, Race, Class, and Sex: Women Redefining Difference," 1980, *Sister Outsider* (Freedom, Calif.: The Crossing Press, 1984) 115.

2. Contending Forces (pp. 55–89)

1. Gwendolyn Brooks, "The Third Sermon on the Warpland," *Riot* (Detroit: Broadside Press, 1969) 15.
2. Samuel R. Delany, *Dhalgren* (1975; New York: Vintage, 2001) 15. All further citations from this text are noted in parentheses.
3. "Afrofuturism: Afrofuturist Literature," 2 June 2001, <http://www.afrofuturism .net/text/lit.html>.

4. Quoted in Mark Dery, "Black to the Future: Interviews with Samuel R. Delany, Greg Tate, and Tricia Rose," *Flame Wars: The Discourse of Cyberculture,* ed. Mark Dery (Durham: Duke UP, 1994) 190.

5. Quoted in Dery 190.

6. For more on this phase of Delany's life and career, see *Heavenly Breakfast: An Essay on the Winter of Love* (1979; Flint, Mich.: Bamberger Books, 1997).

7. Quoted in Seth McEvoy, *Samuel Delany* (New York: Ungar, 1984) 98.

8. "Author Q & A: Samuel R. Delany on *Dhalgren,*" Mar. 2001, 13 June 2001, <http://www.randomhouse.com/vintage/catalog/display.pperl?isbn=0375706682&view=qa>.

9. McEvoy 97, 98.

10. Gerald Jonas, "SF," review of *Dhalgren* by Samuel R. Delany, *New York Times Book Review,* 16 Feb. 1975: 27.

11. Theodore Sturgeon, "Galaxy Bookshelf," review of *Dhalgren* by Samuel R. Delany, *Galaxy* Mar. 1975: 154–55.

12. Harlan Ellison, "Breakdown of a Breakthrough Novel," review of *Dhalgren* by Samuel R. Delany, *Los Angeles Times,* 23 Feb. 1975: 64.

13. Darrel Schweitzer, "Dully Grinning Delany Descends to Disaster," review of *Dhalgren* by Samuel R. Delany, *Justworld* Sixth Anniversary Issue (27) ed. Bill Bowers (North Canton, Ohio 1976) 1041, 1042.

14. Quoted in Jane Branham Weedman, *Samuel R. Delany* (Mercer Island, Wash.: Starmont House, 1982) 14.

15. Quoted in Weedman 14.

16. McEvoy 102.

17. Samuel R. Delany, "The Semiology of Silence: The *Science Fiction Studies* Interview," 1987, *Silent Interviews* (Hanover, N.H.: UP of New England/Wesleyan UP, 1994) 35.

18. Jean Mark Gawron, introduction, *Dhalgren,* by Samuel R. Delany (Boston: Gregg Press, 1977) x.

19. Douglas Barbour, *Worlds Out of Words: The SF Novels of Samuel R. Delany* (Frome, UK: Bran's Head Books, 1979) 90.

20. McEvoy 102.

21. Gawron x.

22. William Gibson, "The Recombinant City," 1996, foreword, *Dhalgren,* by Samuel R. Delany (New York: Vintage, 2001) xi.

23. Barbour 114.

24. Gawron xxxiv.

25. Gawron xlii.

26. Gawron v.

27. Samuel R. Delany, "Of Sex, Objects, Signs, Systems, Sales, SF," *The Straits of Messina* (Seattle: Serconia, 1989) 35.

28. Gawron xxix. There appears to be at least some confusion surrounding Kid's racial make-up in the extant criticism on *Dhalgren.* It is agreed that he is half Native American: "My mother was a full Cherokee . . ." he tells Tak (37). But there are varying opinions as to his other "half." Although Gawron calls Kid "half-Indian, half-white," Rudi Dornemann says that he

is "African and Native American" (Review of *Dhalgren, Rain Taxi* 1.4 [Fall 1996] 1, 31.), whereas Robert Elliot Fox simply cites Kid's journal's description of his race as "ambiguous" (753) ("'This You-Shaped Hole of Insight and Fire': Meditations on Delany's *Dhalgren,*" *Ash of Stars: On the Writing of Samuel R. Delany,* ed. James Sallis [Jackson: UP of Mississippi, 1996] 105). However, in an "Artist's Synopsis" in a journal from 1973, Delany writes that "[Kid's] mother was an American Indian; [and] his father was 'a little ballsy, blue-eyed Georgia Methodist.'" (Boston University, Mugar Library, Dept. of Special Collections, Samuel R. Delany Collection (1025), Part I, Box 16, Journal #55. England 1973.)

29. Gawron xiv.
30. Barbour 108–12. See also Fox 105.
31. Weedman 63–65.
32. Barbour 102.
33. Jane Branham Weedman was the first to assert that Delany's blackness is an important context for reading his works. See also Mary Kay Bray, "Rites of Reversal: Double Consciousness in Delany's *Dhalgren,*" *Black American Literary Forum* 18.2 (1984): 57–61; Sandra Y. Govan, "The Insistent Presence of Black Folk in the Novels of Samuel R. Delany," *Black American Literature Forum* 18.2 (1984): 43–48; and Robert Elliot Fox, "'This You-Shaped Hole of Insight and Fire': Meditations on Delany's *Dhalgren,*" 104.
34. James A. Snead, "Repetition as a Figure of Black Culture," *Black Literature and Literary Theory,* ed. Henry Louis Gates Jr. (New York: Routledge, 1984) 68, 69, 67. Robert Elliot Fox's "Meditations" makes a similar point about repetition as a black figure in Delany's novel that emphasizes Amiri Baraka's "the changing same" and Henry Louis Gates Jr.'s reference to "repetition with a difference" (106).
35. Snead 67.
36. Samuel R. Delany, *The Einstein Intersection* (1967; Hanover, N.H.: UP of New England/Wesleyan UP, 1998) 120.
37. Snead 68. Delany wrote two articles for *Seventeen* magazine on music in the early 1960s, the second of which, "All that Jazz" (Aug. 1961), was never published. Delany opens the article by stating "My name is Chip Delany, and I don't like jazz." By the end of the article, however, he is convinced that jazz "is a language, and in order to understand it . . . the best way to find out what it's all about is to listen to it carefully." Boston University Mugar Library Dept. of Special Collections, Samuel R. Delany Collection (1025), Part II, Box 46: Bernard Kay Collection of Samuel R. Delany Papers. A. Manuscripts and Published Writings, Typescript (f. 1).
38. Barbour 104. K. Leslie Steiner [Samuel R. Delany], "Some Remarks Toward a Reading of *Dhalgren,*" *The Straits of Messina,* 59.
39. Barbour 105.
40. Quoted in David Jones, preface to *The Anathemata* (London: Faber and Faber, 1952) 35.
41. Snead's discussion of the perceived accidental nature of repetition includes a brief foray into Freudian and Lacanian psychoanalysis. A psychoanalytic approach to *Dhalgren* would surely yield useful readings of the novel, es-

pecially given Kid's problems with memory, his questions and fears about his own sanity, and Delany's identification of Foucault's *Madness and Civilization* as one of his novel's influences in "Sex, Objects" (37).

42. See Barbour 108, Gawron xxxvii, and Bray 61. Another of Delany's "mobius texts" is "On the Unspeakable" in *Shorter Views: Queer Thoughts and the Politics of the Paraliterary.* (Hanover, N.H.: UP of New England/Wesleyan UP, 1999) 58–66.

43. Samuel R. Delany, Unpublished "Author's Note" to *Dhalgren,* Boston University Mugar Library Dept. of Special Collections, Samuel R. Delany Collection (1025), Part II, Box 1: I. Manuscripts, A. Novels, 1. *Dhalgren,* a. Drafts of front matter-Typescript with holograph corrections, 44 pp. (f. 1).

44. For more on the role of repetition in hip-hop see Tricia Rose, *Black Noise* (Hanover, N.H.: UP of New England/Wesleyan UP, 1994) 66–74.

45. Snead 59.

46. Barbour 111.

47. Barbour 104–05.

48. Delany, "Sex, Objects" 38.

49. Samuel R. Delany, Unpublished "Author's Note."

50. McEvoy 112.

51. Steiner 71–72. In the preface to the collection of critical essays entitled *The Straits of Messina,* Delany explains that he originally created K. Leslie Steiner to function as the author of requisite "scholarly exegeses, medical disclaimers, and apologiae—many of them, of course, bogus" for *Hogg,* a pornographic novel (x). Steiner later came in handy for Delany's reviews in the journal *Venom,* which was dedicated to scathing reviews and required each of its contributors to pan one of his or her own works (xii). The opinions and readings attributed to the Steiner persona are somewhat fictive; that is, although they are highly instructive, they do not necessarily represent Delany's "true" or "real" opinions or intentions, any articulation of which might not be trustworthy and would not deserve to be privileged anyway, especially since Delany ostensibly intended her as a "joke" (xiii). (See also Michael W. Peplow and Robert S. Bravard, Introduction, *Samuel R. Delany: A Primary and Secondary Bibliography: 1962–1979* (Boston: G.K. Hall, 1980) 48.) This book treats Steiner as a separate critical entity from Delany.

52. Steiner 79.

53. Snead 68.

54. Steiner 75.

55. Steiner 75, 79.

56. Steiner 75.

57. Bray 59. Bray sees Kid's race—"half–Native American and half-white" (58)—as relevant to the novel's interrogation of "classic" American narratives.

58. Steiner 79.

59. Samuel R. Delany, "Forward to an Afterword," *The Complete Nebula Award–Winning Fiction* (Toronto: Bantam, 1986) 406.

60. Delany, "Sex, Objects" 50.

61. McEvoy 106.
62. Delany, "Sex, Objects" 40.
63. Delany, "Sex, Objects" 39.
64. Delany, "Sex, Objects" 48.
65. Delany, "Sex, Objects" 41.
66. Foucault's full statement reads as follows: "I think that we have to get rid of the more or less Freudian schema—you know it—the schema of interiorisation of the law by the self" (163), and its source is not "Pastoral Power and Political Reason" from his Stanford University lectures, as noted in "Sword and Sorcery, S/M and the Economics of Inadequation" (*Silent Interviews* 139), but instead "About the Beginning of the Hermeneutics of the Self" from his 1980 lectures at Dartmouth College. See *Religion and Culture*, ed. J. Carrette (New York: Routledge, 1999).
67. Fox 104.
68. Fox 104.
69. Delany, "Sex, Objects" 51.
70. Barbour 100.
71. Steiner 62.
72. Steiner 61.
73. Bray 61.
74. Gawron xxiv.
75. Fox 105.
76. Fox 105.
77. Kobena Mercer, *Welcome to the Jungle* (New York: Routledge, 1994) 132.
78. Delany, "Sword and Sorcery" 140.
79. Essex Hemphill, introduction to *Brother to Brother: New Writings by Black Gay Men*, ed. Essex Hemphill (Boston: Alyson Publications, 1991) xviii.
80. Delany, "Shadow and Ash," *Longer Views* (Hanover, N.H.: UP of New England/Wesleyan UP 1996) 153.
81. Delany, "Shadow and Ash," 153.
82. Delany, "The Rhetoric of Sex/The Discourse of Desire," *Shorter Views* 24.
83. See "Reading Racial Fetishism: The Photographs of Robert Mapplethorpe" in Mercer's *Welcome to the Jungle*.
84. A letter in Delany's *1984* reveals that Helen Adam's surrealistic 1961 musical *San Francisco's Burning* (Brooklyn: Hanging Loose Press, 1985) was an influence on *Dhalgren* (327). What June desires from George parallels what Adams's Laura desires from Spangler Jack: "Black angel frowning, / My sense drowning. / Oh! At last, a ruthless blow. / Come closer, stranger. / Give me danger. / Love me low, dear, love me low. / Don't love me kindly. / Love roughly, blindly, / Till the hour when the black cocks crow. / Let danger take me. / Let terror shake me. / Love me low, dear, love me low" (147). June's father, Arthur Richards, is a ghost-worker, a man who goes to work every day despite the disorder outside his door and the fact that no one else is at the office. He bears some resemblance to Adams's The Nameless Man, who laments, "One more day in the morning / I'll wake, and dress, and eat, / And take the trolley, and go to work, / And when my work's complete, / I'll read

the paper, and get to bed. / It certainly won't be gay. / Nothing is forever. / I can't stand it one more day" (39). The chaos during the earthquake that rocks San Francisco at the conclusion of the musical is similar to the catastrophe at the end of Chapter VI in *Dhalgren*.

The distinction between rape and consensual sex acts is made repeatedly in Delany's works, including the Return to Nevèrÿon series and the short story "Citre et Trans," another example of the "sex reverses society" thesis. The story details, among other things, the rape of a young African American writer named Sam by a pair of Greek sailors. The rape is nothing but a violent, hurtful attack; but when "Sam" later masturbates to its memory—and, thereby, masters its memory—he experiences pleasure.

85. Angela Y. Davis, *Women, Race & Class* (1981; New York: Vintage, 1983) 182.

86. David Ian Paddy, review of *Dhalgren*, by Samuel R. Delany, *Review of Contemporary Fiction* 17.1 (Spring 1997) 181.

87. Karen J. Bartlett, "Subversive Desire: Sex and Ethics in Delany's *Dhalgren*," *New York Review of Science Fiction* 76 (1994): 7.

88. Bartlett 684.

89. Govan 47.

90. Steiner 65.

91. For a description of Delany's high school acquaintanceship with Stokely Carmichael/Kwame Turé, see Delany's *The Motion of Light in Water* (79–80).

92. William L. Van Deburg, *New Day in Babylon: The Black Power Movement and American Culture, 1965–1975* (U of Chicago P, 1992) 11.

93. Samuel R. Delany, "Some *Real* Mothers . . . : The *SF Eye* Interview," 1987, *Silent Interviews* 171.

94. Robert Gooding-Williams, "Introduction: On Being Stuck," *Reading Rodney King, Reading Urban Uprising*, ed. Robert Gooding-Williams (New York: Routledge, 1993) 11.

95. Delany, "Sex, Objects" 41.

96. Delany, "Sex, Objects" 42.

97. Fox 101.

98. Steiner 58.

99. Gibson, "The Recombinant City," xii.

100. Fox 98.

101. Bayard Rustin, "The Watts Manifesto," 1966, *Urban Racial Violence in the Twentieth Century*, ed. Joseph Boskin (Beverly Hills: Glencoe Press, 1976) 118.

102. Gerald Horne, *Fire This Time* (Charlottesville: U of Virginia P, 1995) 340.

103. Nathan Wright, Jr., *Ready to Riot* (New York: Holt, Rinehart and Winston, 1968) 4.

104. "Newark: On the Salt Marshes of the Passaic River," *Report of the National Advisory Commission on Civil Disorders, 1968, Urban Racial Violence in the Twentieth Century*, ed. Joseph Boskin (Beverly Hills: Glencoe Press, 1976) 123.

105. Fox 105.

106. Quoted in Godfrey Hodgson, *America in Our Time,* 1976 (New York: Vintage, 1978) 432.

107. Hodgson 434.

108. "An American Tragedy—Detroit," 1967, *Urban Racial Violence in the Twentieth Century* 132.

109. Peter H. Rossi, introduction to *Ghetto Revolts,* by Peter H. Rossi (New Brunswick, N.J.: Transaction Books, 1970) 5.

110. Gibson, "The Recombinant City," xii, xiii.

111. William Gibson, "Burning Chrome," *Burning Chrome,* 1982 (New York: Ace, 1987) 186.

112. Quoted in Dery 193–94.

113. Melvin L. Oliver, James H. Johnson, Jr, and Walter C. Farrell Jr., "Anatomy of a Rebellion: A Political-Economic Analysis," *Reading Rodney King, Reading Urban Uprising* 118.

114. Jerry G. Watts, "Reflections on the Rodney King Verdict and the Paradoxes of the Black Response," *Reading Rodney King, Reading Urban Uprising* 241.

115. Judith Butler, "Endangered/Endangering: Schematic Racism and White Paranoia," *Reading Rodney King, Reading Urban Uprising* 15. Similar points are made in Patricia J. Williams's "The Rules of the Game" and Kimberlé Crenshaw and Gary Peller's "Reel Time/Real Justice," both in the same volume as Butler's essay. Bill Nichols's *Blurred Boundaries: Questions of Meaning in Contemporary Culture* (Bloomington: U of Indiana P, 1994) features a chapter on the trial that also provides a detailed analysis of the defense's attempt to build "an interpretive frame" of the Holliday tape by way of claims of "Rodney King's control of the situation and the officer's operational obedience to policy and procedure" (29), as well as a sincere call for a "transformative social praxis" (42) in response to the trial and the civil unrest that followed.

116. Quoted in Ruth Wilson Gilmore. "Terror Austerity Race Gender Excess Theatre," *Reading Rodney King, Reading Urban Uprising* 29.

117. Delany, "Sex, Objects" 51.

118. Thomas L. Dumm, "The New Enclosures: Racism in the Normalized Community," *Reading Rodney King, Reading Urban Uprising* 191.

119. Hodgson 361.

120. Hodgson 361.

121. "Uprising and Repression in L.A.: An Interview with Mike Davis by the *CovertAction* Information Bulletin"; and Michael Omi and Howard Winant, "The Los Angeles 'Race Riot' and Contemporary U.S. Politics." Both in *Reading Rodney King, Reading Urban Uprising* 100, 104.

122. Delany, "Semiology" 36.

123. For more, see Cedric J. Robinson, "Race, Capitalism, and the Antidemocracy" and Oliver et al. in *Reading Rodney King, Reading Urban Uprising.*

124. Horne 360.

125. Michael Omi, and Howard Winant. *Racial Formation in the United States: From the 1960s to the 1990s* (New York: Routledge, 1994) 123.

126. Hodgson 266.

127. Omi and Winant, *Racial Formation* 124.

128. John F. Galliher and James L. McCartney, *Criminology: Power, Crime, and Criminal Law* (Lexington: Ginn, 1977) 55–56.
129. Galliher and McCartney 57.
130. Gawron vi, vii.
131. Gawron xxi.
132. Martin Duberman, *Stonewall,* (New York: Dutton, 1993) 170.
133. "Grendel" is also the name given to a member of the commune/band in Delany's *Heavenly Breakfast*.

3. The Empire of Signs (pp. 90–149)

1. Orlando Patterson, *Slavery and Social Death* (Cambridge: Harvard UP, 1982) 12.
2. Samuel R. Delany, *Tales of Nevèrÿon* (1979; Hanover, N.H.: UP of New England/Wesleyan UP, 1993) 239. All further citations from this text are noted in parentheses.
3. *Neveryóna* was originally published by Bantam in 1983 as *Neveryóna, or the Tale of Signs and Cities; Return to Nevèrÿon* was originally published by Arbor House in 1987 as *The Bridge of Lost Desire*.
4. Samuel R. Delany, "The Semiology of Silence: The *Science Fiction Studies* Interview," 1987, *Silent Interviews* (Hanover, N.H.: UP of New England/ Wesleyan UP, 1994) 46.
5. Samuel R. Delany, "*Alyx*," 1976, *The Jewel-Hinged Jaw* (New York: Berkley, 1978) 194.
6. Delany included Lieber's Fafhrd and the Grey Mouser in his scripts for two issues of DC Comics' *Wonder Woman*, #201–202 (1972).
7. Samuel R. Delany, "The Kenneth James Interview," Silent Interviews, 237.
8. Samuel R. Delany, "Sex, Race, and Science Fiction: The *Callaloo* Interview," 1990, *Silent Interviews* 225–26.
9. Gerald Jonas, review of *Tales of Nevèrÿon* by Samuel R. Delany, *New York Times Book Review* 28 Oct. 1979: 16.
10. Gerald Jonas, review of *The Bridge of Lost Desire* by Samuel R. Delany, *New York Times Book Review* 7 Feb. 1988: 22.
11. Kathleen Spencer, "Deconstructing *Tales of Nevèrÿon*: Delany, Derrida, and the 'Modular Calculus, Parts I–IV,'" *Essays in Arts and Sciences* 14 (1985): 67.
12. K. Leslie Steiner (Samuel R. Delany), "*Tales of Nevèrÿon*," *The Straits of Messina* (Seattle: Serconia, 1989) 160.
13. K. Leslie Steiner (Samuel R. Delany), "Return . . . a preface," *Tales of Nevèrÿon* 14.
14. Robert Elliot Fox makes this point about *Tales of Nevèrÿon* in *Conscientious Sorcerers* (Westport, Conn.: Greenwood Press, 1987) 108.
15. Delany, "Sex, Race" 226.
16. Derek Attridge, ed., *Acts of Literature* by Jacques Derrida (New York: Routledge, 1992) 221.

17. Steiner, "Return" 12.
18. Steiner, "Return" 11, 13.
19. S. L. Kermit (Samuel R. Delany), "Appendix: Some Informal Remarks Towards the Modular Calculus, Part Three," appendix to *Tales of Nevèrÿon* 247.
20. Also in Samuel R. Delany, *Return to Nevèrÿon* (1987; Hanover, N.H.: UP of New England/Wesleyan UP, 1994) 220. All further citations from this text are noted in parentheses.
21. Samuel R. Delany, *Flight from Nevèrÿon* (1985; Hanover, N.H.: UP of New England/Wesleyan UP, 1994) 234. All further citations from this text are noted in parentheses.
22. Samuel R. Delany, *Neveryóna* (1983; Hanover, N.H.: UP of New England/Wesleyan UP, 1993) 142. All further citations from this text are noted in parentheses.
23. Samuel R. Delany, "The *Black Leather in Color* Interview," 1994, *Silent Interviews* 118.
24. Patterson viii.
25. According to Morrill, Delany chose an anagram of the artist's name—ROWENA M.—for the name of this creature. *The Art of Rowena* (London: Paper Tiger, 2000) 52.
26. The Return to Nevèrÿon series is hardly the only example of the whitening of black characters on the covers of SF books. The novels of other African American SF authors have received similar makeovers. Although Lilith Iyapo, the heroine of Octavia Butler's *Dawn* (1987) is explicitly described as a woman of African descent, the first Questar editions of the novel feature a white woman on the cover.
27. Delany, "Semiology" 47.
28. *Having Our Say* (New York: Dell, 1993), by Delany's aunts Sarah L. and A. Elizabeth Delany, includes the story of Henry Beard Delany, Samuel R. Delany's paternal grandfather, who was born in 1858 before the American Civil War and grew up during Reconstruction.
29. Arna Bontemps, introduction to *Black Thunder* by Arna Bontemps (1968; Boston: Beacon, 1992) xxi.
30. Deborah E. McDowell and Arnold Rampersad, introduction to *Slavery and the Literary Imagination,* eds. Deborah E. McDowell and Arnold Rampersad (Baltimore: Johns Hopkins UP, 1989) viii, vii.
31. Hazel Carby, "Ideologies of Black Folk: The Historical Novel of Slavery," *Slavery and the Literary Imagination,* eds. Deborah E. McDowell and Arnold Rampersad (Baltimore: Johns Hopkins UP, 1989) 125–26.
32. Delany, "Semiology" 47.
33. Henry Louis Gates Jr., introduction to *The Slave's Narrative,* ed. Henry Louis Gates Jr. (Oxford UP, 1985) xxiii.
34. Patterson 5.
35. Samuel R. Delany, "The Necessity of Tomorrows," 1978, *Starboard Wine: More Notes on the Language of Science Fiction* (Pleasantville, N.Y.: Dragon Press, 1984) 35.

36. Quoted in Mark Dery, "Black to the Future: Interviews with Samuel R. Delany, Greg Tate, and Tricia Rose," *Flame Wars: The Discourse of Cyberculture,* ed. Mark Dery (Durham, N.C.: Duke UP, 1994) 190–91.

37. Gates xxvi, xiii.

38. James Olney, "The Founding Fathers—Frederick Douglass and Booker T. Washington," *Slavery and the Literary Imagination,* eds. Deborah E. McDowell and Arnold Rampersad (Baltimore: Johns Hopkins UP, 1989) 3.

39. Samuel R. Delany, *The Motion of Light in Water* (1988; New York: Kasak, 1993) 14.

40. Robert B. Stepto, "The Reconstruction of Instruction," *Afro-American Literature: The Reconstruction of Instruction,* eds. Dexter Fisher and Robert B. Stepto (New York: MLA, 1978) 18.

41. Frederick Douglass, *Narrative of the Life of Frederick Douglass, an American Slave,* 1845, *The Classic Slave Narratives,* ed. Henry Louis Gates Jr. (New York: Mentor, 1987) 303.

42. Quoted in Janet Duitsman Cornelius, *"When I Can Read My Title Clear": Literacy, Slavery, and Religion in the Antebellum South* (Columbia: U of South Carolina P, 1991) 3.

43. Henry Louis Gates Jr., introduction to *The Classic Slave Narratives* (New York: Mentor, 1987) ix. Other key commentaries on slave narratives' illustrations of the relationship between literacy and freedom include Houston A. Baker in *Blues, Ideology, and Afro-American Literature* (U of Chicago P, 1984), and William L. Andrews in *To Tell a Free Story* (Urbana: U of Illinois P, 1986).

44. Douglass 274–75. Literacy and education were just as important for former slaves during Reconstruction as well, a fact that Delany's forebears knew first-hand. *Having Our Say* notes that those ancestors "fared better than most [freed slaves]. Because they had been 'house niggers,' the Delanys had been forced to endure relatively fewer privations than those who had labored in the fields. Most important, they could read and write, and were better able than many former slaves to make a niche for themselves in the chaos of Southern life" (31–32). Sarah and Elizabeth Delany were fortunate enough to grow up on the campus of St. Augustine's School (now College), a black school their father helped develop and served as an Episcopal minister and vice-principal: "Growing up in this atmosphere, among 300 or so college students, reading and writing and thinking was as natural for us as sleeping and eating" (62). However, they also attest to the desire of numerous blacks at the turn of the century to learn: "Often there were people in the class who were grown men and women who lived nearby who wanted to learn to read and write," Sarah Delany states, "I never saw people try harder to improve themselves than these grown men and women wanting to read and write" (73). The Delany sisters also reveal that at St. Augustine's, the favorite hobby of their father, the grandfather of the first Nebula and Hugo Award–winning African American science fiction author, was astronomy (75).

45. Douglass 294.

46. Gates xiii and Olney 5.

47. Mikhail Bakhtin, *Rabelais and His World*, trans. Helene Iswolsky (1968; Bloomington: Indiana UP, 1984) 7.
48. Bakhtin 10.
49. Peter Stallybrass and Allon White, introduction, *The Politics and Poetics of Transgression*, eds. Stallybrass and White (Ithaca: Cornell UP, 1986) 7.
50. Douglass 299.
51. Karen Hohne and Helen Wussow, introduction, *A Dialogue of Voices: Feminist Literary Theory and Bakhtin*, eds. Hohne and Wussow (Minneapolis: U of Minnesota P, 1994) xii.
52. Douglass 300.
53. Patterson 2.
54. Quoted in Patterson 3.
55. Patterson x.
56. Steiner, "Return" 11.
57. Patterson 3, 5, 5, 44.
58. Patterson 26, 5.
59. Patterson 38, 7.
60. Patterson ix.
61. Patterson 97, 100.
62. Herbert Aptheker, *American Negro Slave Revolts* (1943; New York: International Publishers, 1969) 106.
63. Herbert Aptheker, *Abolitionism: A Revolutionary Movement* (Boston: Twayne Publishers, 1989) xi, xii, xii.
64. Introduction to Edmund S. Morgan, "Slavery and Freedom: The American Paradox," 1972, *Slavery in American Society*, ed. Lawrence B. Goodheart, et al. (Lexington: D.C. Heath, 1993) 69.
65. Elizabeth Hand, "Some Impertinent Remarks toward the Modular Calculus, Part One," *Science Fiction Eye* 4 (Aug. 1988): 36.
66. Patterson 34.
67. Ferdinand de Saussure, *Course in General Linguistics*, eds. Charles Bally et al., trans. Wade Baskin (New York: McGraw-Hill, 1966) 6.
68. Foucault, Michel, *This Is Not a Pipe*, 1973, ed. and trans. James Harkness (Berkeley: U of California P, 1983) 20.
69. Saussure 10, 66, 16. Saussure was not the only linguist to identify the arbitrary nature of the sign. American William Dwight Whitney supplied rudimentary theorizations in this direction in *Language and the Study of Language* (1867) and *The Life and Growth of Language* (1875), which were a major influence on Saussure's *Course*. See Jonathan Culler, *Ferdinand de Saussure*, 2d ed. (Ithaca: Cornell UP, 1986) 82; and Wade Baskin, Introduction to *Course in General Linguistics* by Ferdinand de Saussure (xv).
70. Jonathan Culler, *The Pursuit of Signs: Semiotics, Literature, Deconstruction* (Ithaca: Cornell UP, 1981) 23–24.
71. Delany, "Semiology" 23. Jonathan Culler's observation that scholars "have given the name of *semiotics* or *semiology*" to the investigation of linguistic and non-linguistic signs (*Pursuit* 22) suggests that the two names are practically interchangeable. However, Delany prefers the term "semiology" because it "suggests an area of study in which, by the very nature of such

study, we will always be inclined to seek a system, a law, a 'logos' ("Reading and the Written Interview," introduction, *Silent Interviews* 15). Delany finds Roland Barthes's description of "semiology" particularly useful: "The labor that collects the impurities of language, the wastes of linguistics, the immediate corruption of any message: nothing less than the desires, fears, expressions, intimidations, advances, blandishments, protests, excuses, aggressions, and melodies of which active language is made" (quoted in Delany, "Reading" 15).

72. Quoted in Steiner 15.
73. Spencer 88.
74. Saussure 118–19.
75. Steiner, "Return" 13.
76. Terry Eagleton, *Literary Theory: An Introduction* (Minneapolis: U of Minnesota P, 1983) 97.
77. Eagleton, *Theory* 127.
78. Jacques Derrida, "Différance," 1972, *Margins of Philosophy*, trans. Alan Bass (U of Chicago P, 1982) 11.
79. Saussure 14.
80. Eagleton 128.
81. Jacques Derrida, *Of Grammatology*, 1967, trans. Gayatri Chakravorty Spivak (Baltimore: Johns Hopkins UP, 1974) 7. The technique of identifying a binary relationship, revealing it to be a hierarchical relationship, and showing how the distinction between the two terms involved is not absolute, is a characteristic of the critical method known as deconstruction. Kathleen Spencer makes an excellent argument when she asserts that *Tales* is set up to deconstruct a host of binary oppositions: "civilization/barbarism, freedom/slavery, master/slave, man/woman, and literature/criticism" (74).
82. Samuel R. Delany, "Toto, We're Back! The *Cottonwood Review* Interview," 1986, *Silent Interviews* 71.
83. Samuel R. Delany, "The Susan Grossman Interview," *Silent Interviews* 254.
84. Culler, *Saussure* 105, 135, 139.
85. Karl Marx, From *Capital I* on Alienation, *Karl Marx: A Reader*, ed. Jon Elster (Cambridge UP, 1986) 63, 68.
86. Delany, "Semiology" 28.
87. Delany, "Semiology" 28.
88. Marx 66.
89. Spencer 79.
90. Booker T. Washington, *Up From Slavery*, 1901, *Three Negro Classics* (New York: Avon Books, 1965) 148.
91. Culler, *Saussure* 117.
92. Roland Barthes, *Mythologies*, trans. Jonathan Cape Ltd., 1957 (New York: Noonday, 1993) 11.
93. Sausurre 68. In another passage, Saussure backs off from this radical stance, claiming that "unlike language, other human institutions—customs, laws, etc.—are all based in varying degrees on the natural relations of things" (75).
94. Culler, *Saussure* 108.

95. Eagleton 135.

96. Culler, *Saussure* 108.

97. Antonin Artaud, *The Theater and Its Double* (New York: Grove Press, 1958) 30.

98. Patterson 38, 37, 8.

99. Saussure 68.

100. Jacques Derrida, "Signature Event Context," 1972, *Limited Inc.* (Evanston: Northwestern UP, 1988) 7, 12.

101. Jacques Derrida, "Limited Inc a b c . . ." 1977, *Limited Inc.* 40, 53.

102. Eagleton 129.

103. Robin Kelley's "Looking B(l)ackward," a dystopic look at African American academia in the twenty-first century, features, among other things, some humorous musings on the associations scholars make between plantation slavery and S/M. See *Race Consciousness: African American Studies for the New Century*, eds. Judith Jackson Fossett and Jeffrey A. Tucker (New York: New York University Press, 1997) 1–16.

104. Samuel R. Delany, "Sword and Sorcery, S/M, and the Economics of Inadequation: The *Camera Obscura* Interview," *Silent Interviews* 140.

105. Anne McClintock, *Imperial Leather* (New York: Routledge, 1995) 143.

106. Terry Eagleton, "Brecht and Rhetoric," 1982, *Against the Grain* (London: Verso, 1986) 167, 168, 169.

107. McClintock 144, 148, 144, 144, 146.

108. Much more remains to be said about Delany's treatment of both psychoanalysis and issues of gender in the *Return to Nevèrÿon* series. Suffice it to say here that Delany engages in a critique of gender identity that challenges both the patriarchal normalization of the male gender as well as feminist responses that simply invert the male/female hierarchy.

109. Samuel R. Delany, "Of Sex, Objects, Signs, Systems, Sales, SF," *The Straits of Messina.* (Seattle: Serconia, 1989) 41.

110. The contextuality of the sign is also relevant in Delany's *Stars in My Pocket Like Grains of Sand* (1984).

111. Eagleton, "Brecht" 171.

112. Delany, "Grossman" 251.

4. The Window of Autobiography (pp. 150–98)

1. Saunders Redding, "The Problems of the Negro Writer," *Black and White in American Culture*, eds. Jules Chametzky and Sidney Kaplan (Amherst: U of Massachusetts P, 1969) 361.

2. Samuel R. Delany, *The Motion of Light in Water*, 1988 (New York: Kasak, 1993) 327. All further citations from this text are noted in parentheses.

3. Silvio Gaggi, *Modern/Postmodern* (Philadelphia: U of Pennsylvania P, 1989) 83.

4. bell hooks, "Postmodern Blackness," *Yearning: Race, Gender, and Cultural Politics* (Boston: South End, 1990) 23.

5. hooks 23.

6. Ross Posnock, *Color and Culture: Black Writers and the Making of the Modern Intellectual* (Cambridge: Harvard UP, 1998) 23.
7. hooks 26, 28.
8. Redding 361, 362.
9. Stuart Hall, "New Ethnicities," (1989) *Stuart Hall: Critical Dialogues in Cultural Studies,* ed. David Morley and Kuan-Hsing Chen (New York: Routledge, 1996) 443.
10. Stuart Hall, "Ethnicity: Identity and Difference," *Radical America* 23.4 (Oct.–Dec. 1989) 17.
11. Hall, "New Ethnicities" 444.
12. Joyce A. Joyce, "'Who the Cap Fit': Unconsciousness and Unconscionableness in the Criticism of Houston A. Baker Jr. and Henry Louis Gates Jr." *New Literary History* 18:2 (Winter 1987): 378.
13. Joyce A. Joyce, "The Black Canon: Reconstructing Black American Literary Criticism," *New Literary History* 18:2 (Winter 1987): 341, 341–42.
14. Joyce, "'Who the Cap Fit'" 379.
15. Diana Fuss, *Essentially Speaking: Feminism, Nature and Difference* (New York: Routledge, 1989) 77.
16. Mark Dery, "Black to the Future: Interviews with Samuel R. Delany, Greg Tate, and Tricia Rose," *Flame Wars: The Discourse of Cyberculture,* ed. Mark Dery (Durham: Duke UP, 1994) 190.
17. Posnock 5, 266.
18. Fuss 104.
19. Cornel West, "Identity: A Matter of Life and Death," *Prophetic Reflections: Notes on Race and Power in America* (Monroe, Maine: Common Courage Press, 1993) 164.
20. Donna Haraway, *Simians, Cyborgs, and Women* (New York: Routledge, 1991) 150. Delany provides a most rigorous analysis of the "cyborg," the central trope of Haraway's "Manifesto," in "Reading at Work," *Longer Views,* (Hanover, N.H.: UP of New England/Wesleyan UP, 1996) 87–118.
21. Stuart Hall, "Ethnicity: Identity and Difference," *Radical America* 23.4 (1989): 16.
22. Fuss 103.
23. Thomas Disch, "This Is Not a Review," review of *The Motion of Light in Water* by Samuel R. Delany, *American Book Review* March 1988: 1.
24. Roy Pascal, *Design and Truth in Autobiography* (London: Routledge and Kegan Paul, 1960) 67, 68.
25. Pascal 61, 18–19, 70, 83.
26. Larry McCaffery, introduction, *Postmodern Fiction: A Bio-Bibliographical Guide,* ed. Larry McCaffery (New York: Greenwood, 1986) vii.
27. Posnock 283.
28. Jacques Derrida, "The Law of Genre," *Acts of Literature,* ed. Derek Attridge (New York: Routledge, 1992) 230.
29. Pascal 133, 96.
30. Jean Mark Gawron, introduction, *Dhalgren,* 1975 (Boston: Gregg Press, 1977) xv.
31. Posnock 9.

32. Pascal 5.
33. Robert F. Sayre, "Autobiography and the Making of America," *Autobiography: Essays Theoretical and Critical,* ed. James Olney (Princeton: Princeton UP, 1980) 148.
34. Posnock 262.
35. Thomas Keenan, "Windows: of vulnerability," *The Phantom Public Sphere,* ed. Bruce Robbins (Minneapolis: U of Minnesota P, 1993) 124, 127, 133–34.
36. Keenan 125.
37. This subtitle is taken from the title of Dany Laferrière's *Why Must a Black Writer Write About Sex?,* trans. David Homel (Toronto: Coach House, 1994).
38. Audre Lorde, "Uses of the Erotic: The Erotic as Power," 1978, *Sister Outsider* (Freedom, Calif.: The Crossing Press, 1984) 54.
39. Gerald Jonas, review of *The Motion of Light in Water* by Samuel R. Delany, *New York Times Book Review* 24 Jul. 1988: 25.
40. Posnock 261, 266. The latter citation comes from Delany's "Aversion/Perversion/Diversion," 1995, *Longer Views* 142.
41. Samuel R. Delany, "The 'Gay' Writer/'Gay Writing'. . . ?" *Shorter Views* (Hanover, N.H.: UP of New England/Wesleyan UP, 1999) 113, 112.
42. Joseph Beam, "Samuel R. Delany: The Possibility of Possibilities," *In the Life: A Black Gay Anthology,* ed. Joseph Beam (Boston: Alyson, 1986) 204.
43. Delany, "Aversion/Perversion/Diversion" 142.
44. Fuss 97.
45. Fuss 97.
46. Steven Seidman, "Identity and Politics in a 'Postmodern' Gay Culture: Some Historical and Conceptual Notes," *Fear of a Queer Planet,* ed. Michael Warner (Minneapolis: U of Minnesota P, 1993) 105, 135. 137.
47. Eve Kosofsky Sedgwick, *Epistemology of the Closet* (Berkeley: U of California P, 1990) 40–41.
48. Samuel R. Delany, "Racism and Science Fiction," 1999, *Dark Matter,* ed. Sheree R. Thomas (New York: Warner/Aspect, 2000) 396.
49. Sedgwick 1.
50. Cindy Patton, *Fatal Advice: How Safe-Sex Education Went Wrong* (Durham: Duke UP, 1996) 158.
51. Samuel R. Delany, *Heavenly Breakfast: An Essay on the Winter of Love* (1979, Flint, Mich.: Bamberger Books, 1997) 12, 20.
52. Samuel R. Delany, *1984: Selected Letters* (Rutherford, N.J.: Voyant, 2000) 103.
53. Joan W. Scott provides an analysis of the St. Mark's Baths episode as part of an analysis of "experience" as a basis for history and politics in "Experience," *Feminists Theorize the Political,* eds. Judith Butler and Joan W. Scott (New York: Routledge, 1992) 22–40.
54. Patton 158.
55. By making a connection between Rosenblatt's comments on black autobiography, which emphasize the importance of "choice," and narratives about gay experiences, I do not intend to suggest that homosexuality is a

"choice," or that it is simply a "lifestyle" that people choose to pursue. As *Motion* illustrates, such is not the case. Instead I seek to point out that, in general, both of these types of text share an investment in ideals of freedom and in speaking out against oppression.

56. Roger Rosenblatt, "Black Autobiography: Life as a Death Weapon," *Autobiography: Essays Theoretical and Critical,* ed. James Olney (Princeton: Princeton UP, 1980) 170.

57. William L. Andrews, introduction, *African American Autobiography: A Collection of Critical Essays* (Englewood Cliffs, N.J.: Prentice Hall, 1993) 1.

58. James Olney, "Autobiography and the Cultural Moment: A Thematic, Historical, and Bibliographical Introduction," *Autobiography: Essays Theoretical and Critical,* ed. James Olney (Princeton: Princeton UP, 1980) 13.

59. Quoted in Andrews 1.

60. Henry Louis Gates Jr., introduction, *The Classic Slave Narratives,* ed. Henry Louis Gates Jr. (New York: Mentor, 1987) xiv.

61. Olaudah Equiano, *The Interesting Narrative of the Life of Olaudah Equiano, or Gustavus Vassa, the African, Written by Himself* (1789), *The Classic Slave Narratives.* 12.

62. Quoted in Seth McEvoy, *Samuel Delany* (New York: Ungar, 1984) 94.

63. Posnock 285.

64. Gates xiv.

65. Werner Sollors, introduction, *The Interesting Narrative of the Life of Olaudah Equiano, or Gustavus Vassa, the African, Written by Himself* (1789; New York: Norton, 2001) xix, xxiv.

66. I am referring specifically to Marlon Riggs's film *Black Is, Black Ain't* (1995); Kendall Thomas's "'Ain't Nothing Like the Real Thing': Black Masculinity, Gay Sexuality, and the Jargon of Authenticity," *The House That Race Built: Black Americans, U.S. Terrain,* ed. Wahneema Lubiano (New York: Pantheon, 1997) 116–35; and Phillip Bryan Harper's *Are We Not Men?: Masculine Anxiety and the Problem of African American Identity* (New York: Oxford UP, 1996).

67. Rosenblatt 170, 171.

68. Posnock 285.

69. Rosenblatt 176.

70. E. Guereschi, review of *The Motion of Light in Water* by Samuel R. Delany, *Choice* 26 (1989): 938.

71. Scott 35.

72. Rudi Dornemann and Eric Lorberer, "A Silent Interview with Samuel R. Delany," *Rain Taxi* 5.4 (2001), 7 Mar. 2001, <http://www.raintaxi.com/delany.html>. See also *Silent Interviews.*

73. Essex Hemphill, introduction, *Brother to Brother: New Writings by Black Gay Men,* ed. Essex Hemphill (Boston: Alyson Publications, 1991) xvii–xviii.

74. Keith Boykin, *One More River to Cross: Black and Gay in America* (New York: Anchor Books, 1996) 270.

75. Samuel R. Delany, "Coming/Out," *Shorter Views* 89.

76. Samuel R. Delany, "The *Black Leather in Color* Interview," *Shorter Views* 115.

77. Delany, "The *Black Leather in Color* Interview" 115.

78. Delany, "Coming/Out" 95, 94.

79. Martin Duberman, *Stonewall* (New York: Dutton, 1993) 183.

80. Thom Beame, "Interview: BWMT Founder—Mike Smith," *Black Men, White Men,* ed. Michael J. Smith (San Francisco: Gay Sunshine Press, 1983) 188.

81. Robert F. Reid-Pharr, "Dinge," *Women and Performance: A Journal of Feminist Theory* 8.2 (16): 1996, 77.

82. Delany, "A Bend in the Road," *Shorter Views* 104.

83. Delany, "Citre et Trans," *Atlantis: Three Tales,* (Hanover, N.H.: UP of New England/Wesleyan UP 1995) 192.

84. Gayle Wald, *Crossing the Line: Racial Passing in Twentieth-Century U.S. Literature and Culture* (Durham: Duke UP, 2000) 14.

85. Wald 18. See also Phillip Brian Harper, *Are We Not Men?* (Oxford UP 1996).

86. Wald ix.

87. Judith Butler, *Bodies That Matter* (New York: Routledge, 1993) 172, 168.

88. Captain Elmer and Ron, the third crew member, appear as a transport crew that Comet Jo joins on his quest in *Empire Star* (1966). Some of Delany's other experiences on the Gulf Coast appear as those the Kid has had in *Dhalgren* (304–5).

89. Butler 171.

90. Wald ix, 9, 6.

91. Hall, "New Ethnicities" 444, 445–46.

92. Fuss 104.

93. Starobinski, Jean, "The Style of Autobiography," *Autobiography: Essays Theoretical and Critical,* ed. James Olney (Princeton: Princeton UP, 1980) 78.

94. Michael Eric Dyson, "Michael Jackson's Postmodern Spirituality," *Reflecting Black: African American Cultural Criticism* (Minneapolis: U of Minnesota P, 1993) 35.

95. Delany, *1984* 317.

96. Posnock 10, 45, 261, 284.

97. Quoted in Posnock 285.

98. Hall, "Ethnicity" 19.

99. The tables are turned somewhat in *Bread and Wine* (New York: Juno Books, 1999), Delany's graphic novel with art by Mia Wolff. The author's previously homeless love interest, Dennis, reveals that before agreeing to move in with Delany, he had the author "checked out" by friends "'cause [Delany] *could* have been . . . a crazy *psycho* cuttin' me up in little pieces . . . and *buryin'* 'em all over every which where" (30). For more interrogations of a discourse that links homosexuality and psychopathic killers see Douglas Crimp, "Right On, Girlfriend!" *Fear of a Queer Planet* 300–20 and Diana Fuss, "Oral Incorporations: *The Silence of the Lambs,*" *Identification Papers* (New York: Routledge, 1995) 83–105.

100. Stephen Butterfield, *Black Autobiography in America* (Amherst: U of Mass-achusetts P, 1974) 3, 107.

101. Jane Gallop, *The Daughter's Seduction: Feminism and Psychoanalysis* (Ith-aca: Cornell UP, 1982). Delany cites this passage from Gallop in "Aversion/ Perversion/Diversion" (142–43), as does Fuss in *Essentially Speaking* (104). Delany has noted that many readers "misread" the Central Park episode, which he characterizes as a youthful "mistake." See "A Silent Interview with Samuel R. Delany," *The Poetry Project Newsletter* 175 (June 1999): 8–11.

102. Hall "Ethnicity" 18.

103. It could be argued that Delany does not present this particular encounter as a "violation" because he does not use the word "rape" in describing what happened and that my reading of Delany's muteness as disempowering is based on the traditional "kinds of conceptions of black masculinity" inter-rogated by a work like *Motion*. When Delany leaves the apartment to go out and (pretend to) be "Snake" in public he is looking for some sort of interpersonal contact: "What I hoped—realized, indeed, I'd been hoping it for several days—was that someone, maybe not too different from me, might simply start speaking to me, warmly, understandingly" (125). And he is perfectly open to the possibility that this contact might be sexual: "If there was something sexual in the meeting, it would be silent and known" (125). However, what happens in the flower booth was most likely not what he had in mind. Although his response to the clerk's initiatory groping is neutral—"I was surprised to realize his interest was sexual. I looked at him, and I don't think I smiled or frowned. I was more curious than anything. And numb" (127)—*Motion*'s language indicates that he was being coerced and injured: "I wasn't really sure if I wanted to do that. . . . Even though he didn't get in, he shoved hard enough to hurt. I wasn't sure what I should do" (127). Delany leaves the flower booth wondering "if this was what happened to the mute or simple-minded wandering New York" (128). Compared to *Motion*'s numerous accounts of consensual anonymous sex, the incident in the flower booth looks like a violation.

104. Posnock 285.

105. Derek Attridge, ed. Jacques Derrida, *Acts of Literature* 221.

106. Gawron xxi.

107. Fuss 103, 102, 36, 96, 98.

108. Sayre 149.

5. Magic, Memory, and Migration (pp. 199–229)

1. Jean Toomer, "Bona and Paul," *Cane* (1923; New York: Norton, 1988) 75–76.

2. Samuel R. Delany, *Atlantis: Model 1924, Atlantis: Three Tales* (Hanover, N.H.: UP of New England/Wesleyan UP, 1995) 117. All subsequent cita-tions from this text are noted parenthetically.

3. Steven Moore, review of *Atlantis: Model 1924* by Samuel R. Delany, *Re-view of Contemporary Fiction* 15 (Spring 1995): 175.

4. Moore 176.

5. Rose Kernochan, review of *Atlantis: Three Tales* by Samuel R. Delany, *New York Times Book Review* 100 (29 Oct. 1995): 42.

6. Alain Locke, "The New Negro," *The New Negro* (1992; New York: Atheneum, 1992) 4, 6.

7. Samuel R. Delany, "Atlantis Rose . . . : Some Notes on Hart Crane," *Longer Views: Extended Essays* (Hanover, N.H.: UP of New England/Wesleyan UP, 1996) 189.

8. Sigmund Freud, *Civilization and Its Discontents* (New York: Norton, 1989) 16.

9. Freud 17.

10. Freud 18.

11. Margaret E. Gray, *Postmodern Proust* (Philadelphia: U of Pennsylvania P, 1992) 1.

12. Hal Foster, introduction, *The Anti-Aesthetic: Essays on Postmodern Culture,* ed. Hal Foster (Port Townsend, Wash.: Bay Press, 1983) xi.

13. Larry McCaffery, introduction to *Postmodern Fiction: A Bio-Bibliographical Guide,* ed. Larry McCaffery (New York: Greenwood, 1986) xii, xiii, xvi.

14. Jacques Lacan, "The Agency of the Letter in the Unconscious, or Reason Since Freud," *Écrits* (New York: Norton, 1977) 147.

15. Lacan 148.

16. Malcolm Bowie, *Freud, Proust, Lacan: Theory as Fiction* (Cambridge UP, 1987) 109.

17. Jacques Derrida, *Of Grammatology* (1967; Baltimore: Johns Hopkins UP, 1976) 7.

18. Terry Eagleton, *Literary Theory: An Introduction* (Minneapolis: U of Minnesota P, 1983) 128.

19. Mark Dery, "Black to the Future: Interviews with Samuel R. Delany, Greg Tate, and Tricia Rose," *Flame Wars: The Discourse of Cyberculture* (Durham, N.C.: Duke UP, 1994) 191.

20. James Thomson, "The City of Dreadful Night," *Poems and Some Letters of James Thomson,* ed. Anne Ridler (Carbondale: Southern Illinois UP, 1963) 200.

21. Farah Jasmine Griffin, *"Who Set You Flowin'?": The African American Migration Narrative* (Oxford UP, 1995) 3.

22. Samuel R. Delany, *Flight from Nevèrÿon* (Hanover, N.H.: UP of New England/Wesleyan UP, 1994) 193.

23. Griffin 3.

24. Griffin 69, 51–52, 73.

25. Griffin 52.

26. Griffin 4.

27. Sarah L. and A. Elizabeth Delany, with Amy Hill Hearth, *Having Our Say* (New York: Dell, 1993) 128.

28. Darwin Turner, *In a Minor Chord,* (Carbondale: Southern Illinois UP, 1971) 20.

29. Griffin 102, 106.

30. Julia Kristeva, *Powers of Horror,* 1980 (New York: Columbia UP,1982) 12.

31. Griffin 5, 23.
32. Delany, "The Semiology of Silence: The *Science Fiction Studies* Interview," *Silent Interviews* (Hanover, N.H.: UP of New England/Wesleyan UP, 1994) 51.
33. Delany, Delany, and Hearth, 14 and caption to seventh photo page.
34. Posnock 289.
35. Delany, Delany, and Hearth xv.
36. Griffin 23–24, 44.
37. Michel Foucault, *Madness and Civilization* (1965; New York: Vintage, 1988) 21, 39.
38. Samuel R. Delany, *The Motion of Light in Water* (1988, New York: Richard Kasak, 1993) 319–20.
39. Turner 27.
40. Delany, *Motion* 319.
41. Excerpts from Morrison, Larsen, Wright, and Toomer are quoted in Griffin, 171, 154, 160, 147 respectively.
42. John's comment may be more accurate than he realizes. The juxtaposed columns of text in Lewy's journal and in *Atlantis* itself approximate the appearance of the Talmud, which features the Torah, the codification of Jewish religion and law, surrounded by ancient rabbinical commentary. I am indebted to Jonathan Waldauer for this insight.
43. In 1915, Leo Frank, a Jewish factory manager, was lynched after being convicted of the 1913 murder of teenager Mary Phagan in Atlanta, although another man had been seen hiding Phagan's body. The trial of Frank led to the founding of the Anti-Defamation League. Frank was posthumously pardoned in 1986.
44. Delany, *Motion* 182.
45. Samuel R. Delany, "Science Fiction and Criticism: The *Diacritics* Interview," *Silent Interviews* 203.
46. Jean Toomer, "Song of the Son," *Cane* (1923; New York: Norton, 1988) 14.
47. Toomer, "Kabnis," *Cane* (1923; New York: Norton, 1988) 98.
48. Stuart Hall, "Ethnicity: Identity and Difference," *Radical America* 23.4 (1989): 19.
49. Posnock 286, 292–93.
50. Posnock 32.
51. Quoted in Turner 34.
52. Turner xxii.
53. "A Silent Interview with Samuel R. Delany," *The Poetry Project Newsletter* 175 (June 1999): 8–11.
54. Posnock 292.
55. Posnock 292.
56. W. E. B. DuBois, *Dusk of Dawn, Writings,* ed. Nathan Huggins, (1940; New York: Library of America, 1986) 665, 666.
57. Henry Louis Gates Jr. "Two Nations . . . Both Black," 1992, *Reading Rodney King, Reading Urban Uprising,* ed. Robert Gooding-Williams (New York: Routledge, 1993) 252.

58. W. E. B. DuBois, *The Souls of Black Folk* (1903; *Writings,* ed. Nathan I. Huggins, New York: Library of America, 1986) 438.

59. DuBois, *Dusk of Dawn* 665.

60. Posnock 263–64, 293.

61. Robert Hayden, "[American Journal]," *Collected Poems: Robert Hayden* (New York: Liveright, 1996) 192.

62. Robert Hayden, "El-Hajj Malik El-Shabazz," *Collected Poems: Robert Hayden* (New York: Liveright, 1996) 89.

63. Robert Hayden, "Words in the Mourning Time," *Collected Poems: Robert Hayden* 98.

64. Arnold Rampersad, introduction, *Collected Poems: Robert Hayden* (New York: Liveright, 1996) xxxiii, xxiv.

65. Rampersad hypothesizes that Hayden "tightly embraced black history" in order to avoid the confessional mode other poets of his time were using and cites Hayden correspondent Pontheolla Taylor Williams, who "identified homoeroticism and bisexuality—which Hayden never acknowledged—as a troubling source of guilt and shame for the poet" (xxviii).

66. Rampersad xxiv–xxv.

67. Samuel R. Delany, "Introduction to a Reading of Robert Hayden's 'Middle Passage,'" in Honor of *The Norton Anthology of African American Literature,* 92nd St. YM/WHA, New York, 27 Feb. 1997.

68. Delany, "Atlantis Rose" 224.

69. Delany, "Introduction to a Reading of Robert Hayden's 'Middle Passage.'"

70. Foucault 11.

71. John Edgar Wideman, *Fatheralong* (New York: Vintage 1994) xxv.

72. Samuel R. Delany, *Motion* 52.

73. Samuel R. Delany, "Introductory Remarks to 'Smoke, Lilies, Jade,' by Richard Bruce Nugent," *The James White Review* 16.1 (Winter 1999) ed. Patrick Merla, 21.

74. Samuel R. Delany, "Beatitudes," *Crimes of the Beats,* eds. The Unbearables (Brooklyn, N.Y.: Autonomedia, 1998) 120.

75. Delany, "Atlantis Rose" 187, 188–89.

76. Delany, "Atlantis Rose" 197.

77. Delany, "Atlantis Rose" 201.

78. Thomson 178.

79. Delany, "Atlantis Rose" 241.

80. Delany, "Atlantis Rose" 174.

81. Posnock 290.

82. Eric Garber suggests that racial difference was not always an impassable barrier between straight African Americans and gay whites in 1920s New York City: "Many White [sic] lesbians and gay men felt a kinship with Harlem's residents. . . .White homosexuals found sanctuary and a sense of camaraderie uptown in Harlem." "T'ain't Nobody's Bizness: Homosexuality in 1920s Harlem," *Black Men, White Men,* ed. Michael J. Smith (San Francisco: Gay Sunshine Press, 1983) 10, <http://www.gaysunshine.com/exc_black-white.html>.

83. Quoted in Gordon Hunter, ed. "The Situation of American Writing 1999," *American Literary History* 11.2 (1999) 352.
84. Ken James, "Extensions: An Introduction to the Longer Views of Samuel R. Delany," *Longer Views* by Samuel R. Delany xxxiv.
85. Wideman 63.
86. Delany, "Atlantis Rose" 246.
87. Neil Gaiman with illustrations by John Bolton, *The Books of Magic,* Book One: "The Invisible Labyrinth" (New York: DC Comics, 1990) 26.

6. A Revolution from Within (pp. 230–75)

1. Cornel West, "Black Sexuality," *Race Matters* (Boston: Beacon Press, 1993) 90.
2. Samuel R. Delany, *The Mad Man*, rev. ed. (Rutherford, N.J.: Voyant, 2002) 5. All further citations from this text are noted in parentheses.
3. Quoted in Richard Elovich, "Beyond Condoms . . . : How to Create a Gay Men's Culture of Sexual Health," *POZ* June 1999, 8 Oct. 2000, <http://www.thebody.com/poz/features/6_99/beyond.html>.
4. Joint United Nations Programme on HIV/AIDS and the World Health Organization, *AIDS Epidemic Update* (December 2002) 24 May, 2003, <http://www.who.int/hiv/facts/epiupdate_en.pdf> 3. All further citations from this text are noted in parentheses.
5. With regard to the etiology of AIDS, current mainstream medical discourse has identified HIV infection as the principal agent. According to the CDC, HIV has been proven to be the cause of AIDS in a number of ways including the following: "Tests for HIV antibody in persons with AIDS show that they are infected with the virus. HIV has been isolated from persons with AIDS and grown in pure culture. Studies of blood transfusion recipients before 1985 documented the transmission of HIV to previously uninfected persons who subsequently developed AIDS." Moreover, HIV infection is the only common factor among people with AIDS throughout the world. CDC Divisions of HIV/AIDS Prevention, "HIV Causes AIDS," 23 March 2003, 8 May 2003, <http://www.cdc.gov/hiv/hivinfo/overview/htm>.
   According to the National Institute of Allergy and Infectious Diseases and the National Institutes for Health, HIV can be spread a variety of ways: "most commonly by having unprotected sex with an infected partner . . . through contact with infected blood . . . among injection drug users by the sharing of needles or syringes . . . [and] from mother to child during pregnancy or through the breast milk of mothers infected with the virus." (NIAID/NIH Fact Sheet, "HIV Infection and AIDS: An Overview," Aug. 2002, 8 May 2003, <http://www.niaid.nih.gov/factsheets/hivinf.htm>. There have been challenges made to the theory that HIV leads to AIDS by biologist Peter Duesberg in *Inventing the AIDS Virus* (Washington, D.C.: Regnery, 1996), and by South African President Thabo Mbeki. It appears that such arguments have yet to definitively repudiate the connection between HIV and AIDS, but they persist and sustain debate and discussion on the issue.

6. CDC Divisions of HIV/AIDS Prevention, "Basic Statistics," 31 March 2003, 7 May 2003, <http://www.cdc.gov/hiv/stats.htm#cumaids>.
7. CDC Divisions of HIV/AIDS Prevention, "Table 1. Persons reported to be living with HIV infection and with AIDS, by state and age group, reported through December 2001." *HIV/AIDS Surveillance Report* 13.2, 24 Sept. 2002, 9 May 2003, <http://www.cdc.gov/hiv/stats/hasr1302/table1.htm>.
8. NIAID/NIH Fact Sheet, "HIV Infection and AIDS: An Overview."
9. CDC Divisions of HIV/AIDS Prevention, "Table 7: AIDS cases by sex, age at diagnosis, and race/ethnicity, reported through December 2001, United States," *HIV/AIDS Surveillance Report* 13.2, 24 Sept. 2002, 9 May 2003, <http://www.cdc.gov/hiv/stats/hasr1302/table7.htm>.
10. CDC Divisions of HIV/AIDS Prevention, "Table 20: Deaths in persons with AIDS, by race/ethnicity, age at death, and sex, occurring in 1999 and 2000; and cumulative totals reported through December 2001, United States," *HIV/AIDS Surveillance Report* 13.2, 24 Sept. 2002, 8 May 2003, <http://www.cdc.gov/hiv/stats/hasr1302/table20.htm>.
11. CDC Divisions of HIV/AIDS Prevention, "Table 7."
12. CDC Divisions of HIV/AIDS Prevention, "Table 9: Male adult/adolescent AIDS cases by exposure category and race/ethnicity, reported through December 2001, United States," *HIV/AIDS Surveillance Report* 13.2, 25 Sept. 2002; 18, 9 May 2003, <http://www.cdc.gov/hiv/stats/hasr1302.pdf>.
13. CDC Divisions of HIV/AIDS Prevention, "Table 11: Female adult/adolescent AIDS cases by exposure category and race/ethnicity, reported through December 2001, United States," *HIV/AIDS Surveillance Report* 13.2, 24 Sept. 2002, 9 May 2003, <http://www.cdc.gov/hiv/stats/hasr1302/table11.htm>.
14. Robert N. Anderson, "Table 1. Deaths, percent of total deaths, and death rates for the 10 leading causes of death in selected age groups, by race and sex: United States, 1999–Con.," *National Vital Statistics Reports* 49.11 (12 Oct. 2001) Hyattsville, Md.: National Center for Health Statistics, 31, 33, 12 May, 2003, <http://www.cdc.gov/nchs/data/nvsr/nvsr49/nvsr49_11.pdf>.
15. National Minority AIDS Council. *HIV/AIDS and African Americans* (October 1999) 8, 24 May 2003, <http://www.nmac.org/publications/policypubs/factsheets/hivaids_and_african_americans.pdf>.
16. Stuart Hall, "Cultural Studies and Its Theoretical Legacies," *Cultural Studies,* ed. Lawrence Grossberg, Cary Nelson, and Paula Treichler (New York: Routledge, 1992) 284, 285.
17. Ross Chambers, *Facing It: AIDS Diaries and the Death of the Author* (Ann Arbor: U of Michigan P, 1998) vii.
18. Paula Treichler, *How to Have Theory in an Epidemic: Cultural Chronicles of AIDS* (Durham: Duke UP, 1999) 4.
19. Susan Sontag, *Illness as Metaphor* (1978) and *AIDS and Its Metaphors* (New York: Anchor, 1989) 181–83.
20. Treichler 316.
21. Laurie Anderson, "Language Is a Virus," *Home of the Brave,* Warner Bros., 1986. See also Cindy Patton, *Fatal Advice: How Safe-Sex Education Went Wrong* (Durham, N.C.: Duke UP, 1996) 14.

22. Treichler 150, 11.
23. Simon Watney, *Policing Desire: Pornography, AIDS, and the Media* (Minneapolis: U of Minnesota P, 1987) 9.
24. Phillip Brian Harper, *Private Affairs* . (New York UP, 1999) 92.
25. Treichler 18, 70–72. See also Steven Epstein, *Impure Science* (Berkeley: U of California P, 1996.)
26. Douglas Crimp, "AIDS: Cultural Analysis, Cultural Activism," *AIDS: Cultural Analysis, Cultural Activism,* ed. Douglas Crimp (Cambridge, Mass.: MIT Press, 1987) 3, 7, 4, 5.
27. Samuel R. Delany, "The Thomas L. Long Interview," *Shorter Views,* (Hanover, N.H.: UP of New England/Wesleyan UP, 1999) 125.
28. The neologism "pornotopic fantasy" has generated more than a little confusion about *The Mad Man,* which is set in mid–1980s New York City, as opposed to, say, the empire of Nevèrÿon. Delany's explanation of the novel's generic identity and the terms he uses to describe that identity is as follows:

> "Pornotopia" is not the "good sexual place." (That would be "Upornotopia" or "Eupornotopia.") It's simply *the* "sexual place"—the place where all can become (apocalyptically) sexual.
> "Pornotopia" is the place where pornography occurs—and that, I'm afraid, is the world of *The Mad Man*. It's the place where any relationship can become sexualized in a moment, with a proper word or look—where every relationship is potentially sexualized even before it starts. In *The Mad Man* I try to negotiate pornotopia more realistically than most . . .
> *The Mad Man* is a serious work of pornography. I suppose I ought to be flattered by some readers' confusing it with realism. But, finally, it *is* a pornographic work. Its venue is pornotopia, not a realistic portrayal of life on New York's Upper West Side, for all I have used that as the basis for what I wrote. Those who say it is not a pornographic work (and that I am being disingenuous by saying that it is) are, however well-intentioned, just wrong. (Delany, "The Thomas L. Long Interview" 133).

29. Treichler 5.
30. Cathy J. Cohen, *The Boundaries of Blackness: AIDS and the Breakdown of Black Politics* (Chicago: U of Chicago P, 1999) 228.
31. Hall 285.
32. LeRoy Whitfield and Esther Kaplan with Shana Naomi Krochmal, "The Fire This Time," *POZ* Jan. 1999, 8 Oct. 2000, <http://www.thebody.com/poz/features/1_pp/leaders.html>.
33. Cohen's *Boundaries of Blackness* features more information on the service and activist efforts by African American AIDS organizations such as Black AIDS Mobilization (BAM!) and Voices of Color against AIDS and for Life (VOCAL), as well as African American Gay and Lesbian organizations such as Advocates of Gay Men of Color, the Audre Lorde Project, SALSA Soul Sisters, Bay Area Black Lesbians and Gays, the DC Coalition of Black Gays, the National Coalition of Black Lesbian and Gays, Black Coalition on AIDS–

San Francisco, and Gay Men of African Descent. The Los Angeles-based African American AIDS Policy and Training Institute (AAAPTI) is currently one of the most important organizations at the forefront of the battle against AIDS.

34. Whitfield et al.
35. Whitfield et al.
36. Cohen 258, 259, 97–98, 264.
37. Whitfield et al. See also Cohen's *Boundaries of Blackness* for a detailed analysis of African American political and religious organizations' responses to AIDS.
38. Cohen 254, 299, 310.
39. Cohen 118–20; 11; 13; x, 15; 15–16; 19.
40. Cohen xi.
41. Jan Zita Grover, "AIDS: Keywords," *AIDS: Cultural Analysis, Cultural Activism*, 18.
42. Douglas Crimp, "How to Have Promiscuity in an Epidemic," *AIDS: Cultural Analysis, Cultural Activism*, 249.
43. Cohen 124, 122–25.
44. Cohen 121, 160–61, 166, 240, 228–29.
45. Cohen 34.
46. West 85.
47. Frantz Fanon, *Black Skin, White Masks* (1952, New York: Grove Press, 1967) 202.
48. Kobena Mercer, *Welcome to the Jungle*, (New York: Routledge, 1994) 146.
49. Cohen 63, 71, 72.
50. Phillip Brian Harper, *Are We Not Men?: Masculine Anxiety and the Problem of African American Identity*, (New York: Oxford UP, 1996) 12, 10, 19.
51. Mercer 137.
52. Toni Morrison, *Beloved* (1987; New York: Plume, 1988) 108–09. Charles I. Nero argues that *Beloved* is itself a heterosexist and homophobic text, because in the absence of women, Paul D and the other Sweet Home men practice bestiality but do not engage in homosexual sex. See "Toward a Black Gay Aesthetic: Signifying in Contemporary Black Gay Literature," *Brother to Brother*, ed. Essex Hempill (Boston: Alyson Publications, 1991) 229–52.
53. Mercer 137.
54. Amiri Baraka, "Black Art," *The Norton Anthology of African American Literature*, ed. Henry Louis Gates Jr. et al. (New York: Norton, 1997) 1884.
55. Quoted in Harper, *Are We Not Men?* 50.
56. Larry, Neal, "The Black Arts Movement," 1968, *Within the Circle: An Anthology of African American Literary Criticism from the Harlem Renaissance to the Present*, ed. Angelyn Mitchell (Durham: Duke UP, 1994) 190, 195.
57. Mercer 139.
58. Harper, *Are We Not Men?* 11.
59. Kendall Thomas, "'Ain't Nothing Like the Real Thing': Black Masculinity, Gay Sexuality, and the Jargon of Authenticity," *The House That Race Built:*

Black Americans, U.S. Terrain, ed. Wahneema Lubiano, (New York: Pantheon, 1997) 128. Thomas's essay features more information on homophobia in hip-hop and black nationalist narratives of racial authenticity.

60. Mercer 158.
61. Frances Cress Welsing, "The Politics Behind Black Male Passivity, Effeminization, Bisexuality, and Homosexuality," 1974, *The Isis Papers,* (Chicago: Third World Press, 1991) 86, 89, 91. Welsing is only one of a number of black intellectuals who have posited highly problematic theories about black homosexuality. Ron Simmons identifies similar statements by Haki Madhubuti, Molefi Asante, Nathan and Julia Hare, Robert Staples, and others. See "Some Thoughts on the Challenges Facing Black Gay Intellectuals," *Brother to Brother,* 211–28.
62. Simmons 213.
63. Cohen 14.
64. Harper, *Are We Not Men?* 37–38.
65. Harper, *Are We Not Men?* 11.
66. Delany's 1986 interview with Anthony Davis, "Anthony Davis—A Conversation," appears in *Silent Interviews* 289–311.
67. Delany, "Aversion/Perversion/Diversion," 1995, *Longer Views: Extended Essays,* (Hanover, N.H.: UP of New England/Wesleyan UP, 1996) 126–28.
68. Delany, "Aversion/Perversion/Diversion," 137.
69. Delany, "Aversion/Perversion/Diversion," 141.
70. Delany, "The Rhetoric of Sex/The Discourse of Desire,"1993, *Shorter Views* 16.
71. Samuel R. Delany, *Flight from Nevèrÿon* (1985, Hanover, N.H.: UP of New England/Wesleyan UP, 1994) 160.
72. Samuel R. Delany, *Return to Nevèrÿon* (Hanover, N.H.: UP of New England/Wesleyan UP, 1994) 181.
73. Samuel R. Delany, *Neveryóna,* (1983, Hanover, N.H.: UP of New England/ Wesleyan UP, 1993) 97.
74. Darryl Towles, "Black and Gay: One Man's Story," *Black Men, White Men,* ed. Michael J. Smith (San Francisco: Gay Sunshine Press, 1983) 92.
75. According to Essex Hemphill, such jargon reveals a contradiction between an assumed sophistication regarding race in the gay social scene, and the reality of racial segregation among gays outside of it: "Terms such as 'dinge queen,' for white men who prefer black men, and 'snow queen,' for black men who prefer white men, were created by a gay community that obviously could not be trusted to believe its own rhetoric concerning brotherhood, fellowship, and dignity." (Essex Hemphill, Introduction to *Brother to Brother* xix.) Delany, however, includes these terms among the "ordinary day-to-day homosexual argot" that "however mildly pejorative . . . represented an active perversion." Samuel R. Delany, "Coming/Out," 1996 in *Shorter Views* 82.
76. Delany, "Sword and Sorcery, S/M, and the Economics of Inadequation: The *Camera Obscura* Interview," 1989, *Silent Interviews* 135, 136.
77. Delany, "Sword and Sorcery" 137.

78. Delany, "Sword and Sorcery" 138.
79. Samuel R. Delany, "Of Sex, Objects, Signs, Systems, Sales, SF," *The Straits of Messina* (Seattle: Serconia, 1989) 39.
80. Delany, *Flight* 64.
81. Harper, *Private Affairs* 142. One of Harper's essays in this volume, entitled "'Take Me Home.': Location, Identity, Transnational Exchange," features an extended reflection on the meaning of interracial gay male "trade," particularly as represented in *The Mad Man*.
82. Samuel R. Delany, *1984: Selected Letters* (Rutherford, N.J.: Voyant, 2000) 179.
83. The name of the novel's narrator-protagonist approximates that of Johnny Marr, guitarist for the 1980s British rock band, The Smiths. Among their hits was "Ask," which featured these lyrics, penned by lead singer Morrissey: "So if there's something you'd like to try/If there's something you'd like to try/Ask me, I won't say 'no,' how could I?" One interpretation of the lyrics is that they approximate the attitudes of John Marr and Timothy Hasler to their sexual partners. (The Smiths, "Ask," *Louder Than Bombs*, WEA/Warner Brothers, 1987.)
84. Delany, *Neveryóna* 180.
85. Dany Laferrière, *How to Make Love to a Negro* (Toronto: Coach House Press, 1987) 76.
86. Regarding the "truth" of the "content" of his fictions, Delany identifies many standard literary tropes as "lies about the world": "Not *every* woman who had an abortion died. (This is before abortions were legal.) Not *every* time two men had sex together did one of them have to go off and within three weeks smash his car drunkenly and fatally into a tree. Not *every* time two people fell in love from different social strata did the person from the lower—if he was a man—find himself driven to strangle the woman from the upper, through nothing more that the torments of social inadequacy and his subsequently compromised masculinity." "The Naropa Interview" (Boulder, 2001: unpublished).
87. Quoted in Samuel R. Delany, "Sword and Sorcery, S/M, and the Economics of Inadequation," *Silent Interviews* 139.
88. Harper, *Private Affairs* 143.
89. Thom Beame, "Interview: BWMT Founder—Mike Smith," *Black Men, White Men* 187–95.
90. Robert F. Reid-Pharr, "Dinge," *Women and Performance: A Journal of Feminist Theory*, 1996, 8: 2 (16): 76.
91. Harper, *Private Affairs* 140–41.
92. Quoted in Treichler 86.
93. *Black Is, Black Ain't*, dir. Marlon Riggs, ITVS, 1995. The "family" metaphor is Riggs's, however I employ it with the knowledge that, as Michael Warner explains, such expressions "can either be a language of exile for queers or a resource of irony." Michael Warner, Introduction to *Fear of a Queer Planet*, ed. Michael Warner (Minneapolis: U of Minnesota P, 1993) xviii.
94. Harper, *Are We Not Men?* xi–xii.

95. Reed Woodhouse, *Unlimited Embrace: A Canon of Gay Fiction, 1945–1995* (Amherst: U of Massachusetts P, 1998) 221.

96. Cohen 3. Some such claims may not be without merit. According to Keith Boykin, "the largest recipient of government AIDS-related funds" in Washington D.C.—where "most AIDS cases occur in the African American population"—went to the Whitman-Walker Clinic, a white-run health service provider for homosexuals, until the 1993 intervention of United Response to Black America's Needs (URBAN) began challenging for city resources. Keith Boykin, *One More River to Cross: Black and Gay in America* (New York: Anchor Books, 1996) 222–23.

97. Leo Bersani, "Is the Rectum a Grave?" *AIDS: Cultural Analysis, Cultural Activism* 204. Jose Muñoz criticizes "the race and gender troubles" of, in *Homos*, Bersani's description of "coalitions between gay men and people of color or women as 'bad faith'" in "Ghosts of Public Sex: Utopian Longings, Queer Memories," *Policing Public Sex*, ed. Dangerous Bedfellows (Boston: South End Press, 1996) 357.

98. Cindy Patton, "Resistance and the Erotic: Reclaiming History, Setting Strategy as We Face AIDS," *Radical America* 20.6: 68. Quoted in Crimp, "How to Have Promiscuity in an Epidemic," 252. And Patton, *Fatal Advice* 83.

99. Mercer explains that "the documentary film *Before Stonewall* shows how the American gay community learned new tactics of protest through their participation in the Civil Rights struggles for equality, dignity and autonomy led by figures like Martin Luther King Jr. As Audre Lorde points out in the film, the black struggle became the prototype for all the new social movements of the time–from women's and gay liberation, to the peace, antiwar and ecology movements as well" (132).

100. Hall 285.

101. Treichler 12–13, 38. No. 9 is an allusion to Michael Crichton's 1969 novel *The Andromeda Strain,* about a satellite that crashes to earth with a deadly micro-organism.

102. In his 1996 interview with Thomas L. Long, Delany states that by 1986— when metaphors such as "plague" and "victim" were being criticized in the gay press—neither he "nor . . . anyone else with a shred of social responsibility" (137) would have used "plague" in this context. Delany came up with his story's title in 1980 (137); the composition of *The Tale of Plagues and Carnivals* was completed in 1984, and the story was first published in 1985.

103. Delany, *Flight* 187.

104. Delany, "The Thomas L. Long Interview" 125.

105. Crimp, "AIDS: Cultural Analysis, Cultural Activism" 12.

106. Dwight Garner, "Pulp Friction," *Salon.com* 29 July 1996, 25 August 2000, <http://www.salon.com/weekly/kasak960729.html>.

107. Joe McKenna, "The Best Gay Smut of the Last 1000 Years," *Inches* 14.5 (Jan. 2000): 28.

108. Michael Warner, *The Trouble with Normal: Sex, Politics, and the Ethics of Queer Life* (Cambridge: Harvard UP, 1999) 16.

109. Delany, "Aversion/Perversion/Diversion" 139.

110. Samuel R. Delany, "The Phil Leggiere Interview," *Shorter Views* 312.

111. Delany, *Flight* 363.

112. Crimp, "AIDS: Cultural Analysis, Cultural Activism" 13.

113. Bersani 197.

114. Warner 2, 3.

115. Samuel R. Delany, "Aye, and Gomorrah . . ." 1967, *Aye, and Gomorrah* (New York: Vintage, 2003) 97.

116. Warner 5.

117. Delany, *The Motion of Light in Water* (1988, New York: Richard Kasak, 1993) 269–70.

118. Samuel R. Delany, *Times Square Red, Times Square Blue* (New York: NYU Press, 1999) 83.

119. Julia Kristeva, *Powers of Horror* (1980, New York: Columbia UP, 1982) 69.

120. Samuel R. Delany, "Toto, We're Back! The *Cottonwood Review* Interview," *Silent Interviews* 71.

121. Mary Douglas, *Purity and Danger* (London: Routledge and Kegan Paul, 1966) 121. Quoted in Kristeva 69.

122. Woodhouse 214. "Leaky" also suggests "leakage," a term used in AIDS discourse to describe "the insidious movement of the disease or infection outside its 'natural' limits." Jan Zita Grover notes that the terms "*spread* and *leakage* share common sexual and polluting connotations, which are carried over into media descriptions of gay male sexual practices and social haunts" (28).

123. Kristeva 69; Douglas quoted in Kristeva 69.

124. Delany, *Times Square Red, Times Square Blue* 126, 139. Delany states that such relations are "dangerous [to the status quo, in that] they represent lines of communication, fields of interest, and exchanges of power" ("Sword and Sorcery" 137).

125. William Haver, "Of Mad Men Who Practice Invention to the Brink of Intelligibility," *Queer Theory in Education,* ed. William F. Pinar (Mahwah, N.J.: Lawrence Erlbaum Associates, 1998) 350.

126. Woodhouse 218.

127. Haver 352.

128. Delany discusses this distinction in "The Thomas L. Long Interview" 132–33.

129. Delany, *Motion* 369.

130. Warner 217.

131. Steven Seidman, "Identity and Politics in a 'Postmodern' Gay Culture: Some Historical and Conceptual Notes," *Fear of a Queer Planet,* ed. Michael Warner (Minneapolis: U of Minnesota P, 1993) 124.

132. Delany, *Return* 65.

133. Delany, *Times Square Red, Times Square Blue* 56.

134. According to Gay Men's Health Crisis, only certain bodily fluids transmit HIV, and only in certain ways: "HIV can be transmitted through certain body fluids: blood, semen, vaginal secretions and breast milk. There is no evidence that the virus is transmitted through saliva, tears or sweat. HIV enters the body through mucous membranes (the lining of the rectum, the walls of the vagina, or the inside of the mouth and throat) or through direct

contact with the bloodstream. The virus cannot enter through the skin, unless the skin is broken or cut and another person's infected body fluids enter the bloodstream. The virus cannot be transmitted through the air by sneezing or coughing. This is why there is absolutely no danger in casual contact with people with HIV." GMHC, "HIV and AIDS—The Basics," 5 Jul. 2000, <http://www.gmhc.org/basics/hiv/trans.html>.

135. Kristeva 4, 3.
136. Delany, *Flight* 332.
137. Woodhouse 212–13.
138. Woodhouse 213.
139. "Diamonda" is a variation of the first name of avant-garde vocalist/performance artist Diamanda Galás, whose recordings and performances, in various ways, address AIDS, which took the life of her brother, playwright and poet Philip Dimitri Galás. From <http://www.diamandagalas.com/biography.htm>, 15 Dec. 2000.
140. Delany, *Flight* 189.
141. Ben Williams, interview with Samuel R. Delany, Citysearch.com., Aug. 1999, <http://newyork.citysearch.com/E/F/NYCNY/0010/04/49/#interview>.
142. Haver 360–61.
143. Haver 359. Haver's essay provides a more thorough reading of Mad Man Mike's game and its significance to the novel.
144. Haver identifies "*ekpyrosis*" as a Heraclitean term marking "a certain ultimate extremity . . . the all-consuming fire of an absolutely undifferentiated pure difference (at the very limit of thought . . .)" (353).
145. Ellis Hanson, "Undead," *Inside/Out: Lesbian Theories, Gay Theories,* ed. Diana Fuss (New York: Routledge, 1991) 324.
146. Woodhouse 218.
147. Kitchens of Distinction, "Prize," *Love Is Hell,* One Little Indian/A & M Records, 1989.
148. Crimp, "AIDS: Cultural Analysis, Cultural Activism" 15.
149. Delany, *Flight* 364–65.
150. Delany, *Flight* 363.
151. Delany, "Street Talk/Straight Talk," *Shorter Views* 41.
152. Delany, "The Rhetoric of Sex/The Discourse of Desire" 5, 33. See also "Closures and Openings," Delany's Appendix to *Return to Nevèrÿon* (275–76).
153. Delany, "Street Talk/Straight Talk" 41.
154. Delany, *Flight* 361.
155. Delany, *1984* (317). Of the mystical experience at the Variety Photoplays, Delany says that "it rates with that incident I told you [Bravard] about that occurred when I was sixteen or seventeen, that morning in Central Park, when sitting on the bench in that somewhat overcast dawn, I had that revelation of my multiply marginal/ambiguous status as to race, sex, and social position: a black man, a gay man, a writer" (317), a significant life event described in *The Motion of Light in Water.*
156. Woodhouse 221.
157. The National Coalition for the Homeless has identified a connection between AIDS and homelessness. Affordable housing can be an issue for people

who have lost work due to AIDS/HIV–related illness or discrimination. Estimates of HIV among the nation's homeless have ranged from 3 percent to 20 percent. And many homeless people, particularly young people, exchange sex for food, clothes, or shelter. National Coalition for the Homeless, "NCH Fact Sheet #9: HIV/AIDS and Homelessness," April 1999, 27 Oct. 2000, <http://nch.ari.net/hivaids.html>.

158. Treichler 172.
159. Crimp, "AIDS: Cultural Analysis, Cultural Activism" 6.
160. Delany, "The Rhetoric of Sex/The Discourse of Desire" 20, 35.
161. Delany, "Street Talk/Straight Talk" 56.
162. Delany, *Flight* 215. See also Delany, *1984* (14).
163. Delany, *Flight* 341.
164. Delany, "The Rhetoric of Sex/The Discourse of Desire" 36.
165. Delany, "The Rhetoric of Sex/The Discourse of Desire" 37.
166. Delany, "Street Talk/Straight Talk" 56.
167. Delany, "The Rhetoric of Sex/The Discourse of Desire" 38, 26.
168. Delany, "Street Talk/Straight Talk" 53.
169. Delany, "Street Talk/Straight Talk" 53–54.
170. Delany, "The Rhetoric of Sex/The Discourse of Desire" 35.
171. Delany, "Street Talk/Straight Talk" 41, 42, 43–44.
172. Delany, "Street Talk/Straight Talk" 53–54.
173. Delany, *Flight* 303.
174. Delany, "Street Talk/Straight Talk" 54.
175. Delany, "Street Talk/Straight Talk" 48.
176. Delany, "Street Talk/Straight Talk" 50.
177. Delany, "Street Talk/Straight Talk" 53. Strictly speaking, one does not "transmit" AIDS, which is a syndrome, "a set of symptoms which occur together; the sum of signs of any morbid state; a symptom complex" (Grover 18–19). One transmits or is infected by a virus, HIV.
178. Delany, "Street Talk/Straight Talk" 56.
179. Delany, "Sword and Sorcery" 161. Brian Lampkin, "The Motion of Going Down: Samuel Delany on HIV and AIDS," *Voices* May 1998: 5. Delany, *Flight* 366.
180. Delany, "Street Talk/Straight Talk" 56.
181. Treichler 174.
182. Such criticisms are described in Lampkin 5.
183. See, for example, *Flight* 364–65.
184. CDC Divisions of HIV/AIDS Prevention, "Primary HIV Infection Associated with Oral Transmission," Feb. 2001, 9 Dec. 2001, <http://www.cdc.gov/hiv/pubs/facts/oralsexqa.htm>. In response to the question, "How do you know if the study participants were telling the truth about their sexual history?" The fact sheet states, "Oral transmission of HIV is very difficult to single out as the only way that HIV is transmitted because few people engage exclusively in oral sex. A number of specific questions were asked by a trained evaluator. The participants' risk behaviors were assessed by using clinical interviews, counselor intervention, epidemiologic interview, partner interview when possible, and final disposition of transmission risk. Of the

8 cases, 4 reported protected anal intercourse, without the condom break-ing, with persons who were either HIV infected or had an unknown serosta-tus. Men in this study who reported that they were uncertain if the condom was used properly were eliminated from this study." Though not a "moni-tored study," it took some measures to insure the accuracy of the partici-pants' reports regarding the mode of their sexual activity.

185. Kimberly Page-Shafer, et al. "Risk of HIV infection attributable to oral sex among men who have sex with men and in the population of men who have sex with men," *AIDS: Official Journal of the International AIDS Society* 16 (17), 22 Nov. 2002: 2350–52.

186. Centers for Disease Control and Prevention Divisions of HIV/AIDS Pre-vention, HIV/AIDS Update, "Preventing the Sexual Transmission of HIV, the Virus that Causes AIDS: What You Should Know about Oral Sex," De-cember 2000, 26 May, 2003, <ftp://ftp.cdcnpin.org/Updates/oralsex.pdf>.

187. Lawrence A. Kingsley, et al., "Risk Factors for Seroconversion to Human Immunodeficiency Virus Among Male Homosexuals," *The Lancet* 14 Feb. 1987. Appendix to Delany, *The Mad Man* 495–96.

188. University of California at San Francisco HIV InSite, "Oral Sex: Using Your Head," 1 Oct. 1997, 8 Oct. 2000, <http://hivinsite.ucsf.edu/prevention/safer_sex_info/2098.32ac.html>.

189. Page-Shafer, et al.

190. Gay Men's Health Crisis, "Beyond Condoms: Let's Talk about It," 17 Oct. 2000 (http://www.gmhc.org/basics/men/beyond.html).

191. Gay Men's Health Crisis, "Beyond Condoms."

192. Gay Men's Health Crisis, "Frequently Asked Questions—and Some An-swers—about Gay Sex," 17 Oct. 2000, <http://www.gmhc.org/basics/men/gayfaq.html>.

193. Warner 217.

194. Warner 217.

BIBLIOGRAPHY

Adam, Helen. *San Francisco's Burning.* 1961. Brooklyn: Hanging Loose Press, 1985.

"Afrofuturist Literature." *Afrofuturism.* 2 Jun. 2001. <http://www.afrofuturism .net/text/lit.html>.

Albertini, Bill, Ben Lee, et al. "Introduction: The End of Identity Politics?" *New Literary History* 31.4 (Autumn 2000): 621–26.

"An American Tragedy—Detroit." *Urban Racial Violence in the Twentieth Century.* Ed. Joseph Boskin. Beverly Hills, Calif.: Glenroe Press, 1976. 132–42.

Anderson, Laurie. "Language Is a Virus." *Home of the Brave.* Warner Brothers, 1986.

———. "Sharkey's Night." *Mister Heartbreak.* Warner Brothers. 1984.

Anderson, Robert N. *National Vital Statistics Reports* 49.11 (12 Oct. 2001). Hyattsville, Md.: National Center for Health Statistics, 31, 33. 12 May 2003. <http://www.cdc.gov/nchs/data/nvsr/nvsr49/nvsr49_11.pdf>.

Andrews, William L. Introduction. *African American Autobiography: A Collection of Critical Essays.* Ed. William L. Andrews. Englewood Cliffs: Prentice Hall, 1993.

———. *To Tell a Free Story.* Urbana: U of Illinois P, 1986.

Appiah, Anthony. "The Uncompleted Argument: Du Bois and the Illusion of Race." *"Race," Writing, and Difference.* Ed. Henry Louis Gates Jr. U of Chicago P, 1986. 21–37.

Appiah, K. Anthony and Amy Gutmann. *Color Conscious: The Political Morality of Race.* Princeton UP, 1996.

Aptheker, Herbert. *Abolitionism: A Revolutionary Movement.* Boston: Twayne Publishers, 1989.

———. *American Negro Slave Revolts.* 1943. New York: International Publishers, 1969.

Artaud, Antonin. *The Theater and Its Double.* Trans. Mary Caroline Richards. 1938. New York: Grove, 1958.

Asimov, Isaac. *I, Robot.* 1950. Greenwich, Conn.: Fawcett Crest, 1970.

Atlantis and Other New York Tales: Samuel R. Delany Reads at the Judson Church. Dir. Eric Solstein. DMZ/Voyant, 2001.

Attridge, Derek, ed. *Acts of Literature.* By Jacques Derrida. New York: Routledge, 1992.

Auden, W. H. "In Memory of Sigmund Freud." *Collected Poems: W. H. Auden.* New York: Vintage, 1991. 273–76.

"Author Q & A: Samuel R. Delany on *Dhalgren.*" Mar. 2001. 13 Jun. 2001. <http:// www.randomhouse.com/vintage/catalog/display.pperl?isbn=0375706682& view=qa>.

Baker, Houston A. *Blues, Ideology, and Afro-American Literature.* Chicago: U of Chicago P, 1984.

Bakhtin, Mikhail. *Rabelais and His World.* Trans. Helene Iswolsky. 1968. Bloomington: Indiana UP, 1984.

Baraka, Amiri. "Black Art." *The Norton Anthology of African American Literature.* Ed. Henry Louis Gates Jr. et al. New York: Norton, 1997. 1883–84.

Barbour, Douglas. *Worlds Out of Words: The SF Novels of Samuel R. Delany.* Frome, England: Bran's Head Books, 1979.

Barthes, Roland. *Mythologies.* Trans. Jonathan Cape, Ltd. 1957. New York: Noonday, 1993.

Bartlett, Karen J. "Subversive Desire: Sex and Ethics in Delany's *Dhalgren.*" *New York Review of Science Fiction* 76 (1994): 1, 3–7.

Baskin, Wade. Introduction. *Course in General Linguistics.* By Ferdinand de Saussure. 1959. Ed. Charles Bally, et al. New York: McGraw-Hill, 1966.

Beam, Joseph. "Samuel R. Delany: The Possibility of Possibilities." *In the Life: A Black Gay Anthology.* Ed. Joseph Beam. Boston: Alyson Publications, 1986. 185–208.

Beame, Thom. "Interview: BWMT Founder, Mike Smith." *Black Men, White Men.* Ed. Michael J. Smith. San Francisco: Gay Sunshine Press, 1983. 187–95.

Bersani, Leo. "Is the Rectum a Grave?" *AIDS: Cultural Analysis, Cultural Activism.* Ed. Douglas Crimp. Cambridge, Mass.: MIT Press, 1988. 197–222.

"Beyond Condoms: Let's Talk about It." *Gay Men, Sex, and HIV.* Gay Men's Health Crisis (GMHC). 17 Oct. 2000. <http://www.gmhc.org/basics/men/beyond.html>.

Black Is, Black Ain't. Dir. Marlon Riggs, ITVS, 1995.

Bontemps, Arna. Introduction. *Black Thunder.* By Arna Bontemps. 1968. Boston: Beacon Press, 1992.

Bowie, Malcolm. *Freud, Proust, Lacan: Theory as Fiction.* Cambridge: Cambridge UP, 1987.

Boykin, Keith. *One More River to Cross: Black and Gay in America.* New York: Anchor Books, 1996.

Bray, Mary Kay. "Rites of Reversal: Double Consciousness in Delany's *Dhalgren.*" *Black American Literary Forum* 18.2 (1984): 57–61.

Brooks, Gwendolyn. "The Third Sermon on the Warpland." *Riot.* Detroit: Broadside Press, 1969.

Butler, Judith. *Bodies That Matter.* New York: Routledge, 1993.

———. "Endangered/Endangering: Schematic Racism and White Paranoia." *Reading Rodney King, Reading Urban Uprising.* Ed. Robert Gooding-Williams. New York: Routledge, 1993. 15–22.

———. *Gender Trouble.* New York: Routledge, 1990.

Butler, Octavia E. *Dawn.* New York: Warner Books, 1987.

Butterfield, Stephen. *Black Autobiography in America.* Amherst: U of Massachusetts P, 1974.

Carby, Hazel V. "Ideologies of Black Folk: The Historical Novel of Slavery." *Slavery and the Literary Imagination.* Ed. Deborah E. McDowell and Arnold Rampersad. Baltimore: Johns Hopkins UP, 1989. 125–43.

Centers for Disease Control and Prevention Divisions of HIV/AIDS Prevention. "Basic Statistics." March 31, 2003, 7 May 2003. <http://www.cdc.gov/hiv/stats.htm#cumaids>.

Centers for Disease Control and Prevention Divisions of HIV/AIDS Prevention. "HIV Causes AIDS." 23 March 2003, 8 May 2003. <http://www.cdc.gov/hiv/hivinfo/overview/htm.>

Centers for Disease Control and Prevention Divisions of HIV/AIDS Prevention. *HIV/AIDS Surveillance Report* 13.2 Sept. 24, 2002. Tables 1, 7, 9, 11, 20. 9 May 2003. <http://www.cdc.gov/hiv/stats/hasr1302.htm> and <http://www.cdc.gov/hiv/stats/hasr1302.pdf>.

Centers for Disease Control and Prevention Divisions of HIV/AIDS Prevention. HIV/AIDS Update. "Preventing the Sexual Transmission of HIV, the Virus that Causes AIDS: What You Should Know about Oral Sex." December 2000. 26 May 2003. <ftp://ftp.cdcnpin.org/Updates/oralsex.pdf>.

Centers for Disease Control and Prevention Divisions of HIV/AIDS Prevention. "Primary HIV Infection Associated with Oral Transmission." Feb. 2001, 9 Dec. 2001. <http://www.cdc.gov/hiv/pubs/facts/oralsexqa.htm>.

Chambers, Ross. *Facing It: AIDS Diaries and the Death of the Author.* Ann Arbor: U of Michigan P, 1998.

Chan, Edward K. "(Vulgar) Identity Politics in Outer Space: Delany's *Triton* and the Heterotopian Narrative." *Journal of Narrative Theory* 31.2 (Summer 2001): 180–213.

Clute, John and Peter Nicholls, eds. *The Encyclopedia of Science Fiction.* New York: St. Martin's Press, 1993.

Cohen, Cathy J. *The Boundaries of Blackness: AIDS and the Breakdown of Black Politics.* Chicago: U of Chicago P, 1999.

Cornelius, Janet Duitsman. *"When I Can Read My Title Clear": Literacy, Slavery, and Religion in the Antebellum South.* Columbia: U of South Carolina P, 1991.

Crenshaw, Kimberlé and Gary Peller. "Reel Time/Real Justice." *Reading Rodney King, Reading Urban Uprising.* Ed. Robert Gooding-Williams. New York: Routledge, 1993. 56–70.

Crimp, Douglas. "AIDS: Cultural Analysis, Cultural Activism." *AIDS: Cultural Analysis, Cultural Activism.* Ed. Douglas Crimp. Cambridge, Mass.: MIT Press, 1987. 3–16.

———. "How to Have Promiscuity in an Epidemic." *AIDS: Cultural Analysis, Cultural Activism.* Ed. Douglas Crimp. Cambridge, Mass.: MIT Press, 1987. 237–71.

———. "Right On, Girlfriend!" *Fear of a Queer Planet.* Ed. Michael Warner. Minneapolis: U of Minnesota P, 1993. 300–20.

Crossley, Robert. Introduction. *Kindred.* By Octavia Butler. Boston: Beacon Press, 1988.

Culler, Jonathan. *Ferdinand de Saussure.* Second ed. Ithaca: Cornell UP, 1986.

———. *The Pursuit of Signs: Semiotics, Literature, Deconstruction.* Ithaca: Cornell UP, 1981.

Davis, Angela Y. *Women, Race and Class.* 1981. New York: Vintage, 1983.

Davis, Mike. "Uprising and Repression in L.A.: An Interview with Mike Davis by the *Covert Action* Information Bulletin." *Reading Rodney King/Reading Urban Uprising*. Ed. Robert Gooding-Williams. New York: Routledge, 1993. 142–54.

Davis, Ray. "Delany's Dirt." 1995. *Ash of Stars: On the Writing of Samuel R. Delany*. Ed. James Sallis. Jackson: UP of Mississippi, 1996. 162–88.

Davis, Thulani. "The Future May Be Bleak, But It's Not Black." *The Village Voice* 1 Feb. 1983: 17–19.

Delany, Samuel R. Afterword. *Stars in My Pocket Like Grains of Sand*. By Samuel R. Delany. New York: Bantam, 1990. 376–85.

———. *"Alyx."* 1976. *The Jewel-Hinged Jaw*. New York: Berkley, 1978. 191–209.

———. "An Interview with Samuel R. Delany." Interview with Charles H. Rozell. *Callaloo* 23.1 (2000). 247–67.

———. "Anthony Davis—A Conversation." *Silent Interviews*. Hanover, N.H.: UP of New England/Wesleyan UP, 1994. 289–311.

———. *Atlantis: Model 1924*. *Atlantis: Three Tales*. Hanover, N.H.: UP of New England/Wesleyan UP, 1995. 1–121.

———. "Atlantis Rose . . . : Some Notes on Hart Crane." *Longer Views: Extended Essays*. Hanover, N.H.: UP of New England/Wesleyan UP, 1996. 174–246.

———. "Author's Note" to *Dhalgren*. Samuel R. Delany Collection (1025), Part II, Box 1: I. Manuscripts, A. Novels, 1. Dhalgren, a. Drafts of front matter-typescript with holograph corrections, 44 pp. (f. 1). Mugar Library, Dept. of Special Collections, Boston University.

———. "Aversion/Perversion/Diversion." 1995. *Longer Views: Extended Essays*. Hanover, N.H.: UP of New England/Wesleyan UP, 1996. 119–143.

———. "Aye, and Gomorrah . . ." 1967. *Aye, and Gomorrah*. New York: Vintage, 2003. 91–101.

———. *Babel-17*. 1966. New York: Vintage, 2001.

———. "Beatitudes," *Crimes of the Beats* (Brooklyn: Autonomedia, 1998) 117–29.

———. "A Bend in the Road." *Shorter Views: Queer Thoughts and the Politics of the Paraliterary*. Hanover, N.H.: UP of New England/Wesleyan UP, 1999. 98–110.

———. "The *Black Leather in Color* Interview." *Shorter Views: Queer Thoughts and the Politics of the Paraliterary*. Hanover, N.H.: UP of New England/Wesleyan UP, 1999. 115–22.

———. *Bread and Wine*. New York: Juno Books, 1999.

———. "Citre et Trans." *Atlantis: Three Tales*. Hanover, N.H.: UP of New England/Wesleyan UP, 1995. 173–212.

———. "Closures and Openings." *Return to Nevèrÿon*. 1987. Hanover, N.H.: UP of New England/Wesleyan UP, 1994. 269–91.

———. "Coming/Out." *Shorter Views: Queer Thoughts and the Politics of the Paraliterary*. Hanover, N.H.: UP of New England/Wesleyan UP, 1999. 67–97.

———. "Critical Methods/Speculative Fiction." 1970, 1971. *The Jewel-Hinged Jaw*. New York: Berkley, 1977. 119–31.

———. *Dhalgren*. 1975. New York: Vintage, 2001.

———. "*Dichtung und* Science Fiction." *Starboard Wine.* Pleasantville, N.Y.: Dragon Press, 1984. 165–96.

———. *The Einstein Intersection.* 1967. Hanover, N.H.: UP of New England/ Wesleyan UP, 1998.

———. *Empire Star.* 1966. New York: Vintage, 2001.

———. *Flight from Nevèrÿon.* 1985. Hanover, N.H.: UP of New England/Wesleyan UP, 1994.

———. Foreword. *Black Gay Man.* By Robert F. Reid-Pharr. New York UP, 2001.

———. "Forward to an Afterword." *The Complete Nebula Award–Winning Fiction.* Toronto: Bantam, 1986. 405–408.

———. "The 'Gay' Writer/'Gay Writing'. . . ?" *Shorter Views: Queer Thoughts and the Politics of the Paraliterary.* Hanover, N.H.: UP of New England/Wesleyan UP, 1999. 111–14.

———. *Heavenly Breakfast: An Essay on the Winter of Love.* 1979. Flint, Mich.: Bamberger Books, 1997.

———. Introduction. *Empire* by Samuel R. Delany and Howard V. Chaykin. New York: Berkley, 1978.

———. "Introduction: Reading and the Written Interview," *Silent Interviews.* Hanover, N.H.: UP of New England/Wesleyan UP, 1994. 1–17.

———. "Introduction to a Reading of Robert Hayden's 'Middle Passage.'" In Honor of *The Norton Anthology of African American Literature.* 92nd St. YM/WHA, New York. 27 Feb. 1997.

———. Introduction. *Shade: An Anthology of Fiction by Gay Men of African Descent.* Ed. Bruce Morrow and Charles H. Rowell. New York: Avon, 1996.

———. "Introductory Remarks to 'Smoke, Lilies, Jade,' by Richard Bruce Nugent." *The James White Review* 16.1 (Winter 1999). Ed. Patrick Merla.

———. Journal #55. England 1973. Samuel R. Delany Collection (1025), Part I, Box 16. Mugar Library, Dept. of Special Collections, Boston University.

———. "The Kenneth James Interview." *Silent Interviews.* Hanover, N.H.: UP of New England/Wesleyan UP, 1994. 233–49.

———. *The Mad Man.* Rev. ed. Rutherford, N.J.: Voyant, 2002.

———. Manuscripts and Published Writings, Typescript [f. 1]. Samuel R. Delany Collection (1025), Part II, Box 46. Bernard Kay Collection of Samuel R. Delany Papers. Mugar Library, Dept. of Special Collections, Boston University.

———. *The Motion of Light in Water.* 1988. New York: Kasak, 1993.

———. "The Naropa Interview." (Boulder, 2001: unpublished)

———. "The Necessity of Tomorrows." 1978. *Starboard Wine: More Notes on the Language of Science Fiction.* Pleasantville: Dragon Press, 1984. 23–35.

———. *Neveryóna.* 1983. Hanover, N.H.: UP of New England/Wesleyan UP, 1993.

———. *1984: Selected Letters.* Rutherford, N.J.: Voyant, 2000.

———. *Nova.* 1968. New York: Vintage, 2002.

———. "Now It's Time for Dale Peck." *Shorter Views: Queer Thoughts and the Politics of the Paraliterary.* Hanover, N.H.: UP of New England/Wesleyan UP, 1999. 384–87.

———. "Of Sex, Objects, Signs, Systems, Sales, SF." *The Straits of Messina.* Seattle: Serconia, 1989. 33–55.

———. "On the Unspeakable." 1987. *Shorter Views: Queer Thoughts and the Politics of the Paraliterary.* Hanover, N.H.: UP of New England/Wesleyan UP, 1999. 58–66.

———. "The *Para • doxa* Interview." 1995. *Shorter Views: Queer Thoughts and the Politics of the Paraliterary.* Hanover, N.H.: UP of New England/Wesleyan UP, 1999. 186–217.

———. "The Phil Leggiere Interview." *Shorter Views: Queer Thoughts and the Politics of the Paraliterary.* Hanover, N.H.: UP of New England/Wesleyan UP, 1999. 311–14.

———. "The Politics of Paraliterary Criticism." 1996. *Shorter Views: Queer Thoughts and the Politics of the Paraliterary.* Hanover, N.H.: UP of New England/Wesleyan UP, 1999. 218–70.

———. Preface. *The Straits of Messina.* By Samuel R. Delany. Seattle: Serconia, 1989.

———. "Racism and Science Fiction." 1999. *Dark Matter.* Ed. Sheree R. Thomas. New York: Warner/Aspect, 2000. 383–97.

———. "Reading at Work." *Longer Views: Extended Essays.* Hanover, N.H.: UP of New England/Wesleyan UP, 1996. 87–118.

———. *Return to Nevèrÿon.* Hanover, N.H.: UP of New England/Wesleyan UP, 1994.

———. "The Rhetoric of Sex/The Discourse of Desire." *Shorter Views: Queer Thoughts and the Politics of the Paraliterary.* Hanover, N.H.: UP of New England/Wesleyan UP, 1999. 3–40.

———. "Science Fiction and Criticism: The *Diacritics* Interview." *Silent Interviews.* Hanover, N.H.: UP of New England/Wesleyan UP, 1994. 186–215.

———. "The Second *Science Fiction Studies* Interview." 1990. *Shorter Views: Queer Thoughts and the Politics of the Paraliterary.* Hanover, N.H.: UP of New England/Wesleyan UP, 1999. 315–49.

———. "The Semiology of Silence: The *Science Fiction Studies* Interview." 1987. *Silent Interviews.* Hanover, N.H.: UP of New England/Wesleyan UP, 1994. 17–58.

———. "Sex, Race, and Science Fiction: The *Callaloo* Interview." 1990. *Silent Interviews.* Hanover, N.H.: UP of New England/Wesleyan UP, 1994. 216–29.

———. "Shadow and Ash." *Longer Views: Extended Essays.* By Samuel R. Delany. Hanover, N.H.: UP of New England/Wesleyan UP, 1996. 144–73.

———. "Shadows." 1977. *Longer Views: Extended Essays.* Hanover, N.H.: UP of New England/Wesleyan UP, 1996. 251–323.

———. "A Silent Interview with Samuel R. Delany." *The Poetry Project Newsletter* 175 (June 1999): 8–11.

———. "Some Queer Notions About Race." *Dangerous Liasons.* Ed. Eric Brandt. New York: The New Press, 1999. 259–89.

———. "Some *Real* Mothers . . . : The *SF Eye* Interview." 1987. *Silent Interviews.* Hanover, N.H.: UP of New England/Wesleyan UP, 1994. 164–85.

———. *Stars In My Pocket Like Grains of Sand.* 1984. New York: Bantam Books, 1990.

———. "Street Talk/Straight Talk." 1991. *Shorter Views: Queer Thoughts and the Politics of the Paraliterary.* Hanover, N.H.: UP of New England/Wesleyan UP, 1999. 41–57.

———. "The Susan Grossman Interview." *Silent Interviews.* Hanover, N.H.: UP of New England/Wesleyan UP, 1994. 250–68.

———. "Sword and Sorcery, S/M, and the Economics of Inadequation: The *Camera Obscura* Interview." *Silent Interviews.* Hanover, N.H.: UP of New England/Wesleyan UP, 1994. 127–63.

———. *Tales of Nevèrÿon.* 1979. Hanover, N.H.: UP of New England/Wesleyan UP, 1993.

———. "The Thomas L. Long Interview." *Shorter Views: Queer Thoughts and the Politics of the Paraliterary.* Hanover, N.H.: UP of New England/Wesleyan UP, 1999. 123–38.

———. *Times Square Red, Times Square Blue.* New York: New York UP, 1999.

———. "Toto, We're Back! The *Cottonwood Review* Interview." 1986. *Silent Interviews.* Hanover, N.H.: UP of New England/Wesleyan UP, 1994. 59–82.

———. *Trouble on Triton.* 1976. Hanover, N.H.: UP of New England/Wesleyan UP, 1996.

———. "Wagner/Artaud." 1988. *Longer Views: Extended Essays.* Hanover, N.H.: UP of New England/Wesleyan UP, 1996. 1–86.

Delany, Sarah L., A. Elizabeth Delany, and Amy Hill Hearth. *Having Our Say.* New York: Dell, 1993.

Derrida, Jacques. "Différance." 1972. *Margins of Philosophy.* Trans. Alan Bass. U of Chicago P, 1982. 1–27.

———. "The Law of Genre." *Acts of Literature.* Ed. Derek Attridge. New York: Routledge, 1992. 221–52.

———. "Limited Inc a b c . . ." 1977. *Limited Inc.* Evanston: Northwestern UP, 1988. 29–110.

———. *Of Grammatology.* 1967. Trans. Gayatri Chakravorty Spivak. Baltimore: Johns Hopkins UP, 1974.

———. "Signature Event Context." 1977. *Limited Inc.* Evanston: Northwestern UP, 1988. 1–23.

Dery, Mark. "Black to the Future: Interviews with Samuel R. Delany, Greg Tate, and Tricia Rose." *Flame Wars: The Discourse of Cyberculture.* Ed. Mark Dery. Durham: Duke UP, 1994. 179–222.

Diamanda Galás Biography. Diamanda Galás.com. 15 Dec, 2000. <http://www.diamandagalas. com/biography.htm>.

Disch, Thomas. "This Is Not a Review." Review of *The Motion of Light in Water,* by Samuel R. Delany. *American Book Review* March 1988: 1.

Dornemann, Rudi and Eric Lorberer. "A Silent Interview with Samuel R. Delany." *Rain Taxi Review of Books* 7 Mar. 2001 (Winter 2000/2001). <http://www.raintaxi.com/delany.html>.

Douglas, Mary. *Purity and Danger.* London: Routledge and Kegan Paul, 1966.

Douglass, Frederick. *Narrative of the Life of Frederick Douglass, an American Slave.* 1845. *The Classic Slave Narratives.* Ed. Henry Louis Gates Jr. New York: Mentor, 1987. 243–331.

Duberman, Martin. *Stonewall*. New York: Dutton, 1993.

DuBois, W. E. B. *Dusk of Dawn*. 1940. *Writings*. Ed. Nathan I. Huggins. New York: The Library of America, 1986. 549–802.

———. *The Souls of Black Folk*. 1903. *Writings*. Ed. Nathan I. Huggins. New York: The Library of America, 1986. 357–547.

Duggan, Lisa. "Dreaming Democracy." *New Literary History* 31.4 (Autumn 2000): 851–56.

Dumm, Thomas L. "The New Enclosures: Racism in the Normalized Community." *Reading Rodney King, Reading Urban Uprising*. Ed. Robert Gooding-Williams. New York: Routledge, 1993. 178–95.

Dyson, Michael Eric. "Michael Jackson's Postmodern Spirituality." *Reflecting Black: African American Cultural Criticism*. Minneapolis: U of Minnesota P, 1993. 35–60.

Eagleton, Terry. "Brecht and Rhetoric." 1982. *Against the Grain*. London: Verso, 1986. 167–72.

———. *Literary Theory: An Introduction*. Minneapolis: U of Minnesota P, 1983.

Ellison, Harlan. "Breakdown of a Breakthrough Novel." Review of *Dhalgren* by Samuel R. Delany. *Los Angeles Times* 23 Feb. 1975: 64.

Ellison, Ralph. *Invisible Man*. 1952. New York: Vintage, 1989.

Elovich, Richard. "Beyond Condoms . . . : How to Create a Gay Men's Culture of Sexual Health." *POZ* June 1999, 8 Oct. 2000. <http://www.thebody.com/poz/features/6_99/beyond.html>.

Epstein, Steven. *Impure Science*. Berkeley: U of California P, 1996.

Equiano, Olaudah. *The Interesting Narrative of the Life of Olaudah Equiano, or Gustavus Vassa, the African, Written by Himself*. 1789. *The Classic Slave Narratives*. Ed. Henry Louis Gates Jr. New York: Mentor, 1987. 1–182.

Eshun, Kodwo. "Black Britain's Planetary Humanists: 4Hero and Nitin Sawhney are charting the future of black British music." *The Fader* 11 (Spring 2002).

Fanon, Frantz. *Black Skin, White Masks*. 1952. New York: Grove Press, 1967.

Farred, Grant. "Endgame Identity? Mapping the New Left Roots of Identity Politics." *New Literary History* 31 (Autumn 2000): 627–48.

Foster, Hal. Introduction. *The Anti-Aesthetic: Essays on Postmodern Culture*. Port Townsend, Wa.: Bay Press, 1983. ix–xvi.

Foucault, Michel. "About the Beginning of the Hermeneutics of the Self." *Religion and Culture*. Ed. J. Carrette. New York: Routledge, 1999.

———. *Madness and Civilization*. 1965. New York: Vintage, 1988.

———. *This Is Not a Pipe*. 1973. Ed. And Trans. James Harkness. Berkeley: U of California P, 1983.

Fox, Robert Elliot. *Conscientious Sorcerers: The Black Postmodernist Fiction of LeRoi Jones/Amiri Baraka, Ishmael Reed, and Samuel R. Delany*. New York: Greenwood Press, 1987.

———. "'This You-Shaped Hole of Insight and Fire': Meditations on Delany's *Dhalgren*." *Ash of Stars: On the Writing of Samuel R. Delany*. Ed. James Sallis. Jackson: UP of Mississippi, 1996.

Freedman, Carl. *Critical Theory and Science Fiction*. Hanover, N.H.: UP of New England/Wesleyan UP, 2000.

"Frequently Asked Questions—and Some Answers—about Gay Sex." *Gay Men, Sex, and HIV.* Gay Men's Health Crisis (GMHC). 17 Oct. 2000. <http://www.gmhc.org/basics/men/ gayfaq.html>.

Freud, Sigmund. *Civilization and Its Discontents.* 1961. New York: Norton, 1989.

Fuss, Diana. *Essentially Speaking: Feminism, Nature and Difference.* New York: Routledge, 1989.

———. "Oral Incorporations: *The Silence of the Lambs.*" *Identification Papers.* New York: Routledge, 1995. 83–105.

Gaggi, Silvio. *Modern/Postmodern.* Philadelphia: U of Pennsylvania P, 1989.

Gaiman, Neil. Illustrations by John Bolton. "Book One: 'The Invisible Labyrinth.'" *The Books of Magic.* New York: DC Comics, 1990.

Galliher, John F. and James L. McCartney. *Criminology: Power, Crime, and Criminal Law.* Lexington: Ginn, 1977.

Gallop, Jane. *The Daughter's Seduction: Feminism and Psychoanalysis.* Ithaca: Cornell UP, 1982.

Garber, Eric. "T'ain't Nobody's Bizness: Homosexuality in 1920s Harlem." *Black Men, White Men.* Ed. Michael J. Smith. San Francisco: Gay Sunshine Press, 1983. <http://www.gaysunshine.com/exc_black-white.html>.

Garner, Dwight. "Pulp Friction." *Salon.com* 29 July 1996. 25 August 2000. <http://www.salon.com/weekly/kasak960729.html>.

Gates, Henry Louis Jr. Introduction. *The Classic Slave Narratives.* Ed. Henry Louis Gates Jr. New York: Mentor, 1987.

———. Introduction. *The Slave's Narrative.* Ed. Henry Louis Gates Jr. Oxford: Oxford UP, 1985.

———. "Two Nations . . . Both Black." 1992. *Reading Rodney King, Reading Urban Uprising.* Ed. Robert Gooding-Williams. New York: Routledge, 1993. 249–54.

Gawron, Jean Mark. Introduction. *Dhalgren.* By Samuel R. Delany. 1975. Boston: Gregg, 1977.

Gibson, William. "Burning Chrome." 1982. *Burning Chrome.* New York: Ace, 1987.

———. "The Recombinant City." Foreword. 1996. *Dhalgren.* By Samuel R. Delany. New York: Vintage, 2001.

Gilmore, Ruth Wilson. "Terror Austerity Race Gender Excess Theatre." *Reading Rodney King, Reading Urban Uprising.* Ed. Robert Gooding-Williams. New York: Routledge, 1993. 23–37.

Gilroy, Paul. *Against Race.* Cambridge: Harvard UP, 2000.

Gooding-Williams, Robert. "Introduction: On Being Stuck." *Reading Rodney King, Reading Urban Uprising.* Ed. Robert Gooding-Williams. New York: Routledge, 1993.

Gordon, Avery and Christopher Newfeld. "White Philosophy." 1994. *Identities.* Ed. Kwame Anthony Appiah and Henry Louis Gates Jr. U of Chicago P, 1995. 380–400.

Govan, Sandra Y. "The Insistent Presence of Black Folk in the Novels of Samuel R. Delany." *Black American Literature Forum* 18.2 (1984): 43–48.

Gray, Margaret E. *Postmodern Proust*. Philadelphia: U of Pennsylvania P, 1992.

Griffin, Farah Jasmine. *"Who Set You Flowin?"*: *The African American Migration Narrative*. New York: Oxford UP, 1995.

Grover, Jan Zita. "AIDS: Keywords." *AIDS: Cultural Analysis, Cultural Activism*. Ed. Douglas Crimp. Cambridge, Mass.: MIT Press, 1987. 17–30.

Guereschi, E. Review of *The Motion of Light in Water* by Samuel R. Delany. *Choice* 26 (1989): 938.

Hall, Stuart. "Cultural Studies and Its Theoretical Legacies." *Cultural Studies*. Ed. Lawrence Grossberg, Cary Nelson, and Paula Treichler. New York: Routledge, 1992. 277–94.

———. "Ethnicity: Identity and Difference." *Radical America* 23.4 (1989): 9–20.

———. "New Ethnicities." 1989. *Stuart Hall: Critical Dialogues in Cultural Studies*. Ed. David Morley and Kuan-Hsing Chen. New York: Routledge, 1996. 441–49.

———. "On Postmodernism and Articulation: An Interview with Stuart Hall." Ed. Lawrence Grossberg. 1986, *Stuart Hall: Critical Dialogues in Cultural Studies*. Ed. David Morley and Kuan-Hsing Chen. New York: Routledge, 1996.

Hand, Elizabeth. "Some Impertinent Remarks toward the Modular Calculus, Part One." *Science Fiction Eye* 4 (Aug. 1988): 32–39.

Hanson, Ellis. "Undead." *Inside/Out: Lesbian Theories, Gay Theories*. Ed. Diana Fuss. New York: Routledge, 1991. 324–40.

Haraway, Donna. *Simians, Cyborgs, and Women*. New York: Routledge, 1991.

Harper, Phillip Bryan. *Are We Not Men?: Masculine Anxiety and the Problem of African American Identity*. New York: Oxford UP, 1996.

———. *Private Affairs*. New York: New York UP, 1999.

Hassan, Ihab. "Pluralism in Postmodern Perspective." *Critical Inquiry* 12 (Spring 1986): 503–20.

Haver, William. "Of Mad Men Who Practice Invention to the Brink of Intelligibility." *Queer Theory in Education*. Ed. William F. Pinar. Mahwah, N.J.: Lawrence Erlbaum Associates, 1998. 349–64.

Hayden, Robert. "[American Journal]." *Collected Poems: Robert Hayden*. New York: Liveright, 1996. 192–95.

———. "El-Hajj Malik El-Shabazz." *Collected Poems: Robert Hayden*. New York: Liveright, 1996. 86–89.

———. "Words in the Mourning Time." *Collected Poems: Robert Hayden*. New York: Liveright, 1996. 90–100.

Hebdige, Dick. *Hiding in the Light*. London: Routledge, 1988.

Hemphill, Essex. Introduction. *Brother to Brother: New Writings by Black Gay Men*. Ed. Essex Hemphill. Boston: Alyson Publications, 1991.

Henderson, Stephen. *Understanding the New Black Poetry*. New York: Morrow, 1973.

"HIV & AIDS—The Basics." *HIV & AIDS—The Basics*. Gay Men's Health Crisis (GMHC). 5 July 2000. <http://www.gmhc.org/basics/hiv/trans.html>.

Hodgson, Godfrey. *America in Our Time*. 1976. New York: Vintage, 1978.

Hohne, Karen and Helen Wussow. Introduction. *A Dialogue of Voices: Feminist Literary Theory and Bakhtin*. Ed. Karen Hohne and Helen Wussow. Minneapolis: U of Minnesota P, 1994.

hooks, bell. "Postmodern Blackness." *Yearning: Race, Gender, and Cultural Politics*. Boston: South End, 1990. 23-31.

Horne, Gerald. *Fire This Time*. Charlottesville: U of Virginia P, 1995.

Hutner, Gordon, ed. "The Situation of American Writing 1999." *American Literary History* 11.2 (1999): 215-353.

Jackson, Earl Jr. *Strategies of Deviance*. Bloomington: Indiana UP, 1995.

James, Ken. "Extensions: An Introduction to the Longer Views of Samuel R. Delany." *Longer Views: Extended Essays*. By Samuel R. Delany. Hanover, N.H.: UP of New England/Wesleyan UP, 1996. xiii-xl.

Jameson, Fredric. *Postmodernism, or the Cultural Logic of Late Capitalism*. Durham: Duke UP, 1991.

Johnson, Charles. *Being and Race*. Bloomington: Indiana UP, 1988.

Joint United Nations Programme on HIV/AIDS and the World Health Organization. *AIDS Epidemic Update* (December 2002) 24 May 2003. <http://www .who.int/hiv/facts/epiupdate_en.pdf>.

Jonas, Gerald. Review of *The Bridge of Lost Desire* by Samuel R. Delany. *New York Times Book Review* 7 Feb. 1988: 22.

———. Review of *Dhalgren* by Samuel R. Delany. *New York Times Book Review* 16 Feb. 1975: 27.

———. Review of *The Motion of Light in Water* by Samuel R. Delany. *New York Times Book Review* 24 July 1988: 25.

———. Review of *Tales of Nevèrÿon* by Samuel R. Delany. *New York Times Book Review* 28 Oct. 1979: 15-18.

Jones, David. Preface. *The Anathemata*. By David Jones. London: Faber and Faber, 1952. 35.

Joyce, Joyce A. "The Black Canon: Reconstructing Black American Literary Criticism." *New Literary History* 18.2 (Winter 1987): 335-44.

———. "'Who the Cap Fit': Unconsciousness and Unconscionableness in the Criticism of Houston A. Baker Jr. and Henry Louis Gates Jr." *New Literary History* 18.2 (Winter 1987): 371-84.

Keenan, Thomas. "Windows: of vulnerability." *The Phantom Public Sphere*. Ed. Bruce Robbins. Minneapolis: U of Minnesota P, 1993. 121-41.

Kelley, Robin. "Looking B(l)ackward." *Race Consciousness: African American Studies for the New Century*. Ed. Judith Jackson Fossett and Jeffrey A. Tucker. New York: New York UP, 1996. 1-16.

Kermit, S. L. (Samuel R. Delany). "Appendix: Some Informal Remarks Towards the Modular Calculus, Part Three." *Tales of Nevèrÿon*. By Samuel R. Delany. Hanover, N.H.: UP of New England/Wesleyan UP, 1993. 247-60.

Kernochan, Rose. Review of *Atlantis: Three Tales* by Samuel R. Delany. *New York Times Book Review* 29 Oct. 1995: 42.

Kingsley, Lawrence A., et al. "Risk Factors for Seroconversion to Human Immunodeficiency Virus Among Male Homosexuals." *The Mad Man*. By Samuel R. Delany. New York: Richard Kasak, 1995. 603-21.

Kitchens of Distinction. "Prize." *Love Is Hell*. One Little Indian/A & M, 1989.

Knight, Damon. "The Classics." *In Search of Wonder*. Second ed. Chicago: Advent, 1967. 9-21.

Kristeva, Julia. *Powers of Horror*. 1980. New York: Columbia UP, 1982.

Lacan, Jacques. "The Agency of the Letter in the Unconscious, or Reason Since Freud." *Écrits*. 1966. New York: Norton, 1977. 146–78.

Laferrière, Dany. *How to Make Love to a Negro*. Toronto: Coach House Press, 1987.

———. *Why Must a Black Writer Write about Sex?* Toronto: Coach House Press, 1994.

Lampkin, Brian. "The Motion of Going Down: Samuel Delany on HIV and AIDS." *Voices* May 1998: 6–7.

LeGuin, Ursula K. Introduction. *The Norton Book of Science Fiction*. Ed. Ursula K. LeGuin and Brian Attebery. New York: Norton, 1993. 15–42.

Lejeune, Philippe. "The Autobiographical Pact." *On Autobiography*. Ed. Paul John Eakin. Trans. Katherine Leary. Minneapolis: U of Minnesota P, 1989. 3–30.

Leonard, John. "Gravity's Rainbow." *The Nation* 15 Nov. 1993: 580–88.

Lerner, Michael and Cornel West. *Jews and Blacks*. New York: Grosset/Putnam, 1995.

Lipsitz, George. *The Possessive Investment in Whiteness*. Philadelphia: Temple UP, 1998.

Littlefield, Emerson. "The Mythologies of Race and Science in Samuel Delany's *The Einstein Intersection* and *Nova*." *Extrapolation* 23.3 (1982): 235–42.

Locke, Alain. "The New Negro." *The New Negro*. 1922. New York: Atheneum, 1992.

Lorde, Audre. "Age, Race, Class, and Sex: Women Redefining Difference." 1980. *Sister Outsider*. Freedom, Calif.: The Crossing Press, 1984. 114–23.

———. "Uses of the Erotic: The Erotic as Power." 1978. *Sister Outsider*. Freedom, Calif.: The Crossing Press, 1984. 53–59.

Lott, Eric. "After Identity, Politics: The Return of Universalism." *New Literary History* 31.4 (Autumn, 2000): 665–78.

Lubiano, Wahneema. "Shuckin' Off the African American Native Other: What's 'Po-Mo' Got to Do with It?" *Cultural Critique* 18 (1991): 149–86.

Lyotard, Jean-Francois. *The Postmodern Condition: A Report on Knowledge*. 1979. Minneapolis: U of Minnesota P, 1984.

Marx, Karl. From *Capital I*, on Alienation. 1967. *Karl Marx: A Reader*. Ed. Jon Elster. Cambridge: Cambridge UP, 1986. 62–100.

McCaffery, Larry. "The Desert of Reality." Introduction. Ed. Larry McCaffery. *Storming the Reality Studio*. Durham, N.C.: Duke UP, 1991.

———. Introduction. *Postmodern Fiction: A Bio-Bibliographical Guide*. Ed. Larry McCaffery. New York: Greenwood Press, 1986.

McClintock, Anne. *Imperial Leather*. New York: Routledge, 1995.

McDowell, Deborah E. and Arnold Rampersad. Introduction. *Slavery and the Literary Imagination*. Ed. Deborah McDowell and Arnold Rampersad. Baltimore: Johns Hopkins UP, 1989.

McEvoy, Seth. *Samuel Delany*. New York: Ungar, 1984.

McKenna, Joe. "The Best Gay Smut of the Last 1000 Years." *Inches* 14.5 (January 2000): 28.

Mercer, Kobena. *Welcome to the Jungle*. New York: Routledge, 1994.

Moore, Steven. Review of *Atlantis: Model 1924* by Samuel R. Delany. *Review of Contemporary Fiction* 15 (Spring 1995): 175.

Morgan, Edmund S. "Slavery and Freedom: The American Paradox." 1972. *Slavery in American Society.* Ed. Lawrence B. Goodheart, et al. Lexington, Ky.: D.C. Heath, 1993. 69–82.

Morrill, Rowena. *The Art of Rowena.* London: Paper Tiger, 2000.

Morrison, Toni. *Beloved.* 1987. New York: Plume, 1988.

———. "Unspeakable Things Unspoken: The Afro-American Presence in American Literature." 1990. *Within the Circle: An Anthology of African American Literary Criticism from the Harlem Renaissance to the Present.* Ed. Angelyn Mitchell. Durham, N.C.: Duke UP, 1994. 386–98.

Morrow, James. "*Para • doxa* Interview with James Morrow." Interview with Samuel R. Delany. *Para • doxa* 5.12 (1999): 132–49.

Mosley, Walter. "Black to the Future." *New York Times Magazine.* 1 Nov. 1998. 32.

Moylan, Tom. *Demand the Impossible.* New York: Methuen, 1986.

Muñoz, Jose Esteban. "Ghosts of Public Sex: Utopian Longings, Queer Memories." *Policing Public Sex.* Ed. Dangerous Bedfellows. Boston: South End Press, 1996. 355–72.

National Coalition for the Homeless, "Fact Sheet #9: HIV/AIDS and Homelessness." April 1999, 27 Oct. 2000. <http://nch.ari.net/hivaids.html>.

National Institute of Allergy and Infectious Diseases/National Institutes for Health. Fact Sheet: "HIV Infection and AIDS: An Overview," Aug. 2002, 8 May 2003. <http://www.niaid.nih.gov/factsheets/hivinf.htm>.

National Minority AIDS Council. *HIV/AIDS and African Americans* (October 1999) 24 May, 2003. <http://www.nmac.org/publications/policypubs/factsheets/hivaids_and_african_americans.pdf >.

Neal, Larry. "The Black Arts Movement." 1968. *Within the Circle: An Anthology of African American Literary Criticism from the Harlem Renaissance to the Present.* Ed. Angelyn Mitchell. Durham: Duke UP, 1994. 184–98.

Nero, Charles I. "Toward a Black Gay Aesthetic: Signifying in Contemporary Black Gay Literature." *Brother to Brother.* Ed. Essex Hemphill. Boston: Alyson Publications, 1991. 229–52.

"Newark: On the Salt Marshes of the Passaic River." *Report of the National Advisory Commission on Civil Disorders.* 1968. *Urban Racial Violence in the Twentieth Century.* Ed. Joseph Boskin. Beverly Hills: Glencoe Press, 1976. 123–32.

Nichols, Bill. *Blurred Boundaries: Questions of Meaning in Contemporary Culture.* Bloomington: U of Indiana P, 1994.

Nicholls, Peter and Cornel Robu. "Sense of Wonder." *The Encyclopedia of Science Fiction.* Ed. John Clute and Peter Nicholls. New York: St. Martin's Press, 1993. 1083–85.

Oliver, Melvin L., James H. Johnson Jr. And Walter C. Farrell Jr. "Anatomy of a Rebellion: A Political-Economic Analysis." *Reading Rodney King, Reading Urban Uprising.* Ed. Robert Gooding-Williams. New York: Routledge, 1993. 117–41.

Olney, James. "Autobiography and the Cultural Moment: A Thematic, Historical, and Bibliographical Introduction." *Autobiography: Essays Theoretical and Critical.* Ed. James Olney. Princeton: Princeton UP, 1980. 3–27.

————. "The Founding Fathers—Frederick Douglass and Booker T. Washington." *Slavery and the Literary Imagination*. Ed. Deborah E. McDowell and Arnold Rampersad. Baltimore: Johns Hopkins UP, 1989.

Omi, Michael and Howard Winant. "The Los Angeles 'Race Riot' and Contemporary U.S. Politics." *Reading Rodney King, Reading Urban Uprising*. Ed. Robert Gooding-Williams. New York: Routledge, 1993. 97–114.

————. *Racial Formation in the United States: From the 1960s to the 1990s*. New York: Routledge, 1994.

"Oral Sex: Using Your Head." *University of California at San Francisco HIV InSite*. 1 Oct. 1997. University of California at San Francisco. 8 Oct. 2000. <http://hivinsite.ucsf.edu/prevention/safer_sex_info/2098.32ac.html>.

Outlaw, Lucius. "Toward a Critical Theory of 'Race.'" *Anatomy of Racism*. Ed. David Theo Goldberg. Minneapolis: U of Minnesota P, 1990. 58–82.

Paddy, David Ian. "Dhalgren." *Review of Contemporary Fiction* 17.1 (Spring 1997): 181–82.

Page-Shafer, Kimberly et al. "Risk of HIV infection attributable to oral sex among men who have sex with men and in the population of men who have sex with men," *AIDS: Official Journal of the International AIDS Society* 16 (17), 22 Nov. 2002: 2350–52.

Palumbo-Liu, David. "Assumed Identities." *New Literary History* 31.4 (Autumn 2000): 765–80.

Pascal, Roy. *Design and Truth in Autobiography*. London: Routledge and Kegan Paul, 1960.

Patterson, Orlando. *Slavery and Social Death*. Cambridge: Harvard UP, 1982.

Patton, Cindy. *Fatal Advice: How Safe-Sex Education Went Wrong*. Durham, N.C.: Duke UP, 1996.

Peplow, Michael W. and Robert S. Bravard. *Samuel R. Delany: A Primary and Secondary Bibliography: 1962–1979*. Boston: G.K. Hall, 1980.

Posnock, Ross. *Color and Culture: Black Writers and the Making of the Modern Intellectual*. Cambridge: Harvard UP, 1998.

Rampersad, Arnold. Introduction. *Collected Poems: Robert Hayden*. By Robert Hayden. New York: Liveright, 1996.

Redding, Saunders. "The Problems of the Negro Writer." *Black and White in American Culture*. Ed. Jules Chametzky and Sidney Kaplan. Amherst: U of Massachusetts P, 1969. 360–71.

Reid-Pharr, Robert F. *Black Gay Man*. New York UP, 2001.

————. "Dinge." *Women and Performance: A Journal of Feminist Theory* 8.2 (16) (1996): 75–85.

Robinson, Cedric J. "Race, Capitalism, and the Antidemocracy." *Reading Rodney King, Reading Urban Uprising*. Ed. Robert Gooding-Williams. New York: Routledge, 1993. 73–81.

Rose, Tricia. *Black Noise*. Hanover, N.H.: UP of New England/Wesleyan UP, 1994.

Rosenblatt, Roger. "Black Autobiography: Life as a Death Weapon." *Autobiography: Essays Theoretical and Critical*. Ed. James Olney. Princeton, N.J.: Princeton UP, 1980. 169–80.

Ross, Andrew. Introduction. *Universal Abandon?* Ed. Andrew Ross. Minneapolis: U of Minnesota P, 1988.

———. *Strange Weather.* London: Verso, 1991.

Ross, Marlon B. "Some Glances at the Black Fag: Race, Same-Sex Desire, and Cultural Belonging." *Canadian Review of Comparative Literature* (March-June, 1994): 193–219.

Rossi, Peter H. Introduction. *Ghetto Revolts.* By Peter H. Rossi. New Brunswick: Transaction Books, 1970.

Russ, Joanna. "Towards an Aesthetic of Science Fiction." 1975. *To Write Like a Woman: Essays in Feminism and Science Fiction.* Bloomington: Indiana UP, 1995. 3–14.

Rustin, Bayard. "The Watts Manifesto." 1966. *Urban Racial Violence in the Twentieth Century.* Ed. Joseph Boskin. Beverly Hills: Glencoe Press, 1976. 116–22.

Saunders, Charles. "Why Blacks Don't Read Science Fiction." *Brave New Universe: Testing the Values of Science in Society.* Ed. Tom Henighan. Ottawa: Tecumseh, 1980. 160–68.

———. "Why Blacks Should Read (and Write) Science Fiction." *Dark Matter.* Ed. Sheree Thomas. New York: Warner/Aspect, 2000. 398–404.

de Saussure, Ferdinand. *Course in General Linguistics.* 1915. Trans. Wade Baskin. New York: McGraw-Hill, 1966.

Sayre, Robert F. "Autobiography and the Making of America." *Autobiography: Essays Theoretical and Critical.* Ed. James Olney. Princeton, N.J.: Princeton UP, 1980. 146–68.

Schweitzer, Darrel. "Dully Grinning Delany Descends to Disaster." Review of *Dhalgren* by Samuel R. Delany. *Justworld.* Sixth Anniversary Issue (27). Ed. Bill Bowers. North Canton, OH (1976): 1041–42.

Scott, Joan W. "'Experience.'" *Feminists Theorize the Political.* Ed. Judith Butler and Joan W. Scott. New York: Routledge, 1992. 22–40.

Sedgwick, Eve Kosofsky. *Epistemology of the Closet.* Berkeley: U of California P, 1990.

Seidman, Steven. "Identity and Politics in a 'Postmodern' Gay Culture: Some Historical and Conceptual Notes." *Fear of a Queer Planet.* Ed. Michael Warner. Minneapolis: U of Minnesota P, 1993. 105–42.

Simmons, Ron. "Some Thoughts on the Challenges Facing Black Gay Intellectuals," *Brother to Brother.* Ed. Essex Hempill. Boston: Alyson Publications, 1991. 211–28.

Smiths, The. "Ask." *Louder Than Bombs.* WEA/Warner Brothers, 1987.

Snead, James A. "Repetition as a Figure of Black Culture." *Black Literature and Literary Theory.* Ed. Henry Louis Gates Jr. New York: Routledge, 1984.

Sollors, Werner. Introduction. *The Interesting Narrative of the Life of Olaudah Equiano, or Gustavus Vassa, the African, Written by Himself.* By Olaudah Equiano. 1789. New York: Norton, 2001.

Sontag, Susan. *Illness as Metaphor* (1978) and *AIDS and Its Metaphors.* New York: Anchor, 1990.

Spencer, Kathleen. "Deconstructing *Tales of Nevèrÿon*: Delany, Derrida, and the 'Modular Calculus, Parts I–IV.'" *Essays in Arts and Sciences* XIV (1985): 59–89.

Stallybrass, Peter and Allon White. Introduction. *The Politics and Poetics of Trans-gression*. Ed. Stallybrass and White. Ithaca: Cornell UP, 1986. 1–26.

Staples, Robert. *Black Masculinity: The Black Man's Role in American Society*. San Francisco: Black Scholar Press, 1982.

Starobinski, Jean. "The Style of Autobiography." *Autobiography: Essays Theoret-ical and Critical*. Ed. James Olney. Princeton, N.J.: Princeton UP, 1980. 73–83.

Steiner, K. Leslie (Samuel R. Delany). "Return . . . a preface." *Tales of Nevèrÿon* by Samuel R. Delany. Hanover, N.H.: UP of New England/Wesleyan UP, 1993. 11–21.

———. "'The Scorpion Garden' Revisited." *The Straits of Messina* by Samuel R. Delany. Seattle: Serconia, 1989. 17–31.

———. "Some Remarks Toward a Reading of *Dhalgren*." *The Straits of Messina* by Samuel R. Delany. Seattle: Serconia, 1989. 57–91.

———. "*Tales of Nevèrÿon*." *The Straits of Messina* by Samuel R. Delany. Se-attle: Serconia, 1989. 159–60.

Stepto, Robert B. "The Reconstruction of Instruction." *Afro-American Litera-ture: The Reconstruction of Instruction*. Ed. Dexter Fisher and Robert B. Stepto. New York: Modern Language Association, 1978. 8–24.

Sturgeon, Theodore. Review of *Dhalgren* by Samuel R. Delany. *Galaxy* Mar. 1975: 154–55.

Suvin, Darko. *Metamophoses of Science Fiction*. New Haven: Yale UP, 1979.

Tate, Greg. "Ghetto in the Sky: Samuel Delany's Black Whole." 1985. *Flyboy in the Buttermilk*. New York: Simon and Schuster, 1992. 159–67.

Thomas, Kendall. "'Ain't Nothing Like the Real Thing': Black Masculinity, Gay Sexuality, and the Jargon of Authenticity." *The House that Race Built: Black Americans, U.S. Terrain*. Ed. Wahneema Lubiano. New York: Pantheon, 1997. 116–35.

Thomson, James. "The City of Dreadful Night." *Poems and Some Letters of James Thomson,* Ed. Anne Ridler. Carbondale: Southern Illinois UP, 1963. 177–205.

Toomer, Jean. *Cane*. 1923. New York: Norton, 1988.

Towles, Darryl. "Black and Gay: One Man's Story." *Black Men, White Men*. Ed. Michael J. Smith. San Francisco: Gay Sunshine Press, 1983. 92–95.

Treichler, Paula. *How to Have Theory in an Epidemic: Cultural Chronicles of AIDS*. Durham, N.C.: Duke UP, 1999.

Turner, Darwin. *In a Minor Chord*. Carbondale: Southern Illinois UP, 1971.

Van Deburg, William L. *New Day in Babylon: The Black Power Movement and American Culture, 1965–1975*. Chicago: U of Chicago P, 1992.

Walcott, Rinaldo. "Queer Texts and Performativity: Zora, Rap, and Commu-nity." *Queer Theory in Education*. Ed. William F. Pinar. Mahwah, N.J.: Lawrence Erlbaum Associates, 1998. 157–71.

Wald, Gayle. *Crossing the Line: Racial Passing in Twentieth-Century U.S. Litera-ture and Culture*. Durham, N.C.: Duke UP, 2000.

Warner, Michael. Introduction. *Fear of a Queer Planet*. Ed. Michael Warner. Min-neapolis: U of Minnesota P, 1993.

———. *The Trouble with Normal: Sex, Politics, and the Ethics of Queer Life*. Cambridge: Harvard UP, 1999.

Washington, Booker T. *Up From Slavery*. 1901. *Three Negro Classics*. New York: Avon Books, 1965. 23–205.

Watney, Simon. *Policing Desire: Pornography, AIDS, and the Media*. Minneapolis: U of Minnesota P, 1987.

Watts, Jerry G. "Reflections on the Rodney King Verdict and the Paradoxes of the Black Response." *Reading Rodney King, Reading Urban Uprising*. Ed. Robert Gooding-Williams. New York: Routledge, 1993. 236–48.

Weedman, Jane Branham. *Samuel R. Delany*. Mercer Island, Wash.: Starmont House, 1982.

Welsing, Frances Cress. "The Politics Behind Black Male Passivity, Effeminization, Bisexuality, and Homosexuality." 1974. *The Isis Papers*. Chicago: Third World Press, 1991. 81–92.

West, Cornel. "Black Sexuality." *Race Matters*. Boston: Beacon Press, 1993. 83–91.

———. "Identity: A Matter of Life and Death." *Prophetic Reflections: Notes on Race and Power in America*. Monroe, Me.: Common Courage Press, 1993.

Whitfield, LeRoy, Esther Kaplan and Shana Naomi Krochmal. "The Fire This Time." *The Body: An AIDS and HIV Information Resource*. Body Health Resource Corporation. 8 Oct. 2000. <http://www.thebody.com/poz/features/1_pp/leaders.html>.

Wideman, John Edgar. *Fatheralong*. New York: Vintage, 1995.

Williams, Ben. Interview with Samuel R. Delany. Citysearch.com. Aug. 1999. <http://newyork.citysearch.com/E/F/NYCNY/0010/04/49/#interview>.

Williams, Patricia J. "The Rules of the Game." *Reading Rodney King, Reading Urban Uprising*. Ed. Robert Gooding-Williams. New York: Routledge, 1993. 51–55.

Wolfe, Gary K. *Critical Terms for Science Fiction and Fantasy*. New York: Greenwood Press, 1986.

Woodhouse, Reed. *Unlimited Embrace: A Canon of Gay Fiction, 1945–1995*. Amherst: U of Massachusetts P, 1998.

Wright, Nathan Jr. *Ready to Riot*. New York: Holt, Rinehart and Winston, 1968.

Young, Robert. *White Mythologies: Writing, History, and the West*. London: Routledge, 1990.

INDEX

abjection, 259–60

ACT-UP, 231–32, 253–54

Adam, Helen, 289–90n

African American Studies, 48–49, 50–54, 90, 93–117, 152–54, 179–80, 237

AIDS, 96, 254, 255; activism, 4, 233–34, 234–35, 265; African Americans and, 231, 234–40; art about, 186, 233, 253–54; etiology of, 306n; and discursive analysis, 232, 265–73, 275; the humanities and, 231–33; homophobia and, 237, 252–53; media representation of, 234, 236–37, 238; risk factors, 231; science fiction characterizations, 253; statistics, 230–31. *See also* HIV

Akomfrah, John, 50

"[American Journal]" (Hayden), 225

Analog magazine, 51, 57

Anderson, Laurie, 54, 232

Andrews, William, 179

antipornography, 3. *See also* pornography

Appiah, Kwamé Anthony, 8–9, 10, 11, 17, 18, 23, 24, 25

Aptheker, Herbert, 114

Artaud, Antonin, 2, 4, 137

articulation, 47–48, 50, 228–29

Asimov, Isaac, 28, 29

Atlantis: Model 1924 (Delany), 3, 14, 61, 199–229, 238; articulation in, 228–29; genre of, 199; Hart Crane, 219–20, 225–28; memory in 201–8; as migration narrative, 208–21; racial identity in, 220–229; representations of racism in, 201, 214, 218; sexuality in, 211–17

"Atlantis Rose . . . : Some Notes on Hart Crane" (Delany), 226, 227

Attridge, Derek, 197

Auden, W. H., 31, 158, 225

autobiography, 3, 156, 164, 184, 198;

African American, 154, 164, 179–82; and architecture, 169; the erotic in, 173; and identity, 161; memory and, 159, 160, 161, 162; subversion of expectations in, 186, 190; vulnerability of subject in, 169–70

"Aversion/Perversion/Diversion" (Delany), 176, 242–43

"Aye, and Gomorrah . . ." (Delany), 57, 255

Babel-17 (Delany), 41, 157, 181

Baker, Houston A., 154

Bakhtin, Mikhail, 106–7

Baldwin, James, 12, 19, 181, 240, 241, 248

The Ballad of Beta-2 (Delany), 40

Baraka, Amiri (LeRoi Jones), 191, 239

Barbour, Douglas, 58–59, 61, 63, 64, 65

Barthes, Roland; and authorship, 29; *Barthes*, 161; fluidity of meaning, 181, 193, 197; *Mythologies*, 34, 132–134

Bartlett, Karen J., 77, 78

Baudrillard, Jean, 127

Beam, Joseph, 175, 188, 248

Beloved (Morrison), 239, 240, 242, 246

"A Bend in the Road" (Delany),187–88

Bernal, Martin, 96

Bersani, Leo, 252, 255, 256

The Birth of a Nation (dir. Griffith), 201, 214, 218

bisexuality, 61, 69, 178

Black Arts Movement, 13, 239–240

Blackberri, 186

Black Is, Black Ain't (dir. Riggs), 252, 300n

Black Power, 25–26, 79, 85, 158

Blassingame, John, 180

"The Blue Meridian" (Toomer), 223

Bontemps, Arna, 99, 222

2, 39, 47, 55–89, 157, 158, 164,
168, 175, 183, 187, 197, 200, 209,
211, 238, 245–46, 247, 286–87n,
288n; "*Dichtung und* Science Fiction," 33–34; *The Einstein Intersection*, 1–2, 5, 39, 40, 62, 208,
283n; *Empire*, 32; *Empire Star*, 39,
44–46, 61, 63, 157, 209; *Equinox*,
3–4; *The Fall of the Towers* Trilogy,
157, 280n; *Flight from Nevèrÿon*
(see also *Return to Nevèrÿon* Series), 61, 94, 95, 97, 100, 105, 107,
108, 114, 119, 138, 140, 209, 233,
243, 246, 260, 262, 265, 268–69,
271; "The 'Gay' Writer/ 'Gay Writing' . . . ?" 175; *Heavenly Breakfast*, 79, 178; *Hogg*, 4; *The Jewels
of Aptor*, 91, 157, 160, 196; *The
Mad Man*, 2, 3–4, 145, 187, 211,
230–75; *The Motion of Light in
Water*, 3, 50, 104, 150–98, 174,
216, 219, 200, 222–24, 226–27,
228, 243, 254, 255, 258–59, 302n;
"The Necessity of Tomorrows," 18,
19–20, 28, 34, 102–3, 131; *Never-
ÿóna* (see also *Return to Nevèrÿon*
Series), 90, 94–97, 99, 107–9, 104–
5, 109, 114–19, 121–25, 132–36,
138, 142–45, 204, 210, 243–44,
247, 292n; *1984: Selected Letters*,
178, 233, 246, 266, 268; *Nova*, 2,
20–21, 35, 39, 40–41, 51, 83,
214, 222, 263; "Of Sex, Objects,
Signs, Systems, Sales, SF, and Other
Things," 60–61, 65, 69–70, 80–81,
84, 144; "Racism and Science Fiction," 177; *Return to Nevèrÿon* (see
also *Return to Nevèrÿon* Series), 2,
39, 61, 92, 101, 103, 105, 113,
114, 117, 121, 132, 137, 139, 140,
145, 146–47; "The Rhetoric of
Sex/The Discourse of Desire," 76,
233, 243, 269; "Shadow and Ash,"
75; *Stars in My Pocket Like Grains
of Sand*, 35, 42, 49; "Street Talk/
Straight Talk," 233, 268, 270, 272;
Tales of Nevèrÿon (see also *Return
to Nevèrÿon* Series), 39, 42, 92, 97,

101, 113, 106, 120, 121, 130–32,
137, 139, 141, 147, 148; *Times
Square Red, Times Square Blue*,
257, 259, 262, 266–67; *Trouble on
Triton*, 42–44; "Wagner/Artaud,"
4, 16

Delany, Sarah, 199, 211, 294n
Del Rey, Lester, 57
Derrida, Jacques, 30; and deconstruction, 125–27; *différance*, 123, 125–
27, 205; on genre, 15, 164, 197; on
iteration, 137–38
Dery, Mark, 50
Dhalgren (Delany), 2, 39, 55–89, 157,
158, 164, 175, 197, 200, 211, 286–
87n; and black sexuality, 69–78, 183,
238; contesting narratives in, 66–69,
72–74, 76–78, 158; creation of, 56;
decentering in, 69, 89; narrative
shape, 62, 63–65, 66–69, 209; optic
chain, 47–48, 168; reception, 56–57;
repetition in, 62–66; schema of law
and sex, 69–70, 187, 245–46, 247;
self-referentiality, 60; subversion of
expectations 57–61; and urban uprising, 80, 81–83, 83–88
"*Dichtung und* Science Fiction" (Delany), 33–34
différance, 123, 125–27
difference: intraracial, 37–38, 152–53,
234, 275; politics of, 35–39, 46–48;
theme in Delany's works, 35–38,
40–48, 95, 198
différend, 262
Disch, Thomas, 156
discourse, 66, 69, 170, 174; on
HIV/AIDS 233, 265–66, 268, 273
Dixon, Thomas, 238
double consciousness, 3, 18, 61, 68, 79,
165, 181, 185
Douglas, Mary, 256, 257
Douglass, Frederick, 105, 106–9, 114,
160, 180, 181, 182
Dove, Rita, 29–30, 200
Duberman, Martin, 88, 175, 186
DuBois, W. E. B., 8, 11, 16, 18, 25, 68,
224
Duchamp, Marcel, 45

Duggan, Lisa, 252
Dylan, Bob, 158
Dyson, Michael, 192

Eagleton, Terry: on semiotics, 123, 125, 126, 133, 138, 141, 149, 205; on utopianism, 27
Eighteen Happenings in Six Parts (Kaprow), 151–52, 163, 181
Einstein, Albert, 158, 202
The Einstein Intersection (Delany), 1–2, 5, 39, 40, 62, 208, 283n
"El-Hajj Malik El-Shabazz" (Hayden), 225
Eliot, T. S., 228
Ellison, Harlan, 57
Ellison, Ralph, 26, 180, 212
Empire (Delany), 32
Empire Star (Delany), 39, 44–46, 61, 63, 157, 209
Enlightenment, 47, 113
Equiano, Olaudah, 180–81, 182
Equinox (Delany), 3–4
Escher, M. C., 63, 67
"Ethnicity: Identity and Difference" (Hall), 21, 22, 156
exchange value, 127

The Fall of the Towers Trilogy (Delany), 157, 280n
Fanon, Frantz, 10, 238
fantasy. *See* sword-and-sorcery
Farnham's Freehold (Heinlein), 96
Farred, Grant, 24, 25–27, 38
fetishism: and commodification, 127; sexual, 75–76, 187–89, 242–51
Flight from Nevèrÿon (Delany), 61, 209, 233, 243, 246, 260, 265; "The Mummer's Tale," 61, 97, 243; "The Tale of Fog and Granite," 95, 97, 105, 119, 138, 140, 246; *The Tale of Plagues and Carnivals*, 94, 100, 107, 108, 114, 233, 260, 262, 265, 266, 268–69, 271. See also *Return to Nevèrÿon* Series; semiotics; sexuality; slavery
Folsom, Bob, 157–58, 173, 177, 180, 187, 188
"For the Marriage of Faustus and Helen" (Crane), 229

Foucault, Michel, 92; on authorship, 29; on discourse, 265; and heterotopia, 42; and identity, 6; on madness, 215, 226; on representation and semiotics, 118, 127, 133; on schema of law and sex, 70, 247, 289n
Fox, Robert Elliot, 2, 3, 41, 49; on multiplexity, 44; on race in Delany's works, 54, 70–71, 73, 74; on urban uprisings, 82, 83
Frank, Waldo, 222, 228
Franklin, V. P., 104
Freedman, Carl, 41–42, 49, 50
Freud, Sigmund, 201–2
Fuss, Diana, 6, 21, 154, 155, 156, 176, 191, 197–98
futurism, 9–10, 26–27

Gaggi, Silvio, 151
Gaiman, Neil, 229
Galliher, John, 87
Gallop, Jane, 196
Garrison, William Lloyd, 114
Gates, Henry Louis, Jr., 200, 224; interviewed by Delany, 28, 29; and poststructuralism, 154; on slave narratives, 103, 104, 106, 181
Gawron, Jean Mark, 57, 59–61, 63, 73, 87–88, 164–65, 197
"The 'Gay' Writer/'Gay Writing' . . . ?" (Delany), 175
gender, 6, 7, 37, 78, 130, 197
genre, 14–15, 16, 136, 184, 197
Gernsback, Hugo, 39
Gibson, William, 29, 58, 82, 83–84
Gide, Andre, 4, 171
Gilroy, Paul, 9–10, 12, 18, 20, 26
Gooding-Williams, Robert, 80
Govan, Sandra Y., 54, 287n, 290n
Gray, Margaret, 203
Greenberg, Samuel Bernhard, 219–20
Griffin, Farah Jasmine, 208, 209–12, 214–15, 217

Hacker, Marilyn, 150, 180, 194, 219; poetry of, 47, 162–63; relationship with Delany, 155, 157–58, 160, 161, 162–63, 168, 173, 177, 182–84, 192
Hall, Stuart: on AIDS, 231, 236, 253;

on articulation, 47–48, 50; on critiques of identity, 5–7, 21–22, 153–54, 156, 191; on cultural recovery, 194, 222; on necessity of identity, 22, 196

Hanson, Ellis, 264

Haraway, Donna, 156

"Harbor Dawn" (Crane), 227

Harper, Phillip Brian: on AIDS, 232, 238; on black authenticity, 37, 188, 238, 240, 241, 252; on racial fetishism, 246, 248, 249

Hassan, Ihab, 35

Havens, Richie, 158

Haver, William, 257, 258, 262, 263

Having Our Say (Elizabeth Delany, Sarah Delany, and Hearth), 199, 211, 215, 294n

Hayden, Robert, 207, 208, 225

Heavenly Breakfast (commune/band), 56, 79, 178

Heavenly Breakfast (Delany), 79, 178

Hebdige, Dick, 9, 35

Hegel, Georg Wilhelm Friedrich, 16, 113

Heinlein, Robert A., 19, 29, 96

Hemphill, Essex, 75, 185, 188, 241, 248

Henderson, Stephen, 5

Hersey, John, 83

heterotopia, 42–44

Himes, Chester, 19

hip-hop, 228, 240, 241, 248

HIV, 4, 21, 69, 174; statistics, 230–31; transmission and its prevention, 265–75, 306n, 313–14n. *See also* AIDS

Hodgson, Godfrey, 83, 86, 87

Hoffman, William M., 186

Hogg (Delany), 4

Hohne, Karen, 107

homophobia, 76, 156, 176, 258; as impediment to AIDS activism, 237–38, 252–53; and racial authenticity, 235, 237–40; and racism, 48, 186, 228

homosexuality, 69, 74, 227, 254, 264; former medical discourse on, 170, 233; and heterosexuality, 15, 33; minoritizing representation of, 177, 178–79; myths of, 179, 187, 188, 301n; race and, 185–86, 240–42, 244, 246–53; racism and, 75–76, 186–88; universalizing representation

of, 177–78, 244. *See also* identity politics, sexuality

hooks, bell, 152–53

Hopkinson, Nalo, 55

Horne, Gerald, 86

How to Have Theory in an Epidemic (Treichler), 232, 233

Howard, Robert E., 91

Hughes, Langston, 222, 241

identity, 5, 163, 223–24; critiques of, 3, 6–7, 16–17, 21–22, 37, 43, 152, 154–56, 191; and difference, 15, 198; dual vision of, 155–56, 174–76; as effect of language, 167, 170, 195; multiplicity of, 3, 24–25, 27, 29–30, 176, 184, 193, 197–98; public and private, 169–70. *See also* homosexuality; identity politics; race; sexuality

identity politics, 27, 198; history of, 6, 24, 26–27, 38, 252–53; importance of, 152–53; skepticism toward, 2, 5, 6, 11–12, 15, 21, 24–26. *See also* homosexuality; identity; race; sexuality

"In Memory of Sigmund Freud" (Auden), 31

In Search of Wonder (Knight), 31

The Interesting Narrative of the Life of Olaudah Equiano (Equiano), 180, 181, 182

Invisible Man (Ellison), 7, 26, 65, 180, 212

iteration, 64–66, 137–38, 139, 228, 248

Jackson, Earl, Jr., 34, 41, 43

James, Kenneth, 34–35, 50, 54, 229

Jameson, Fredric, 35, 36, 90, 92

jazz, 62, 287n

The Jewels of Aptor (Delany), 91, 157, 160, 196

Johnson, Charles, 1, 13

Johnson, James Weldon, 180

Jonas, Gerald, 56, 92, 173

Jones, David, 63

Joyce, Joyce Ann, 154, 155

Julien, Isaac, 186

Kallman, Chester, 158

Kaprow, Allan, 151, 163, 181

74, 211–17. *See also* fetishism; homosexuality; identity
"Shadow and Ash" (Delany), 75
Shelley, Percy Bysshe, 220
Simmons, Ron, 240
slave narratives, 102, 103–9, 180, 181–82
slavery, 3; abolitionist activism against, 113–17; in American history, 103, 207; in American literature, 99–100; the carnivalesque and, 106–8; and Delany family, 98, 294n; and fetishism, 137–49, 251, 297n; in Nevèrÿon, 95, 100–2, 106–8; sociology of, 108–13, 114–15; violence endemic to, 90, 108–9. *See also* slave narratives
Slavery and Social Death: A Comparative Study (Patterson), 90, 96, 102, 108–13, 116–17, 137, 140
Smith, Michael J., 248
Snead, James, 62–64, 66, 138
Sollors, Werner, 181
"Song of the Son" (Toomer), 217
Sontag, Susan, 232
Soul on Ice (Cleaver), 240
The Souls of Black Folk (DuBois), 68, 224, 229
Spencer, Kathleen, 92, 130
Spivak, Gayatri, 92
split subjectivity, 3, 12, 76, 167, 172, 179, 197
Stallybrass, Peter, 107
Starobinski, Jean, 191
Star Trek, 10, 284–85n
Starship Troopers (Heinlein), 19–20, 28
Stars in My Pocket Like Grains of Sand (Delany), 35, 42, 49
Steiner, K. Leslie, 3, 49–50; description of, 93; on *Dhalgren* 66, 68–69, 72, 78, 82; origin of, 288n; on *Return to Nevèrÿon* Series, 92, 93, 110, 121
Stepto, Robert, 104, 180
Sterling, Bruce, 1
Stonewall uprising, 15, 79, 88, 253, 254, 312n
"Street Talk/Straight Talk" (Delany), 233, 268, 270, 272
Sturgeon, Theodore, 56–57
Sullivan, Andrew, 230
suspension, 14, 192–93, 195–97, 222–24

Suvin, Darko, 14, 32, 33
sword-and-sorcery, 2, 91, 97–98, 101, 117, 128, 136, 149

The Tale of Plagues and Carnivals. See *Flight from Nevèrÿon*
Tales of Nevèrÿon (Delany): "The Tale of Dragons and Dreamers," 113, 121, 141; "The Tale of Gorgik," 39, 92, 101, 121, 132, 137, 139, 147; "The Tale of Old Venn," 106, 120, 148; "The Tale of Potters and Dragons," 42, 97, 120, 130–32; "The Tale of Small Sarg," 111, 120, 139. See also *Return to Nevèrÿon* Series; semiotics; sexuality; slavery
Tate, Greg, 53
"The Third Sermon on the Warpland" (Brooks), 55, 86
Thomas, Kendall, 48, 240
Thomson, James, 228
The Tides of Lust. See Equinox
Times Square Red, Times Square Blue (Delany), 257, 259, 262, 266–67
Tolkein, J. R. R., 91
Tom Corbett: Space Cadet, 46
Toomer, Jean, 219, 222–23, 228; *Cane*, 199, 200, 201, 212, 214, 217, 221
Towles, Darryl, 244
transgressive fiction, 3
The Treachery of Images (Magritte), 118
Treichler, Paula, 232, 233, 253, 268, 273
Trouble on Triton (Delany), 42–44
Turé, Kwame. See Carmichael, Stokely
Turner, Darwin, 212, 221, 222, 223
Turner, Nat, 114

universalism, 9–10, 12, 14, 61, 177, 222–23, 225
"Unspeakable Things Unspoken" (Morrison), 53
urban uprisings, 2, 79–80, 82–87; in Detroit, 83, 87; differences between, 86–87; in Los Angeles, 84, 86; in Newark, 83, 86; political response to, 87; in Watts, California, 82, 86, 87. *See also* Stonewall uprising
utopia, 42–44

ABOUT THE AUTHOR

Jeffrey Allen Tucker is Assistant Professor of English at the University of Rochester. He is co-editor of *Race Consciousness: African-American Studies for the New Century.*